THE HUB

THE HUB

BOOK TWO OF THE DERIVATES RISING
TRILOGY

LIV EVANS

The Hub
First published by Liv Evans in 2021
ISBN 9780648812258

© 2021 by Liv Evans

For any enquiries please visit www.livevans.com.au

Cover: Piere d'Arterie (Instagram @piere_d_arterie)

Editing: Nicole Zoltack (www.nicolezoltack.com)

For my parents.
To my mother, for being a living example of the importance of empathy and kindness.
To my father, for teaching me to take neither shit nor prisoners.
Xx

1

———

FLIT

"WARNING, the self-destruct sequence will commence in five minutes!"

The pleasant, automated voice echoed through the empty communications network room. Flit bit her lip. Link, Tweak, and Swipe froze. The overhead lighting, previously a cool white, started pulsating, bathing the slick silver walls an eerie crimson hue. Rows of cabinets twice as tall as Flit lined the room, wires, circuit boards, and cooling systems filling it with that unique scent of operating electronics.

Flit sank onto the balls of her feet, crouching closer to the top of the motherboard tower. Her fitted black tights and smooth white tank clung to her form as she gave the others an apologetic shrug. "Oops?"

"Oops?" Swipe snapped, her blonde braid flicking like a whip when she turned to narrow her eyes at Flit. "You trigger a self-destruct sequence, and all you can say is *oops?*"

Flit jutted her chin towards Tweak. "I thought you checked for pressure detectors."

Tweak raised his hands defensively. "You said *pressure* detectors. That," he jabbed his finger in the direction of the case Flit had teleported on top of, "was clearly a *motion* detector. There is probably a sensor somewhere in the room, but you didn't ask me to check for those."

"Here I was thinking that good general micro detection was a given." Flit shook her head.

"Hey, I do what I'm told, unlike other people in this team," Tweak grumbled.

"I don't know what you're talking about." If Flit was closer to Tweak, she would have cuffed him across the back of his head. "Right. Well, the emergency alarm has been triggered. Are there any other sensors or traps around? Feel free to use your initiative this time."

"Roger that, Captain." Tweak gave a lackadaisical salute before pressing his hand against the electrical control panel by the door. As he used his powers, his gaze lost focus.

"Warning! The self-destruct sequence will commence in four minutes and thirty seconds."

Flit's shoulders tensed at the updated warning. Depending on the nature of the surveillance and security protocols, it could take Tweak a good minute to get it cleared. "Link, we don't have time to wait."

Link nodded, smooth raven strands of hair falling out of her braid and framing her heart-shaped face. "I'll give you live updates." She rested her hand on Tweak's shoulder. As the team's resident telepath, she was often a conduit for information so others could keep working without distraction. "You've blown the all the sensors. You might as well keep moving. There may be some electrical security fields, but they are all at ground level, at the back of the room." Link paused. Tweak flinched. "He's working on those now. There are power points beneath the covers on the top of each tower. The info we need should be in Six-Alpha."

"Great, thanks," Flit called out before turning her attention to Swipe. "Start peeling the covers back, please. I'll jump over once you've worked them up a bit."

"Has anyone ever told you how bossy you are?" Swipe threw up her hands, and there was a wail of rending metal as one of the covers on top of the tower to Flit's right bent back on itself.

Flit teleported across to the newly exposed target. "Kinda the point of being a team leader, or did you not get the memo?" Flit read the serial number above the data port. "Nope, not this one."

"Oh, I got the memo." Swipe tore another cover open with a careless flick of her wrist. "I just don't like it."

"Good thing your opinion doesn't matter." Flit teleported to the next tower between sentences. "You just need to do what you're told."

Swipe let out a bitter laugh. "Poor Scraps. Are you this insufferable with him?"

"You can ask him yourself when we rescue him from this place." Flit turned to face her. "By the way, you've got two hands, so shut your mouth and peel these back faster. We'll never get anything at this rate."

Then again, Flit thought, that probably didn't bother Swipe. She would do anything to mess with Flit's chances of becoming the leader of the Blue Team. However, there was one thing Swipe valued more than taking pot shots at Flit, and that was her pride. After questioning her speed, she had something to prove, and Flit's jab was enough to force Swipe to peel back motherboard towers faster, creating a symphony of groans around them.

"Warning! The self-destruct sequence will commence in four minutes!"

"Tweak's isolated the fields and is working on dismantling them, but someone is trying to swipe access at the back door. He's holding off the security approval for now, but it's slowing down his other work," Link called out.

"Good work, Tweak. Keep doing what you're doing. Swipe?" Flit called out. "Faster!"

Swipe complied without argument. The covers flew back almost as quickly as Flit could teleport. All they needed was to find the right tower, and then they could figure out where they were holding Scraps and get him back.

Gritting her teeth, Flit moved to the next tower and read the last two parts of the serial number. *Four-Foxtrot.*

She swore under her breath and teleported again. *Three-Echo.* She straightened up and looked at the metallic carnage around her. There were so many exposed towers now. If she had to check all of them, the place would blow before she got a quarter of the way through.

They had to work smarter, not faster.

She took a deep breath and considered what she knew, ignoring the instinctive urge to rush in the flashing warning lights. The solution was right there. She could feel it. She just needed to—

"It's a grid format!" Flit pointed at the rows while she counted them. Three across and five forward. "That one!" she called out to Swipe.

Swipe paused, mid-motion. "I can't see what you're—"

One moment, Flit was standing on top of the towers. The next, she appeared by Swipe's side. "Don't squirm," she commanded, pressing her body up against Swipe's taller and slimmer form. She held one hand against the nape of her neck, the other at the base of her spine.

"Wait, just give me—"

Blink.

"A minute!"

Swipe groaned and pulled away from Flit, doubling over at their sudden reappearance on top of the towers. Her smooth creamy skin was tinged green, and her fingers trembled.

"Warning! The self-destruct sequence will commence in three and a half minutes!"

Flit put a hand on Swipe's shoulder and turned her around, helping her stay balanced on top of the server tower. "That one!" She pointed to the cover she wanted removed.

All it took was a jarring push of Swipe's hand, and the cover a couple of metres away tore free of its holdings and bounced down from tower to tower with a clanging cacophony.

Flit was over and standing on top of the tower before the cover hit the ground. "Got it. Six-Alpha!"

Despite the overwhelming urge to do a victory lap, Flit sank to her knees. She reached into her bra, yanked out the datastick she'd tucked in there for safe-keeping, and then rammed it into the port. The light on the side flashed red.

"Tweak said the program will take a minute to collect the information," Link called out. Flit was far enough away from the door now that she couldn't see her teammates.

Flit stood and looked towards the door at the back of the room. "How are those fields going?" she asked.

"Still up," Link replied. "They've got some pretty fancy coding. Tweak's swearing up a storm in his head."

"Warning! The self-destruct sequence will commence in three minutes!"

They were running out of time.

"What'll get fried if they are set off?" Flit barked.

"It's won't fry anything, but it'll be sore. It'll affect anyone touching the floor and the walls. The towers should be fine," Link said warily.

"And are there still people trying to get in the back door?"

"Yes," Link confirmed.

Flit smirked. "Great. Tweak, release the access to the back door. When I say now, you trigger the fields."

"You want me to what?" Tweak scoffed.

"Trust me!"

There was grumble of reluctance, but the door at the back of the room slid open with an electronic hiss.

Flit teleported over to Swipe and wrapped her arms around her. "Ready for a fight?" she hissed under her breath.

Swipe's face set in fierce determination. "Always."

A man and a woman appeared at the back of the room. Their plain black fatigues were worse for wear, but the visors covering their faces were fully blacked out, hiding their identities. They each had a grip on the elbow of the man between them, whose hands were cuffed behind his back.

He had a black bag over his face, but Flit would know Scraps anywhere.

"What is this?" Flit grumbled, rolling her eyes at the sight of the bag. "Some shitty retro kidnapping movie?"

"Warning! The self-destruct sequence will commence in two and a half minutes!"

The man and woman's heads moved as they scanned the room, and Flit held Swipe closer. The man tentatively placed his foot on the floor of the tower room.

"Now!" Flit cried.

"No!" The woman tried to pull her partner back, but it was too late.

With a snap and a sizzle, the flavour of ozone pierced the air. The man holding Scraps grunted. Scraps and the woman on the other side jumped back at the conducted charge.

"Shield's fully discharged!" Link called out.

Flit teleported herself and Swipe to stand in front of the captors. "Hope that wasn't too much of a shock to your system," she taunted as she swung a fist at the man's shielded face.

With a grunt, her opponent let go of Scraps and stumbled to the side, holding the side of his visor and swearing. He barely had time to straighten up before Flit teleported behind him and slammed her foot against the back of his knee, sending him tumbling to the floor.

"Tweak, shut off the self-destruct sequence! Link, get your arse over here to help Swipe," Flit called out. She teleported in front of Scraps and yanked the hood off his head. His dazed red eyes landed on her, and a smile tugged at the corner of his lips.

Beside them, Swipe sent a shower of motherboard covers flying towards the female assailant. The woman cried out and darted behind a tower to avoid the onslaught.

The man, who received the worst of the shock, started crawling towards Flit. Instead of sticking around, she wrapped her arms around Scraps and teleported to the far side of the row and then to the door where Tweak was standing.

"Partial as I am to you having your hands tied behind your back, let's get these cuffs off you," Flit said, letting go of Scraps.

Scraps blinked. "You like it when my hands are tied behind my back?"

"Warning! The self-destruct sequence will commence in two minutes!"

Tweak laughed. "She can explain it later," he said, without looking away from the panel.

He held his hand out, and Flit helped Scraps manoeuvre his bound hands to the microkinetic. The instant Tweak touched the cuffs, the lights around the wristbands switched off, and they clattered to the floor.

"You get back to Swipe. I've got a datastick to recover." Flit ran a hand through his tousled hair before she looked up at the nearest tower and teleported, aiming for a spot above the top of it.

The inevitable freefall that followed only lasted a moment before Flit's feet slammed onto the metal case, and she fell into a crouch. She peered around, counting the towers, and then jumped to Six-Alpha. The light on the side of the datastick blinked a solid green, so she yanked it out and shoved it back down her bra. A few seconds and several teleports later, she was back by Scraps' side. In the time that it took her to get the datastick, he, Swipe, and Link had subdued his captors. They were on the ground. Swipe had her foot on the small of the woman's back, and Link straddled the man's waist, holding his arms pinned down to the floor either side of his head.

Flit was about to demand her opponents turn off the emergency sequence when the lights overhead flicked off, and they were plunged into darkness.

'Attention! The self-destruct sequence has been deactivated. Have a nice day.'

The room flared to life again with bright, white lights.

Everyone fell silent when a loud, slow clapping filled the room. One of the side walls, previously shiny and white, turned to clear glass, and Flit peered through the pain in her eyes to see Posthoc with his hands raised in applause. Hawkeye stood beside him, disgruntled.

"A total of six minutes and twenty-one seconds," Posthoc announced. "Almost a whole five minutes faster than Hawkeye's run."

Flit smirked to herself and jabbed her toe into the male assailant's leg. Link released his hands and sat back on him.

"Looks like you owe me a couple of chocolate bars, Sway," Flit teased.

Sway pulled the visor off and looked up at Link, who was still straddling his waist. "Sorry, babe," he groaned.

"You lose one more chocolate bar, and I'm dumping you." Link sighed, the threat holding absolutely no weight. They were perfect for each other, and everyone knew it. That was why Sway got away with so much mischief. Link would forgive him for anything.

"Surely there's a penalty for activating the emergency self-destruct sequence and winding up only two minutes away from being blown to smithereens," Swipe said. She took her foot off her captive's back.

Clarity sat up, taking her own visor off and rubbing her eyes. "And for getting us electrocuted."

Flit ignored them. "Both mission objectives were completed, and we did it in record time." She shrugged and returned her attention to Posthoc, ignoring how Hawkeye seethed at his side. "I'd say that makes me team leader material."

"Only if we want to end up fried or splattered against the walls." Swipe sneered.

Flit teleported over to the viewing window. "You know, if anything, I should get bonus points for dealing with Swipe's shit and Tweak's purposeful lack of initiative."

"Hey!" Tweak laughed, walking over to join her. "Team members don't always have to do what you say. You're the worst."

"Which is why I need to be leader," Flit said, pointing out the obvious, "because I was designed to make the good calls, not follow shitty ones."

"I don't make shitty calls!" Hawkeye snapped, glaring at Flit through the glass.

"Of course not." Flit smiled at him, consoling. "Just slow ones."

"For the love of—" Posthoc trailed off into a muttering string of swear words that gave even Flit's extensive vocabulary a run for its money. "Some of the other department managers and I will review the footage and give you our decision tomorrow. For now, everyone, get some rest. It's been a long day."

Flit suppressed a groan. It was hard enough having to wait until the end of her test for an announcement. The Blue Team hadn't had a Team Leader since they'd lost Rook, and her application to take the role was deeply personal. She knew Hawkeye would do a good job, but she wanted to have the opportunity to fill the space Rook had left behind, and she was ready for more than just patrols. She figured the extra responsibility would scratch the itch growing inside her. Besides, Hawkeye had been called out by Shadow a couple of times in the months since the incident with Heft and the weapon. He wasn't necessarily a reliable choice.

Still, Posthoc had to do what he thought was best for the team, and he was clearly done arguing.

Posthoc walked out of the observation room with Hawkeye following in his wake.

A hand settled on Flit's shoulder, and she turned to come face-to-face with Link.

"We'll see you later, yeah?" Link asked, looking deep into Flit's eyes.

Is everything set for tonight? Flit thought.

Link gave her a subtle nod.

"Yeah, we'll be at dinner as usual. My folks aren't coming back tonight, so we'll eat with the team," Flit lied.

"Great!" Link's lips twisted into a secretive smile before she turned to Sway and the others. "All right. I'm hitting the showers."

Sway fell out of the quiet conversation he was having with Swipe immediately. "Ooh, take me with you!"

Everyone laughed as he followed Link out of the room. Tweak, Clarity, and Swipe went along with them.

"So," Scraps said slowly, leaning against the observation window and treating her to her one of his cute, half-cocked smiles. "Would you care to explain what you meant before about me having my hands tied behind my back?"

Flit's smile turned into a wicked grin. "Better yet, let me show you."

2

———————

SCRAPS

SCRAPS LAY IN HIS BED, propped up on his elbows, and covered in nothing but a sheet.

"Come on! I'm starving. Get dressed so we can get to dinner." Flit was even more impatient than usual as she retrieved her clothes from the back of his chair.

"You are terribly confusing. No more than an hour ago, you were telling me to hurry up and get undressed," Scraps teased, watching Flit expertly hook the clasp of her bra behind her back before tugging her shirt over her head.

Flit winked at him, hazel eyes sparkling. "That was different, and you know it."

Scraps did know it, and he had particularly enjoyed the part when she'd showed him what she had meant about tying his hands up. He never thought he would enjoy being unable to touch Flit, but he still learned something new every day. Still, as hungry as he was from their day of training and then their evening romp, he wasn't ready to interrupt the post-copulation bliss just yet.

"If you were that hungry, we should have just gone for an early dinner. Then, we would have had all night to relax," he muttered.

Even though Flit's illogical choices left him shaking his head, he slipped out of bed. Getting to his feet, Scraps went about the business of looking for his clothes. As usual, Flit had flung them all around the room in her haste to be rid of them. He would much prefer it if she'd laid them over the back of his chair, the way he did with hers, but old habits were difficult to break. He finally located his underwear and pants, both of which had fallen between his desk and wardrobe. Once he retrieved them and tugged them on, he looked up to see Flit glaring at him. She had crossed her arms and popped her hip out to one side, his T-shirt bundled in her clenched fist.

Uh-oh. He knew that look.

"Uh, I mean, well… It was fun, obviously, but I like taking a break after…" Scraps stopped, his justification falling on deaf ears as Flit tapped her foot impatiently.

He decided to change tactics.

Scraps walked over, leaned down, and pressed a soft kiss against her wryly twisted lips before straightening up. "Or kissing. I like lying in bed after and just kissing you."

For a moment, Scraps thought he had failed. Then, slowly but surely, Flit's shoulders softened and sagged, and her frown turned into more of an exasperated grimace.

"You know, you won't always be able to win me over with a kiss or a compliment," she warned, poking his chest. The tone she used reminded Scraps of the one parents in the Underground favoured when they reprimanded their children.

"You are right." Scraps pretended to be suitably apologetic. "I am sorry, Flit. Next time, I will try and point out the flaws in your time-management logic *before* they become an issue."

Flit narrowed her eyes at him, and he had to hold back a smirk, proud of the satire he'd injected into his remark.

Without warning, Flit turned around and pressed her hand against the panel to open his door. "Come on. Food time!" she called over her shoulder as she teleported into the hallway with his top.

"My shirt!"

Flit turned on her heel and strode off, leaving him bare-chested and with no other choice but follow.

"YOU SAID we were going to dinner," Scraps grumbled.

"Oh, we are," Flit promised. "I just need to stop by the training room first. I forgot something in there."

Flit held his hand tight as they made their way down the familiar, stark grey corridors of the training area. When they reached the training room, the observation window was frosted over. Scraps could have sworn Posthoc had deactivated that setting before they had left for the afternoon. Thanks to the deaths caused by the tunnel explosions a few months ago, there had been a reshuffling of staff in the Underground, so he wouldn't have been surprised if the training room had been used by someone else afterwards.

When Flit opened the door, the room beyond was pitch black, without even a hint of emergency lighting. It was unusual and alarming. He was about to warn Flit to watch herself when—

"Surprise!" A raucous cheer of voices went up.

The lights overhead flared on, temporarily blinding him. Scraps' stomach twisted, and adrenaline surged through his veins. Instinctively, he threw an arm up to shade his eyes as he pushed Flit behind him.

"I told you the lights and screaming were a stupid idea."

Scraps lowered his arm at the familiar voice and blinked against the lights, following the sound to see Swipe standing to the side of the room, shaking her head. Beside her were two long dining tables pushed together and loaded with enough food to feed an army. There were chairs scattered between his standing teammates and some of the other people he had come to think of as good friends. His brows furrowed in confusion as Flit's soft hand settled onto his shoulder, and she stepped out from behind him.

Flit smiled sheepishly. "Surprise?"

She might be a troublemaker, but when she looked at him like that, something inside of Scraps softened.

"Surprise indeed." Scraps glanced between Flit and the gathered people in confusion. They were all watching him expectantly. "What is this?"

"Well, one year ago today, Hawkeye and I were on patrol together in some Surface-level tunnels and heard weapons fire down below. I made the incredibly wise—"

"Wise, my arse!"

Flit rolled her eyes at Hawkeye's interruption and continued, "The incredibly wise decision to go down there and check it out. Happy anniversary, Scraps. You've made it to a full year in the Underground!"

Any lingering sense of alarm melted away in an instant. Scraps slid his arm around Flit's waist and skimmed his gaze over the people gathered. Just under two hours ago, the room had been a minefield of server towers and bent metal covers. There wasn't a single training prop in sight. They had cleaned up, moved in different furniture, and brought food all the way from the kitchens. All for him. All to celebrate the fact that he had been with them for a year.

"I… I don't know what to say," Scraps admitted, his voice catching in his throat. His heart swelled three times its normal size with affection for the group of rebels.

"Good, don't say anything more. We don't need a speech. Get the fuck over here so we can eat. I'm starving!" Sway jeered.

Scraps chuckled, agreeing with the sentiment. Flit took his hand and led him over to the table. In addition to the members of the Blue Team, Posthoc, Patch, Honey, Bookworm, and Acumen had joined them. Fit and Scraps took the spare seats between Link and Hawkeye.

The group fell into light conversation as Link pulled Scraps into a tight hug. "Happy anniversary, Scraps. I'm glad Flit can't follow protocol. It's been great having you down here," she said.

Sway reached across the table, shaking Scraps' right hand in both of his. "I'm not gonna go all soft on you, but it's been a pleasure."

A warm flush crept over Scraps' cheeks at the gratuitous attention and kindness from his friends.

"Although you, Flit… What the hell took you so long? Did you forget where the training room was? I though you said you'd be here like half an hour ago," Tweak said, taking a neatly cut chicken wrap off the platter in front of him and shoving it in his mouth, accentuating his point.

"Flit and I took a detour through Tunnel Forty-Two on the way here. It was a very satisfying route, even if it made us a little late." Scraps' voice was so deadpan that Sway and the others just looked at him for a moment, trying to figure out if he knew what he was saying.

Flit elbowed him. "Scraps!"

The tension in the room broke, and laughter filled the space.

Scraps looked down at Flit and shrugged, trying to mimic her fake-innocence from earlier. "What? It is true."

Flit just rolled her eyes and grabbed his T-shirt collar, pulling him in for a kiss. The cheers went up again in the room, and Scraps' blush deepened. He wondered whether he should have been at least a little bashful about it, but then he realised he didn't care. He considered every person in the room to be a close friend. This party was proof they accepted and valued him. It was safe for Scraps to enjoy himself around them.

After their very public display of affection, everyone started on dinner. It was a lively event full of good food, banter, and the occasional splurge of powers. Scraps and Swipe did their best to get the platters moving up and down the table so people didn't have to reach over each other to get their food. Tweak, Patch, and Bookworm pitched in by using their microkinesis to keep the food hot. When everyone had what they wanted on their plates, the table was a little less chaotic. The lull didn't last for long, though, as some people finished earlier and insisted on swapping seats with others to have different conversations.

"Hi, buddy." Acumen patted Scraps on the back between bites of potato as he shoved Link aside with his hip and stole her seat.

Perking up, Scraps swallowed the water he had just sipped and smiled at the mind reader. "I have not seen you in a while," Scraps said.

"Tell me about it," Acumen agreed. "I've been doing a lot of gardening with the kids lately, and they are missing you. I was gonna pull you out of training today to stop the whining, but Posthoc said you had something important."

Scraps laughed. The children were insistent when they wanted to be, which was most of the time. "Once the new Team Leader is chosen and the patrol routes are settled, I will start gardening again," he promised.

"Are you sure you want to stick with the Security Team? You've got quite the green thumb."

Scraps frowned, looking down at his hands and wondering if he had gotten anything on them.

Beside him, Acumen sighed. Scraps was just about to ask if there was anything wrong when the door to the training room opened.

The conversations around the table spluttered to a stop as Shadow, the Head of Intelligence, stepped into the room. He opened his mouth to speak, but before he could get a word out, Tweak jumped out of his seat.

"Shadow! So glad you could join us. Come and sit down. I'll get you a plate. There's plenty of food left." Tweak pulled his chair aside and snatched an empty plate off the table.

Acumen chuckled under his breath. "Someone's angling for a role in Intelligence."

"Don't bother, Tweak. Thank you, though." Shadow cleared his throat. "I'm sorry to interrupt, but I need to speak to Flit and Hawkeye."

Scraps and Flit exchanged glances. He could see she was curious about what Shadow had to say, but she didn't jump up right away.

"Do you mind?" she whispered.

Scraps shook his head. "No. Why would I?"

Shadow was one of the Department Heads. If he was asking, it had to be important. Scraps would never presume to tell one of his superiors not to take his girlfriend away from his party.

"Is this about the Team Leader role?" Sway asked, leaning forward and shaking his chicken drumstick bone at Shadow. "Because, if it is, you need to know that I wholeheartedly support—"

"No." Posthoc cut Sway off before he could finish. "That's my decision. Shadow is here on other business."

"Oh, ok." Hawkeye took a quick sip of his drink and walked around the table, nodding towards Flit. "You coming, or what?"

Flit leaned over and kissed Scraps' cheek before teleporting to Shadow's side. Hawkeye joined them, and they left the room in silence.

When the door was shut behind them, Scraps leaned closer to Acumen and whispered, "Flit's not in trouble again, is she?"

Acumen cocked an eyebrow at him. "Should she be?"

Scraps purposefully emptied his mind. "Er—no. Of course not."

But he wasn't entirely sure. One could never know with that girlfriend of his.

3

___

FLIT

WHEN THE DOOR slid shut behind them, Shadow gestured for Hawkeye and Flit to follow him. "We'll go to the training room next door. There's no need to go all the way into Intelligence."

As much as Flit enjoyed being allowed into the Intelligence tunnels, they had upped their security procedures lately, and she hardly felt like going through the full rigmarole so late in the evening. She'd lost almost an entire night of sleep in anticipation for the Team Leader test, and then, instead of having a nap before Scraps' anniversary dinner, they'd worked off some of the nervous energy she still had bouncing about.

She didn't regret it, though. She was more than happy with what she and Scraps had gotten up to, but it didn't help her flagging energy levels. She suppressed a yawn as they made their way into the training room. Shadow gestured to the bench against the wall. Flit teleported across the room and slumped onto the seat while Hawkeye trudged over. Shadow decided to walk and picked up a chair along the way. He waited for the younger man to sit before he set the seat down in front of the bench so that he could look at them both as he spoke.

"So, to what do we owe the pleasure of your visit? Especially at this hour." Flit leaned against the wall.

Shadow sat, straight backed, and looked between the two. "I want to talk to you both about a reassignment. I was under the impression you would work well together, but after seeing the competitiveness you displayed today in your ploy for the Team Leader role, I'm not so sure. I need two agents that complement one another, not try to get one up on them." Shadow's face was unreadable.

Flit perked up in her seat a little.

"What do you mean?" Hawkeye tilted his head in interest.

"Before we seconded you to Intelligence, Hawkeye, I heard you two were quite the partnership." Shadow glanced between them.

"We're still good," Hawkeye insisted. "We might have differences of opinion, but when it matters, we're a team."

Flit snorted in amusement.

"Do you disagree, Flit?" Shadow turned his piercing gaze on her.

"No, not really. I think we're just out of practice." Flit shrugged. She hadn't been on patrol with Hawkeye since she'd been assigned as Scraps' partner. A lot had changed since then.

Shadow watched them both for a minute. The only sign that he was thinking was a wry twist in the left corner of his lips. "I am confident you will work it out for the sake of a mission. Two of our undercover operatives in Eastbay, Newton and Vista, need to be recalled."

"Are they ok?" Flit asked, concerned. She vaguely remembered the pair before they had been sent on assignment a couple of years back.

"Vista is pregnant. It is still early stages, but in the interest of safety, it is best to recall her. Divvy insists it would be cruel to recall Vista without Newton," Shadow explained.

Even though Shadow made it sound like an inconvenience, Flit was happy for the remote viewer and her microkinetic husband. Flit would never bring kids into the mess of a world they lived in, she had chosen to use a long-acting contraceptive implant for just that reason, but she didn't begrudge others for trying.

Shadow continued, "We are forging a transfer for their aliases to the Hub. We will alter their data so you and Hawkeye can take over. Eastbay is far enough away that it is unlikely you'll run into any of their old workmates."

Flit thought it over. Accepting a brand-new assignment was one thing, but taking on a transfer and identity switch seemed extra risky. "Why are you keeping their identities?"

"They've gained a clearance level that will be nearly impossible to get if you two start from scratch in the Hub. We don't have time for that." Shadow nodded, and that wry twist turned to something more approving. "They were initially paired based on their abilities: remote viewing and microkinesis. Even though your skills, Flit, lend you better to a different type of intelligence, I believe your knowledge of the Hub will balance it out."

Flit's insides churned with anticipation. The time had come. Shadow was offering her the assignment of her dreams.

"When do we start?" Hawkeye asked.

"Newton and Vista will be here in two weeks. We have organised for a week of personal leave to handle their *relocation*. If you accept, you will start general Intelligence training immediately, with one week of intensive handover when they arrive, so the mission will commence in approximately three weeks."

Three weeks? Considering Flit hadn't been expecting a reassignment, that felt awfully soon. She was chuffed to be offered the transfer, but she had only just settled back into the Underground, and she and Scraps—

Flit froze. Scraps. With the exciting prospect of a new assignment, she had forgotten why she hadn't been hungering for one in a while. Things with Scraps were going so well, but accepting any assignment would mean leaving him behind. Her stomach lurched.

"Perfect!" Hawkeye chirped, and he slung his arm around her shoulders.

"How long is the assignment?" Flit asked.

Hawkeye frowned at her. "What?"

"It is indefinite. Recall is based on a number of factors: mission success or redundancy, safety concerns in the Hub, extenuating personal circumstances…" Shadow trailed off.

"And is it a full dark operation?" Flit probed.

Shadow nodded. "No contact with base other than mandated check-ins or emergency alerts."

That would mean Flit might not speak to her parents, or Scraps, ever again.

"I'll need some time to think it over," Flit blurted.

"Flit?" Hawkeye gawked at her, aghast. "Are you kidding? This is what we've wanted ever since we were little."

"I know." Flit nudged his legs with her knees to shut him up. "I just… I just need to think about it, ok?"

"Flit—"

"You have until tomorrow morning after breakfast to decide," Shadow interrupted. He got up and levelled a serious look at them. "Think about it. Offers like this do not come up very often. I don't know when the next chance at a suitable intelligence assignment will arise for you, Flit."

Flit went to tell him she understood, but he faded from view. She slumped back in her seat and sighed.

"What is there to think about?" Hawkeye asked, slipping from his place on the bench and onto Shadow's vacated chair. He put his hands on her knees, and his green eyes met hers, full of hope and excitement. "This is our dream, Flit!"

"It *was*." Flit shook her head. "It *was* our dream, Hawkeye. Things have changed a lot lately. I can't just jump into this."

"Are you kidding? You jump into everything! It's your bloody trademark."

"I know! Just…" Her body tensed as she pulled away from him. "Give me some space, all right?"

Hawkeye sat back and rubbed his eyes. "Look, I get that you've got Scraps now, and you probably don't want to leave him behind, but you need to think logically. Opportunities like this are once in a lifetime. You can't give up on your dreams like that. You could do so much good up there, and relationships don't last forever, you know."

That last phrase dumped an ice-cold bucket of water over Flit's head. "You don't need to remind me of that."

Flit teleported from her seat over to the door. She slammed her hand on the control panel.

Hawkeye flinched and turned around. When his eyes fell on her, they were wide and filled with awareness of the implication of his words. "Flit, please, that's not what I meant."

"Oh, I know what you meant. Don't worry," Flit snapped, teleporting out before he could say anything else.

As much as Flit wanted to return to her room to have some

time alone to think, Hawkeye would probably try and follow her, so, instead of leaving, she returned to the party. The food was almost finished, and someone had started pumping music through the speakers. When Flit looked around, she noticed that Acumen, Bookworm, and Posthoc had left, which explained why Sway and Tweak were leaned over, heads together, messing with the projection console to get some fun lighting going to match the music.

"Flit, is everything all right?"

A warm hand slid onto the small of her back, and Flit forced a smile onto her face. Scraps looked at her with such concern in his eyes that her heart melted.

"No." She sighed melodramatically. "I leave for fifteen minutes, and the vultures here devoured most of the dessert." She flung her arm towards the table.

Scraps perked up. "Oh, don't worry. I knew you wouldn't want to miss it." He flicked his own hand towards the table, and an upturned dish flipped over to reveal an untouched bowl of cake and ice cream.

With a genuine laugh, Flit swivelled towards Scraps and took both of his cheeks in her hands. She pulled him down for a kiss that was longer and more intimate than their surroundings allowed for. When she pulled away, she said breathlessly, "You, Scraps, are the best boyfriend a girl could ask for."

Flit linked her arm through Scraps' and dragged him back to the table. The two fell into a recount of the leadership trials and how they think Flit went, as she fed them both dessert, alternating spoonfuls between them.

4
____

SCRAPS

IT WAS LATE by the time the party finally wrapped up. The group, full of good food and cheer, were walking around and gathering any rubbish or dishes that needed to be dealt with. Everyone pitched in to make it light work, including Scraps, who used his telekinesis to float a stack of four tables to the storeroom.

Just as Scraps had the tables leaning properly against the wall, Sway stepped up beside him. "Mate, why don't you and Flit head off? We've got this." Sway gestured to the remaining chairs that needed to be stacked and put into storage, and the plates that had to be taken back to the Mess.

Scraps frowned. "It does not feel right to leave you all to clean up after you organised such a great party for me."

"That's the point, though. The party is in your honour. You shouldn't have to lift a finger. Just chill. We've got it. I promise." Sway's voice was earnest.

Scraps lowered his hand and turned to his friend. "Well, if you are sure... I think Flit would appreciate the early night."

"I'm sure she will," Sway scoffed, the implication clear in his tone.

Scraps looked over to where Flit and Hawkeye were standing in the corner of the room, engaged in what looked like a rather heated whispered argument, while they stacked trays of leftover food. Scraps hoped the end of the Team Leader testing would be enough to pause their growing rivalry, if only for a little while, but it seemed his hopes were premature.

"There is only one thing that will make the night better," Scraps said, drawing his words out as he turned back to Sway.

Sway cocked an eyebrow at him. "A return trip through Forty-Two?"

"No." Scraps shook his head. "Well, yes, but that is not what I am referring to. I meant those chocolate bars you owe Flit for losing your wager. If anything will make Flit happy, it's chocolate."

"You need to up your game if chocolate would make her happier." Sway shoved his hand into his pocket and retrieved two bars of chocolate. He surrendered them to Scraps with a disgruntled frown. "Link's so mad at me for losing those."

Scraps pocketed the bars and patted Sway on the shoulder. "If you cannot distract Link after losing two chocolate bars, perhaps it is you who needs to up his game."

With that, Scraps turned and made his way to Flit, leaving Sway muttering something about smart-arse upstarts in his wake. When Scraps approached, Flit stiffened and snapped something at Hawkeye. The remote viewer's eyes settled on Scraps.

"I'll see you both tomorrow. Don't forget, Flit. You've got until breakfast." Hawkeye's tone was tight, his face drawn. He gave Scraps a nod of farewell before he went over to join the others as they stacked chairs.

"What have you got until—"

"Come on. Let's get out of here." Flit linked her arm with his and dragged him out of the training room before he could finish his question.

On the return trip, Flit walked much faster than her usual, casual saunter. If they hadn't spent their evening in each other's arms, he would have almost thought she was eager for them to get back to bed. Given how satisfied she had appeared before she had gotten dressed, he seriously doubted it. Either way, there was a concerning energy bubbling up insider her, and as they got closer to the Residence, it got harder and harder to keep his questions at bay.

Thankfully, Scraps did not have to wait long with the breakneck pace Flit set. He didn't even mind that she lured him into the *organ-*

ised chaos of her room, rather than his own immaculate one. He picked his way across the clothing on the floor and sank onto her bed.

As the door slid shut behind her, Flit stood there, looking rather lost.

"What is on your mind?" Scraps asked, sitting on the edge of the bed and leaning forward. "Is it anything I can fix with these?" He reached into his pocket and pulled out the two bars of chocolate.

The set of Flit's shoulders softened, but she shook her head. "Not tonight, I'm afraid."

Scraps frowned, his strong jawline sitting askance as he grew more concerned. It must be bad if chocolate couldn't fix it. "Then why don't you sit down and talk to me about it?" He patted the bed.

Flit teleported over and then kicked off her shoes. The bed sank slightly with her weight when she settled beside him, curling her legs under her. She let out a heavy sigh and rubbed her eyes. He put his arm around her and drew her close.

"Shadow wanted to meet with Hawkeye and I earlier because he has an assignment for us."

That certainly got Scraps' attention. His back straightened, and the soft concern on his face turned into something more curious. "And?"

He loved having Flit as a patrol partner, but he knew how important her career was to her. She told him so many times that she had always dreamed of working in Intelligence, and given her talents, she would be an amazing addition to their team.

"He offered us an undercover assignment up in the Hub."

Scraps' eyes widened. That, according to the gossip in the Underground, was the gold standard of Intelligence missions, the place where someone could really make a difference.

"That is fantastic. This is what you have been waiting for!" Scraps pulled her into a hug, excited for her.

Flit shook her head and wiggled out of his embrace. "I'm not so sure anymore."

Scraps blinked. "What?"

Flit raked a hand through her hair and looked away. "It's full dark, and there is no recall date. Scraps, if I go up there, I…" She choked on her own words.

Turning to face her properly, Scraps urged, "You what?"

"I won't be able to see you or talk to you, or my parents, or anyone. I could be up there for years. Hell, I could be up there for the rest of my life."

Scraps considered her concerns. Given how ecstatic she had been to move down to the Underground only twelve months ago, he should have expected some hesitation from her. Still, she must have known what it involved when she had let her dreams take hold all those years ago.

He refused to let her wallow in the what ifs. If she was not ready to be enthusiastic about the new posting, he would support her by being optimistic on her behalf. "If they have asked you to go, you must be the best for the job. They are giving you the opportunity you have been working so hard for. Imagine the difference you could make! When do you have to leave?"

Flit bit her lip, looking up at him from under her lashes. "I haven't said yes yet."

"You haven't?" Scraps stared at her as though she had grown a second head. He considered calling Patch to check her temperature. "Why not?"

"Because I'll miss you!" she spluttered, throwing her hands in the air. "We've only just gotten together, and the last few months have been the best of my life! I stopped thinking about getting into Intelligence and was just enjoying our time together, but… having to leave now? Scraps, I can't leave you behind. I haven't felt so… so… so *complete* since before I lost Rook."

It took Scraps several long, tense, silent moments to process this. "I do not understand… You would give up this incredible opportunity and let yourself get stuck in the Underground because of me?"

The hazel in Flit's eyes darkened to a shade that told Scraps he had hurt her feelings. He wasn't sure how or why, but he tilted his head to the side as he tried to figure out what he should do, what she wanted him to do.

"You've always said that this is bigger than all of us, that the goal of the Underground used to be, and still should be, to find a way to get us back into the real world. Isn't that what you tell people all the time?"

"Yes!" Flit's voice was raised and edged with something sharp. She blinked rapidly as moisture built in her eyes, making her lashes dewy. "I… I still believe that, ok? I still want to do it, but—"

Scraps leaned forward, brushing a strand of deep brown hair out of her eyes and taking her hands in his. "But what?"

"Won't you miss me?" Flit's voice was uncharacteristically small.

She watched him, and suddenly, the room felt ten degrees hotter. Her question was a test and not one he had studied for. He let go of her hands and tugged at his collar, the weight of her unreadable expectations settling over him. She was right, of course. He did not know what the Underground would be like without her, but he knew what her dreams were, and he would never put himself before those.

He hesitated, trying to find the right words. "I would understand. You would be doing something you love."

"I don't love the stupid fucking mission, Scraps. I love you!"

The words fell between them with all the gravity of a lead balloon. Scraps had no idea how to respond. His mouth flapped open and closed uselessly, and he had the sudden urge to escape.

5

———

FLIT

FLIT'S HAND flew to cover her mouth.

Poor Scraps looked like he had been hit by a hover truck.

Panic rose inside of Flit then, a gnarled, vicious coiling that strangled her stomach and clawed at her lungs. She would give anything to wind back time and stop herself from blurting out those words. No matter how true they were, she knew he wasn't ready for them yet.

The seconds of spluttered confusion felt like hours of agony. The pounding of her heart became so powerful she could hear the blood rushing through her head.

She couldn't take it anymore.

Flit teleported to her feet.

"Flit, no—" Scraps reached out, grabbing her hand and trying to tug her back down.

"I… I need to think. I'm sorry. I, uh, I'm going to have a shower," Flit stammered, pulling her hand out of his grasp and stumbling back. She turned and teleported into her small en suite and slid the door shut between them.

THE NEXT MORNING, Flit sat in Shadow's office with Hawkeye at her side. The room was small, with all four walls lined with screens, any space between painted the light grey of the Intelligence sector. The screens were all switched off, but Flit had seen them used to display all sorts of views, from the Underground to Government offices in the Hub. The desk they were at had an interactive surface as well, and she avoided touching it, not wanting to get her fingerprints all over the glossy screen. She and Hawkeye had made their way over right after breakfast, but Shadow's assistant had let them into the office, explaining that he would be with them shortly, after he finished dealing with some more urgent matters.

Flit swallowed, trying to keep down the small amount of breakfast she had eaten before resigning to push the rest around on her plate. She was tired enough that she could fall asleep upright in her chair. If it wasn't bad enough that she had to decide whether to accept the mission, she also had to deal with the tension caused by blurting out 'I love you'. Not that Scraps had said anything, of course. When she had emerged from the shower, he had pressed a kiss to her cheek and gone in to clean up for himself. He'd come out, and they slipped into bed and slept together like they had for the past several months. No mention was made of the short but weighty words she had dropped, no more talk of the mission. Just a lukewarm goodnight and a casual arm slung around her waist as he had fallen asleep behind her.

While Scraps had slept, Flit had thought. And thought. And then thought some more.

It was a long night, the longest she'd had since Rook died. She hated that she could even draw that comparison, because in some ways, the idea of this mission felt like another kind of grieving. Either way, she stood to lose something important to her.

Hawkeye shifted uncomfortably in his seat beside her as they waited. She looked at the clock on the corner of the large screen behind the desk and frowned. They had only been waiting ten minutes, but it felt like hours.

"You look tired," Hawkeye ventured, no doubt chafing at the tense silence.

"No shit."

Hawkeye winced and rubbed the back of his neck. "I'm just trying to make conversation."

"When has using 'you look tired' to start a conversation with a woman ever worked for anyone?" Flit snapped, fixing Hawkeye with a disparaging look.

"Oh, for fu—" Hawkeye caught himself mid-curse and let out a slow breath, raking his fingers through his hair. "Let's try this again… Have you decided what you want to do?"

"Yes."

"Yes, you've decided, or yes, you're coming on the mission?"

Flit looked down at her nails, pretending that the chip on one bothered her more than her breaking heart. "Yes, to both."

Despite the frostiness in the room, Hawkeye's face lit up with excitement. He seemed like he was about to hug her, but he sat back in his seat, probably thinking better of it when Flit's shoulders tensed.

"How did Scraps take it?"

"He seemed pleased that I would be doing something I loved." Flit purposefully hedged around the truth.

"And?"

"That's all."

"Oh." Hawkeye's lips closed into a concerned frown, and he tore his gaze from Flit's. "Did he—"

Hawkeye's question was cut short as Shadow appeared in the room and glanced between them. "Do you two have your answers for me?"

Flit's heart thundered in her chest, and her throat went dry. She knew what she was supposed to say, but she couldn't make the words come out. Saying yes to Shadow was far more official than telling Hawkeye her intentions.

"We're in," Hawkeye responded for them both, sitting forward in his seat, eyes alight with excitement.

Shadow looked to Flit for confirmation, and she nodded numbly.

"Very well, then. Shall we begin?" Shadow settled into his seat on the opposite side of the desk and tapped the screen that took up most of the surface. He opened several virtual files and flicked them across to Hawkeye and Flit.

Despite her reservations, Flit's curiosity caused a hairline fracture to crack through her hesitation. She leaned forward, shoulder brushing Hawkeye's as Shadow pulled up schematics of a weapon that looked far too familiar.

"That's it," Flit blurted, muscles twitching at memories of the purple spray of lights. "You found it!"

Shadow leaned back in his seat. "We found evidence of it," he conceded, "but not much. A weapon like that should have a decent paper trail behind it. Beyond the schematics and a few documents claiming some of the mechanisms inside as proprietary tech, our agents were unable to get anything we could work with."

Flit reached out, pinch-zooming the schematics and spinning them around to get a closer look. Not that she really knew what she was looking for. From her basic understanding of weapons, the only thing she could note about this one was a lack of ammunition chamber.

"Is that what we're looking for up there? More information about the weapon?" Hawkeye asked.

"Yes." Shadow closed the file. "Our usual channels for this kind of investigation have failed, so we were hoping to use Newton and Vista's clearance to take a more *indirect* route."

Flit did not like the lilt in Shadow's tone. She crossed her arms over her chest. "*Indirect?*"

"Newton and Vista's aliases work for the Government department responsible for reviewing policies and procedures, and monitoring compliance," Shadow explained.

Any kindling sense of excitement Flit felt for the mission drained right out of her. "Reviewing policies and procedures?"

She couldn't think of anything more soul-destroying.

Hawkeye shot her a warning glare.

"This might come as a surprise to you, Flit, but reviewers have access to more sensitive information than any other agents we've got." Shadow's voice was firm and free of irony. "In Eastbay, the policies and procedures mostly related to the day-to-day running of some of the peripheral Government departments. The reviewers in the Hub will have access to critical organisational systems, standard and specialised operating procedures of every department, compliance checks for restricted manufacturing facilities…"

Flit connected the dots. "So, we go in and investigate the facilities in question?"

Active investigations were good. She could do that.

"No, you mind your cover and wait for the right jobs to cross your desk. Then, you gather information and report it back. Our other agents will conduct the physical investigations."

It was then that Flit realised disappointment had a flavour. It was a mix of the metallic tang of regret and the hallmark bitterness of fading dreams. She tried to swallow it down, but like her decision, it could not be undone.

"Let me show you what your clearances will be." Shadow opened a new document on the tabletop and widened it for Flit and Hawkeye to see.

Flit leaned in, telling herself this was still her dream and that she would be able to find ways to make a difference, regardless of what her Hub job would be.

WHEN FLIT and Hawkeye left Shadow's office, Flit's head was spinning. After showing them their clearances, Shadow had walked them through their anticipated training schedule. Most of it would be self-study, so they could familiarise themselves with key policies and procedures, but the rest was fast-tracked intensive field instruction to enhance their abilities and improve their teamwork. Even though he had stressed that their aliases were used more for information gathering than physical investigation, they had to be ready for everything.

Hawkeye was too busy chatting about their agenda for the next three weeks to realise she checked out the moment Shadow had handed it to them.

"Flit?" Hawkeye stopped walking and looked at her.

Flit stumbled to a stop. "Huh? Yeah?" They had reached a fork in the tunnel that would lead them to the Residence or to the training rooms. She must have been tuned out for a while if they had come that far.

"I asked if you wanted to come to my room so we can start on the reading? I know we've technically got the rest of the day off, but it can't hurt to try and get our heads around it all," Hawkeye offered.

"Can we meet after lunch? I didn't get much sleep last night. I can barely think straight." Flit's tone held a hint of apology.

"Sounds like a plan. I might head to the gym for a while, then." Hawkeye stepped closer and gently squeezed her upper arm. "I know this can't have been an easy decision for you. For what it's worth, you're doing the right thing. There's a fire in you, Flit. You won't be able to rest while things are the way they are. This is your chance. Our chance. We'll finally be somewhere we can make a difference."

Flit patted Hawkeye's hand. "Thank you, Hawk." She sighed, trying to get herself back together. "Of all the buffoons down here, I'm glad I'll be going up with you."

While he might not be her first choice, he was the indisputable second, and she had a feeling he understood that.

"Me too. Someone's gotta watch your back while you're doing your crazy shit," Hawkeye teased, pulling her in for a hug.

Flit rested her head against his shoulder as she forced a laugh. "Yeah, good luck with that."

Hawkeye's insistence that Flit needed someone to look after her was a constant point of contention between them. The banter, old as it was, was enough to put a smile on her lips for the first time that day. That had to count for something.

6

———————

SCRAPS

EVERY TIME SCRAPS thought he had gotten his head around the mystery of Flit, something happened to show him just how wrong he was. Things had been going so smoothly for them over the past few months that Flit's moodiness when she'd told him about her reassignment had taken him aback. From the first day he'd met her, she had been so determined to make a difference. She had been so critical of the Underground's lack of action on the surface. He assumed she would jump at the chance to take the mission. As someone who had always put work and duty first, Scraps could understand.

What Scraps couldn't understand, however, was love.

He had talked to various people about the topic, and no one could give him a solid answer. The most concrete conclusion he could draw was that he would know it when he felt it, and that if he loved Flit, he would find the idea of living without her unpalatable.

Really, though, he was just pleased she would get a chance to follow her dreams. His own career aspirations had ground to a dizzying halt when he had been captured by the Underground, but that had turned out to be a good thing. It would be a genuine tragedy if Flit allowed herself to get stuck on Security patrols for the rest of her life. Flit was the kind of person who refused to be contained, and if anyone had the passion and tenacity to bring the Government to their knees, it was her.

Scraps tried not to think about it too much as he reported for duty after breakfast. Hawkeye was in the same meeting as Flit, so Posthoc had assigned Swipe as his patrol partner. Scraps hadn't spent any time alone with Swipe since the rather spectacular fist-fight she and Flit had months ago, so he was not really looking forward to half a day of patrolling with her.

The patrol started quietly enough as they made sporadic but polite conversation along their route. Around half-way through, Scraps had almost started to enjoy it, but that enjoyment was cut short when they stopped just outside of one of the deeper caves.

The cavern was tall, perhaps the equivalent of four stories. Normally, the stalactites were illuminated by filtered red lighting. Fresh water from the tunnel above looked like blood dripping down the rock formations. It was almost impossible to see the natural protrusions as bat shrouded all the lights. As black as the depths of the caverns themselves, the creatures hung upside down, leathery wings wrapped around coarsely furred bodies. Scraps hadn't seen many of the mutant bats before, but he could see why Flit professed a particular dislike for the creatures. They were easily each the size of a small child, and the claws at the ends of their wings had a wicked curve to them. There had to be hundreds of them roosting on the ceiling.

"Stud, what's on the level above us?" Swipe whispered, stepping gingerly into the cavern and turning around in a slow circle.

Even with her years of patrolling, she still deferred to Scraps to know exactly where they were. His rote memorisation of the labyrinthine maps was a point of pride for the Blue Team. Unlike the others, who knew certain routes or could figure them out quickly from the markers, he knew them all by heart.

"A subterranean river runs through the network directly above us. It's why these caverns are so damp all the time," Scraps explained, his nose twitching at the moist, earthy scent hanging in the air around them. "The river veers off towards the north, and the caverns there—which I have been told normally house bats—collapsed after one of the explosions last year."

"So… they're looking for a new home?" Swipe asked.

Scraps nodded at her assessment. "That sounds probable."

"And unfortunate." Swipe sighed and stepped back to join him in the shelter of the corridor. "Isn't this one of the tunnels that leads to an emergency exit at the foothills between Old City and the eastern part of the Hub?"

"It is indeed." Scraps leaned into the tunnel again, looking up and trying to get a better count. He pulled his visor down and switched the green shades of night-vision to a heat-sensing field. His stomach dropped at the sheer mass of bright red above their heads. "I suppose that means that we will need to clear it out?"

Swipe swore under her breath. "Yep. We can't leave them up there." She looked around, and her lips twisted in a wry frown. "If we hold the exits that lead back to the habitation levels, then we can muster them out the exit over there. That will lead them away from our emergency route, right?"

"Correct." Scraps ran his hand over his belt. "The bats dislike light. If we use our flares and fire grenades, we should be able to get them to move without getting too close."

Even with the bats involved, Scraps was sure Flit would be upset at missing out on the chance to wantonly cast her fire grenades around.

Swipe groaned. "Buckle up, Stud. This is about to get very messy."

AN HOUR AND A HALF LATER, they returned to the armoury covered in bat guano. The stench was so tart that Scraps was struggling to keep his breakfast down, and the black tar-like substance burned where it touched his skin. He tried to be thankful that the fire grenades and flares had been enough to stop the bats from swiping at them with razor sharp claws, but he could have done without the putrid waste they had dropped in shock when the flames had roared to life beneath them.

"Woah." Clarity let out a low whistle as she looked between them. "Rough patrol, huh?"

Swipe dumped her belt on the steel preparation bench and bent over to retrieve a box of rags. She took a few out before handing the box to Scraps. "You could say that." She scrunched up her nose and cleaned some muck off her belt.

"Why were you on Deep Level? I thought you and Hawk were assigned to Surface," Tweak asked.

"Flit and Hawkeye had a meeting to attend," Scraps supplied, taking his own belt off and assessing it for grime.

"Speaking of meetings," Clarity said as she put her patrol gear in her locker and leaned back against the door, "Posthoc came by earlier. He wants the whole team in Training Room Three in half an hour."

Scraps frowned. He could probably spend the whole day scrubbing himself and his gear and still not feel clean enough to be around other people, but orders were orders. If he wanted to have a shower before the meeting, he would need to get a move on. He redoubled his effort and concentrated a little harder on getting the bat faeces out of the cracks between his grenade cradles.

"Has the decision about the Team Leader role been made?" Swipe asked.

Scraps' hand slipped on his belt, and he frowned at it. Of course, in all the talk about Flit's Intelligence mission last night, he had all but forgotten about the Team Leader role. If both Hawkeye and Flit left the team, not only would they be short-staffed, but they still be without a leader. It was a pity too. He had been looking forward to seeing either one of them flourish in the new position. For a moment, Scraps wondered if Flit might stay behind for it, if being a leader of a Security Team would give her what she was looking for.

Clarity shrugged. "I think so."

"Who do you think it'll be?" Tweak asked. Clarity went to answer, but he elbowed her. "Not you. You have an unfair advantage."

"Hawkeye, obviously." Swipe snorted, shaking her head.

"What do you think, big guy?" Tweak tapped the table in front of Scraps.

Scraps started. "Think about what?"

"The Team Leader position," Tweak repeated. "You gonna be sleeping with the boss?"

"I think…" Scraps wasn't sure what he should say. It hit him that Flit hadn't told him what she intended to do before they had parted ways that morning. "I think I need to take a shower." Scraps turned, dumping the rags into the bin and throwing his belt into his locker.

As Scraps made for the door, Clarity called out behind him, "Don't forget. Training Room Three. You've got twenty-five minutes."

7

———

FLIT

ALL FLIT WANTED WAS A NAP.

After she and Hawkeye had gone their separate ways, Flit retreated to her room and curled up in bed. She tossed and turned for what felt like an hour, and when she finally fell into that blissful state of nothingness, a shrill ringing pierced through her slumber.

"Fucking alarm," Flit groaned, rolling over and pulling her pillow over her head. "Off! Turn off!"

The alarm continued to blare despite her impassioned protest.

With a heavy sigh, and a great deal of effort, Flit restrained her temper and lowered her voice. "Alarm, off."

It didn't work.

Flit sat up, about to find a shoe to throw at the comm system when she noticed Posthoc's name flashing on the screen, indicating an incoming call.

In the blink of an eye, Flit teleported over. She tapped the screen. "Hello?"

"Flit, Posthoc here."

"What can I do for you?" Flit leaned against the wall and yawned as his face appeared on the unit.

"Shadow tells me that you and Hawkeye have accepted a reassignment to Intelligence." His eyes narrowed ever so slightly, and he pressed his lips together.

Flit rubbed her eyes with the heels of her hands. "Uh, yeah. We'll be going up in three weeks. I know it's terrible timing, given we just went through the process of applying for the Team Leader role and stuff."

"You're right about that," Posthoc huffed. "The team are expecting a decision from me today. I don't have one to give them, but you and Hawkeye might as well come down here and tell them why."

Flit's gut churned at the thought of announcing what she was struggling to get her own head around. "I was going to tell them at dinner."

Posthoc shook his head. "Not going to work, I'm afraid. I need to get things sorted for patrols tomorrow and to assign a few temp team members to the roster. If I start messing with the schedule, they'll ask questions, so you might as well tell them beforehand."

As much as Flit hated to admit it, there was no point delaying the inevitable. "Sure. Whatever. I'll be there."

"Training Room Three. See you in ten minutes," Posthoc said before ending the call.

With a low groan, Flit leaned forward, resting her forehead against the cool wall. She had a hard enough time coming to terms with the fact she had agreed to go on the mission, to leave Scraps and her parents behind. She had hoped for a little bit more time to get her feelings and thoughts in order before announcing it to everyone else, but even if she was tired, even if she was leaving them, the Blue Team had to come first. They were all going to be pulling extra hours until they got some new recruits, so the least she could do was be upfront.

With a growing sense of trepidation, Flit went to the bathroom and washed her face, hoping to appear little more alert. She took her hair out of the messy braid and combed her fingers through it before tying it into a high ponytail. Then, knowing there was little she could do to improve the bags under her eyes, she turned and made her way to the meeting.

The observation window of Training Room Three was already opaque, but the door was still open. When she walked in, everyone was standing around and laughing about something that had happened earlier in the day. It looked like they were just waiting on Hawkeye.

Flit picked up on a few words that made her scrunch her nose in distaste. "Bat shit?" she asked, teleporting to stand beside Scraps. "Whose patrol was that on?"

"Lean in closer to lover boy, and you might be able to tell for yourself," Sway teased, drawing a round of laughter from everyone except for Swipe and Scraps.

"I wasn't even supposed to be on that damned route," Swipe muttered under her breath, turning her nose up.

Flit almost leaned in to tell Scraps that he smelled wonderful and fresh, but she remembered the night before and kept her thoughts to herself. They would have to talk about what had happened at some point, but now was not the time.

Hawkeye finally walked in, and Flit was glad for the reprieve. Posthoc perked up and gestured for him to come over. When Hawk stood on Flit's other side, Posthoc cleared his throat. "Thanks for coming, everyone. You know I hate dragging you into meetings after you've been on shift, but you're all waiting on a certain announcement, one that I unfortunately cannot make today."

"But we've got bets riding on this!" Sway protested.

The way Posthoc glared at Sway was enough to make the perky telecoercionist shrink back into petulant silence. "Believe me, I'm frustrated too. I've spent a great deal of time considering the best person for the position, but the reason why is not mine to tell." Posthoc glanced pointedly at Flit and Hawkeye.

Hawkeye cleared his throat. "Thanks, Posthoc. I appreciate the thoughtfulness," he announced. He stepped closer to Flit's side, and the warmth of his skin radiated against her left arm. "Flit and I have been reassigned to Intelligence. We'll be heading out on a full dark mission in a couple of weeks. We start training immediately."

The announcement was met by stunned hush. As her teammate's eyes widened in surprise, Flit could almost hear their hearts breaking in their hitched breaths and shuffling feet.

After an uncomfortable twitch contorted Link's lips into a deep frown, she broke the silence. "For how long for?"

"It's a long-term gig," Flit admitted. Her voice sounded distant, even to her.

"So, you're just gonna leave—" Swipe's protest ended when she looked at Scraps and then shook her head.

On any other day, Flit might have urged Swipe to continue, encouraged her to speak her mind, maybe picked a fight over whatever she clearly had a problem with, but she wasn't in the mood right now.

Clarity, always the optimist, played with the end of her braid as she forced a smile. "We'll miss you both, obviously, but… you've been wanting this since we were kids, so congratulations, I suppose."

Hawkeye slung his arm around Flit's shoulder. "Thanks!" His tone was far too chirpy for the moment.

"However, that means this team is now down two members and still leaderless. I've been playing around with the roster, and while the outcome is not ideal, it should allow everyone to get enough rest between shifts," Posthoc said. He walked over to the window in the training room and activated the projection screen, bringing up the patrol timetable. "Flit, Hawk, I'm sure you guys have plenty to do. You don't need to stick around for this. Thanks for dropping by."

The dismissal landed like a punch in the gut. It took Flit a moment to catch her breath at how quickly things were changing. "Right. Thanks," she muttered, forcing her chin high as she walked out, Hawkeye by her side.

"Wait!" Sway spluttered. Flit and Hawkeye stopped. "Posthoc, can you at least tell us how who you would have picked as Team Leader?"

The natural, competitive beast that slumbered inside of Flit reared its head at the question. She turned back to Posthoc, but the postcognitive shook his head. "Not a chance. You're just going to have to find another way to win Link's chocolates back. That is, if they haven't already been eaten. Sorry."

Sway groaned, leaving the others laughing at his expense.

Sensing that there would be no resolution on the matter, Flit left the training room.

"So, snacks and then study?" Hawkeye asked.

Flit sighed heavily. "I hate that word."

"Snacks?" Hawkeye needled her.

She shot him a warning look before teleporting a few metres ahead.

"Oh, come on! I'm just trying to lighten the mood," Hawkeye called after her, jogging to catch up.

8

———

SCRAPS

THE DAYS that followed Flit's decision to accept the role in Intelligence were busy for both her and Scraps. Having two less team members meant that he had to take on extra patrols, and even though he would never admit it to Flit, he'd come to take her teleporting shortcuts for granted. He and Swipe had to check each and every tunnel in the labrynthine network, even the ones that terminated in dead ends or cave-ins.

Even if he was not pulling extra shifts, Scraps would not be spending his spare time with Flit anyway. Her training schedule was just as intensive as she said Shadow had promised it would be. When her full day of training was over and they met up in the Mess for dinner, she barely made it through their meal without yawning. They would retreat to either one of their rooms, and then spend some time talking and kissing, or more, before falling asleep. In reality, the most time they spent together was with their eyes closed.

Scraps had been with Flit long enough to have a good understanding of her moods. When she got tired, she was verbally snappy but physically affectionate. Extra sarcasm indicated frustration, but the guarded conversation and hard kisses were new. He had a feeling it had something to do with the night she had made her decision, but when he brought it up, she shut it down by going to sleep or stealing the concerns away with her lips.

Scraps straightened his jacket as Flit walked into the Mess. She looked around, smiling when she spotted him at a table near the food, and teleported over.

"Are you sure you want me to have dinner with you?" Scraps asked as she appeared right beside him.

Flit sank into the seat beside his and slipped her hand onto his thigh under the table. "I'm sure. I need the moral support. But if you'd rather eat with the others, I'd understand."

"That is not what I meant—"

"I know," Flit interrupted, shaking her head. "I'm just worried the conversation will get a bit awkward."

Whenever Scraps joined Flit and her parents for dinner, the conversation inevitably fell into bickering about trivial things. Their friends swore it was just part of normal family dynamics, but he never quite knew how to engage with it. If he took Flit's parents' side, Flit would hold it against him later. But if he took Flit's side, he was worried her parents would disapprove of him, and while Flit was tempestuous, he could curb her fire with a few well-placed kisses. Tinker, though? Well, she was terrifying.

"Although," Flit said, drawing him out of his internal dilemma, "I want you here so you know that when I'm gone, my parents will have your back. They like you, and if you can't talk to me, you can always seek them out."

Scraps blinked, his heart warming with affection. He had always attended dinners with Flit's parents out of respect for her, but he had never considered building his own relationship with them to be a priority. With the way Flit said it, though, he knew she was right. He was close to the others in the Blue Team, but not nearly as close as he was to her. When she left, he would need a new confidant. As intimidating as she could be, Tinker had always been a good listener. Even Stride seemed to have come around to the fact he was dating Flit.

"That is a lovely idea. Thank you."

"Flit, Scraps!" Tinker's voice cut through their conversation, and the middle-aged woman pulled her daughter into a tight hug. Scraps smiled while he watched, wondering what it would be like to have parents, to have someone that adored you no matter how many mistakes you made. Parents, he thought, had to be the most forgiving kind of people there were.

Then, Tinker did something unexpected. She let go of Flit and gave Scraps a tight but quick hug. Scraps was so surprised that he didn't think to return the embrace until it was too late. He didn't have time to mull over it, though, as Stride reached out his good hand for Scraps to shake.

"Good to see you again, mate," Stride said with a firm nod.

"Likewise, Sir."

Flit rolled her eyes. "Scraps…"

"Someone's gotta have a little respect around here." Stride poked her playfully in the ribs. "But honestly, Stride is fine. Sir makes me feel old."

"You are old."

"Flit, we've been at the table for less than ten seconds." Tinker cast her daughter an exasperated look.

"And yet, I still haven't broken the record!" Flit sighed melodramatically.

Scraps had to pick up his water and take a sip to stop himself from laughing. He was on Tinker's good side right now, and he had no desire to ruin that.

"So, what is new with you two?" Stride settled down into his seat with a groan of relief.

"I've been reassigned to Intelligence," Flit said in an overly chirpy voice.

Tinker and Stride's faces ran through a gamut of emotions.

"You… you've been what?" Tinker put a hand over her heart.

"I've been given a full dark mission," Flit said. Scraps got the feeling Tinker's question was rhetorical. "No recall date." Her parents paled.

Stride reached across the table, taking his daughter's hand. "When do you leave?"

"Two and a half weeks," Scraps blurted. Flit's parents looked at him as though they had forgotten he was there. He froze, realising he had spoken out of turn, but their faces softened.

"Are you going together?" Tinker asked, some measure of hope returning to her gaze.

Scraps shook his head. "No. Hawkeye is going with Flit."

Tinker glanced between Scraps and Flit for a few seconds as she digested the revelation.

Beside him, Scraps felt the vibration of Flit's left leg bouncing up and down under the table. He gently settled his hand on her knee to help keep her steady. She gave him a grateful smile, and he resisted the urge to kiss her.

"Well… I…" Tinker stopped, clearing her throat and blinking furiously. "I don't suppose there is anything an old medic can do to stop her daughter from going on some crazy mission, is there?"

"Nope. Not unless I go and get myself hurt," Flit said with a frown and an innocent shrug, her voice completely devoid of her typical cheeky charm.

Scraps saw a flicker in Tinker's eyes and swore she was considering something dangerous.

He leaned in closer. "There is still time," he whispered conspiratorially. "She always finds ways to get herself into trouble."

For a moment, Tinker and Stride just stared at him, but then, Flit started to laugh. Stride joined her and then Tinker.

"Well, we should make the most of this dinner then, shouldn't we?" Stride said, voice choked with emotion.

Everyone else nodded in agreement.

"Thank goodness." Flit sniffed. "Here I was thinking you were gonna start sobbing, Old Man."

Stride pointed a finger at his daughter. "Enough with this old business, ok? At least pretend to be nice to me in the time we've got left."

THE NEXT DAY ON PATROL, Sway and Link found another roost of bats in several of the key emergency exit tunnels. Despite the fact that there had not been any cave-ins or explosions for months, it was concerning to think that anyone trying to flee the Underground might end up running straight into a leathery-winged, sharp-teethed flock of flying death. When Posthoc found out, he decided that the team needed to clear them out once and for all. The natural network in that area was littered with tunnels, caves, and switchbacks that would make it hard to muster the bats in the desired direction. It was a job that would take a lot of planning, and not a single team member argued when Posthoc handed the task to Scraps. After all, he knew the tunnel routes the best.

After discussing the particulars with Posthoc, Scraps retired to the common area in the Residence to start strategising. He had gotten as far as finding the ideal exit route for the bats when a familiar voice shattered his concentration.

Without an invitation, Acumen sank down onto the couch beside him. "Scraps, buddy, good to see you. How's the planning going?"

The older man wiped his soil-covered hands on the thighs of his trousers, and Scraps winced as he realised he had forgotten all about helping out with the gardening.

"Good. I think I have the best route sorted. I am pleased to have a chance to coordinate it." Scraps held the datapad out for Acumen to see.

Acumen leaned forward, ice blue eyes scanning over the maps and notes that Scraps had made. "That bat colony showing up there was weird, all right. I daresay Posthoc is glad to have you on side. With Hawkeye gone, the Blue Team has lost their most tactical mind."

"It is unfortunate." Scraps set the datapad down on his lap so that he could talk to Acumen without distraction. "But we should have the required abilities within the team to make sure the mission is a success. We may need to ask a few people from Red to join us, but I will leave that up to Posthoc."

"Oh, I'm sure you're all more than capable." Acumen waved a dismissive hand in the air. "I just meant for the overall team-planning side of things. There are so many new recruits to train thanks to the events of the past six months. It's not a great time to lose any team members, let alone the most experienced. Now, with Flit and Hawkeye gone, you're going to wind up doing a lot more stuff like this. The other Blue Team members are good, but somehow, your knowledge still puts them all to shame."

"Knowledge?" Scraps chuckled, shaking his head. "I think it is more the time that I dedicate to studying while they play in the VR suite or gamble."

Acumen chuckled. "That's probably true." He leaned against the back of the couch, resting his hands behind his head and looking at Scrap appraisingly. Scraps couldn't help but wonder what Acumen was thinking. "You know that's my forte, not yours… the mind-reading thing?" Acumen teased.

"Thank goodness for that. I would not like to be in anyone's head. I can barely get my mind around my own thoughts," Scraps muttered.

"It can get chaotic at times," Acumen acknowledged, his tone turning serious. "How are things going for you, though?"

"Good," Scraps said simply.

A cocked eyebrow was all it took for Scraps to know that Acumen didn't believe him.

"Why would it be any other way?" Scraps' brows knitted together in confusion.

"Oh, I don't know. Something about the fact your girlfriend is going on a top-secret mission for an indeterminant amount of time." Acumen drummed his fingers on his chin in an approximation of deep thought.

Scraps let out a huff of annoyance. "I have been feeling the lack of her presence on patrol, but I do not see the point in worrying about something that is going to happen in the future. Besides, I have spent most of my life without her. I am sure I will survive well enough."

Acumen frowned, the sparkle in his blue eyes dimming into something more sombre. "Buddy, do me a favour, please?"

It was the last thing Scraps expected Acumen to say, but he nodded all the same. He had a lot of respect for the man. He would do whatever he could to help him.

"Of course."

"Please don't pull out the 'I've spent most of my life without you' line in front of Flit. She's barely managed to put her heart back together. It would be cruel to break it like that before she leaves," Acumen said. With a groan, he pushed himself out of his seat and patted Scraps' shoulder. "When things settle on you, feel free to come and find me for a chat. I know it all seems over the top now, but feelings have a way of creeping up on us when we least expect them."

Scraps watched Acumen walk away. He went to reach for his datapad, but his excitement for mission planning had fizzled out after their conversation. He might have been in the Underground for a full year, but times like these made him feel further away from understanding it than ever.

9

FLIT

FLIT ENJOYED STUDYING PRECISELY one time in her life.

It had been several months earlier, when Scraps was revising for his orienteering test and she had made it her mission to distract him. Granted, it wasn't her doing the studying, and, really, not much had gotten done… but she found it infinitely more entertaining than slogging through the material she needed to know for her Intelligence mission.

"Ugh!" Flit threw the datapad onto her bedside table and flopped back onto her bed.

"Is that a good *I am loving this study so much I can't possibly take any more* ugh, or an *I am so bored I want to scratch my eyes out* ugh?" Scraps peered at Flit over the top of his own datapad as he sat at her small dining table.

"It's a *why the hell did I think this was ever going to be possible* ugh!" Flit replied, exasperation nibbling away at each of her words.

Scraps got up and walked over. He gently patted her hip, and she scooted over to make room for him. "If I can memorise the entire Underground tunnel network in under three months, then I am sure you can manage that." He waved his hand towards the discarded datapad.

"I appreciate your confidence. I really do." Flit shifted onto her side and rested her head in his lap. Scraps begun to idly stroke her hair, his fingers moving in a soothing, gentle rhythm. "But I'm not you. I don't do studying. Of all of the jobs I could have been assigned to, reviewing safety protocol procedures is the absolute worst."

Scraps hand froze over her brow.

She craned her neck to look up at him, her lips twisting in confusion. "What?"

"You weren't supposed to tell me that." Scraps' voice was low, disconcerted.

"What?"

"That your new position will be reviewing safety protocol and procedures. Is that not classified?"

Flit winced. He was right. "I suppose it is. Oops." She shrugged, pleased she had managed to keep it from him that long.

"Flit, you have to be careful. The information is restricted for a reason." Scraps shook his head.

"Oh, Scraps, it's fine." Flit chuckled. "It's you, not some Government office worker. You're not going to go telling anyone."

Scraps just stared at her in disbelief. "Please promise me you'll be more careful."

Rolling over and sitting up so that she was facing him, Flit smirked. "Well… now that you know, I don't suppose you could help me figure out how to get my head around it all?"

Her request for study assistance burned away any rebuke he might have had for her not promising to be more careful. "You want me to help you study?"

Flit smiled, wide and bright. "Yes, please."

"If I agree, will you allow me to create a study schedule?"

"Knock yourself out."

"And if I make it, will you follow it?" Scraps' narrowed his eyes at her.

Flit shrugged. "Uh, sure. Why not?"

Scraps scoffed, "Flit!"

She rolled her eyes, but she didn't blame him for milking the situation. This, she knew, was what he had been born for. In her idle moments, when she daydreamed about what they would do in an alternate reality where they didn't have to hide in the Underground, Flit thought Scraps would make an excellent teacher.

"Probably not as faithfully as you'd like, but I will try my hardest. There is so much shit to learn."

"It is not shit!"

"Ok, crap." Flit amended, and Scraps groaned. "I figure I actually have a chance if you help me."

Scraps reached out to pull her into his harms and stole a sweet, lingering kiss. Just as she begun to enjoy the playfulness, reality washed over her, and her mood turned sombre. Sure, they would have fun studying together, but every minute of that took her closer to leaving. An iron fist grabbed her heart when she realised that she had just under two and a half weeks before she would have to say goodbye to him. Maybe forever.

"Well, I can't say no to that. If you must go up there, I want you to be prepared. The more you can learn now, the better," Scraps agreed with a firm nod. He used his telekinesis to float her datapad into his hands. "I'll get started on the timetable immediately."

"No!" Flit blurted, prising the datapad from his grip. Her heart thundered in her chest. "We can sort that out over breakfast in the morning. I am not doing any more study tonight."

To emphasise her point, Flit got to her knees on the soft blanket and leaned forward, pressing her lips against his. Scraps groaned into the kiss. This was a much better way to use their precious time together.

They ended up spending much of the night moving in each other's arms. Sleep took enough of a back seat that Scraps woke up starving. However, his excitement at the idea of creating a study timetable for her meant that he was as alert and perky as ever. He sat at his table and ate his breakfast while he worked. Flit reclined on the bed and caught up on the news.

"This material is fascinating!" Scraps' voice was garbled between bites of cereal. He moved the various policy and procedure document titles around in the timetable he was setting up for her. "Storage of 'Biohazards in Medical Facilities'? 'Personal Protective Equipment in Arms Manufacturing'? 'Avoiding detection by Registered temporal sensing and mind reading'? So much potential."

Flit looked up from the video she was watching with a single eyebrow cocked in disbelief. "It depends on whether I get to review any of those. Who knows? I may be stuck using the 'Appropriate Cleaning Strategies for Silicone-Based Tech Chips' review." Instead of returning her attention to her video, she dragged her gaze from the eager look on his face down to his shirtless chest. "Are you sure you don't wanna skip the timetabling and jump back into bed before we start our day?"

Scraps' expression was so unimpressed that she shrank back and raised her hands, creating a buffer between them. "Hey, you look hot without a shirt on! Can't blame a girl for trying."

"I may look 'hot' shirtless, but that will not save me from Posthoc's disappointment if I do not complete my mission proposal," Scraps tutted. "Because of your seductive distraction and creating your timetable, I actually have a lot of work to do this morning."

Flit had spent much of her life arguing, so she knew a thing or two about picking her battles. Even she was not foolish enough to try and pull Scraps away from his work when he used *that* tone. Instead, she figured she would use the extra time to get to training early, rather than stumbling in just after they were supposed to begin. It might even put her on Shadow's good side for once.

10

SCRAPS

SCRAPS HAD an hour after Flit left to finish putting together his mission proposal for Posthoc. He worked quickly, aware that the distractions of the past twenty-four hours meant he was not as far along in the process as he would have liked. In an ideal world, the last hour before submitting any proposal would be spent making final checks on the most important aspects. When he had been Registered, he had plenty of spare time to study and plan, all without interruptions. It had been a simpler life in many ways. Not that he would trade it, but he did miss the straightforwardness from time to time.

With a grim smile, Scraps put his datapad to sleep and stood. He twisted from side to side and stretched out his arms and legs, regretting that he did not have time for his morning exercise routine, although before he had started studying with Flit over breakfast, she had helped him wake up in a different way.

A call came through the comms unit in Flit's room, and Scraps walked over to answer it.

Posthoc's face appeared on the screen, relief washing over it. "Ah, there you are," he said. "I figured if you weren't in your room, you were either in Flit's or at the gym. I'm glad I didn't have to go chasing after you."

"I skipped the gym this morning," Scraps admitted. "I wanted to put the final touches on my plans for the mission."

"It's done?"

Scraps nodded.

"Great, but we're going to have to put it on hold." Posthoc rubbed the stubble on his chin. His normally sharp eyes were underscored with dark bags. "We've just received some new information from Control and Intelligence. Don't bother coming to meet with me now. I need you and Swipe to head out on your patrol early, and when you get back, report straight to Control."

Any disappointment Scraps felt at having his proposal pushed aside was obliterated by the serious-sounding nature of Posthoc's request. "Copy that. See you then."

Posthoc grunted a farewell, and Scraps freshened up and got changed before heading out. Instead of making straight for the armoury, he decided to stop by Swipe's room to see if she was ready. He still remembered the way to her room from when he had escorted her there on the day she had tried to kiss him.

He shook off those memories and knocked on her door.

"Who is it?"

"It is Scraps. I wanted to make sure you heard from Posth—"

Before he could finish, the door slid open to reveal Swipe pulling a skin-tight white tank top over her head. Scraps' cheeks flared with heat, and he turned away quickly, but not before catching an eyeful of the beige bra she wore and how it barely managed to contain her assets.

"Yes, I'm getting ready now. Come in. I've just got to plait my hair," she said, pulling her honey blonde locks free of her top. Her room was much the same size and layout as his own, but like Flit's, it was lived in. Not messy, just decorated with the evidence of many years spent in the same place. She gestured to her bed. "Take a seat."

Scraps looked at the bed and shook his head. "Uh, I am fine standing here, but thank you."

"If you'd prefer standing in the doorway to sitting, be my guest." Her tone held a hint of exasperation. She retrieved a brush from her bedside table and ran it through her hair a few times. "Did Posthoc give you any extra information? I asked what this was all about, but he brushed me off."

"I did not ask," Scraps admitted. "We will find out after our patrol."

Swipe chuckled. "You are far more patient than you ought to be." She reached behind her head and started to work her hair into a neat braid. Her amusement turned into something more sombre. "How did your mission planning go? I suppose you've got more time on your hands now that you and Flit aren't really a thing anymore."

Mind whirring to a stop, Scraps stepped into the room properly. The door slid shut behind him. "Not really a thing anymore?" he repeated. "What do you mean?"

"Uh, well, Flit's leaving." Swipe paused mid-movement, fingertips tangled in her silky strands. "One of you is going to have to end it."

"End it?"

Swipe let go of her braid to gesture to him. "Your relationship." She spoke slowly, giving him a chance to catch on. "You can't date someone who's moving to the Surface for an indeterminate amount of time."

Scraps pressed his lips together. He supposed proximity played an important part in their relationship, but he was not ready to end things. He had developed genuine feelings for Flit.

"Fuck, Scraps…" Swipe trailed off, walking over to him, the progress she made on her braid coming undone. "Please don't tell me you're going to wait for her to come back."

Scraps had not really considered any other option. When Patch had asked him a while ago whether he could see himself with another woman in the Underground, he said no. The other ladies were lovely, and some of them rather attractive, but he was not interested in spending time with them like he did with Flit.

Gently grasping his biceps, Swipe looked into his eyes. She was around the same height as him, so neither had to crane their neck to make it comfortable. "Scraps, Stud, that isn't going to work. She's going up with Hawkeye. He may pretend he's over her, but when it's just the two of them, no end date in sight…"

The memory of Hawkeye kissing Flit in the Mess flashed through Scraps' mind. Hot, ugly jealousy reared deep in his gut, and his back stiffened, his teeth clenching. "Flit would not do that."

With a heavy sigh, Swipe let go of his arms and shook her head, taking up her braid again. "I don't want to be accused of meddling, but someone's gotta give it to you straight. Agents sent on missions of unspecified lengths rarely come back. I get it if you're both just clinging onto things for as long as you can, but make sure you cut it off clean before she leaves. You deserve better than to be left down here, pining over someone who won't return."

Scraps wanted to argue. He wanted to tell Swipe that she was indeed meddling. He wanted to provide her with several logical, well-phrased rebuttals that would put her argument to rest.

But he had nothing. Swipe was right. He had not given enough thought to what would happen beyond their remaining two-and-a-half weeks. There was no telling how long Flit would be gone. He was confident she would not give in to Hawkeye's advances, if he made any, but Scraps supposed it did seem unrealistic for either of them to commit to holding on to the wisps of their relationship for five, ten, maybe forty years.

"Come on. Let's get this patrol done so we can find out whatever it is Posthoc discovered." Swipe brushed past him as she walked out of her room.

Scraps turned, rushing to catch up as he got lost in his own thoughts.

INSTEAD OF FOCUSING on their patrol, Scraps became preoccupied by his earlier conversation with Swipe. Thankfully, it was an uneventful day in the tunnels. As much as he wished he did not have to think about the changes his relationship with Flit would face, he was glad to have something to consider beside the odd, overly dramatic video series Swipe insisted on talking about.

When they returned, they walked straight through the painted periwinkle habitation tunnels and into a dense warren of sleek white passages. They stopped at the heavy metal blast door that led to Control, and Swipe leaned towards it, keeping her eyes wide as the retina scan activated and the access panel blinked with a *Requesting access, please stand by* message. A few seconds later, the words changed to *Access granted,* and the doors hissed open.

Inside, the main war-room-like space was busy, the fullness exacerbated by his friends and teammates milling about in the middle of the room. The Control workers nearby cast the Blue Team disgruntled looks as they disrupted the working environment with their chatter.

When Swipe and Scraps approached, Posthoc stepped forward. Scraps noticed that Flit was leaning against a vacant console behind him, with Hawkeye at her side.

"A team reunion already?" Swipe asked as they came to a stop by the group. "Surely it's too early for that."

"You would think so, but we got some information, and it looks like you'll all have one last hurrah," Posthoc said. Everyone perked up at the idea, and Posthoc chuckled. "Shadow and I booked a meeting room. I'll give you more information once we're all settled in."

Without further delay, Posthoc turned and led the group to the exit at the rear of the room. They walked down the long corridor lined with heavy, dull metal doors, and Posthoc stopped at one about half-way down. He pressed his hand against the reader, and the door slid open to reveal a larger meeting space that Scraps had not been into before. A dozen chairs circled a projection-enhanced tabletop. Shadow was already waiting for them, and he looked up at the incomers, nodding slightly.

"Thank you all for coming. Please, sit. You're in for quite a briefing." Shadow gestured to the empty seats.

Skirting around Swipe, Scraps stepped up to Flit's side. She flashed him a half-smile in greeting as they sat down together.

"Looks like we get one last mission together." The usual sparkle that would be in Flit's eyes at such an opportunity was dulled by something he could not read.

Scraps took her hand under the table. "I'm already looking forward to it."

"Ugh, you two," Tweak groaned, settling into the seat on the other side of Scraps. "It's a mission, not a bloody date."

Scraps chose to ignore him, a resolve made even easier when Posthoc activated the table and the surface started glowing with green light, ready to project. Silence fell in the room, and everyone leaned in, waiting to see what the two leaders had for them.

"Before I begin, I need you all to know that this mission is unique. As members of the Security department, your interests and routes have always remained firmly within the boundaries of the Underground," Posthoc began, his voice was low and serious, and he looked around the table, making eye contact with each of them in turn. "What Shadow and I are asking of you goes beyond your job description. You have every right to decline to participate, and if you do, it will not be held against you."

If anything, Posthoc's phrasing and the inherent sense of danger only made the members of the Blue Team lean in closer. Scraps was not surprised. His colleagues were all as skilled as they were spirited. Being so closed off from the outside world, anything out of the ordinary in the Underground was highly coveted. Scraps doubted anyone sitting at the table would walk away no matter what Posthoc revealed next.

"Everyone here has a good idea of what happened with Heft a few months ago, while Flit and Scraps were on patrol," Posthoc said. "Shadow and I have been working together to try and find clues about what really happened, and we've finally had a break-through."

Flit sat up straighter, her hand tensing in Scraps' grasp. He caught her gaze out of the corner of his eyes, and she seemed reen-ergised by the news. Whenever their talk had turned to what happened with Heft, she had sworn there was more going on. Scraps sincerely hoped there wasn't, as he had come to enjoy the peace and quiet, but it looked like Flit was right. As usual.

"We found some tech on the bodies of the men Heft was working with," Shadow explained. "Two of them were carrying devices encrypted with Dead Man's switches. The internals were decimated, but with Posthoc's help, our micros had a good idea of what it was all supposed to look like. They spent the last few months reconstructing the hardware from the atomic level up and then patched the software."

Tweak let out a slow whistle. "That's pretty impressive. Who did you have working on it?"

"It was team effort. I'll be sure to pass on your admiration." Shadow's voice was dry as he tapped the tabletop. A wireframe projection of a familiar, crumbled skyline assembled itself before them. "We initially tracked the communications Heft sent out to locations scattered around the city." With a gesture, a dozen points of red light glowed on the wireframe, nestled in various parts of the city. "Unfortunately, we reached a dead end following those. They were intercepted by hand-held devices so we had nothing to investigate, but this is where the reconstruction of the tech on the bodies came in handy."

This time, Posthoc pinched part of the cityscape with both fingers and then dragged them apart, zooming in on a building in the heart of the ruined metropolis.

"Their tech contained data with various geotags. Thanks to the analysis of Shadow's team, we believe this is the location they were using as their base."

"Shit…" Flit whispered beside Scraps, almost bouncing in her seat. It was not the word Scraps would use to express his awe at the discovery, but he wholeheartedly concurred with the sentiment.

"Now, if you follow the old subway network that heads east in sector T, there is a good access point here." Posthoc circled a spot a few blocks away from the target building with his fingertip, and it lit up blue as well. "Depending on Government drone surveillance at the time, you've got the option of one of three safe routes."

Shadow tapped the table a few times, and three jagged pathways ran through the map, each one a different shade of yellow. "We need your team to run reconnaissance on the site and report back to us."

Silence fell in the room. Everyone seemed to be looking at the map before them with varying degrees of interest and wariness as they processed the information.

"Why isn't the Intelligence team running head on this?" Sway asked, breaking the pensive atmosphere.

"The operatives I have down here are better suited to more a more covert calibre of mission and work better in specialised pairs," Shadow explained, leaning back in his seat.

Posthoc made a sweeping movement with his arms. "You guys, however, are used to working as a team. We don't know what to expect at this site, but we need it investigated ASAP, and we need a good range of powers represented. We don't have time to train another team, so… you're the best we've got."

Clarity laughed nervously. "You make it sound like we're a consolation prize," she said, paling.

"No, please do not misread my tone." Posthoc's voice was gentler as he regarded her. "Divvy assessed the possible outcomes of several team combinations, and you guys have the highest chance of success. I regret having to ask you to do this because it is not what you signed up for. I don't like putting you at undue risk either, but you are the most skilled and synergetic team in my department, and this is a matter of dire urgency."

"My people retrieved and collated the information early this morning, and we intend to have our chosen operatives leave before sunrise tomorrow." Shadow swiped his hand through the holographic projection, and it blinked off. The room felt much darker in its absence. "We need to act swiftly because we are concerned that whatever is up there poses a very real threat to the Underground."

Sway looked at Link, but her expression remained unreadable. "How long do we have to decide?"

"We'll give you the room and return in ten minutes." Shadow stood up and straightened the collar on his shirt.

Posthoc got to his feet, expression solemn, and then the two exited the room, leaving the Blue Team to carry the weight of the decision on their own.

11

———

FLIT

WHEN FLIT HAD WOKEN up that morning, she'd had a few ideas of how her day would pan out. This was not one of them. As she sat beside Scraps, she peered around the table at her teammates—*former* teammates—and wondered who would break the silence first. She was already on track for a riskier assignment, and this new mission fed into it perfectly. She needed to be there.

"So…" Tweak sat back in his chair and crossed his arms over his chest. "Is this an all-or-nothing gig? If some of us want to drop out, is that an option?"

Beside him, Clarity shifted in her seat and looked down at her hands, eyes glazing over.

"Until those two dorks left us, we were a team." Sway jutted his chin towards Flit and Hawkeye. "And a good team sticks together."

"They said they wanted a full complement of powers," Link supplied, glancing towards the door. "And… if you guys decided to go, I couldn't stay behind. You'd make a complete mess of it without me around."

The rare jibe from Link caused a spluttered laugh to spill from Clarity's lips. She let out a low sigh. "If they had Divvy project it, then this really must be the best option. She's the best precog on record."

Awe suffused Clarity's tone, a professional sense of wonder for someone who excelled at their gift. Flit felt the same way towards

Shadow. At least, she had until he'd started training her, and she'd learned he was just as much a pain in the arse as all the other leaders down here, even if he did teleport like a boss.

"Old City's a damn mess." Swipe gestured towards the now smooth surface of the projection table. "We came through it on our way from Longbeach. It's unstable as all hell, and Government drones are everywhere."

Hawkeye's frown deepened. "Which means it's even more important to make sure the right people go up. I know it sounds dangerous, but… what choice do we have? If we don't go, who will? I don't fancy getting spotted by a Government drone, but I don't know if I could live with myself if I let someone else go up in my place, and they got caught instead."

"That's not your fault, though," Clarity argued, shaking her head. "That's just the risk you take when you accept an assignment, and the risks attached to this are huge."

Sitting up straighter, Scraps squared his shoulders. "Should we write down a list of risks versus reasons we should go for comparison?"

Swipe tapped the edge of the table, and the time flashed across the surface. "We've only got a couple of minutes. That discussion would go on for hours."

Flit leaned forward. "So, we take a vote."

Scraps turned to her. "How do we decide if the vote succeeds? Does it need to be unanimous, or is a majority acceptable?"

"The thing about this team," Hawkeye said slowly, "is that you've all become my family. I think that if some of us go, we should all go. We work well together for a reason."

"So, it's all or nothing," Flit announced, not wanting to draw the process out by further debate. "I might as well start. I'm in."

Swipe rolled her eyes. "Of course you are."

Flit didn't even bother nipping at the bait.

"It sounds important, and if Flit is going, so am I," Scraps said, nodding decisively.

Flit smiled and patted his leg under the table.

Hawkeye leaned forward. "If there's a threat to the Underground, I want to help."

Sway straightened up, about to speak, when he looked at Link.

He waved his hand towards her, and she bit her lip before saying, "Like I said, you lot are gonna need me up there to keep you together. I don't really want to throw myself into danger, but it seems that's just par for the course these days."

The wariness in Sway's expression turned into pride. He slung his arm around his girlfriend's shoulder. "My answer's obvious."

That just left Clarity, Tweak, and Swipe. The three looked at each other, waiting to see who would speak first.

In the end, Tweak threw his hands up in the air. "I tried to give you two a chance to speak so it wouldn't be solely on your shoulders, but you chickened out. I'm in. I've always wanted to see what Old City is like up close, and I can't remember the last time I tasted fresh air. I'll put up with a bit of danger for that."

"If Divvy thinks we are the best option, then I'm in," Clarity said softly.

With an indignant flick of her hair, Swipe narrowed her eyes at everyone around the table. "Of course, it comes down to me."

Flit shrugged. "You could have spoken up sooner."

"What difference would it make? If I don't agree, I'll be the selfish one." Swipe let out a bitter laugh. "But hey, if we die, at least we die in the sun, right?"

Tweak pointed a finger at her, pretending to be hurt. "Don't you dare underestimate the power of a tan."

"I guess that answers the question," Flit said, looking around at her friends. They all returned her gaze, resolute. She teleported over to the door and pressed her palm against the reader. Out in the hall, Shadow and Posthoc were talking in hushed voices. "We're all in. Blue Team reporting for our last hurrah."

Posthoc's expression turned steely as he turned to Flit. "Then let's get planning. We don't have a moment to waste."

THE NEXT MORNING, Flit and Scraps woke up early. Despite a late night of planning and spending some quality time together before sleeping, Flit didn't yell at her alarm. The instant the piercing squall broke through her vague dreams, she knew what they were waking for. A flurry of excited pre-mission butterflies set in, and she sat up quickly enough to startle Scraps. His red eyes were wide as he peered around warily. She shrugged sheepishly. "Sorry. Didn't mean to startle you."

"Is everything ok?" His voice was endearingly thick with sleep as he rubbed his eyes.

Flit teleported out of bed. "Yeah, all good. Just looking forward to today."

Scraps threw the blanket off himself and slid out of bed. "You must be if you didn't yell at the alarm," he noted with a yawn. "Or did you? Did I sleep through it?"

"No yelling at the alarm today."

Scraps turned around to tuck the sheets in and smooth everything down before he made his way towards the bathroom. While he sorted himself out, Flit got their clothes organised and brushed then braided her hair. She retrieved a couple of protein bars they had taken from the Mess the night before and started eating while she waited for her time in the bathroom. She was grateful for their foresight because if they had to go to breakfast, they would have had to wake up a good half hour earlier.

"All right, your turn," Scraps said when he stepped out, a towel wrapped around his waist, water dripping down his chest.

"Bloody hell. Do you not dry yourself properly on purpose?" she groaned through a mouthful of breakfast.

Scraps tilted his head to the side and looked down at himself. "I do not want to monopolise the bathroom."

Flit swallowed the last of the protein bar and teleported right in front of him. She pressed her hands against his shower-warmed chest and leaned in to kiss a stray drop of water off his neck. "Next time, we should go in together. Save water and all that."

Scraps shook his head. "You have said that before, and I know not to fall for it." His expression turned serious, and he stepped aside, letting her hands fall off him. "We should not get distracted. We cannot be late for this mission."

"Spoil sport." Flit rolled her eyes, making sure to brush against his flushed skin on her way past him.

After a cold shower, Flit walked out of the bathroom to see Scraps dressed and studying their path through Old City on his datapad. Technically, Flit was in command of the mission, but she knew to play to the strengths of the team. There wasn't a single person she would trust more to navigate them safely through the streets if their tech failed.

Scraps was so absorbed in his task that he didn't even notice she walked out of the bathroom naked. As she pulled on her clothes, including grey camouflage cargo pants, a fitted white singlet, and a dark grey jacket, Flit looked over at him. "You got it down?"

"Roger that, Captain," he said with a roguish smile as he finally dragged his eyes away from the screen.

"Hmm," Flit huffed, straightening and walking over to retrieve her boots. "I like the sound of that."

"You just like being in charge," Scraps pointed out as he got up. He set his datapad back on the bedside table and walked over to the door.

"True." Flit put her boots on and pulled the straps tight then teleported over to Scraps' side. "Let's get going."

The trek to the armoury was unusually quiet. On any other day, Scraps would be filling Flit in on some new development he had read about in the Underground information repository, or she would share gossip about some of the social shenanigans happening.

It wasn't until they were a few turns away from the armoury that Scraps finally broke the silence. "Flit?"

"Mmm?"

"You said that your mission had no set recall date."

They had already discussed that matter, but his tone indicated he was looking for confirmation. In the flurry of planning for the trip to Old City, she had been able to ignore her internal conflict about going on her mission, but it slammed back into her with full force.

"Yeah, that's right. The position we're in is not an easy one to transition in and out of. I'm not holding my breath for a recall."

"But Vista and Newton were recalled." Scraps stopped walking, his back stiff and shoulders squared. For most people, it would have been a confident posture, but Flit had been with him long enough now to know that it was a default for him, the same pose he would have assumed when he took orders from the Government. It was more of a sign that he was readying himself for something unpleasant than taking control.

Flit shrugged. "That's because Vista's pregnant."

"If you became—" Scraps stopped almost as quickly as he begun, his face a picture of discomfort.

Despite his expression, Flit's heart warmed. It was a regrettable thing, the relief that was borne of his discomfort. She saw where his question was going and was grateful he did not want to finish the thought. The only way she would become pregnant was if she slept with someone else on her mission, and it clearly did not sit well with him.

"Don't worry." She reached up, cupping his cheek and rubbing her thumb over the smoothly-shaven skin there. "I have no plans to get pregnant."

Especially not with Hawkeye as her mission partner. She loved the man, sure, but not like that. He was her best friend. Anything more just felt wrong.

"But then you may not come back." The words came out in a sudden splutter that sliced right through Flit's heart. "And I do not want our relationship to end."

"Why would it have to end?" Flit asked, uncertain where the fatalistic thinking came from.

"Swipe said—"

Flit sighed. "Fuck Swipe." She took a deep breath to stop herself from swearing some more. "Look, I am sure it seems like a good idea to some, but just because I'll be up there doesn't mean we have to end things between us."

"Then how will it work?" Scraps looked so perplexed that any annoyance Flit felt towards Swipe melted away.

"Don't worry about that, ok?" She gently guided his face down until their foreheads were touching. Then, she whispered, "I won't be up there for long. Every spare second I have on the surface will be spent finding a way to bring the Government down. Once that is sorted, I will not let anything else take me from your side. I promise."

"Flit—" Scraps protested, but she silenced his words with a fierce kiss that left them both breathless.

When she pulled away, Scraps just looked at her. She could see the cogs of his mind turning behind his eyes and wondered what he was thinking. Then, the hard set of his shoulders settled, the creases in his brows smoothed out, and his eyes shone with approval. "In that case, I am already looking forward to seeing you again."

If Flit let herself dwell on the utter confidence in his words, it would tear her apart, so she slipped her hand into his and tugged him down the tunnel. They couldn't get caught up in the moment. They had a mission to complete.

Flit and Scraps were the first to arrive at the armoury, but it wasn't that way for long. The others trickled into the space in a steady stream until they all stood around the preparation bench, talking about the mission.

The air in the room was thick with a curious mix of concern and excitement, as none of them had ever embarked upon an adventure quite like this. Any sort of action above ground was undertaken in small groups of two or three and usually for a specific purpose. Growing up, Flit could remember seeing people leaving to raid abandoned Government production plants or to procure the necessary components to make weapons or technology that they could not manufacture for themselves. It had, at least to Flit's knowledge, been at least a year and a half since one such raid. The Underground had gotten quite good at meeting their own needs. Their own tech was behind that of the Government's, but the abilities of their micros more than made up for it.

"Flit… that's a lot of grenades," Tweak observed as he buckled his weapons belt around his hips.

Flit tucked another small metal sphere into her bandolier. "I've only got…" She ran her hands over the devices, counting them. "Eight."

"Yeah, across your chest." Clarity laughed. "What about the ones on your belt?"

Flit tugged on her jacket so the sides fell to cover the weapons on her hips. "Your point is?"

"We're not trying to blow Old City up. We're just running recon," Hawkeye pitched in, but his tone was more resigned than exasperated. He knew not to get between Flit and her flame grenades.

Flit finished putting two more grenades in the bandolier, making each move precise so that the metal spheres settled into their holders with an audible pop. "What can I say? I'm preparing for every outcome."

"Well, I volunteer to take the tail. I don't want to be near you when those things go off." Tweak shook his head in disapproval.

"Not all of us can explode things with our mind, you know," Sway muttered to his friend. "Grenades may not be my style, but I'm packing extra."

Scraps cleared his throat as he slipped a pistol into his thigh holster. "Given that this group is linked to the weapon that temporarily robbed Flit of her powers, I think it is wise to gear up."

Flit thought Scraps wanted to say more, but he focused on reaching for a new dagger and testing the edge.

"If we have to decide between more or less weapons, more is the safer option." Flit's voice was firm and held a note of authority. She hadn't exactly ordered them to pack heavy, but she would if she had to. She checked that she was all buckled up, and she hadn't forgotten anything. Then, she picked up a light pack with provisions of food and water in it, slinging it over her shoulder. "Right. Are we gonna sit here and argue about weapons, or can we get this show on the road?"

12

———

SCRAPS

EVEN SURROUNDED by the eerie wasteland that was Old City, the fresh air was invigorating. Scraps wasn't the only one refreshed by it. After a long morning trek through musty tunnels, everyone else in the team stood taller when they navigated the crumbled subway station stairs to stand on the street. The blue and orange hues of dawn were startling, even though the warmth of the sun hadn't yet thawed the chill of the night before. As the light cascaded over the once-grand metropolis, it cast long and unusual shadows along the fractured sidewalk.

"According to the map, we go east from here," Scraps said in a low voice.

He narrowed his eyes against the sunrise and peered around them. He scanned above street level, looking past the shells of the tumbled skyscrapers and into the sky. Shadow and Posthoc had made it clear that Government drones were just as much a threat out here as the unstable landscape, and he did not wish to be caught out by either.

"It's all clear. Let's move." Flit waved her hand to the others and gestured for them to follow her lead. "Watch out for roots. There are trip hazards all over this place."

Scraps had never been this far into Old City before, and what he saw amazed him. Nature was doing its best to reclaim the landscape. For every building façade that had crumbled, there was another being held up by thick, wooded vines or scaffolded by twisted trees stretching for the sun. The salty scent of powdered cement and tang of shattered glass were filtered through a fresh zest of greenery.

The terrain of Old City was an unusual one to navigate for the Blue Team, who were used to dark tunnels and still air. Clarity and Link, who were walking directly behind Scraps, jumped at every stray breeze that danced past them, and Tweak was muttering something about *bloody nature* and his sinuses.

"Hawk, how are we looking?" Flit called back over her shoulder without turning around.

Hawkeye, who was with Sway and Swipe in the rear guard of the group, called back, "So far, so good. The ground isn't the most stable, but I can't see anything that's going to crumble underneath us or fall down on top of us."

Scraps was pleased by that assessment.

At least, he was until Hawkeye added, "Yet."

"Loving the positivity, Hawk. Keep it coming." Flit continued onward, unperturbed. Scraps supposed it was easier for a tele-porter. If the ground started to crumble beneath her feet, she could jump herself to safety in less than the time it took to blink. It made her far more daring than most other people would be in situations like this.

The group walked through the streets, weaving between vehi-cles that had been abandoned and left to rust and chunks of concrete or metal that had fallen to the street. As the sun rose, the wind picked up and rushed through the shattered building windows and hanging vines with a keening whistle. It was an odd, unearthly sound, and Scraps could swear some of the buildings groaned in protest.

"Hold up," Hawkeye called.

Everyone stopped immediately. Scraps turned to look at the remote viewer. In the absence of marching feet and clattering weapons belts, the noises of the city were amplified. Hawkeye's gaze became unfocused, and he held up his hand. Everyone watched and waited, holding their breath. After a few tense moments, he came back to the vicinity with a blink and a shake of his head.

"What is it?" Flit asked.

Hawkeye pointed ahead, where the road opened into a cross-shaped intersection. "We're supposed to turn left up there, correct?"

"Yes." Even though Flit answered, she still looked to Scraps for confirmation. He nodded.

"A building has come down around the corner that wasn't showing on the map Shadow gave us. I think it's pretty recent, as all the ground and buildings around it are still adjusting to the shift of weight," Hawkeye informed her.

"Can we go through it?" Sway asked as everyone stepped closer to form a tighter circle.

"I don't think it's worth the risk," Hawkeye muttered.

Flit turned to him. "Is there another way?"

"The more time we are up here, the higher our risk of exposure," Clarity said, shifting from foot to foot as she looked back over her shoulder in the direction of the Hub.

"Did you see something?" Flit asked.

Clarity shook her head. "Our surroundings are so volatile I can't get a good read of the possible outcomes. It's unnerving."

Scraps couldn't blame Clarity for being concerned. While things seemed calm enough now, there was no telling when that would change. Between the crumbling city, the uncertainty around what awaited them at their destination, and the high likelihood of running into Government surveillance, Scraps assumed it was probably the greatest challenge Clarity had faced in a while. Still, standing around talking about it would not help their situation.

"We can overshoot that street and take the next left," Scraps suggested, pausing for a moment to bring the map back to mind. "There should be an alley between two buildings we can use, so we do not have to go all the way around that city block."

"Let's do it," Flit decided.

When Clarity looked like she would protest, Sway put a hand on her shoulder. "Every option is dangerous. I don't have to be a precog to know that," he said in an uncharacteristically soft tone. "But we need you on your game. Take a deep breath, centre yourself, and then exhale some of those worries."

The instructions were laced with a light, calming thread of telecoercion. Clarity closed her eyes and did as Sway instructed. When she opened them again, she seemed more focused.

"See, we've got this!" Sway patted Clarity's shoulder and straightened up. "Right, Flit?"

"Of course we do," Flit said nonchalantly before returning her attention to the whole team. "All right, let's keep the group tight. Hawk, those Government drones should be sweeping over any time now."

"I'll keep a lookout," Hawkeye promised.

The Blue Team resumed their trek. As they walked through the intersection where they were supposed to turn, several voices uttered hushed swear words. An entire building had fallen to block the street. Fragments of shattered glass and brick littered the rest of the street, and unnerving crumbling sounds came at odd intervals as the debris tried to settle through the bushes and vines that had pushed up through the concrete sidewalks.

In a mind-bending view, Scraps looked through one of the broken windows of the fallen building and saw straight out the other side. Sway's question about going through made more sense, but there was no way it felt like a safe idea. He was relieved Hawkeye had vetoed it.

The destruction on their new route was far older, old enough that any broken buildings had already been blanketed with nature, and a small pond had formed in the upturned and hollowed out shell of a water-tank that must have fallen off a nearby roof.

Falling into step behind Flit, the Blue Teem peered around themselves with more interest as they pushed through the tall grass that grew along the network of fault lines in the bitumen. The echo of their footsteps was interspersed by the occasional pitter-patter of falling debris and cracking of concrete. This entire street had fared poorly in the past hundred years, with more buildings fallen than the others they had passed. Scraps just begun to wonder why when a hissed "Holy shit!" from Sway drew his attention to the left foot-path. At first, he couldn't make out much beyond an upturned dumpster and a large round cylinder, but as he spent more time studying the shapes and size, he recognised something from his history lessons. A tank.

"Do you think it's still got ammo in it?" Tweak whispered to Sway, slowing down as they passed.

"Nah, surely someone's raided it already," Sway replied, but it didn't stop him from lingering.

Tweak stopped. "Maybe we can just—"

"Don't even think about it," Flit snapped, turning to narrow her eyes at them. "If you wanted more explosives, you should've packed 'em." She patted the flame grenades on her belt for emphasis. "Right now, we've got bigger priorities. Keep moving."

Scraps was quite impressed with Flit's restraint. If he was entirely honest with himself, he would have bet a chocolate bar on her being the first one trying to find a way into the tank to see if there was anything left inside, but being in control gave her something else to focus on, something even more important. Scraps liked this side of her.

The alley they needed to turn down was only one building past the tank.

"Ah, dang it," Link groaned, voicing what everyone must have been thinking when they saw what lay before them.

The alley was narrow, the ground piled high with bricks, steel sleepers, and other debris that had fallen from the buildings either side of it. They would need to climb over the mess or find another way around.

"Hawkeye, is there another route?" Link asked as she looked around, putting her hands on her slim hips.

Hawkeye looked like he was about to answer when Clarity interrupted. "Flit, don't—"

But then, Flit was gone.

"Flit?" Scraps called out.

"Over here!"

Everyone looked up to see Flit standing on what remained of a fire escape, precariously attached to the side of one of the buildings four stories up. The bottom half was lost somewhere in the rubble below.

"This mess isn't as stable as you think!" Tweak called out, a deep frown etched on his lips.

"But this is." Flit jumped up and down on the fire escape. Her footsteps clanged, and Scraps winced, but the platform held. "And

I've got a good view of the other side from here. It'll take a minute, but I can leapfrog everyone over there. No need to waste time going around."

"Fuck, I knew I should have skipped breakfast," Swipe groaned, clutching her stomach.

"So, who's first?" Flit asked before she teleported back to the spot she left moments ago. The team was so used to her darting about that no one flinched.

"We should keep one macro either side to stabilise the platform," Clarity suggested with an appraising glance at the fire escape.

Flit looked between Scraps and Swipe.

"I'll go first." Scraps stepped forward before Swipe had a chance to volunteer. If there was danger on the other side, he would not want to dump her right into the middle of it. She could handle herself, but he would rather face the danger than let one of his colleagues go in alone.

In a flutter of warm arms and sweet citrus bodywash, Flit wrapped herself around him. The instant one of her hands settled behind his neck and the other on the small of his back, his body instinctively prepared for what was to come. In the time it took to blink twice, he was on a perforated metal platform and then back on solid ground.

Both Flit and Scraps took the next few seconds to look around and make sure the coast was clear before Flit cupped his cheek and pulled him down for a swift kiss. "I'll be right back," she promised. Then, after a firm swat on his behind that made him jump, she was gone.

In the silence that followed, Scraps drew out his pistol and kept his eyes peeled. When Tweak joined him, the microkinetic watched the street, and Scraps turned to keep an eye on the staircase Flit was using as a mid-way point. He tucked his gun away to keep his hands free and held his palms towards the area. He used his powers to push up gently beneath the metal platform, figuring that anything he could do now to prevent it falling was worthwhile.

Flit appeared and reappeared on the platform several more times, and more of their teammates arrived on his side of the alley. Clarity stumbled away from Flit the second her feet touched the footpath and vomited behind a nearby fire hydrant. Link took it much better.

"Flit, baby, any time you want an excuse to cuddle up to me, just ask," Sway said as he landed, even though he looked a little green.

Scraps stiffened at the insinuation.

"Your girlfriend is right there, you sleazeball." Flit laughed, pointing at Link and shaking her head as she wiggled out of his arms.

"I don't mind," Link teased with a playful chuckle, "so long as I get to watch."

"Kinky bastards, the lot of you," Flit muttered before she teleported back to the platform and out of teasing range.

Sway patted Scraps' shoulder. "Don't worry, buddy. You can watch too."

Scraps had to work hard to blink away the image of Flit and Sway tangled in that same embrace but with a lot less clothes on. His facial features must have given away his consternation. Sway laughed to himself as he drew his own weapon and turned to face the street.

There was a groan beside Scraps a few seconds later. "Never. Again." Hawkeye stumbled over to the wall of the nearby building and slumped against it, rubbing his face.

"Take slow, deep breaths," Scraps advised, watching the micro-kinetic struggle to keep his breakfast down.

Hawkeye nodded and gave it a try. He had teleported with Flit far more often than Scraps, but Scraps had learned long ago that some people took longer to get used to things than others. The reaction to teleporting along with Flit seemed to have a lot more to do with the vestibular system. Mental preparation could only go so far when you ceased to exist in one spot and reappeared in another one far away.

"I think she did this on purpose, you know," Tweak said idly behind him. "Find a situation to make us all queasy before we left. It's just the kind of thing she would do."

"Yeah, I snuck up here last night and planted enough explo-sives to bring that building down in our path," Flit said as she reappeared with Swipe and completed the team. "You know, just for shits and giggles."

With everyone reunited on this side of the alley, Scraps stepped in beside Flit, and they regrouped into formation.

Just before they went to move out, Hawkeye held up a hand, a frown tugging at his lips. "There are drones on the horizon. Looks like a sweep is about to begin."

Flit squared her shoulders and looked around at the team. "Then let's get moving. Everyone up for a morning run?"

There was a chorus of, "Copy that", "Roger, boss", and an "Ugh, I hate running", and then the team were off, sprinting through the streets of the crumbled metropolis and hoping they were fast enough to avoid the gaze of the Government's cameras potentially headed their way.

13

FLIT

THE STREET WAS COVERED with a dangerous mix of fractured concrete, broken brick, and bent structural steel beams, all littered with glittering, razor sharp glass. Running from their entry point to the building they needed to investigate was no easy feat. The constantly shifting rubble presented a problem, even for Flit. On several occasions, her teleports landed her on something unstable, and she had to jump out again before she got her feet under her or risk falling flat on her arse.

When they came to the building they had to investigate, everyone was panting. A dozen stories tall, half of the red brick façade had cascaded away over time to reveal the ruins of apartments within. It should be a cut scene of an old architectural manual, except, of course, for the thick vines creeping over the edge of the walls and curling around the rusted and skewed furniture within.

Somehow, the entryway and entire right side of the building were still intact. If Flit held her hand up to cover the left half, she might have been able to ignore all the damage.

"Tweak, Clarity, check for traps and surveillance, please." Flit gestured to the door. "Macros, be prepared for anything that might come flying at us if something is triggered. Hawk, eyes on the street."

Tweak and Flit approached the building, the microkinetic held his hand out towards the intercom system by the door. He screwed up his face in concentration as he used his powers to comply with Flit's request.

"And I mean all traps and surveillance. No smart-arsing around like you did during the leadership test," Flit muttered under her breath, earning her a laugh from Tweak.

"Those drones are doing a wide circuit by the look of it," Hawkeye called out, his face tilted towards the sky. "We're still best to get inside as soon as possible. I'm not sure what kind of sensors they have on them."

"The door's clear. There is power in this area, though. I think they must have connected some solar panels somewhere." Tweak waved his hand, and the magnetic locks holding the building door closed clicked out of place. "The power I sensed goes straight up to the tenth floor."

Flit pushed the door open and gestured for the team to enter. Everyone filed in, with Scraps and Swipe backing in last. They turned around, noting a bank of elevators in the middle of the dusty, mould-coated foyer. Sway pointed out the emergency stairwell, and they made their way over. The staircase itself smelled more offensive than anything Flit had come across underground. Piles of rat droppings and dust were nestled into the corner of each step, but there was an area in the middle that was clearer and spoke of use within the last year.

As they spiralled farther and farther up the spine of the building, Flit wished she was with a group of teleporters. The steep, sometimes slick, inclines of the deep level tunnels were nothing compared to these steps.

"We're going to have some killer glutes after this," Swipe said when they rounded the eighth storey.

Link laughed. "I think my glutes have just about given up."

"Aw, babe. That's sad. Want me to massage them for you?" Sway offered, making the others groan.

"You can on your own time." Flit unbuckled both of her daggers from their holsters. "Everyone, stop."

The rhythmic drumming of their footsteps paused, and it was only their panting echoing in the stairwell.

"Link, are there any signs of life up there?" Flit asked.

"I'll move ahead." Link slipped past her on the stairwell. She disappeared around the bend, and the team all kept their mouths shut so they didn't add in any distractions for her.

After a minute, Link called the all-clear, and they finished the ascent. The landing for the tenth storey was too small for the whole team, so Flit and Scraps stepped up as Link moved back. The door itself was a standard heavy fire escape, although the locking mechanism had been jimmied, and the door was held open with a stray piece of concrete wedged between it and the frame. Flit held her daggers up and readied herself to teleport then nodded at Scraps. He returned the gesture with a grim smile of acknowledgement and held his pistol up with one hand, while he used the other to push the heavy door back.

The instant the door opened, Flit took in the short hallway that ended in a chasm at the other side of the building. There were four doors in the narrow corridor. The closest two on either side were likely the only ones that didn't have crumbled rooms. She scanned the empty space then looked down at the mildewy carpet floors. There were muddy foot tracks back and forth between the apartment on the left and the fire escape, but it was all coated in a sticky layer of dust.

Keeping her weapons at the ready, she gestured for the others to follow her. "Hall's clear. Tracks lead to the left." She crept forward, noting the sogginess of the carpet and how the open end of the building probably allowed rain to soak through regularly. At least that explained the offensive, mouldy odour of the place.

Scraps kept hold of the fire escape door to allow the others through as he followed her, but when Swipe emerged from the staircase, she held out her hand and took over. Flit waited until the transition was clear before she gestured to the apartment door.

Scraps waved towards it, but it resisted his push. "It is locked."

"Not for long." Tweak slid between Flit and Scraps and pressed his hand against the lock. It was barely a second before the tumblers clicked out of place. He ran his hand up the door, head tilted to the side, and then smirked as he found something else. "Tripwire," he whispered. He leaned in a little closer and closed his eyes as he worked on it. After another few seconds, he stepped back. "All clear."

Flit and Scraps repeated the door opening process, but this time, there was not much for Flit to see. The entire apartment had been gutted to bare studwork with heavy quarantine sheets hanging around the perimeter. They could make out vague rectangular shapes through the plastic and cables that ran under the sheets and then into a vent in the wall, but that was all.

Creeping forward and adjusting her grip on her daggers, Flit made a conscious effort to steady the pace of her breathing as Scraps pulled the curtain aside. Inside the area was technology well beyond the era the building. The large console was mostly all screen but with a heavy analogue communications adapter screwed into the side of it. The adapter itself was old-school, but the console was more advanced than most of the gear in Control and, Flit believed, very expensive. The power cables and the line from the communications adapter were the ones running under the plastic curtains and into the vent in the wall.

A flicker of movement in the corner of the room caught Flit's attention and had her poised to move, but she resisted the urge to stab something when a rat scurried out from behind a box and disappeared under the curtains. Alongside the cardboard box, which Flit noted was full of ration bars, were several canteens and other meal-related items. Around the edges of the room was evidence of a camp. Eight sleeping bags covered with a light dusting of mould were lined up along the walls. Each sleeping bag had a backpack beside it, but one in particular caught Flit's attention.

Teleporting over and kicking the bag on its side with the toe of her boot, Flit gasped at what spilled out. "Fuck!" She leaned over, picking up a nondescript grey flak jacket with the tip of her dagger and holding it towards Scraps. Her mind flashed back to the adrenaline-filled moments after Heft and the group of thugs had shot that weapon at her, and her memory snagged on what they were wearing. "This camp did belong to those bastards. There were eight of them, right?"

With a splay of the fingers on Scraps' free hand, the jacket slipped off the end of her dagger and hovered in the air, the arms spreading out as if it were on a hanger. Scraps' expression hardened, and something dangerous flashed behind his deep red eyes as he looked at her. "Yes. This looks familiar."

That was all Flit needed to hear to know they were in the right place.

Flit turned to her best friend and met his serious gaze. "Hawkeye, get us eyes on the roof. Let us know what the drones are doing." She gestured to Sway and Link. "I need you two on the stairs. Link, stick in Hawkeye's head and let us know the second there is something to be concerned about. Sway, you're on lookout."

In a flurry of movement, everyone complied with Flit's orders.

She turned to Clarity. "Head over to one of the windows and watch the street."

Clarity crossed the gutted apartment and disappeared behind the sheet on the opposite side of the room.

"Well, this is getting intimate." Tweak chuckled, looking between Flit and Scraps.

"Actually, I'd prefer you get intimate with those systems over there. We need to know what's on them," she said to the micro before turning to Scraps and Swipe. "Can you search through their stuff, please? See if there is any other evidence."

The two macrokinetics turned and used their powers to start searching.

Flit stood beside Tweak as he worked. The console flared to life, and a password request flashed onto the screen. After all of three seconds, the textbox filled with hidden characters, and Tweak snorted to himself.

"You think they'd encrypt it better." He shook his head. The view shifted to the home screen, and several applications initiated. Different files flashed across the screen as Tweak processed them faster than Flit could follow. Then, a white light filled the room as a secure messaging app opened, and text appeared on screen.

To: Matt McKinley
From: Dept. of Derivate Affairs
Subject: Reward for Derivate Reacquisition
Dear Mr. McKinley,
Thank you once again for your inquiry. Whilst the Government is

firm in its knowledge that the Derivate population is well controlled and accounted for, I can confirm we are interested in any information you happen across. It is highly improbable, if not impossible, that there is something we are unaware of. However, if you believe you have uncovered such intelligence, we are always more than happy to remain in contact with you.

Please note that any claims you make in relation to the existence or whereabouts of, as you called them, *rogue* Derivates, must be substantiated with solid evidence. We will need to know exact numbers and locations. In your correspondences, you offered to recapture them yourself, but we firmly advise against this. If Derivates somehow managed to escape our purview and asset control systems, then they are highly dangerous. The safety of you and your companions is our paramount concern.

Rumours of escaped Derivates are not new. There have been times in the past where similar urban myths fuelled many escapades that inevitably ended in disappointment and wasted resources. As such, if false information leads to the expenditure of Government resources, then you and your companions will be required to reimburse the Government fully for its losses within two business weeks.

Kind regards,

Alexandra Moussa

"Well, fuck me…" Flit gasped as she read the message.

The rustling sounds of Scraps' searching stopped, and his footsteps bounced around the room. Scraps stood beside her and placed his warm hand on her hip.

Tweak moved that message to the side of the screen so Scraps could keep reading it and then opened several more files. The other documents, what Flit believed were log books, were dated in the months before the collapses and explosions began.

The logs told a story of an anonymous tip off about Derivates residing in Old City. There was a map from Eastbay to the Hub, with a note questioning whether Derivates used Old City as an escape route when the Government had their last crackdown there. The group of Citizens formed and, deciding a short stay in the 'radiation' of the city would be worth any reward, set out to create a camp. Suspicious of the Government, they cut communication from the main group out of fears that anything they report could be intercepted. The general concern from the messages, it seemed, was that if they told the Government, they would refuse to pay out, so they wanted to make sure the *rogue Derivates* wouldn't get away. Luckily for them, they stumbled across Heft and forged a deal—a sizeable sum of money and cache of resources in exchange for his assistance bringing down some tunnels.

"The bastards were trying to trap us down there," Tweak said, leaning forward as he found more logs.

After the thugs were sure the rogue Derivates were trapped, they would ensure a reward from the Government by threatening to spread word of what they had found.

Blazing anger roiled in Flit's gut. It was impossible to swallow the outrage and disdain rising up her throat. "We're people, not fucking rats."

Scraps gently squeezed her hip and held her closer to his side.

"What else do they have?" she asked Tweak. "Numbers? Locations?"

Tweak closed the documents. "The other files are locked. It'll take me a while to get through them. Why don't you—"

"Guys!" The door to the apartment burst open, and a hand tore down the white curtain. Link appeared before them, cheeks flushed and panting. "Hawkeye said all the drones turned and are headed this way. We need to move."

Sway and Clarity made their way into the main space as Flit looked at the information on the console and then at Tweak. "Can you do this any faster?"

He raised his hands in the air. "I'm a micro, not a magician."

"Can you wipe the drive?" Flit asked.

"There are all sorts of encryptions. I could do a quick job of it, but any Registered micro would be able to put it back together," Tweak said, still focusing on the console, taking in whatever information he could get.

"I'll take care of it." Swipe stepped forward, holding out her hand.

Tweak yelped and jumped back. "No! That won't help. It could be reconstructed."

"Then how do we destroy it?" Flit snapped, knowing they didn't have time to argue.

Scraps cleared his throat. "Are you sure we need to destroy it? Even if the drones picked up on the activity, they may not deem it worthwhile to expend resources to investigate."

"It's a risk we can't take. They have so much info on us, but it's all local to the server. We need to remove all evidence they found about the Underground. Right, Tweak?" Flit asked.

Tweak tipped his head in her direction. "You got it."

"Ok, so how do we destroy it?" Sway echoed Flit's question, stepping closer and slipping his arm around Link's waist.

Flit patted the veritable stockpile of flame grenades on her belt and bandolier. "Luckily, I came prepared."

14

SCRAPS

"ABSOLUTELY NOT." Swipe shook her head, blonde ponytail flicking behind her like a whip.

Scraps adored Flit and found her shenanigans to be thoroughly entertaining, but even he had to agree with Sway. "Is there another way? A safer, less conspicuous one?"

Tweak rubbed his chin and looked at Flit as Hawkeye ran into the room. "Fire is the best option to ensure nothing can be recovered, and to protect our identity from postcog or micro investigation."

"Fire will draw even more attention," Link insisted.

Flit was about to argue when Clarity held her hand up, her eyes glazing over. She rolled her shoulders and squirmed on her feet a little as she came back to the present. "Fire alone will draw too much attention. The best option is pairing it with a building collapse, those happen all the time around here."

"Bloody hell, are you mad?" Sway spluttered.

"That is a very clever idea," Scraps intoned.

Hawkeye turned to Tweak. "Can you find the weak points in the building?"

Tweak paused, hand still on the terminal, information flying across the screen. "I could try. It would take a good few minutes, though. That kind of thing isn't my forte."

"Don't bother. A building is a building." Flit waved her hand dismissively. "If we hit the foundations and the emergency stairwell, we should be able to bring it down."

"And who knows what else," Hawkeye argued. "This whole block's a mess. We need to be careful." He turned to Clarity for support.

"Don't look at me." Clarity raised both of her hands and took a step back. "There are too many variables right now. I just know that fire and a collapse is our best option. More specific details will take too long to predict."

"I'm not wasting time. Every second we spend up here checking for faults is time the drones spend tightening in around us," Flit said. There was the slightest waver in her voice that made Scraps step closer.

Hawkeye pressed his lips together, and the muscles in his neck strained with frustration. "They aren't so close that we can throw good decision-making out of the window."

It was no secret that Flit believed getting caught by the Government was a fate worse than death. Scraps couldn't help but feel that fear colouring her decision, but it was not his place to argue with her.

Not that it would work if he tried.

Flit and Hawkeye faced off, and tension roiling off them in palpable waves.

"Now is not the time for one of your pissing contests," Sway warned.

As much as Flit disliked the command laced in Sway's tone, she knew he was right. "Three teams," Flit snapped, effectively cutting off the debate. She unclipped some grenades and handed them to Clarity and Hawkeye, who hadn't brought nearly as many. "Swipe, Scraps, and I will take the basement. Hawkeye and Tweak, you get the stairwell sorted. I want a grenade in every doorway. Clarity, Sway, and Link, head outside and find some weak points in the façade to load up."

When Flit finished, Scraps moved to her side. The others went to stand in their teams.

Flit called out, almost as an afterthought, "When you've set the charges, meet at the front door. We'll move somewhere safe before we detonate."

Scraps looked at Clarity. "Can you predict the direction the building will fall?"

Clarity pressed her lips together. "The highest likelihood is towards the street. The exact direction is too close to call. At least, until the charges are set."

"Call it when you get it," Flit said, squaring her shoulders.

Hawkeye stepped in close, leaning down to whisper something in her ear.

She pulled back, glaring at him and shaking her head. Then, she raised her hand and barked, "We need to move."

They team sprinted to the stairwell together, but that was where they split. Hawkeye and Tweak stopped in the doorway to place a grenade on the landing. Flit slipped one arm around Scraps' waist and the other around Swipe's.

"No!" Swipe protested as Flit leaned over the railing and peered down the middle of the stairwell. "I'll run down."

Flit shook her head. "This is quicker. We'll go on three."

Swipe groaned and closed her eyes. "Fuck."

After the promised countdown, the world wobbled on its axis and Scraps' feet slammed against the floor, jolting his entire body. He swayed precariously, but Flit tightened her arm around his waist to steady him. On the other side of her, Swipe tore away and hunched over, bracing one hand against the concrete wall as she vomited in the corner of the stairwell.

"Fucking teleporters," Swipe whined.

"You're welcome." Flit chuckled before teleporting to the basement door. "Now hurry up and get in there."

When Flit pushed the door open, Scraps jogged into the basement. It used to be an under-cover parking lot, with six cracked concrete pillars holding the ceiling up. The line markings had faded, and from the stench, it was evident rodents had taken up residence in the space. A few vintage cars stood, covered in dust, relics from the time when vehicles had been made from steel and plastic and ran on fossil fuels.

"Ooh, I wonder if they have petrol in them." Flit pointed at the cars. "Scraps, can you check? If they do, see if you can pull out the tanks. We could use the extra accelerant." Flit teleported over to the farthest pillar. "Set the charges, Swipe. You take the two at the end."

As a child, Scraps had spent more recreation hours than he could recall studying the schematics of antique vehicles. It was the closest thing he ever had to an interest of his own. He slid under the vehicle and located the fuel tank within seconds, then tapped the steel with his fingers to hear the tell-tale rumble of something in there. Scraps crushed the pipes leading to and from the tank with his telekinesis and yanked it out.

Scraps got to his feet, levitating the tank. "Flit!"

Flit jammed a grenade into a crack in a pillar. "I'll take that to Hawkeye and Tweak." The next instant, she was in front of him, her hands moving fast to unbuckle her grenades and shove them in his pockets. "You deal with these." She pointed to the barred semi-circle window on the wall that would be visible from the street. "And remove the grille from that window there."

Before Scraps had a chance to acknowledge Flit's order, she was gone.

Swipe and Scraps worked quickly to get everything set as instructed, and then ran for the exit. He threw his hand out ahead of them to force the door open. It slammed against the wall with a bang, but he held it back to stop it from rebounding and hitting them on the way out. After they climbed the stairs, they levelled out on the ground floor and heard Tweak, Flit, and Hawkeye not far above them. The sharp tang of petroleum pierced the air in the fire escape.

When Swipe and Scraps tumbled out of the front door, Sway, Link, and Clarity were stuffing charges in between crumbling bricks on the front corner of the façade.

"Where are the others?" Clarity asked, brushing some mortar dust off her hands.

"They'll be out soon. Any idea of which way this building will fall yet?" Scraps asked, stepping away from the buildings.

"Most odds point that way." Clarity jabbed a thumb over her shoulder, down the street, towards the direction they had come from.

"That's if it doesn't fall on our heads first," Swipe muttered.

Clarity snorted. "That's one possible outcome."

Scraps frowned as he looked at her, not sure if she meant it as a joke.

Clearing her throat, Clarity added, "I mean, the chances are slight."

"What do we need to do to avoid it?" Scraps was not interest in the banter. He would rather spend his time making sure they were safe.

Just as Clarity was about to launch into their options, the front door opened, and Flit, Tweak, and Hawkeye spilled out.

"We need to get away from this before we light it up," Clarity pleaded, turning to Flit.

Flit skidded to a stop, taking those words in. She looked over her shoulder at the debris from the window Scraps had torn out. A low buzz sounded overhead as the circle of drones tightened in around them. They were still a radius of a few blocks out, but they could change direction on a moment's notice.

"Swipe, if I give this to you, do you think you can shoot it in that window from the corner of the alley?" Flit asked, holding up the last flame grenade on her belt. Swipe was far better at fine movements and precision than Scraps was, so he understood Flit's decision.

The expression on Swipe's face went from dubious to confident as she levitated the grenade from Flit's hand. "Of course."

"Good. Let's move. Get to the corner, and I'll start teleporting us across the alley right away. We need to get undercover before those drones find us," Flit commanded.

The team didn't hesitate. The pounding of their feet and the hammering of Scraps' heartbeat washed away the awareness of the Government UAVs inching closer. Flit teleported ahead, bouncing from foot to foot as she waited for them. Link was the first to stumble into Flit's arms, and the two were gone as Tweak and Scraps pulled up beside them.

Flit reappeared a moment later and pointed at Hawkeye. "Eyes on the drones," she warned. Then she and Tweak popped out of place.

Scraps looked to the sky while he caught his breath, even though he couldn't see a thing. Beside him, Hawkeye mumbled something about still having plenty of time. Clarity patted his shoulder and plastered him with platitudes about how well they were doing, although Scraps wasn't sure whether it was for Hawk-eye's benefit or her own.

One by one, Flit transported the team to the other side of the alley until it was just Swipe and Scraps left. Flit stepped closer to him, her cheeks flushed and brows glittering with a fine sheen of sweat. She wrapped her arms around him, and, in two blinks, he was on the other side with the majority of the team.

Flit popped a kiss against his cheek before she was gone again. Scraps looked at the great wall of rubble separating them, and an uneasy feeling settled over him. It was the memory of another wall of rubble that came to mind in that moment, but he squashed his concern. Flit was more than capable of handling herself in this—no, in any—environment.

15

———

FLIT

"READY TO THROW?" Flit asked, popping into place beside Swipe. She wiped a sheen of sweat off her forehead with the back of her arm. Flit had forgotten how hot it got standing directly in the mid-morning sun. She wondered if she would have gained some of her usual tan back if she had taken her jacket off.

Swipe rolled her shoulders and sized up the building in the distance. "Yeah, I've got this."

If Flit liked Swipe, she might have added in some words of advice or a general cheer of confidence, but she didn't, so she kept her mouth shut and let Swipe focus.

The other woman took a slow, deep breath before she stepped to the side and sped the walnut-sized silver ball down the street. She stopped it just outside of the window.

"Remember, the impact has to be hard enough to set off the—"

Swipe's sharp gaze snapped towards Flit. "I know how fucking flame grenades work."

"Then hurry up and throw the damn thing."

The flame grenade glinted in the light as Swipe made a sideways flicking motion with her hand and sent it hurtling through the open window. Flit's breath caught in her throat as she waited for the explosion.

For one long, painfully suspended moment, Flit thought they

had messed up. At least, until a loud bang sounded. Then another, and another… The chain reaction was as rapid as Flit's heartbeat.

"Shit," Swipe gasped, blue eyes wide as flames billowed out of the basement window and an unearthly groaning sounded down the street.

Shit is about right, Flit thought as she wrapped her arms around Swipe. "We better jet."

Even Swipe, one of the most reluctant co-teleporters Flit knew, clung to her as the entire concrete and brick mess started to collapse before their eyes.

Flit didn't stick around to see the fallout. When she Swipe teleported onto the landing of the emergency stairwell on their way across the alley, the entire platform shook as bolts popped loose from the brickwork. Flit barely registered it as she caught sight of the team and then teleported over to them. The instant they landed in amongst the group, all eyes were on her.

"What's happening over there?" Tweak asked. "I think we placed enough firepower to bring the whole damn block down!"

Flit laughed and shrugged. The explosions sounded more like fireworks in frequency. "I never claimed to be an explosives expert, just an enthusiast."

"It'll come down. There is literally nothing that can save it now." Clarity had to raise her voice over the groaning of the falling building. Dust and debris started to rain over them.

"We need to move." Hawkeye's voice held a note of utter urgency. Everyone turned to him, wondering what he saw. "The drones have noticed the collapse and are coming in hot—"

Another explosion quaked through the buildings around them.

"Watch out!" Clarity's eyes widened, and she pointed behind Hawkeye's shoulder. With a rattle of falling bolts and a squeal of twisting metal, the staircase they had used to hop across the alley tore away from the building and fell towards him.

Flit didn't even think. She launched herself at her best friend, tackling him and trying to push him out of the way as the staircase plummeted towards them.

A cry of pain escaped her as they hit the ground together. Metal crashed around them. A sickening crack echoed through the din. Flit tried to roll to keep their momentum going, but something stalled their movement. Hawkeye's body was limp against hers, and her head spun.

"Swipe, the staircase!" Scraps' bark came from beyond Flit's view, and the weight of Hawkeye's body eased against hers.

One set of hands slid under Flit's armpits, and another scooped Hawkeye up off her. The staircase was cast aside with matching grunts from Scraps and Swipe. Flit looked up at Tweak as he helped her to her feet, his eyes wide with concern, but Flit wasn't worried about herself. She turned to see Sway lifting Hawkeye.

"No!" Flit ran over, every muscle in her body protesting.

The buzz of drones got more intense as she looked for signs of life in Hawkeye. His breathing was ragged, his legs hanging limply in Sway's arms.

A heavy hand settled on Flit's shoulder, and she shrugged it off.

"Flit!" Scraps' voice shook her out of her single-minded focus. "We need to leave, now."

As much as Flit wanted to check on Hawkeye, as much as she wanted to make sure he was ok, Scraps was right. If they didn't leave now, then all of them would be in grave danger.

"Let's move!" Flit barked through a raw throat and a pounding in her head. "Stick to the shadows and run faster than you ever have before."

Scraps took Hawkeye from Sway, the remote viewer looking floppy in his telekinetically enhanced hold.

Then, they ran.

FLIT DID NOT REMEMBER much about the trip back to the Underground. It was all a mess of ducking and weaving through the shadows and struggling not to stumble on the cracked asphalt.

They had stopped when they hit the dank subway tunnels and retreated to a lower level, where all the steel and concrete above would keep them from being noticed on the scanners of the Government drones. Tweak had only needed a few seconds to determine that Hawkeye was in a critical state. His skin had paled, and his breathing was light and erratic. The team fashioned a stretcher for him out of an old train panel, and Scraps and Swipe used their telekinesis to move it along as smoothly as possible.

Flit teleported ahead as soon as they got to the Underground proper. She traversed the familiar tunnels in a series of blinks faster than any she had used before. When she stumbled into the medbay, Patch looked up at her, frozen in shock at her sudden appearance.

"I'll get the team," Patch promised. He dropped the datapad he was using on the closest bed and activated the emergency panel on the wall. "Take me to them." Patch snatched a medical kit off a hook and stepped closer to Flit.

Thankfully, their route to the Surface had been carefully chosen, so the medical team had their itinerary on file to know exactly where to intercept them. It allowed Flit to grab hold of Patch and get him back into the path of the Blue Team faster. She only hoped she was fast enough.

Meeting back up with Hawkeye and the Blue Team confirmed Flit's worries. Patch's face took on that stern, business-like expression that her mother and all first responders wore when shit got bad. Patch ordered Sway and Swipe to lay Hawkeye on the ground, and Patch fell to his knees beside him. Placing one hand on Hawkeye's chest and the other on his forehead, Patch closed his eyes and got to work.

Flit didn't realise how much her body was shaking until Scraps came over and pulled her against his side. He was a tower of strength and firmness beside her, and she leaned into him. The minutes ticked by, and Hawkeye worsened with every rattling breath he took.

The entire team watched on with horror as the medical emergency crew arrived. They opened up their own stretcher with safety belts and monitors and strapped the still-unconscious Hawkeye to it. Without even a second look at the members of the Blue Team, they left.

After the thundering of the medical team's footsteps receded down the tunnel, the remainder of the Blue Team were left in a tense, painful silence. No one could speak. They didn't look at each other. They just stood there, stunned at how quickly their mission had turned, realising what they stood to lose.

16

———

FLIT

WHEN THE BLUE TEAM got back to base, they barely had time to ask after their friend. They were pulled in by Intelligence for an immediate debrief. Some postcogs reviewed Flit's and Tweak's memories of the information they had found, and by the end of the meeting, everyone was concerned. Not because the secret of their existence wasn't as well kept as they thought, but because they had come so close to losing it all. If those thugs had finished their plan of destroying the exits and alerting the Government, the Underground would have been sitting ducks.

The next few days were touch and go for Hawkeye. The medics agreed that the staircase had done enough damage to crush some nerves that were vital for leg movement. He regained consciousness and retained the use of his hands and arms, but his legs refused to move. The microkinetic healers were trying their best, but even then, there was only so much they could do. They were positive that he would have some level of improvement, but it came with the grim warning that it would be a difficult road.

Flit couldn't help but find it ironic that, only days before, she had still been chafing at the idea of going on her mission. Their find in Old City had renewed her sense of purpose, her eagerness to protect those she loved. Even though her mission partner was injured, Shadow still insisted she continue their schedule. Flit wasn't sure if he was just biding his time or if he still intended to send her, but he refused to give her evidence to speculate on either way.

During the day, when Flit wasn't in intensive training with Shadow, she was in the infirmary with Hawkeye. He offered to help her study, but Flit was reluctant at first. With him out of action, extra study would amount to a peculiar form of torture, but he insisted. Having been the victim of the soul-destroying boredom of a long stay in medical rooms, Flit eventually gave in despite her initial reservations. After all, studying with Hawkeye was much less distracting than studying with Scraps.

"Ugh… I'm out of water," Hawkeye groaned, putting his cup down on the table hard enough to make Flit jump.

Flit looked over at Hawkeye and frowned. "I can get you some," she volunteered. She picked up the cup and teleported to the sink in the corner of the room.

Hawkeye narrowed his eyes at her. "Just like that?"

"What do you mean?" Flit paused, hand hovering just above the sensor for the tap.

"You wanna know what the worst part of being stuck in this bed is?" Hawkeye crossed his arms over his chest.

Flit was left dizzy by the change in subject. "Um, sure?"

"You're being nice to me!" Hawkeye threw his hands up in the air. "I complain about running out of water. You don't demand manners. You don't tell me to stop whining. You just up and run to fill my cup, and then when I ask if you wanna know what is wrong, you say 'sure'. *Sure?*" He raked his fingers through his hair, frustration seeping from every part of him. "Are you kidding? You're never this nice. Stop helping me because you feel sorry for me."

Ouch. Flit tried to tell herself that the comment stung because of the venom in his tone, but the cold hard truth behind it was the real sucker punch. "What do you want me to say? 'No, piss off'?"

"Yes!" Hawkeye snapped.

Flit blinked, puzzled. Her face screwed up in confusion, and she held the cup up between them. "Do you want the water or not?"

Hawkeye's upper body deflated, and he flopped back against his pillow. "Yes, please." Every syllable was laced with defeat.

"No. Go fuck yourself." Flit teleported back to his bedside and slammed the cup onto the side table.

A smile slowly crept onto Hawkeye's lips as Flit glared at him. His eyes shone with amusement and pushed the cup back towards her. "Except… I am actually thirsty."

A loud groan spilled from Flit's lips, and she snatched the cup back up, shaking her head. "You're such an arsehole."

The insult made Hawkeye's smile even wider. She teleported over to the sink and filled up his cup as well as a carafe. When she was done, she returned to his bedside and set both down. "There. Now you can get your own bloody water."

"Perfect." Hawkeye beamed up at her. He reached out, taking her hand and squeezing it.

Flit didn't pull away. She looked down at their hands and sighed. "So… what was the point of that? I'm just trying to help."

"I don't need helpers." Hawkeye let go of her and gently lifted her chin, so she was looking into his green eyes. "I've got a team of fussy medics on my case twenty-four hours a day. I need a friend, someone who won't remind me that I'll be sitting here, letting life fly by, while I wait to see if I'll ever walk again."

After having spent the better part of the past few days shoving down the raging guilt about her best friend getting injured on her watch, Flit's tenuous sense control slipped. Her eyes burned, and suddenly, she hated the timing of it all.

With a sniff and a renewed determination to give Hawkeye what he wanted and not what she thought he needed, she squared her shoulders and sat back in her seat, cocking an eyebrow at him. "Good. Your moping around is starting to shit me. Next time you complain, I'll smother you with a pillow."

Hawkeye choked on the water he was drinking and dissolved into a fit of laughter. He was just wiping some dribbles off his chin when the door to the medbay slid open.

"I trust I am not interrupting anything?" Shadow said, knocking on the door frame.

Both Flit and Hawkeye perked up at his appearance.

"No." Hawkeye shook his head. "Please, come in."

Shadow walked over with a datapad tucked under his arm.

Hawkeye gestured for him to pull up a seat, but he shook his head. "I won't be staying for long."

An iron fist of dread reached inside Flit's stomach, grabbed all her organs, and gave them a mighty twist. Her eyes flicked to her best friend, and she had a feeling she knew what was coming. From the way that Hawkeye's eyes dulled, he did too.

"Hawkeye, I'm sorry to do this, but it will probably come as no surprise. As a member of the Underground, your health is our top priority," Shadow began, his tone business as usual. He gestured to Hawkeye's legs as they lay unmoving on the bed. "The mission you were assigned to is of utmost importance, and we cannot delay it while we wait for your recovery. It is for that reason that we have had no choice but to reassign you."

The breath whooshed from Hawkeye, and he sunk back against the bed. Flit swore his skin paled as he closed his eyes. He stayed like that for what had to have been a full minute before his lids fluttered open. His hand found Flit's and held it tight. "You said that the mission is important. Who will go on it?"

Shadow sighed, suddenly looking much closer to his fifty-something years old than he ever had before. "We are still working on that. Flit's assignment hasn't changed, but we need someone to replace you. Given the sheer amount of information you've both had to take in and the obvious need for mission partner compatibility, it is a challenging one for us to figure out."

Hawkeye held Flit's hand so hard it hurt. She didn't want to let go, though.

"Did you hear that, Flit?" Hawkeye asked weakly. "Shadow basically said that you're such a pain in the arse they can't find anyone else compatible with you."

"Hey!" Flit poked him in the ribs.

"Thanks for coming by and putting me out of my misery, Shadow." Hawkeye turned to nod at the tall man. "I knew this was coming. If there is anything I can do to help, just let me know. I'll do whatever I can to make sure Flit has the best chance up there."

Shadow nodded grimly. "I'll keep your offer in mind. Thank you."

The room was thick with silence as Shadow dissipated from view.

Flit bit her lip as she looked over at her best friend. Her heart ached. It was her fault that he was injured, and now that injury had torn one of his dreams—their dreams—out from under him.

"Hawk, I'm so sor—"

"Don't." Hawkeye shook his head as he leaned back against the bed and closed his eyes. "Just… promise me you'll be ok."

Flit rested her hand on his shoulder. "I don't know how to be any other way," she swore, even though they both knew it was a lie.

AFTER SHADOW LEFT, Flit and Hawkeye played some games on the datapads she had brought to his room. They had always been competitive when they played together, and he enjoyed the escapism of it. She left just before dinner time so she could catch up with Scraps. He and Swipe had been put onto one of the quieter night patrols close to the habitation level because of the strain on their powers from moving the staircase and carrying Hawkeye back to the Underground. Flit was pleased they had an easier route, but it meant Scraps was gone all night and slept most of the day. The small window of time they had to spend with each other just got smaller.

When Flit arrived in the Mess, Scraps was already sitting down with Patch, Honey, Link, and Sway. He gave her a little wave as she walked in, and she gestured towards the food. He came over, greeting her with a tight hug and a kiss on the forehead before they got their trays.

"How was your day?" Scraps asked with a smile while they served themselves dinner.

"I'm not sure how to feel about it, to be honest," Flit conceded, "It was mostly training, then studying with Hawk. When I was in medbay, Shadow stopped by."

Curiosity sparking in Scraps' eyes. "And?"

Flit gestured for him to follow her to a quiet corner of the room so they could talk alone. She wanted to let Hawkeye tell the others in his own time. "They've taken Hawk off the mission."

"Oh."

Flit nodded. "They're trying to figure out who to replace him with."

Frowning, Scraps leaned in a little closer and lowered his voice. "Surely there are plenty of other people who are suitable?"

"I don't know." Flit shrugged. "It depends on how much work they've already put into adjusting the aliases. They also need to make sure whoever they select is compatible with Masquerade."

Scraps' eyebrows furrowed. "Masquerade?"

"Oh, yeah…" Flit trailed off as she realised they never had a reason to talk about it before. He wouldn't know what it was. "It's an injection that they give to people who go to the surface. It carries some hardcore nanotech that attaches to their DNA and makes it read as whatever the nanochips say, rather than what it is. It's how we hide our Derivacy from the Government, even if we wind up in the hospital for whatever reason."

"And since you have lived in the Hub, you are already compatible. Interesting."

Flit wasn't surprised Scraps made the connection so quickly. He was clever like that.

His eyes lit up, and his face shifted to that same expression he got when reading some new policy or procedure. "Why would someone be incompatible with it?"

"There are a few reasons, none of which I have the know-how to explain," Flit said with a flippant shrug. "What I do know is that if your body doesn't like it, you'll be throwing up your guts within four hours, so even though there are probably plenty of other people they could pull from their current postings, there's no guarantee that they can handle the Masquerade. It narrows the pool of candidates."

"Even if they do find someone, their training time will be severely limited." Scraps' eyes narrowed in concern, and the corners of his lips straightened out. "Is that safe? Sending you up there with someone not as well trained as you?"

"They don't have much of a choice. I doubt that they will try and get poor Newton to go back up when Vista will be down here with their baby."

"But… the new person will only have half a week to catch up

on everything before you start your intensive training." Scraps became more disgruntled with each word.

"It's ridiculous, but there's nothing we can do about it." Flit patted his arm. "We should just focus on the things we can control. I don't want this to ruin our time together."

"You are right." Scraps perked up. He held his tray in one hand and slipped his free arm around her waist.

They made their way back to the table and to eat dinner, determined to enjoy the limited time they had together.

17

____

SCRAPS

THE NEXT TWO nights at dinner, Scraps had been expecting Flit to tell him the name of her new partner for her mission. He hoped he would be able to get to know the person a bit better before they started their intense training to make sure that they would know how to keep Flit safe. Not that he didn't trust Flit, of course, but she was rather impulsive at times.

The wait frustrated him, especially because he had so much time to think about it. Hawkeye was the perfect partner for Flit, and Scraps had told himself that at least Flit would be happy with him, but this new person was an uncertainty, and Scraps did not want any unknowns when it came to the woman that he cared so deeply about.

"So, have they asked you yet?" Swipe said, breaking through Scraps' concentration as they stood in the armoury and prepared for their last night patrol of the rotation.

Scraps finished securing his grenades in his belt before he peered over at her. "Has who asked me what?"

"Intelligence. Surely you're at the top of their list to go up with Flit." Swipe expertly manipulated her long, sleek blonde ponytail into a practical bun with a series of hand twists that left Scraps perplexed.

Almost as perplexed as her words. "Why would I be at the top of their list?"

Swipe snorted. "Are you kidding? You have expert, insider knowledge of the Government operations in the Hub and of the city itself. You're a quick thinker, and you're the only person I know other than Rook who can get Flit to shut up and listen to reason."

Scraps did not appreciate how Swipe spoke about Flit. He had learned that the reason Flit never listened to the others is because they were so quick to write her off. To get her to listen, you had to listen to her. He imagined Rook understood that, otherwise he couldn't fathom how it would have worked between them.

"Besides, you could probably memorise all of the mission materials overnight if you had to. They're running out of time." Swipe shrugged as if it was obvious.

"But I've only been here a year. Would they even consider me?"

"I don't know. Why don't you ask them?" Swipe suggested, her eyes holding a challenge as she met his. "Unless you think Flit going on the mission might be a convenient time to cut ties, you've got nothing to lose. The worst they can do is say no."

Scraps stopped moving as he buckled his pistol into his belt, and he considered Swipe's words. He never thought to ask for a change of assignment. He was content with his role in the Security team. The workings of the Underground were much more important than his own personal desire to remain by Flit's side. He didn't think he could justify such a selfish request, but Swipe made some good points. Surely, he wasn't the worst candidate.

He didn't have long to think on it, though, as Tweak and Clarity returned from their patrol and joined them, exchanging information about their own observations of some of the areas to watch out for.

THE NEXT MORNING, Scraps trudged to Flit's room covered in roach guts and stale water. They had gone right up to the Surface Level tunnels in their patrol and run into a rather nasty little nest of the chitinous creatures. Roaches were simple to clear out, even in large numbers, but they always made for a messy time. He was looking forward to getting cleaned off and slipping into bed beside

Flit to hold her body against his for the hour they could be asleep at the same time

Scraps crept across the room, smiling faintly as he looked at Flit, splayed out across the bed, the datapad on her pillow. She was struggling to take in all the material, but she was trying so hard. He admired that about her. Once she set her mind to something, she would make it happen.

As he showered, Scraps finally had time to think about what Swipe had said before their patrol. Suddenly, he wasn't so tired anymore. His mind went from wondering if they would accept him to what it would be like to get out of the shower and not have Flit laying there on the bed. Not this morning or any morning after. His gut twisted with concern hard enough to make him wince.

He switched the shower was off and used his telekinesis to snatch his towel off the rail. He dried himself in record time, and instead of getting dressed in his pyjamas, he pulled on a set of casual clothes. He slipped back out of the room, taking one last look at Flit, sleeping so peacefully.

Swipe was right. What did he have to lose?

At least, that was what he told himself as he threw protocol to the wind and walked towards the Intelligence tunnels. The closer he got, the more reasons his mind conjured for why they would refuse to send him on the mission.

He reached the security door outside Intelligence without seeing another person, and he pressed his palm against it. He stood there for a full minute, waiting. He was just about give up when the screen flared to life with the face of one of the workers.

"Scraps? What can I do for you?" the elderly man asked. Scraps had seen him around a few times but didn't know his name.

"I was hoping to speak to Shadow, please," Scraps requested, voice formal and crisp, just like it was when he had been in the Hub.

"You're lucky Shadow is a workaholic. He's already in. Or, rather, I don't think he left last night. I'll see if he is free to talk to you."

The screen died, and Scraps had to wait for another minute before the door slid open. Shadow was already standing there, and he looked Scraps up and down before he stepped back and gestured for him to enter the main room. It was much like Control's headquarters. Screens covered every available space on the walls, and a skeleton crew of people sat and worked at their consoles.

"I was wondering when you would drop by," Shadow said, leading Scraps through the monitor room and into an office on the right-hand side that had Shadow's name on it.

"Thank you for seeing me without notice."

Scraps peered around Shadow's office as they stepped into it. The large table in the middle had a set of electronic dossiers spread across the screen. One of which, Scraps was surprised to see, was his.

"Please, sit." Shadow pulled a chair at the round table out for Scraps before he walked to the opposite side and sank down. "I have a feeling I already know why you're here… but please, enlighten me."

Scraps settled into the seat he was offered and kept his gaze trained on Shadow rather than the faces looking at him from the files. "I wanted to offer myself as a possible candidate to accompany Flit to the Hub."

Nodding, Shadow turned the files around so that Scraps could see them lined up next to each other. "We have six candidates. It's not an easy choice, which is why I am up so early trying to figure it out. Tell me, Scraps. If you were me, who would you pick?"

Scraps gulped and resisted the urge to say himself immediately. Instead, he swiped through the candidates. He spoke his thoughts aloud to let Shadow know his reasoning for either approving or dismissing a someone as he went along. Flit was on contentious terms with three of them. One was far too old. The other, as much as Scraps loathed to admit it, was a suitable match in personality and age.

"What about you?" Shadow asked, pushing the file towards him when it was the last one left.

Scraps sucked in a slow, steady breath and raised his eyes to meet Shadow's. "Flit and I work well together," he began, figuring that was the most important point. "If the Masquerade is compatible with my system, I already have a sound working knowledge of Government protocol and procedure, and the layout of the Hub.

Whatever I don't know, I am confident I can learn easily enough. Even though I grew up there, with enough phenotypical manipulation, no one would ever know. No one ever looks too closely at Registereds."

"Could you handle being back up there? How do you know it won't be too emotionally triggering?" Shadow asked.

"Because I would be working against it. I cannot pretend to know what it would feel like yet, but I am determined. I have no desire to ever rejoin the ranks of the Government. The Underground is my home now, and I want to do my part to protect it, even if that means that I have to go back to the Hub to do it."

Shadow pushed Scraps' file over to the 'keep' pile and then looked up at him. "So, who should I choose?"

Scrap's heart thundered in his chest. His palms were sweaty, and his throat was suddenly very dry. He did not want to presume to tell the leader of Intelligence what to do, but he also did not want to miss his chance with Flit because he didn't have the courage to back himself.

"Me," Scraps said, voice full of confidence. "If the Masquerade works, I believe I am the best candidate for the position."

Shadow sat back, inscrutable as he watched Scraps. The silence between them was so tense it hummed with an anticipatory energy of its own.

Shadow reached out, tapping the table screen a few times to turn it off.

"Make your way to the medbay and ask someone there to administer you a Masquerade Trial. If it works, the job is yours. If not? I will pick either Nova or Pierce."

Blinking in disbelief, Scraps got up from his seat. They were willing to give him a chance!

He mumbled a thanks to Shadow before he saw himself out. He let his legs lead him to the medbay, and when he got there and knocked on the door, it opened to reveal a yawning Patch. The medic's eyes cleared up as he saw Scraps.

"Morning! What can I do for you?" Patch asked with a tired smile.

Scraps felt bad that he had probably caught Patch at the tail end of his shift. "Shadow asked that I come in and request a Masquerade trial."

"Is that so?" Patch's tired expression quirked with amusement. "I was just about to start my handover, but I'd like to stick around for this. Come in, and make yourself comfortable. It might hurt a little, but we will have the results in a few hours."

Scraps followed the micro. Not even the promise of pain was enough to turn him off this course of action.

As Patch prepared the nastiest-looking syringe Scraps had ever seen in his life, he used the console in the room to send a message to Flit. He told her he'd had a late night and that he was looking forward to seeing her at dinner. If the Masquerade went well, he was sure she wouldn't hold it against him. If it didn't? Well, he would deal with that when it happened.

18

———

FLIT

FLIT SPENT the morning following the independent study timetable Scraps had created for her. It was dreadfully boring, but she was making good progress. When lunch arrived, she was grateful for the break. She'd joined Hawkeye for some food and a few rounds of Virtuball. She kicked his arse even easier than usual, but he didn't seem to care. His injury was finally taking a toll on his mood, and for once, he didn't ask about her mission. She was glad to have some time that she didn't have to think about it.

It was a short reprieve, though. After playing, she had to meet Shadow for another round of intensive training. He had been in a particularly gruff mood since Hawkeye's injury, but even his brusque manner was preferable to studying alone.

When Flit arrived at the training room, she pushed the door open to find Shadow had beaten her there. That was normal, but she tilted her head to the side as she noticed another person in the room.

"Uh, hi…" Flit trailed off as she looked between Shadow and Scraps.

Scraps' lips curled into a smirk. There was an amused glint in his eyes that had her immediately wary.

"You know, Shadow, if you brought my boyfriend here to encourage me to concentrate on studying, you are sorely misguided," Flit tutted. "He is very, very distracting."

Squaring his shoulder, Scraps retorted, "I resent that. You are more than capable of distracting yourself without my assistance."

"This isn't about you, Flit." Shadow waved his hand dismissively. "We have a higher priority: getting your new mission partner up to speed."

She avoided looking at Scraps. She wouldn't even entertain the hope growing in her heart because if she did and she was wrong, it would be utterly soul-destroying.

"Oh?" Flit hummed, feigning nonchalance.

"We don't have much time, but I am good at memorising information. I'm sure I will be able to make up for my late start," Scraps said, stepping closer to her and dipping his head to catch her gaze.

Flit's eyes widened. "You're not serious?" She turned to Shadow for confirmation.

"I do not joke when it comes to covert operations," Shadow sniffed, tone stuffed to bursting with indignance.

Faster than the blink of an eye, Flit went from hovering in the doorway to standing an inch away from Scraps. She threw her arms around him and held him as tight as she could. His low, smooth laugh cascaded around her as he returned the embrace. When she pulled away, she reached up, taking his face in both hands and guiding him down to give him a long, deep kiss.

Flit never would have stopped kissing Scraps if the sound of Shadow clearing his throat didn't shatter the moment.

"Again, I was not joking when I said we had a new priority. Newton and Vista will be here in a couple of days. You two will have plenty of time for canoodling when you are in the Hub," Shadow warned, looking thoroughly unimpressed. "For now, please bring those chairs over here so we can get started on the basics."

The blush on Scraps' carved cheekbones was almost as deep as the red of his eyes. With a casual wave of his hand, he floated a stack of three chairs over to them. He set them down and then arranged them neatly in front of the monitor.

After everyone settled into their seats, Shadow turned to Flit. "Consider this your first test, Flit. Give Scraps a rundown of the material, and we'll see how much you remember."

Flit gulped. How could Shadow expect her to think after he had dropped such a bombshell on her? Then again, she was sure there would be bigger surprises to contend with when she was above ground.

She squared her shoulders and decided to view it as a training opportunity, performing under a different kind of pressure.

FLIT AND SCRAPS didn't get a proper chance to talk until Shadow released them and they were making their way to the Mess for a very late dinner. Flit was surprised at how much she remembered from the files, but Scraps' knowledge would soon eclipse hers. She had no doubt that any concerns Shadow might have about him being unprepared would be blown to smithereens.

"So, when did you find out?" Flit asked as they walked, slipping her hand into Scraps', wondering if he had known for a while but had kept it from her.

"About half an hour before we started training."

Flit tugged on Scraps' hand to pull him to a stop. She looked up into his eyes. "I know I was ridiculously excited about it and all... but pretend you didn't see that reaction. Are you sure this is what you want?"

Scraps' brows furrowed, perplexed. "Why wouldn't I want to go to the Hub with you?"

"Well, because it's the Hub, for one. You only just escaped that place. I can't imagine going back is a particularly thrilling idea."

"It is if it means we get to work towards making changes for ourselves and our fellow Derivates," Scraps replied matter-of-factly.

Flit couldn't help but smile, excited he felt the same way she did, like they had a responsibility to work for change. So many people in the Underground had forgotten about that part, about shaking up the system keeping them in the tunnels.

"Once we are on this mission, we can't just come back down if things aren't working out between us."

He gently squeezed her hand as he frowned. "Why do you assume I would want to leave if things aren't working between us? Who said they won't? Isn't working on problems part of being in a healthy relationship?"

Warm flutters of affection stirred in Flit's chest. "All I'm saying is that we're making a rather permanent decision. When we're up there, we'll be each other's sole confidantes. You've only just gotten a taste for what it is like to live on your own terms, and to explore romance… Are you sure you want to give that up?"

"What would I be giving up?" Scraps scoffed. "I will be working on a mission that excites me, and I will be doing it with you. We can still explore our romance in the Hub, can't we?" The tone of that question made it clear it was rhetorical.

There was no point arguing. Scraps never got caught up the expectations around playing the field when it came to romantic partners. They had talked about it before, and his opinion of the matter was *if it isn't broken, why fix it?*

"So, we're really doing this?" Flit asked, smiling at him.

"Yes, Flit, I believe we are."

Flit balled Scraps' shirt in her fists and pulled him down for a kiss. It was full of love and relief and utter appreciation. After a gasp of surprise, he sank into it, wrapping his arms around her and holding her close. Flit never wanted it to end, but then she remembered once more that he would be the one going to the Hub with her, and the pressure of that ticking countdown in the back of her mind vanished.

THAT NIGHT, despite wanting to celebrate with Scraps, Flit excused herself after dinner and made her way to the medbay. Scraps offered go along with her, but she had gently declined. She wanted to spend some time alone with her best friend. Flit held a small container in her hands a little tighter as she pushed the door open.

Physie was just finishing up an examination on Hawkeye when Flit walked in. The matronly woman straightened up and put her hands on her ample hips. "It is slow going, but you are making good progress."

"Hopefully it stays that way. No offense, Phyie, but I gotta get out of these rooms," Hawkeye agreed with a charming smile.

"I remember a few months back you were telling me to suck it up and be patient because being in the right place to be cared for was more important than my entertainment," Flit tutted as she walked over.

Hawkeye rolled his eyes. "Physie? Can you please ban Flit from medbay? She's a pain in the arse."

Physie spluttered out a laugh. "Tinker has already tried and failed. I have no hope." The older woman shook her head as she walked away.

Flit poked out her tongue out at Physie's retreating back and then narrowed her eyes at Hawkeye. "Do you really want me to go? Because I can turn around right now—"

"Show me what you've got in that container before I decide."

Chuckling, Flit teleported to his bedside and offered him the gift she brought. "Ice cream and two spoons. That means you gotta share." She added the last part as a warning.

Hawkeye looked between Flit and the ice cream, and sighed. "Fine, sit down…" He patted the edge of his bed. "It is really unfair to use ice cream to stop me from kicking you out. It's a real low blow."

Flit just chuckled as she settled down beside her friend and gave him a spoon. They both fell into companionable silence as they ate. That was one thing Flit admired about Hawkeye. He was comfortable with the quiet. As her own mind raced to find questions to ask him or things to tell him, he just enjoyed being there and doing what they were doing. She wished she found it that easy to settle into the present moment.

Finally, after Flit conceded the privilege of scooping out the last dregs of ice cream, Hawkeye broke the silence. "Shadow stopped by before lunch today."

"Oh?" Flit teleported the empty container and spoons to the tray table and settled against the raised back of the bed beside Hawkeye.

"He wanted to get my feedback about your new mission partner. There were a few options, but I told Shadow he should pick Scraps. I should have told him that from the start. I was never the right person to go up with you, but I was selfish because even though I know how much you love him, I didn't want to lose my best friend."

Flit sighed, leaning her head against Hawkeye's shoulder. "You weren't being selfish. You were being a good friend," she clarified. "Just like you were after lunch when you had Scraps' back, as well as mine. Not only because will he be amazing at the role but because he genuinely wants it. I suppose your advice had something to do with it being made official, though, so thank you."

Hawkeye shifted to the side so that he could look at Flit more easily. "Shadow confirmed it?"

She nodded.

Hawkeye's shoulders sagged and pulled her into a firm hug. He didn't say anything. He just held her.

She didn't ruin the moment by talking, either. She knew without a doubt that she would be leaving her best friend behind, and there were no words that could describe how much it hurt.

19

SCRAPS

SCRAPS HAD no idea what Flit was complaining about. The materials they were given to study were thrilling. He would have happily forgone several rounds of VR to dive into the content each night. He was already well-versed in many of the policing and enforcement policies, so getting a chance to read up on the more operational ones was intriguing. It incredibly useful to understand the different rules that applied to manufacturing, medical, and scientific facilities.

One thing Scraps and Flit could agree upon was how much potential their future position had for them to discover useful information for the Underground. This was further confirmed by Newton and Vista when they arrived after a few days, and he and Flit were called into a meeting.

Scraps, Flit, Newton, and Vista were seated around one of the interactive tabletops in a darkened Intelligence meeting room. After a brief introduction, the two operatives had gotten straight down to business, saying there was a lot they wished to cover in the handover and not nearly enough time.

"You're getting access to a lot of highly restricted files," Vista announced, a serious look in her deep brown eyes as she glanced between Flit and Scraps. "One of the biggest obstacles is safely obtaining the right information for the Underground without alerting the security systems. Since neither of you are micros, it will be even tougher. Please be sure you stick to using the devices that Shadow gives you for data transfer. No amount of information is worth blowing your cover."

Scraps leaned in. "Will our access to certain levels of restriction come with the position itself, or does it depend on the jobs assigned?"

"Purely on a need-to-know basis for the job," Newton explained in a deep, almost gravelly voice.

Scraps looked at the man he was supposed to be replacing and couldn't see too many similarities. Newton had deep blue eyes. His hair was several shades lighter than Scraps' and a good deal longer. Their jawlines weren't too different, but Scraps' build was more muscular thanks to his regular training, and Scraps was certain he would damage his vocal chords if he attempted to replicate that voice. He peered down at the dossiers on the table screen for their aliases, *Ava* and *Brian Parkes*.

"What happens if we close a case? Do we lose access to the information we needed for it?" Flit asked, her brows furrowing as she started typing a new note on her datapad.

"Yes, you will have limited time to access certain information. It does put the pressure on when it comes to getting copies of it, but honestly, you'll find ways to work around it." Vista gave Flit a reassuring smile. "Every department has its own demands and culture. You'll find ways to delay closing a case when you need to or opening a linked one to get access to some other side info that you might hope will be useful."

Scraps sat back. Vista had a point. He had experience with two different departments and had seen how some procedures that should have been uniform between them were enacted differently. Most of the time, it came down to the supervisor they were working under. One of the reasons he had been so excited about leading the Crucial Operations Team was because he could finally ensure that all procedures were appropriately complied to.

Scraps was going to ask another question when Vista pressed a closed fist against her mouth. Newton's shoulders tensed, and he turned to face her, his hand on her back. Scraps' eyes widened in concern.

"Are you—" Scraps begun, but Vista got to her feet and raced out of the room.

"Sorry. The nausea's really kicked in," Newton said by way of apology as he stood. "We've given you a lot of reading material. Why don't we call it a day? You two need to get to the medbay to start on the pre-pheno alteration meds anyway."

Scraps waited until Newton left the room and then sighed and sat back, earning him an amused smile from Flit.

"You know, if we didn't have to end the session because Vista was going to throw up, I would almost be excited for the early-mark," Flit said, putting her datapad into sleep mode.

"Almost?" Scraps assumed she would have been ecstatic for the reprieve.

"I say almost because I don't want to deal with the pre-pheno meds. I've heard they're a bitch," Flit informed him.

Frowning, he asked, "How so?"

Flit looked down as she ran her fingers along the edge of the table, a sure sign she was not going to be entirely candid with her response. "Oh, you'll see. I'd hate to give you false preconceptions before we go in there. Just… keep an open mind, is all."

Scraps nodded and got to his feet, stretching his arms and legs. There was no point pressing Flit for information. He would find out why she dreaded the medication soon enough. It wasn't like they could avoid it. After seeing Newton and Vista, it had become clear just how significant the physical alterations they would need to undergo were. He would just have to grin and bear it.

IT TURNED out that Scraps couldn't grin while he endured the side effects of the pre-pheno meds. They came in the form of a long, thick needle injected into the base of his spine, just like an outdated lumbar puncture. Not only were they, as Flit called them, *a bitch*, but they made him feel like he was going to throw up.

From what Scraps understood, they weren't going to be changed completely to look like Newton and Vista. To reduce physical stress and possible side effects, Shadow told them that their new, classified appearances would be somewhere between what they looked like now and Newton and Vista.

Scraps wasn't sure how he felt about Flit's appearance changing. He was quite enamored by her engaging hazel eyes and smooth chocolate hair. He was pleased the team had decided that they didn't have enough time to do anything about either of their heights. It was a risky procedure, apparently, with relatively little gain. It meant that, at the very least, he would still be able to enjoy the feeling of wrapping his arms around Flit's short, curvaceous body. He imagined that, if he closed his eyes, he might not even notice the difference.

"You know, I'm going to miss your red eyes," Flit said, smiling up at him as they lay in the med-bay.

Scraps frowned. "It's the most obvious sign I used to be a Registered Derivate. Why would you miss that?"

"Because it is part of your story." Flit shrugged. "What they do up there will never be ok, but you are you, and I don't want to change a single part of that."

"Not even this?" Scraps' fingers brushed over the tattoo of the Government logo on his neck. It was the only thing he wanted to change. It no longer fitted who he was, and he hoped that others in the Underground would be able to see him better without it clouding their view.

Flit slumped against mattress. "I'm used to seeing you as you are. I love all of it, but my feelings won't change because of the way you look. I like your personality most of all."

"Oh, for the love of—" Physie bustled over, standing between their beds. "That's it. Enough of this sappy stuff. You're not in some tragic romance. You're just getting a few simple physical changes. I can't concentrate on my notes with all the melodrama. Why don't you two head next door and keep poor Hawkeye company? I'll send Patch in to sign you out in half an hour."

Flit snickered at Physie's command and teleported out of bed, but Scraps could see a glint in her eyes telling him that this was the outcome she had been hoping for. They were just waiting out the observation period of the medication before they could head back to Flit's room for the evening.

Scraps slipped off his own bed, head spinning, and followed

Flit from the room. Luckily, it was a very short walk, and there were plenty of spare seats in Hawkeye's room for them to collapse into.

"To what do I owe the pleasure of this visit?" Hawkeye tapped his datapad screen to turn it off and set it aside.

"We're waiting out the observation period of the pheno-prep injection," Flit informed him.

"Oh." Hawkeye's face screwed up in an expression that appropriately mimicked just how Scraps felt.

"Have you had them before?" Scraps asked, leaning over in his seat and looking at Flit's best friend.

Hawkeye shook his head. "Nah, but I've heard all about them from some of the Intelligence crew I was on that mission with last year."

"If the preparation is this bad, I do not want to imagine what the actual manipulation is like," Scraps groaned, trying not to think too hard about it as his lunch did barrel-rolls in his stomach.

Only very specialized microkinetics performed phenotype manipulation. It was a technique where they used their atomic manipulation skills to gently coax DNA to express itself differently, creating permanent but reversible changes to a person's appearance. Any natural changes were possible, including altering hair colour, skin tone, body weight distribution. The bigger the changes, the riskier and slower they were. It was a novelty for some of the Citizens in the Hub but an unnecessary extravagance in the Underground.

"You're under general anesthetic for that, so it's the easy part." Hawkeye chuckled, a smirk tugging at his lips as he looked at Scraps. "You'll just fall asleep then wake up looking different."

That, Scraps though, was a relief.

"So, what have you been playing?" Flit reached out, snatching up the datapad that Hawkeye set aside.

Quick as a flash, Hawkeye tried to take it back off her, but Flit teleported over by the door.

"Oooh, an incoming message from Serenity? I wonder what she has to tell you at this hour—" Flit's fingers poised playfully above the screen, as if she was going to open the message.

"Don't you dare!" Hawkeye leaned forward, but he couldn't move off the bed.

Scraps reached out a hand, telekinetically yanking the datapad out of Flit's hand and floating it over to Hawkeye. Hawkeye gave him a grateful nod, which Scraps returned with a grim smile as Flit groaned.

"Scraps, you've met Serenity before, surely. She's the lovely brunette who works for Control. She was one of the people who came by after our run-in with Heft to offer us debriefing and counselling," Flit said, teleporting back over to her chair and sitting down.

Scraps couldn't help but wonder how Flit managed to move around so much when she had had the same drugs he did. "So then the message from Serenity to Hawkeye must be confidential," Scraps retorted, shaking his head at her antics.

"Thank you!" Hawkeye huffed.

"Not if they are of a personal, not professional, nature," Flit returned.

"Would that not make them even more so?" Scraps asked, bows furrowing.

Flit snorted a laugh. "Not for a best friend. Come on, Hawk. Give a girl some gossip!"

"Wanna hear some gossip?" Hawkeye asked, leaning in towards her. She teleported over and sat on his bed, eager for whatever he had to say. "I shattered your high score on Enviro Quest Two."

"No!" This time, when Flit went to snatch at the datapad, Hawkeye was faster.

"You might have beaten her high score, but there is no way you could top mine." Scraps chuckled smugly, more to himself than anyone else. He had been doing well in that game lately.

"Is that so?" Hawkeye cocked an eyebrow at him. He tapped at his datapad and, after a moment, let out a low, appreciative whistle. Looking up at Scraps, he asked "Wanna try a battleground match? You might be good at the questing, but I'll wipe the floor with you in player-versus-player. Just like I used to in hand-to-hand training."

It was Scraps' turn to snort in amusement. "Not a chance."

Hawkeye reached into his bedside table draw and pulled out a second datapad. He threw it at Scraps, who caught it deftly without using his powers.

"You won't have your remote-viewing to give you advantages in this match," Scraps warned as he logged on.

Flit repositioned her chair so that she could see both screens and let out an amused laugh. He looked up at her questioningly.

She nodded towards the screens. "Come on, you two. Time to back up those threats with action."

Scraps and Hawkeye both logged into the game and got down to playing. When Patch came in to sign Scraps and Flit out, Flit kissed Scraps on the cheek and then hugged Hawkeye before excusing herself. When he went to log out, Flit shook her head and said that he and Hawkeye should keep playing, seeing as they were both enjoying it. Flit wanted to start packing anyway, or so she claimed. Scraps just shrugged and returned his attention to the game, finding Hawkeye a worthy adversary.

"Are you looking forward to going on the mission?" Hawkeye asked when Flit had left the room.

Unsure if this was a distraction technique, Scraps did not look up from his screen. "Yes, thank you. I am sorry it did not work out for you, but I am pleased I can accompany Flit."

The game froze on screen as Hawkeye frowned over at him.

Scraps tensed. "What? Did your game stall?"

"No, I paused it." Hawkeye put his datapad down. "You just… you're going to have trouble fitting in up there if you still sound like a Registered."

Shoulders sagging like a deflating balloon, Scraps asked, "Is it that bad?"

Hawkeye took a moment to think about it, tilting his head from side to side as he weighed his answer. "It's not the worst. They speak more formally than we do, but nowhere near what you do. You need to find a happy medium," he explained, scratching the back of his neck.

"I do not even know where to start," Scraps admitted, game forgotten at Hawkeye's feedback.

Perking up when he spoke, Hawkeye pointed at Scraps. "You can start right there. You need to loosen how you speak, use more contractions. Just… think about how lazily Flit speaks, and aim for, like, ten percent of that laziness." Hawkeye's tone was playful enough to add levity to the critique.

"Do you think you will be able to help me?" Scraps asked, considering it a worthwhile pursuit if it would help him slip into his cover more convincingly.

"I'll do my best," Hawkeye promised, eyes flashing with a new sense of purpose.

Scraps smiled at the change in him and settled in for what became a late night of amusing tuition. It started with contractions, and then spiralled into one of the Underground's favourite past times—swearing. It was far more difficult than he anticipated, but Hawkeye proved to be an enthusiastic teacher, and he promised Flit would be appreciative of the effort.

20

FLIT

HAWKEYE AND SCRAPS were enjoying their gaming so much that Flit didn't have the heart to interrupt them. Besides, things in their budding friendship had taken a downturn since Hawkeye had returned from his Intelligence mission and kissed Flit. Before that, they had been spending time together working out, training, and just generally getting to know one another. It was a little late, but anything she could do to help Scraps bond with the others was good. If anything happened to her on their mission, he would have people to come back down to who would treat him like family.

Packing up her room took a fair deal of concentration, anyway. Given the fact that their mission had no set recall date, there was no sense having her belongings occupying a functional living space. Everything she had accumulated over the years needed to be sorted. She would redistribute what she could and store those things she did not want to part with. She had been working on getting it all packed over the last couple of nights, but there was one item she was reluctant to bring down.

Flit ran her hand over the metal chest where she kept all the items that she collected from her time with Rook. It took a great deal of restraint to leave it closed. If she started looking through it, she might never stop. She bit her lip, hefting it off the shelf in her wardrobe and making for the door and down the corridor. She used her hip to bump the elevator sensor and waited for it to arrive.

On her trip in the elevator, Flit wondered if she was making a mistake. It did not stop her from walking to an apartment she normally avoided. She steeled herself, took a deep breath, and knocked on the door.

There was a good deal of shuffling and muttering, but the door slid open a minute later, revealing Swipe. Standing in her workout gear, with a fine sheen of sweat all over her body, the blonde frowned as she saw Flit standing there. "What do you want?"

Flit gripped the metal chest tighter and took a deep breath. She couldn't rise to Swipe's bait, or her cause would be lost. "Sorry to interrupt. I just wanted to ask you for a favour, please."

Swipe choked on a laugh. Then, realising Flit was serious, she groaned and stood back, gesturing for her to come in.

Swipe's room was tidy, and all the screens on the walls showed reels of images taking at various parties, training sessions, and just around the Underground in general. Flit rarely visited her. They were never close, even when Rook was alive.

"So, were you just planning to nosey around, or are you going to tell me what the favour is?" Swipe snapped, putting her hands on her hips as Flit carefully skirted the exercise mat by the door and the range of dumbbells lined up alongside it.

"You know, there is a perfectly good gym in the training area." Flit nodded towards the set up taking up most of the floorspace.

"Ok, that's it. Get out—"

"Sorry." Flit shrugged innocently and took a breath. "I'm not here to comment on your poor choice of workout venue. I… I was wondering if you would be able to take this for me, please." Flit held out the metal chest. A peace offering.

Swipe eyed it warily and jabbed a finger in its direction. "Is that gonna spontaneously combust and burn everything in here the minute you leave for your mission?"

Flit rolled her eyes and set the chest down on Swipe's desk, resting a hand on it. "No, it has a lot of important stuff in it. I… don't want it to go into storage." Flit flicked open the latches on the outside and pushed the lid up then gestured for Swipe to take a look.

Now more interested, Swipe walked over. She pulled out the shirt that was neatly folded on top of the other items. "Oh…" Her fingers traced over the name patch on the chest, and she looked at Flit, her face softening. "Don't you—oh, I don't know—don't you want to leave this with your parents or something?"

"No." The word tumbled out of Flit's mouth. "They would need to take it back up to the Hub with them. I can't bear to think of it up there, where those bastards might find it. They already took him from me—from us. They can't have these memories too."

The next time Swipe looked away from the shirt in her hands, there was a shine of tears in her eyes. "Are you sure you want me to have these?" Her tone was laced with disbelief.

"It doesn't mean I like you." Flit forced a smirk, making an attempt to crack the layer of icy loss settling over them. "He was your best friend. I know how much you loved him. You will take better care of this stuff than anyone else."

Swipe folded the shirt and put it back in the chest, closing the lid and running her hand over the smooth surface. "I'll take care of it."

"Thank you." Flit cleared her aching throat and took one last look at the chest. Not knowing what else to say, she teleported to the door and pressed the panel to open it. If she didn't walk out now, she would teleport over and take the chest back. Parting with it was harder than she could have imagined.

"Flit?" Swipe called after her.

When Flit stopped, Swipe walked over and pulled her into a hug. "Thank you for trusting me."

Flit blinked back tears, letting Swipe hold her for a moment longer before she let out a low, rough chuckle. "You'd better let go of me before this weirdness turns into the start of an actual friendship."

Swipe pulled away, sniffing. "As if that would ever happen."

Flit turned, but before she could step away, Swipe's hand settled on her shoulder. "Seriously, Swipe. Keep going this way, and the earth will tilt on its axis."

"You're such an idiot." Swipe sighed. "I just wanted to ask for something, in exchange for taking care of Rook's stuff."

Flit's posture sagged, and she rolled her eyes, turning back to the blonde. She should have known it wouldn't be that easy. "Name your price."

"Bring that stud of yours back to the Underground safely when the mission is over. Good guys are hard to come by, and even if you snatch them all up, he deserves to be down here with his people when your mission is over."

Flit's expression turned serious. "That's not a promise I can make," she warned. Swipe narrowed her eyes, but Flit continued, unperturbed. "If things go well, you will be coming above ground to join us, not the other way around." Flit started to walk away.

Swipe called after her, "The Underground has been trying to do that for a century, Flit. You think you're good, but you're not going to be the one to change the world."

"Watch me." Flit teleported the rest of the way to the elevator, ensuring she had the last word on the matter.

THE REST of Flit's and Scraps' time in the Underground sped by. Between intensifying training sessions, the two were pulled a million different ways. Flit had dinner with her parents every night for that last week. Lunches were reserved for Blue Team get togethers, and any other breaks or evenings were spent in the medbay with Hawkeye. As Flit hoped, Scraps and Hawkeye spent more time bonding over games as she crammed in extra study time.

Two days before their anticipated departure date, Shadow teleported directly into medbay, scaring the daylights out of Hawkeye, who dropped his datapad.

"Sorry to interrupt," Shadow said, although he didn't look at all sorry.

Flit sat up as Hawkeye started muttering something about *bloody teleporters* and *giving a guy some warning*. Scraps had a hard time concealing his expression of amusement.

"Shadow, to what do we owe the pleasure?" Flit asked, loud enough to cover Hawkeye's discontent.

"We've moved the timeline forward. The micro performing your phenotype manipulations had something come up. We need to get you up there." Shadow's tone brokered no argument.

Flit's stomach dropped. "What… like, right now?"

Scraps' gaze was a million miles away as he reached out, using telekinesis to lift Hawkeye's datapad off the ground and levitate it back over to the edge of his bed.

"They're not supposed to be leaving for another few days," Hawkeye said, his hand grasping at Flit's as she sat on the edge of his bed.

"Circumstances changed. I expect you both in my office in ten minutes. Tell no one else of your departure."

And, just like that, Shadow teleported out of the room again.

"Fuck… I'm not ready," Flit whispered, her eyes wide.

Scraps was still completely silent.

"Don't be stupid," Hawkeye chided. "You've been ready for this your whole life." He pulled Flit into a tight hug. She wrapped her arms around him.

Scraps cleared his throat, tearing his gaze away from them. "I will wait for you in the hallway, Flit," he said with a nod as he got up. He reached out, taking Hawkeye's hand and shaking it firmly. "I guess this is goodbye for now. Thank you for all the training and wisdom you have shared with me."

"It was my pleasure." Hawkeye graced Scraps with a genuine parting smile as he walked out and left them alone.

"I'm so sorry, Hawk," Flit whispered, blinking away tears. She looked into his familiar green eyes. He cupped her cheek. She leaned into his touch and took a deep, shaking breath.

"If it wasn't for my injury, I'd say that it was better this way," Hawkeye whispered. He let go of her cheek, grunting slightly as he leaned past her to open a draw in his bedside table. Flit held onto his hips so he didn't topple out of bed. "I have something for you. I know you're not meant to have any packed bags… but I think they'll let you take this, so long as you don't tell them what it is."

Hawkeye shut the draw and then flopped back against the headrest of his bed. He held a small box out for her.

Flit bit the inside of her lip. "Hawk, you didn't have to get me anything."

Hawkeye rolled his eyes. "Just take the damn thing."

Flit sniffed and laughed, relieving him of the package. The box itself fit easily into her palm. While it might have been used to hold small pills, the foil had been broken and taped back together. She gently peeled the repaired lid back, and her shoulders sagged with emotion. She reached in and gingerly pulled out the fine silver chain. It was so delicate that it looked likely to break with the barest of force, but it was surprisingly heavy. As it slipped from her fingers to the opposite palm, she noticed a round charm dangling off the clasp. About the size of a pea, it was looked like it was some sort of perfectly polished glass bead with a deep green core. The surface shone with an iridescent polish that caught the light.

"I asked Cogs to make it for you. The green thing in the middle is a locater beacon." Hawkeye carefully took the bracelet from Flit's palm and undid the clasp. "She said the bead is made from the same stuff they use to hide microchips from RFID scanners. No equipment or micro up there should be able to detect what it is without breaking the glass."

Hawkeye fastened the bracelet around Flit's wrist.

"It's beautiful," Flit said, turning her hand over and letting the bead catch the light.

"It is, but it is also a promise," Hawkeye told her, taking her hand in both of his. "If you are ever in danger, break the bead. Bedridden or not, I will find some way to come up and get you, I swear."

Flit collapsed against Hawkeye for what might be the last time. He squeezed her against his chest. "I love you, Hawk," she whispered.

"I love you, too, Flit. Please… be careful."

Flit wanted to hug Hawkeye forever, but the longer she did, the harder she knew it would be to let him go. Finally, she pulled herself away. Hawkeye's fingers brushed over her cheeks, wiping away her tears.

"No more crying now. You have a job to do," Hawkeye whispered, resting his forehead against hers. "You go up there and show those bastards what the Underground is made of."

Flit sat up tall enough to press a soft kiss against Hawkeye's hair before she teleported over to the door. "I'll see you soon," she promised.

A tear slid down his cheek as he nodded.

Flit opened the door, but as she stepped out to see Scraps pacing the hall, Hawkeye called out. "Scraps, can I have a minute, please?"

Scraps stopped pacing, his back ramrod straight, surprised etched on his features. Nevertheless, he stepped into the medbay. The door slid shut between them, and it took all of Flit's composure to stop herself from sagging against the wall. Flit wasn't sure what they were talking about in there, but she didn't spare it too much thought. She was devastated she would miss out on the dinner she had planned with her parents for the following night, that she wouldn't be able to hug her teammates goodbye.

The minutes dragged on, but sure enough, Scraps stepped back out of the medbay. His eyes flicked down to the bracelet on Flit's wrist, and an expression of resolution settled on his face. He turned, giving Hawkeye a crisp salute before he grasped Flit's hand.

"We have already taken longer than we were supposed to. We should go." His voice took on that stiff, formal tone he used whenever he was preparing to face authority or danger.

Strangely enough, the halls were void of people as Flit and Scraps made their way through. For Flit, it felt like wading through an invisible gel of memories. Each hall held something important to her—a conversation, a look, a fleeting memory. She took each one in, noticing the tiny scuffs or markings along the way. She memorised the entire trip, hoping she would one day return to this place that she called home.

Despite her reluctance to leave, the walk opened up something new in Flit. Every step closer to Shadow's office was another step closer to her destiny. It might not have been the high impact mission Flit dreamt of, but that sure as hell wasn't going to stop her from trying to make a difference.

21

———

SCRAPS

WHEN THEY REACHED Shadow's office, the door was open, and the leader was already waiting behind his desk. His dark eyes caught Scraps' as they walked in and settled into their chairs. Flit's hand tightened around Scraps' almost painfully. He ran his thumb over her skin in what he hoped was a soothing motion. Even he was disappointed that they wouldn't get to say their proper good-byes to their friends, so he could only imagine how upsetting it was for Flit.

"Thank you for coming at such short notice. In a couple of minutes, I'll be teleporting us to the doctor's surgery," Shadow informed them, his tone as stiff as always. "In the meantime, Flit, I have prepared the room next door to record a secure message for your parents."

Scraps smiled as Flit's hand softened in his grip. He felt her body shift, coiling, ready to get up and take the opportunity offered to her.

"Scraps, I assume you don't have any messages to record before you leave?" Shadow made it sound like a question, but the subtext was clear. He didn't believe Scraps had made strong enough connections to want to leave a recording.

But Shadow was wrong. There was a message that he would like to store before he left. "Actually, if I could just have a minute or two as well, I would appreciate it."

"You may go after Flit." The only sign of Shadow's surprise was the slight crease of the crow's feet in the corners of his eyes. "I am sure I don't need to remind you that the recording must not contain any sensitive information."

"Of course not," Flit agreed as she teleported over to the door and then out of sight.

Shadow and Scraps sat in stony silence as the minutes dragged. It wasn't broken until Flit returned, dashing tears out of her eyes. As Scraps stood and walked past her, he gave her shoulder a gentle, reassuring squeeze.

The room next door was small and nondescript, furnished with nothing other than a chair and a large monitor on the wall. Scraps leaned forward and opened the message recording panel. He completed the *To* field, left the date blank, and typed an opening requirement in the subject bar before sitting on the chair.

Scraps' throat constricted as he tried to figure out where to begin, but a sense of purpose settled over him and he swallowed his indecision.

"If you are listening to this message, then something must have happened to me…"

ONCE SCRAPS STARTED SPEAKING, the words flowed easily. He left the small recording room a few minutes later, taking three deep breaths to centre himself before returning to Flit and Shadow. They were talking in low tones as he entered, but the moment Flit turned around, her beautiful hazel eyes lit up with warmth as they met his.

"Don't bother sitting. We are leaving right away," Shadow informed Scraps.

The older man materialised to Scraps' left. Flit popped out of her chair and into the space to his right. Scraps reached down, taking her hand as Shadow stepped in and draped an arm around both of their shoulders.

"This is it!" Flit whispered. For the first time since Shadow had appeared to announce their abrupt early departure, there was a spark of excitement in her eyes.

"Don't forget to hold your breath," Shadow warned, looking only at Scraps. Scraps nodded and closed his eyes, preparing to do just that. "Teleporting in three… two…"

Scraps sucked in a deep breath.

"One."

The atomic pull of Shadow's teleportation sucked at Scraps' entire being with a punch and twist that he had never felt with Flit's. His gut protested, and he swallowed down a surge of nausea as he opened his eyes.

"Awesome!" Flit slipped away from him, footsteps echoing on the smooth tiled floors.

Scraps struggled to regain his composure as he took in his surroundings. They were somewhere entirely new, inside a strange mash-up of a medical facility and a fancy waiting room. Three of the four walls were painted a pristine white, and the fourth was opaque electrochromic glass. The dull, muted ambience of the underground tunnels were gone, replaced by the distant evening hustle of a busy city. Scraps' eyes widened. They must have tele-ported aboveground.

Just as Scraps was about to confirm it with Shadow, a large set of glass double doors at the side of the room burst open to reveal a woman and man in clean white scrubs. The bright clinical lights did nothing to hide the spark of recognition in the woman's eyes.

"Ah, Shadow. Right on time." She shook his hand.

"Yavin. Good to see you," Shadow said, a very real smile curling his lips and lighting up his grey eyes.

Scraps was too queasy from the translocation to think much about the uncharacteristic behaviour, but Flit cocked an eyebrow in interest as she playfully elbowed him.

"Yavin, these are the two I told you about. I transferred their necessary medical records to you an hour ago. Their systems received the pre-pheno meds nicely. You have the alteration brief-ing, I assume?" Shadow asked, resuming his business-like manner.

"Right here," Yavin tapped her datapad with a smile. She turned to Flit and Scraps and reached out. She shook both of their hands. "I am Yavin. Please don't tell me your names. I do not need to know them. It's nothing personal, just an attempt to protect your identity."

Scraps nodded but sensed Flit squirming beside him. During training, they had to keep their alias names under wraps for security purposes. In this venue, they were meant to avoid using names all together. Scraps hadn't mentally prepared himself for not being able to call Flit by her name.

"I'll leave them in your hands. I will be back in twenty-four hours to collect them for their assignment. That is the required recovery time, correct?" Shadow asked.

Yavin peered at her datapad. She read off it, her lips moving soundlessly. "Yes. Twenty-four hours is sufficient." She passed her datapad to the man in scrubs behind her. "Come on, let's get started."

Yavin and Shadow gave each other a nod of farewell. Shadow then phased out of view, and Yavin turned on her heels, gesturing for Flit and Scraps to follow her as she pushed back through the double doors.

"I can't believe this is actually happening," Flit whispered.

Scraps gently slid his hand onto the small of her back and held the double door open for her. They were led through a comfortable looking waiting area, and then a series of short, stark white passages until they reached a sterile procedure room with two beds.

Yavin gestured for them to settle in, but before Flit let go of Scraps, she tugged him closer for a deep, loving kiss. Despite the people watching, he gave in and wrapped his arms around her, holding her tight until she pulled away. He looked down at her, eyes raking over her face as his hand tangled in her chocolate hair. He committed every single detail of her to memory before he turned to the doctor and nodded.

"Lay down when you are ready to begin. We will put you under general anaesthetic for the procedure. When you wake up, you will look different. It will be disorienting. You will be together in this room for the procedure and your recovery. We aren't making any vocal changes, so if you need reassurance when you wake, I recommend speaking to one another back-to-back," Yavin explained patiently and as if she had done so a hundred times before.

Scraps walked Flit over to the nearest bed and helped her on before moving to the opposite one and settling onto it for himself. As he lay back, he turned his head. He caught Flit's gaze, and as

Yavin approached her and the assistant moved to him, he thought of nothing other than their next mission together as his breathing slowed and his eyes fluttered shut.

22

———

FLIT

WHEN FLIT WOKE, her eyes were as heavy as lead, her mind was foggy, and she struggled to maintain her tenuous grasp on consciousness. It took a lot of effort, but she opened her eyes, hissing when the artificial lighting burned her retinas mercilessly. She squinted, overwhelmed by a momentary surge of panic at the clinical white walls of the unfamiliar room. Panic seized her and her heart leaped into her throat. She grasped at the crisp sheet covering her as she rolled over on the mattress. She peered across the room, seeing Scraps laying there, curled on his side with his back to her. She rubbed her face, desperately wanting to clear the grit in her eyes so she could see him properly.

"Scraps!" She had to force out his name, her voice scraping against her throat like gravel.

Scraps stirred. He rolled over, and a soft gasp slipped from Flit's dry lips. Instead of being greeted by his deep crimson eyes and short flaxen hair, his new crystal-blue gaze met hers. She looked down at the corded muscles of his neck to see nothing but a bare stretch of skin, free of the Government's brand. Her fingers itched to reach out and run over that smooth space, but she didn't dare move with the way that her head was pounding.

"Flit?" Scraps' voice was just as rough as hers, and his new, tawny brows furrowed as he inspected at her.

She reached behind her head, gently pulling her thick braid

over her shoulder. She blinked. Her normally chocolate brown hair had been replaced by a honey-brown shade with slightly darker highlights.

"I know we were told to expect it, but I was not prepared for how different you look," Scraps confessed.

Flit bit her lip. It was Scraps beneath that face, all right. She saw him in there, behind those foreign blue eyes. His stare still held the intensity and affection that she was familiar with, but it was just masked differently. Nothing in his voice or phrasing had changed, but still, seeing a different face speaking to her like that? It was unsettling.

"Are you okay?" She wanted to say something more, something better, but her words caught in her throat. How could she possibly express the confusion that her mind felt, thinking such tender things about someone who looked so different?

"I'm fine." Scraps pushed the sheet down and tried to sit up, but he grunted and collapsed back against the bed, his shoulders hunching. "Argh… A little sore, but fine," he amended.

There was a soft metallic hiss followed by footsteps as Doctor Yavin entered the room. She was carrying her datapad but observed them both carefully as she stopped between them. "Some discomfort and disorientation are normal. It should clear over the next few hours," she said.

Some discomfort was an understatement, but without something to soothe her scratchy throat, Flit didn't bother to argue.

Yavin walked over to Flit's bed first and tapped the monitor by the headboard. She scrolled down through various feeds. "Your vitals look good," she told Flit before moving over and doing the same to the monitor above Scraps' head. "Both procedures went smoothly. The DNA restructuring was simple enough, and the physical changes have matured well." She peered at Flit's hair and eyes a bit closer before adding. "I managed to achieve the tones required by Shadow. He'll be pleased by the outcome. I am going to get Samson to bring you some dinner and a mirror. If you need anything, please press the help icon on the monitors."

With another satisfied nod, Yavin swiped at her screen one more time and turned, making for the door.

Flit's stomach churned, and she steeled herself, knowing she would have to sit to eat. After a moment of mental preparation, she pushed herself to sitting and turned, looking at the monitor and scanning past the medical data to find the time in the bottom corner.

A low whistle slipped through Flit's lips. "Wow… we've been out nearly eighteen hours."

"That long?" Scraps shook his head and raked his fingers through his hair. "I feel like I have only been asleep for a second. I am so exhausted."

Flit frowned at how worn he sounded. She longed to reach out to him, but their beds were so far apart.

"I hope dinner arrives soon. I don't know about you, but I could eat a whole table full of food," Scraps said, giving her a smile.

Once more, Flit struggled to reconcile his voice and face, but she smiled and laughed all the same at his attempt to lighten the mood. Then, as if summoned by the joking comment, the man who had been assisting Doctor Yavin the previous night walked in carrying a tray with two meals on it. Flit assumed he was Samson.

"Thanks," Flit muttered as he settled the tray on her bedside table. "You've got a small staff here, huh?"

"Only because you two are here," he confessed. "Whenever one of Shadow's requests come in, we need to clear our books. This centre works on the fringe of the law as it is, so we can't risk other patients seeing you. Not that they would know what you—we —are, of course, just by looking at us."

Flit's head tilted to the side. "We?"

"Yes, we." As if to confirm his answer, Samson floated the second meal off the tray over to Scraps and settled it down neatly.

"Ah, a fellow macrokinetic." Scraps smiled as he reached for the food. "Forgive my curiosity, but are we in the Hub now? Is that why you mentioned operating on the fringe of the law?"

Samson shook his head. "I'm not at liberty to answer that." He didn't seem likely to provide any more information as he turned to walk away. "If you need anything, please don't hesitate to call me. I have been told that Shadow will be here this evening. In the meantime, feel free to get up and walk around, but avoid anything strenuous."

Flit nodded, not planning to attempt anything other than sitting up and maybe walking over to Scraps. She wouldn't put it past Scraps, however, to try and get a few push ups in because he had missed his daily morning training session.

THE NEXT FEW hours dragged by. Flit would have called it relaxing if she hadn't spent the entire time waiting for her headache to wear off. After afternoon tea, she discovered that the datapads on their bedside tables had a full suite of games. She told Scraps to scoot over so that she could sit next to him in his bed, and she challenged him to a few rounds of Havcon 5.

When they grew bored with the games, Flit rested her datapad against her lap and turned to properly observe Scraps. She had been avoiding doing so for the entire time they had been playing. If she sat beside him and just listened to his voice, it was almost like nothing had changed. She could pretend it was just any other day, and she wouldn't have to face the disorientation of feeling like she didn't know the man looking back at her.

"Your face is so different," she whispered. She was tempted to reach out, to stroke his skin to at least see if it felt the same when her fingers curled.

His serious expression softened as he took her hand and guided her to touch his face. "I know. So is yours, but we are still the same underneath," Scraps whispered, letting go of her hand so he could run his fingers down the braid resting over her shoulder.

"Would you like to look in the mirror?" Flit asked, gesturing towards the two hand-held mirrors that they had been fastidiously avoiding.

Scraps nodded, so Flit leaned over and grabbed one. As she moved to hold it up for him, she caught a flash of her own new deep brown eyes in her reflection.

Scraps peered into the mirror and rubbed his hand over his neck where the tattoo used to be. He tried to hide it, but his fingertips trembled, and his eyes widened at the clean, smooth flesh there. "I… I do not look like I was ever Registered." He turned his face this way and that to take in his new hair colour. "And my eyes!

Ever since moving to the Underground, I wondered what they would be if the Government hadn't altered them."

"I don't know if they went with what your genetic code said your eyes should have been, but the colour suits you." Flit's smile was tender as she nodded, looking into those new, deep blue eyes of his.

Scraps covered Flit's hand with his own and then lifted it higher and kissed her knuckles. Despite feeling like she was being kissed by someone new, Flit's heart fluttered. Then, with a bit of daring, she leaned forward and claimed his lips with her own. She let her eyes flutter shut, and for a few beautiful moments, she was able to focus on the fact that she was with Scraps. Her Scraps.

As much as Flit would have liked to continue kissing him, voices floated in from outside their small room. She pulled away and looked towards the door just as it slid open.

"Ah," Shadow said as he walked in, his eyes raking over them. Yavin walked in and stopped by his side. "You've done an immaculate job, as always." Shadow strode over, taking his datapad out from where it was tucked under his arm. "I need to take a photo of you both for our files, and then we can get you settled in your new home," Shadow informed them.

Yavin set the screen behind Scraps' bed to a standard white background with the Government logo on it, and then Shadow took the picture. Scraps slid out of bed, watching as Flit took his position. Yavin lowered the height of the logo behind her head, just as it had been for Scraps. After Shadow took the photo, Scraps offered her his hand, and she got to her feet.

"Thank you for this, Doctor Yavin," Flit said with a smile.

"It was nothing." Yavin waved dismissively at her words, but there were dark circles forming under her eyes from what had to have been a very long night and day for the doctor. Just like any other Derivate ability, microkinesis could take quite a toll on the wielder's body.

Flit's mother had spent some time in her youth learning the art of phenotype adjustments but said it was a terribly inefficient and impractical way to use her powers. For the energy it took to lighten someone's hair a few shades, she could have knitted together a puncture wound to the lungs. Flit smiled faintly to herself, regret plucking at her heartstrings at the thought of the not seeing her mother again. They might have argued constantly, but she loved her.

"Yes, thank you," Shadow echoed. He then stepped forward, draping his arms around Flit and Scraps. "Let's leave now so that the good doctor can get some rest, and we can get you to your new home."

Flit excitedly prepared herself for another of Shadows' expert translocations. After the last one, she had felt such a rush of exhilaration. She wished she could do it too. He had taken them from the Underground to somewhere in a big city in the blink of an eye. She had barely felt the strain, and Shadow had appeared no worse for wear. He might be a surly bugger, but Flit had a deep admiration for his precision and control.

Shadow gave the usual countdown, and when they reappeared, they were in yet another new location.

Flit teleported around the room in several rapid hops, taking in the sleek, modern tones of their spacious open-plan living area. The lounges were a smooth grey fabric, and even though the shapes were all clean lines and angles, the cushions shifted nicely as Flit flopped down onto them. They faced a glass wall that spanned the entire width of the space. She perked up and teleported over, running her finger across the glass. Immediately, ripples of pixels disappeared, leaving them with a view of the Hub sprawling out before them. Gleaming skyscrapers spread as far as the eye could see. The height of the buildings dropped away to the west to reveal a watercolour sunset of lilac and orange blazing over the rooftops. Flit sucked in a breath at the beauty of it. She pressed her palm against the cool glass.

Flit had grown up moving between the Underground and the Hub, but she had never been in a home this expensive or this close to the centre of the city. It was a sure sign of the privilege that came with their new jobs.

And a sure sign that they had landed themselves in very risky positions, indeed.

Turning her back on the city, Flit teleported over to Scraps. When she reappeared in front of him, she noted the green tinge of his skin. "Don't you like it?"

Shaking his head, Scraps admitted, "I am still feeling nauseous from the travel." Then, he took a deep breath and finally looked around.

"We are fifty stories up," Shadow informed them.

"And probably only a few blocks from Centre One, if what I saw out of that window is any indication," Flit added.

Scraps skirted past Flit and walked over to take in the view. "We are very close to Government headquarters. These blocks are tightly monitored."

"It makes for an easy walk to work, and it befits the positions that your aliases hold," Shadow said.

"That is true." Scraps left the window and made his way to the kitchen, approaching it like he would an unknown tunnel. "Flit, should you be teleporting around in here?" His wariness was evident as he ran his fingers over the smooth benchtop.

Flit rolled her eyes at his concern.

"It's fine. The apartment is secure. You can both use your powers in here. It is probably a good idea. You should keep them sharp just in case," Shadow suggested.

When Flit poked her tongue out at Scraps, he didn't even crack a smile. He gestured at the stovetop. "Will we be cooking for ourselves?"

"There is enough in your budget to have some meals out, but cooking is the most economical option," Shadow said.

Scraps' frown deepened as he looked at Flit. "Can you cook?"

The surprise in his tone was evidence he didn't consider the fact they might have to feed themselves. Flit supposed it was something he never had to think about. As a Registered, and in the Underground, he had always just been fed.

Teleporting over and leaning on the opposite side of the island bench, she said casually, "Yes, I can cook."

Scraps' shoulders sagged with relief.

"The real question is, can I cook well?" Flit informed him with a wicked smirk.

He narrowed his eyes at her warily. "Can you cook well?"

Flit snorted a laugh. "Nope!" She teleported over to the hallway that led off the living area and sauntered down the hall. "We're having burnt steak for dinner every night!"

23

———

SCRAPS

SCRAPS WINCED at the thought of burned dinners but made to follow Flit all the same.

Before they could get too far, Shadow cleared his throat. "I will leave you both to explore your new home. Now, I would suggest that you start using your alias names immediately. This apartment is the only safe place you can use your real names or discuss anything about the mission. You will have two days to adjust before you are expected to report to Centre One for your first day of work. Use the time to familiarise yourselves with your surroundings, find escape routes, study whatever you didn't manage to cover back home."

With a serious nod, Scraps replied, "Yes, Sir."

Shadow looked at Flit, who gave him a lazy, two-fingered salute.

"Very well. You both know the emergency procedures if you should need anything. I hope you never have to use them. I will check in with you from time to time. Good luck, and remember…" His gaze was so serious that it pinned both Flit and Scraps in place. "Stay safe. Stay hidden. No amount of information is worth your lives or the safety of the Underground."

"We won't forget," Flit promised, her expression grim.

Scraps slid his arm around her waist.

Shadow reached into his pocket and pulled out a small box and set it on the table before he faded from view.

Scraps went to walk over and retrieve the box, but Flit grasped his hand and tugged him down the hall. "Come on, Brian. Let's go and check out our new bedroom!"

Scraps found that having her call him by his alias was worse than having to adjust to her new appearance. Still, he let it sink in as he followed her down the hall and to the left. "Very well, Ava. If it is as nice as the living area, I am sure we will not be disappointed."

Just like the living area, an entire wall of their bedroom was a window. It overlooked the city outside, with the glass of the other buildings catching the burnt orange sunset and reflecting all shades of wonder back at them. The bed was in the middle of the room, already made with fresh, crisp sheets. One wall was the telltale smooth panels of their wardrobe, with a door in the middle that led to a small well-equipped en suite.

Flit let out a squeal of delight and teleported away from Scraps. She reappeared a metre above the bed and let herself fall back onto it with an *oof*. She groaned in relief as she spread out her arms and legs, even though she was too short to touch all four corners. "Well, this is my bed. Where are you gonna sleep?"

Scraps' chuckle came from deep down in his throat. "The couch does look comfortable…"

Flit threw her head back and laughed. She reached one hand out to him. "Stop being ridiculous, and get over here!"

Resistance, Scraps knew, was futile. He kicked his shoes off and dove onto the bed, landing on the end and looking at her body. She didn't move an inch, although he noticed her chest rising and falling a little faster as he crawled up the bed and settled between her legs. He leaned down, kissing her passionately for a moment before he flopped back onto the bed and let out a contented sigh.

"Why did you stop?" Flit rolled onto her side and propped her head up on one hand. "I was enjoying that."

Scraps pressed his lips together in disapproval. "We are not supposed to be doing anything strenuous," he reminded her.

"Strenuous, Brian? Who said it was going to be strenuous?" Flit put her hand on his chest and pushed him back against the mattress. She slid one leg over his hips and straddled him.

When her lips slid to the crook of his neck, Scraps groaned. "Flit…" Her name was as much a plea as a warning.

"You just lay back and relax." Flit kissed her way up the sensitive skin of his neck, over his jawline, and to his lips. Her body sank more heavily onto his, pressing against all the right places.

Doctor Yavin's warnings were lost behind the rush of blood and desire roaring through his veins.

"I promise I won't wear you out," she whispered, her sweet breath mingling with his. He looked up into Flit's now brown eyes, cupping her cheek as he allowed his mind and heart to realign to the new her. Then, that smirk of hers came again as she added, "Too much."

SCRAPS WOKE a couple of hours later to the rumbling of his stomach. Flit was curled up against his side, her head resting on his chest. His arm ached from where she had been laying on it, but as he rubbed his eyes and looked around, he soon forgot about the ache. At some point, the evening had turned into night, and instead of the watercolour sunset, the view outside of their window was now painted with a blanket of darkness and twinkling city lights.

As Scraps stirred, Flit muttered something he couldn't quite understand. He imagined it was some complaint about being disturbed. He laughed quietly and took great care to extricate his arm from under her before he got out of bed. Still naked, he walked through the dark apartment, amazed by how spacious it was. There was even a spare bedroom opposite of theirs they hadn't explored yet.

He went into the kitchen, opening the fridge to see nothing more than a couple of bottles of chilled water. A quick exploration of the cupboards revealed a similar situation. Scraps let out a *hmph* and leaned back against the counter as his stomach rumbled again. He'd never had to worry about where his food was coming from before.

Not that he was overly concerned, of course, as he knew they had money to buy food, but for Scraps, food had always just been there. Whether the tasteless but filling rations at the Government's Derivate facilities or in the Underground, there was always something.

"I've never seen you looking so glum." Flit's voice danced over to him from where she stood in the hall, their sheet wrapped around her otherwise naked body.

"We have no food."

Flit smirked. "Hmm… I guess we have two options." She walked over and wrapped her arms around him, only the thin sheet between them. "We could either order some food for delivery, or we could go out to a restaurant, because there is no way I'm cooking tonight."

"Which is fastest? I'm starving." Scraps rested his chin on top of her head.

"They're about the same, usually. The real question is whether you want to leave the house or not. You've never eaten out before, have you?"

Scraps shook his head. "Never. I never ate anything other than the nutrition rations."

"Well…" Flit sighed, pulling away from him and giving him a long, lurid look up and down. "I suppose that means we should get dressed and go out."

Going out seemed like a horrible option if it involved Flit wearing more than a sheet. Besides, apart from feeling hungry, Scraps was also exhausted. He thought about the effort it would require to get dressed, find somewhere to eat, and be surrounded by Citizens and maybe other Registered Derivates. He would have to be on guard, and he didn't feel like being on guard after the twenty-four hours they'd had.

"Actually, let's just order in. I do not want to go out if it means you have to get dressed."

Cocking an eyebrow at him, she stepped back and looked at the large window of their living area. "Home System, turn on."

"*Home system is on and operational. How can I be of service?*" A professional, computerised voice sounded through the apartment, and the large window screen rippled in acknowledgement.

"We'd like to order a delivery for dinner, please. What are the closest options?" Flit asked.

Flit even treated the AI like a human. Scraps adored that about her. She could see the humanity in anyone, even someone as machine-like as he was when they met.

"*There are twelve restaurants and cafes within a two-block radius that deliver. I am putting the options on the living room screen now,*" the computer replied.

Scraps turned to see a flurry of menus obscuring their view of the skyline. The sheer number of options made him dizzy.

Flit just teleported over and started going through them without an ounce of trepidation. "Ooh, look, this one has freshly made ice cream. Yum!"

"Ice cream is not an adequate dinner food," Scraps tutted, shaking his head as he walked over to her side and slid an arm around her waist.

"Tell that to the mint choc-chip that has my name on it." Flit chuckled as she reached out and tapped the menu to add a serving to their order.

With a fair bit of negotiation, Scraps managed to convince Flit to order proper dinner food to go with their ice cream. When she submitted the order, he walked towards the kitchen to figure out where the crockery and cutlery was but stopped as he passed the box Shadow left on the table. He picked it up.

"What's that?" Flit asked, teleporting over.

She was far fonder of surprises than he was, so he gave it to her to open. "Shadow put it on the table before he left," Scraps told her.

Flit's smile faltered the instant she opened the box.

"What is it?" Scraps asked, leaning over.

Flit held the box out to him and looked away. Nestled inside, between tiny plush fabric cushions, were two plain gold rings.

Scraps plucked one out and looked at it, turning it this way and that in his fingers. "Wedding rings?"

"Ava and Brian are married," Flit muttered.

"True." Scraps went to put the ring on his finger.

"No." Flit reached out, tapping a different finger. "That one."

Scraps slipped it on then retrieved the slightly narrower one and held it out to Flit. She bit her lip and shook her head. "What's wrong?" he asked.

"I don't want to wear it."

"But, our cover—"

"I know!" Flit interrupted. "I… I just always thought the first wedding ring I wore would be my own. I know Ava and Brian are married, but we aren't. You don't even love—" She stopped, lips snapping shut.

Scraps shrunk back. He set the ring and the box back on the table and cleared his throat. "My research never elaborated on the relationship change between being married and not married," he stated simply, hoping Flit would enlighten him. and he could figure out why it was such a problem for her.

"There's no change in the relationship, not really. It's just a way of making it official. Legal. Like, when you're in love with some-one, and you're not afraid to say you want to spend the rest of your life with them," she said, unable to meet his gaze. "It's about commitment."

Marriage was an almost entirely foreign concept for Scraps. Even relationships had seemed impossible a year ago. In truth, he did not understand the purpose. He had already decided he wanted to be with Flit. He didn't see what else marriage had to offer.

"Should we get married?" Scraps asked, "Like, you and I? Not Ava and Brian?"

"Don't ask if we should get married just to make me feel better." Flit pulled out a chair and sank into it, shaking her head. "It has to be built on a foundation of love, not convenience or pity."

"Ah," Scraps hummed. *Love.* There it was again. For such a small word, it sure made a big fuss of itself. "So… you're not going to wear it?"

With a huff, Flit snatched the ring up and shoved it on her finger. Then, she teleported into the kitchen and started opening and shutting cupboard doors with loud bangs, collecting the things they would need to use to eat their dinner with.

Scraps remained standing by the table, wondering if he had done something wrong.

FLIT AND SCRAPS spent the next couple of days relaxing and getting ready for work. Scraps was confident in his and Flit's preparation. They visited the supermarket twice and fully stocked their cupboards. Both trips had been quick, and Scraps had found it odd beyond belief to be out and about as though he was a Citizen. They had walked past one or two Derivates on Law Enforcement patrols, but they had only seen them at a distance. Scraps wasn't sure how he felt about it all, but Flit had been happy to remind him about the purpose for each adventure, and the trips were quick.

After Flit burned their dinner on the second night, he offered to cook on the third. Scraps found the process to be rather meditative. From washing and cutting the ingredients to the actual cooking, it was simple if one just followed the recipe. He tried to explain to Flit that the reason she had burned dinner the night before was likely because she had the cooktop up higher than the recipe suggested, but she just glared at him in response. He kept his cooking tips to himself after that.

Even though they tried to get an early night before their first day of work, Scraps had trouble getting to sleep. He had never really been one for nervous anticipation, but he supposed there had to be a first time. He tossed and turned most of the night, drifting in and out of slumber.

When the shrill piercing of the alarm broke through their consciousness, Flit groaned and pressed her face into his chest. "Off!" she yelled, pulling the sheets up over her head.

Scraps, however, slid out of bed and stretched, glad the night of tossing and turning was finally over. "Ready for our first day of work, Ava?" Scraps asked as he made for their en suite.

"How are you so chirpy?" Flit's groaning was muffled by their sheets.

"Because it is our first day of work. We set our alarm early enough so we could have a good breakfast and take a leisurely stroll to the office. I am looking forward to it," Scraps replied, only partially lying.

There was a string of muttering from the bedroom that Scraps was glad he couldn't hear.

When he got out of the shower, he walked into the kitchen to see Flit holding up a couple of packets of quick-heat food in her hands. "Looks like we have oats, oats… or oats for breakfast. What would you like?" she asked, seeming unimpressed by the options. "Shit, why didn't we buy anything more exciting?"

There were so many options at the supermarket the day before that they had both become overwhelmed. Oats were the closest and cheapest option at hand. Still, he smiled, amused by her dry sense of humour. "We allowed plenty of time to get to work today. Should we purchase something for breakfast from that café on the corner? The one you said looked good."

"Brian, you're a genius!" Flit dumped the packets of oats on the counter and teleported over, taking his cheeks in both hands and pecking his lips excitedly. It still felt odd to have Flit call him Brian, even though they had been practicing it for the past few days. "Right. I'm gonna get ready to brave the world before I decide to barricade myself in here forever."

Flit disappeared into the bathroom as Scraps returned the oats to the pantry and went to put on his work uniform. Half an hour later, they walked out of their apartment and towards the elevator of their building. This part, at least, reminded Scraps of the Residence. The hallways were sleek and modern, but with images of potted plants on wall screens instead of the real things. The elevators were fast, too, and they had never had to wait more than a few seconds for a lift.

Out on the street, Scraps and Flit threw themselves into the morning foot traffic. It was just as busy as Scraps remembered, with people going about their daily business or rushing to work. Usually, he would have been posted on one of the wide street corners, ensuring general order was kept. Traffic—foot and hover—was rarely a problem. The Government had done an excellent job of establishing an effective public transport system. Very few Citizens used private vehicles, as an efficient network of electric trams and underground maglev trains ran like clockwork. Combined with the zoning that ensured that Citizens never lived too far from work, travel was a rather simple affair.

The pair stopped at the café Scraps mentioned for a delicious breakfast of freshly cooked bacon, eggs, and mushrooms on toast.

It felt so indulgent. Scraps only ever had the pleasure of a fully cooked breakfast on special days in the Underground.

After they finished, they had ten minutes to let their food settle and watch the busy world around them before they had to go.

Centre One was the tallest building in the very middle of the bustling capital, and all of its floors contained the most important departments within the Government. It was rumoured that the council of anonymous leaders who oversaw the Government's workings where somewhere in the building, too, but no one could agree on which floor. Scraps had only visited the building a few times in his career, as most Derivates resided and trained in a building five blocks away.

"You look nice in your uniform, Ava." Scraps squeezed her hand as they walked. Even with their alterations, he still found her more attractive than any of other women he had met.

Flit tugged at the hem of the sleek, fitted black skirt she was wearing and the matching silver blouse with the Government logo branded on the high collar. She flicked it with a snort of distaste. "It feels like I'm advertising them or something. I don't know why we can't just wear our own clothes."

Scraps shrugged, looking down at his own crisp black slacks and high collared shirt. It was the same uniform any Citizen who worked for the Government wore. It felt odd to wear it. He was used to the light grey uniform Derivates were required to don. He felt like a fraud, a pretender.

Flit's distaste for her outfit was rather entertaining. He wasn't sure what was wrong with it, apart from the Government logo, of course. It looked nice on her, but he thought she would at least appreciate the compliment. Then, he remembered Hawkeye instructing him on the fact women often liked to turn down compliments on their clothing in his 'how to be a Citizen' training. He was warned that his new co-workers would likely want to chat or laugh about women's delicate fashion sense. Hawkeye told him that participating in banter about how long Flit took to get ready or how many outfits she went through before she left the house would ingratiate him with his peers, but Scraps did not want to speak ill of Flit. Luckily, Hawkeye had given him advice for dodging any kind of socially awkward moment: "Drink more beer and yell some profanity." However, that would not be effective during the workday, as he couldn't drink. Perhaps he would have to talk about the weather instead. Hawkeye had said that was always a good option.

Scraps looked up at the towering glass and metal spires above him as they turned onto the Centre One block. There was nothing new about the sights around him, but seeing them through the eyes of an Underground rebel dressed as an ordinary Citizen somehow made it all look different. The concentration of Registereds was thicker here, and they were such an expected part of the scene that the Citizens all but ignored them. Standing on the corners of the streets or at crossings, they remained unmoving, no different to the data kiosks or lamp posts. They stood at attention with the rigidity he remembered, and his own back straightened instinctively. It was impossible to see their faces behind their visors. When he had worn one himself, Scraps thought it was convenient to have constant access to his HUD. Now, though? He recalled something Flit told him a while ago, and realised she was right. It was nothing more than a way to hide their humanity from anyone who looked upon them.

As Scraps and Flit crossed the street towards the large revolving doors that led to their new place of work, a woman beside them dropped her briefcase. She peered over her shoulder at the Registered on the corner and coughed irritably.

In a flash, the short, grey-uniformed male dashed forward, picking it up and handing it to her without missing a beat. "Your briefcase, Citizen," the man said in a clipped, robotic tone.

The woman could have easily picked it up for herself, but she snatched the case back and turned on her heels, walking away without so much as a blink of appreciation.

"Bitch," Flit muttered under her breath.

Scraps couldn't help but agree. Twelve months ago, he would have seen nothing untoward about the woman's unthinking rudeness, but now he neatly tucked his anger away and pushed through. He had a mission to focus on.

24

———

FLIT

AS FLIT and Scraps walked through the large revolving glass doors of Centre One, the world opened up around them. Outside, surrounded by the soaring buildings, it was hard to think of the city as anything other than crowded. In this building, though, the artistry and technology of architecture came out to play. The tinted windows that had been simultaneously bright and protective on the outside were as clear as clear could be on the inside. They had a perfect view of the street beyond, and if Flit hadn't known that there were windows there, she might have thought the whole bottom level was open air.

The ground floor atrium was light and breezy, even with hundreds of people hurriedly making their way to its core. Everyone was dressed in the same clean, crisp uniforms as Flit and Scraps. Being surrounded by so many Government workers made Flit's fingers twitch for the dagger she usually kept on a weapons belt, but she wasn't on a patrol, and this sure as hell wasn't the Underground. The building itself was cylindrical, with dozens of doors that led out to every part of the landscaped courtyards around it. The heart of the atrium was clear for all to see—a bank of twenty glass elevators that rose straight through the spine of the tower.

As Flit watched, the elevator cars zoomed up and down the transparent shaft, making the room feel as though it was nothing more than a tribute to the throbbing vein of the building above. Several metres away from the centre lifts, there was a neat ring of security scanners. Like everything else in the building, they were minimal, and designed so they didn't detract from the space around them.

Flit slid her hand into Scraps'. "First day at the new job!" she said, nervous excitement creeping in as they joined the surge of people making their way through the scanners.

As the queue for the security scans shrunk, the thought of stepping through the flimsy looking threshold became increasingly intimidating. With fewer bodies between them and the ring, Flit noticed Registereds posted between every scanner. The one closest to them was medium height and stocky, his expression not visible behind his reflective visor. Flit looked for his designation, but none of the Registereds in the area wore the typical patches on their shirts, making it impossible to know what type of powers they had. What if he was a telepath? Instinctively, Flit let her focus slip to the memory of the fun that she and Scraps had in the shower while getting ready. She thought of every detail with painstaking deliberation. If the Registered was a mind reader, that ought to keep him out.

"Floor ninety-eight, wasn't it, Brian?" Flit asked as the woman in front of them stepped through the scanner.

"That's correct. Ninety-eight, section twenty, subsection four." Scraps' elaboration went far beyond what Flit had memorised. She figured that they would show up to reception and be pointed in the right direction. "That way, Ava." Scraps pointed to an elevator bank to their left, with the floors ninety to ninety-nine signposted above them.

Flit's heart hammered when they reached the security scanners. What if something had gone wrong? What if their micros had made a mistake? A vision of red alarms blaring and an army of Derivates gunning for them twisted her stomach into hard knots.

The scanner beeped quietly as it registered their biometric data, and a green light went on over their heads. The Registered didn't even look their way as they moved from the scanners and squeezed into the elevator with two dozen other people. Flit let out a breath of relief, and Scraps gently squeezed her hand.

The ride in the elevator was particularly unpleasant. After spending a month in the Underground, Flit had grown used to the luxury of being in an area where her personal space was a staple part of her day. There were so many workers in the lift that they were all pressed up against each other. Her only comfort was the fact that it was Scraps lining the span of her back. She wanted to talk, just as she always did when her nerves took over, but there were so many people that she didn't dare. Plus, the music playing in the lift sounded horrible enough without awkward conversation as a bonus track.

It wasn't until the fiftieth floor that the elevator started to empty, and Flit could breathe properly again. Every level they passed was designed in a similar, open-plan manner, each one as light and airy as the last. There were minor differences in layout and function, but the architecture and interior design of Centre One flowed just as smoothly as the glass lift.

"Floor ninety-eight," a pleasant, automated voice announced as they finally stopped at their floor.

It was as white, chrome, glassy, and open as the rest of the building. The area immediately surrounding the lift core was dotted with armless couches and potted palms. Beyond that, a long sleek reception desk encircled the entire area. Behind the desk, a wall of seamless grey smoked mirrors kept the space feeling self-contained. There was a man with carefully coiffed black hair standing at the desk, peering at them curiously while they got their bearings.

"New to ninety-eight?" the man asked with a smirk.

Flit put on her brightest smile. "Obvious, huh?" She walked over and leaned against the counter.

"You could say that. What can I help you with?" He was polite enough, but there was a hint of caution in his stiff posture.

"I'm Ava Parkes, and this is my husband, Brian. We are here for our first day of work," Flit explained.

"Ah, our two newest victims!" The man pressed a few buttons on the hidden side of the desk, and a retina scanner popped up from the previously seamless surface. "You know the drill."

Flit nodded and stepped forward. Newton and Vista had filled them in on the sign-in procedures. Flit straightened for the retina scan. A split second later, there was a soft beep, and the man nodded in approval. Flit stepped aside and allowed Scraps to go through the same process.

Scraps was approved without a fuss, and the man said, "Perfect. Follow me." With a tap on his hidden screen, the desk to his right slid back into itself, creating a walk-through. "I'll take you to Jane."

The smoked mirror behind him looked as though it was one wide piece of glass, but when the man pressed his hand against it, the outline of a door appeared, and it slid up into a cavity overhead. Flit and Scraps followed him, and on the other side, she could see perfectly into the reception area from the office side. It made Flit wonder how many of the mirrors in the place were actually one-sided windows.

The office consisted of small settlements of between six and ten work pods, each one housing two desks. Most of the pods were already occupied by people who appeared to be talking or working. There was something about the space that just felt off, but Flit couldn't figure what it was until they passed a pod whose two occupants appeared to be deep in discussion. All she could hear was the low, ambient music playing throughout the entire building. The cubicles were soundproof.

Flit was thoroughly impressed, but she contained her amazement. Her old office on the outskirts of the Hub had nothing more than an open plan desk layout and some big, shared screens.

They continued walking until the large external window wall came into view, displaying a panoramic view of the city below them. The man rapped sharply on the outside wall of a pod about triple the size of the others that held a desk and a meeting table. The door slid open with the slightest electronic hiss.

The woman sitting at the desk looked up from her work. "Ah, Chris. What can I do for you?"

Chris stepped aside so the woman could see Flit and Scraps without obstruction. "I've got our two new recruits, Ava and Brian Parkes."

"Ah, for the good of all," Jane said by way of greeting, her face bright with confidence beneath sideswept red bangs streaked with grey at the sides.

Flit had to stop the full body shudder threatening her composure. It had been a while since she'd heard someone spew out the Government's motto, and she'd forgotten how repulsive it was.

"For the good of all," Scraps returned crisply, most likely on instinct.

Flit swallowed down bile and shifted uncomfortably beside him.

"It's lovely to meet you both. I'm Jane White, the Leading Supervisor of the R&D department. Please, come in."

While Flit and Scraps stepped into the office, Jane thanked Chris for bringing them to her.

"Take a seat," Jane told them, continuing while they got themselves settled. "I'm afraid most of the day will be taken up by your induction. You probably know it all, but procedure is procedure, right?"

Scraps and Jane laughed at her comment, and then Jane got straight down to business. There was an overwhelming amount of information to process. A lot of it was just a rehash of standard Government expectations of workers, followed by more in-depth stuff about their clearance levels and reporting structure. Jane did the mandatory walkthrough of the intranet they were expected to use, and it went right over Flit's head. There were so many different splash pages and log-ins, each area dedicated to one of the three dozen departments they would be required to work with.

About half-way through, Flit zoned out. It was too much information. She knew Scraps would be soaking it in, so she looked around the office, taking in the sights. She noticed who was talking to who and where everyone sat. When people left their pods, they congregated in kitchenette on the opposite side of the floorspace or by a window lounge area with an excellent view of the city. Several times throughout the information dumping, Jane was interrupted by calls on her comms-system. For the most part, she would answer, explain she was busy, and offer to call the person back. Flit kept a mental tally of the names Jane mentioned and established that Amy was impatient, Greg needed his hand held throughout every step of whatever he was working on, and Jane's boss Penny was a micro-manager.

25

____

SCRAPS

JANE WALKED Scraps and Flit through all the necessary induction protocols for the first half of the day. She was going to give them a tour of the office, but her phone refused to stop ringing. Instead, she pointed out the main areas and told them the layout was simple enough that they would be able to figure it out themselves. Compared to the complex network of tunnels in the Underground, learning the orderly arrangement of their floor would be child's play. Their tour turned into a quick escort to their work pod.

"By all reports, you both work exceptionally well together," Jane said, "so we see no reason to give you separate offices. However, if being with each other gets distracting or counterproductive, let me know, and I will reassign office spaces to accommodate a move."

That sounded fair to Scraps, even if he did not intend to make such a request. He was more than used to Flit's methods of distraction, and the most effective of them would be useless in such a public space.

"Your first assignment has already been sent to your work accounts. They are the same as they were at your old job. If there are any questions, Jack in the next pod should be able to handle them. Good luck. We are pleased to have you both on board."

And then, Jane was gone, leaving Flit and Scraps alone in the pod with the screens on their desks blinking at them expectantly.

"Wow, that was a rush." Flit sighed, putting her hands on her hips and looking around.

"Which one do you want?" Scraps asked, gesturing to the desks. One faced the sea of pods, the occupants silent within the confines of their terrariums. The other desk was at a different angle that had a good view of the city.

Flit looked at him, as if assessing his motives. "I'd better take this one." She put her hand on the back of the chair facing their new colleagues. "The view from there is good, but if I don't see other people working, I may forget what I am supposed to be doing."

With what Scraps thought was a rather insightful decision on Flit's behalf, he settled into his new desk and tapped the screen. It flared to life, and he logged in using the credentials Newton and Scry had given them. The system started up, and he smiled. He already had half a dozen mail messages to attend to. He opened the first and saw Jane had pre-prepared a range of policy reviews for him with different workers. In her message she wrote that, once he and *Ava* got to know the other staff members and had settled in, they would be paired together for assignments more tailored to their strengths.

"Looks like we have a lot of work in store for us." Scraps turned, beaming at Flit over his shoulder.

"I haven't even logged in yet." Flit tapped her screen several times with obvious frustration. "Bloody credentials… I could swear I used the right password!"

Scraps chuckled to himself and got out of his seat, walking over to lean past Flit's shoulder and log her into the system using Ava's credentials. "A couple of weeks' holidays and you forget how to log in? It is good we are back at work, Ava."

Flit narrowed her eyes at him, but there was a smile tugging at her lips as she thanked him and opened her inbox.

HALF AN HOUR after they were shown to their workspace, the man in the next pod, Jack, knocked on Scraps' and Flit's door and invited them to join their colleagues for lunch. Scraps had a hard time remembering which name matched which face. He had always been good at remembering other Registereds by matching their designations with their power. The Underground was not so bad because their names were power based, too, but the Citizens? Well, their naming conventions were a free for all.

Flit didn't have that problem. She might not have known the difference between the Cost Mitigation and Cost Mitigation Minimiser policies, but she was using people's names without error or hesitation within minutes of meeting them. Scraps was grateful for it, as it meant he could just sit back and find the best escape routes while she schmoozed their way through the luncheon.

Their colleagues seemed to enjoy asking them a lot of questions. The most popular topic was their most recent position. Flit and Scraps politely explained they were in a similar position, but the details were on a need-to-know basis. The others understood, and Flit's quick thinking allowed the evasion to appear more like professionalism.

Another topic that garnered attention at lunch was how they met. It was already common knowledge that they were a couple or, as Jack had stated, a 'package deal'. Flit spoke about Ava and Brian's chance meeting at their tertiary institution. At that stage, they had been studying different degrees, but by some strange coincidence, they had still been picked for similar positions within the Government's postgraduate program. They served their internships side by side and were inseparable since. Some of their colleagues ooh-ed and ahh-ed in all the right romantic places, and Scraps wondered how much cooing would be going on if Flit told them how they had really met. Flit played the part well, though, and by the end of lunch, there was no doubt that Ava and Brian were as right for each other as they were for their job.

The rest of the day passed in a blink. Flit and Scraps went their own ways to work with their new colleagues on current projects. Scraps was pleased he was assigned to work with Jack, as he was having trouble with the other names. The policies, however, he had a firm handle on. He couldn't help but wonder how Flit was faring with a rather grumpy-looking older man named Michael.

Jane checked in with them about half an hour before the end of their day. She ducked into Jack's pod, where Scraps was sitting, and looked over his shoulder at his screen. She smiled and nodded. "That looks like great progress," she said. Then, she focused on Jack. "Can I expect the final reports on my desk before lunch tomorrow?"

"We're not far from finishing. That should be doable," Jack said, looking between his screen and Scraps'.

Then, Jane was off. Scraps and Jack spent the final half hour trying to get as much of their report written as possible. A mere couple of seconds after a window popped up on Scraps' screen telling him it was the end of the work day, Flit knocked on the door of their pod. Looking up, Jack smiled and gestured for her to come in. Scraps could see the relief of the end of the day etched into her smile.

"How are you guys doing?" Flit asked, stepping into the pod and leaning against the desk.

"I was just about to let your man go, but the problem is that we have an unwritten rule in this office," Jack informed her with an exhausted sigh.

Flit smirked. "Oh? Don't tell me there is some kind of first-day-of-work hazing ritual."

"Worse," Jack whispered. "The team insists on having the newbies join them for a staff dinner at the end of their first day. Sorry, guys, but we're taking you to The Peppered Table tonight."

Scraps looked at Jack, surprised by the revelation. He was under the impression that Citizens could take their meals wherever they liked. He wondered whether this staff dinner, like the ones the Derivates were forced to attend, had assigned seating. If they did, he hoped he would be seated next to Flit.

"Sounds great!" Flit said with such vehement, forced enthusiasm that Scraps tightened his grip on her arm. "What time?"

That seemed to please Jack as he stood there, gathering his things off Flit's desk. "Seven. The Peppered Table is easy to find. It's right at the top of the commercial building in North Two-East Two. We'll be the obnoxiously loud table booked under your names."

"Lovely. See you then," Flit cooed.

Scraps shut his terminal down and stood up. He didn't think he had ever heard Flit say the word *lovely* before and actually mean it.

They had to get out of there before she did something they would both regret.

"Let's go home and get ready for dinner, Ava," Scraps said, warning in his tone as he gently steered her out of the pod.

"Great work today, you two," Jack called out after them with a casual salute. "For the good of all!"

"For the good of all!" Flit replied, her tone a sickly-sweet singsong that immediately made Scraps wary.

"Ava," Scraps muttered through gritted teeth.

Flit chuckled and bumped his side with her hip. "Come on. Let's get home before this bullshit makes my head implode."

That, Scraps thought, was a very good idea.

ONE THING that the Government got right when planning the Hub was that it had a very logical, strict grid layout. All the blocks held a maximum of two buildings and were named for their relative position to Centre One. This presented a problem for Flit and Scraps. Their building, in the block referred to as West Two, was only two blocks away from Centre One. However, The Peppered Table, in North Two-East Two, was quite a distance away. They discussed the idea of catching public transport, but neither of them wanted to spend more time in close confines with others than they had to, so they decided to walk, but it left them will minimal time to get ready after they got home.

Scraps stood in their walk-through closet with Flit as she went through her clothing options. She muttered something about needing to go shopping for some real clothes before snatching an outfit off a hanger and disappearing into the bathroom. Scraps was left in the wardrobe with far too many options and far too little experience. He had no idea what Citizen wore to a dinner with colleagues, so, as he did in other situations he didn't understand, he tried to bring it back to basics. The people they were meeting with were his esteemed colleagues. He needed to impress them. The restaurant was within the highly sophisticated two block radius, where the most influential Citizens resided, meaning it was probably better to be overdressed than underdressed. Given his assumptions, he selected a suitable outfit and took it to the bedroom to dress.

When the door to the bathroom opened with a puff of soap-scented steam, he straightened his collar and turned to Flit, a wide grin on his face. "How do I look?" he asked, throwing his arms out and feeling sleek in the formal suit he was wearing. It was black and cut rather smartly to accentuate his physique. It was, without a doubt, the fanciest thing he had ever worn.

Flit stopped as she twirled a lock of damp hair around her fingers. Her lips parted as she took him in. Scraps caught a familiar flash of appreciation in her gaze before she straightened up and cleared her throat. "You… Uh, you're not wearing that tonight, are you?"

Scraps deflated at her tone. "I was planning to…" he trailed off, crossing his arms over his chest.

Flit's posture softened, making the silky fabric of her crimson camisole strap drop a little lower down her shoulder. It was an effort for Scraps to ignore how it drew attention to her breasts. The flimsy excuse for a top gave way to fitted skirt that hugged her curves in a way that made him want to run his hands over them. Perhaps inappropriate to wear on a formal night out with colleagues, but enchanting nonetheless.

"I didn't mean it like that. You look extremely sexy," Flit purred with a lopsided grin as she slinked over, gently taking his arms and pulling them away from his chest so she could look at him again. "But as nice as you look in this suit, it's a little over the top for dinner." She placed a hand on his chest. "How about we swap the jacket and tie for just a nice shirt instead?"

Ignoring her attempt at flattery, Scraps pressed his lips together. "Flit, this is an important dinner with our new colleagues from our job in the Government Headquarters. We must dress accordingly."

Flit grasped the collar of his jacket and used it to drag him down for a kiss. When she pulled back, she patted his chest. "Take my word on this, ok? I'll follow your lead on the policies and proce-dures. You trust me with the social stuff."

With a flicker of a teleport, Flit landed in the wardrobe and slid a shirt off a hanger. She teleported it in front of him so that he had to catch it to stop it from fluttering to the floor. He held it up to assess her choice. It wasn't terrible, but he would carry his jacket with him, just in case.

"Leave the top two buttons undone," Flit advised him.

Scraps was about to ask whether that was an appropriate thing to do when Flit turned away from him, and he noticed that the back of her camisole was gone. Or, rather, he assumed it never existed. He gulped at how the drapes of red fabric framed her smooth, tanned skin and balled his hands into fists to avoid reaching out to stroke it.

Letting out a low groan, Scraps shook his head and started unbuttoning his jacket. He wasn't sure whether Flit was trying to scandalise or seduce their new colleagues, but whatever it was, she would win them over in a heartbeat looking like that.

26

———

FLIT

THE PEPPERED TABLE was just as fancy as the name and location suggested. Being so close to Centre One, it was modern and fully updated with the latest customer service tech. It was busy, too, so much so that if the waitress hadn't guided them to their table, they might not have seen their colleagues through the sea of people.

There were ten people already seated at the large round booth. The table itself was smooth smartglass, programmed to display the menu and chef's specials for the night. The bench seat surrounding it was divided into segments so two people could sit on each one, and there were two benches left between Jack and Jane.

"We are so glad you could make it," Myriel crooned. As old as Flit's mother and saccharine to a sickening level, the brunette had taken a shine to Flit at lunch and had barely left her alone since. "Take a seat, you two! Have you been here before?"

Flit kept her hand tucked into the crook of Scraps' arm and settled led him to the empty bench seat next to Jane. Flit would have preferred to sit in the bathroom all night, but she had to pretend to give a shit about these Citizens. The moment she and Scraps were seated, the menus on the glossy black table opened and holographic images of the meals they could order danced before their eyes.

Jack rolled his eyes. "Of course they haven't, Myriel. They only just arrived from Eastbay!"

"So? They could have visited the Hub before moving here," Myriel retorted as if it was obvious.

"No, we have not been here before," Scraps said in a distracted tone as the holographic menu shifted to display a different item.

Flit wondered if he had ever seen that sort of tech used for anything so trivial before. She hoped the others would assume his obvious wonder was because he was impressed by the offerings. "We've visited the Hub a couple of times, but we didn't dare try to get into anywhere so fancy," Flit added, sticking to their carefully constructed cover story.

"Well, I'm glad we could impress you on your first night working with us," Jane said with a warm smile.

Flit looked around. "Have you guys ordered yet?"

"We've entered our selections, but we aren't placing the order until Chris and Liana get here," Jane informed them.

Flit nodded. At least they weren't the last to arrive.

Flit waved through the menu options in front of her until she settled on a nice wrap with a side salad. She was able to manipulate the image by turning it and angling it this way and that, getting an impressive preview of what she was hoping to eat. Flit tapped the top of the projection, and it popped out of existence, the screen below it bringing up her choice and asking for confirmation. She pressed her hand against the glass, and the handprint registered her credentials with a small chime and added her selection to the order. She heard the same sound from Scraps and looked over to see him sitting back, his face unreadable. She slipped her hand onto his thigh beneath the table, giving it a gentle squeeze of reassurance. Flit had spent many hours ranting about how frivolous the life of Citizens seemed when people in the Underground didn't even get to see the sun. Being back amongst it all only exacerbated the burden of that knowledge.

After ordering, the conversation quickly turned to how Ava and Brian had enjoyed their first day. With their boss and colleagues at the table, it was a loaded question, but Flit turned on a dazzling smile. "It was lovely, thank you. I was so nervous this morning. I heard that people in the Hub were too busy for the niceties, but it felt just like being with our old team back in Eastbay, only in a much larger building and with much friendlier people!" She winked, and they all laughed appreciatively.

Flit had learned long ago that playful flattery went a long way with most people. She wanted to gag at how easily these sheep gobbled it all up.

"And how about your new apartment? I've heard that the buildings at Eastbay are a lot more… retro than ours," Myriel's tone and constant questions gave Flit a feeling that she was the office gossip.

Well, the Hub is significantly newer than the Underground, so it is a huge upgrade, Flit thought but didn't dare say. "It's gorgeous. We are quite high up so the view is excellent. And we are close enough to walk to work. Can't complain about that!"

"You walked to work?"

The question came from behind her, and Flit turned around to see Chris from reception and a woman named Liana standing beside their booth hand in hand. Liana was tall, with a sheet of silky black hair and friendly green eyes. She had not spoken much at lunch, but she seemed to get along well enough with everyone. At least, at work.

"Yeah, we're close enough," Flit replied with a casual shrug.

The Hub was zoned so that people did not have to waste time on long commutes to work. Each section of the grid came with a certain level of prestige. The closer you lived to Centre One, the higher class you were. When she had lived with her parents, she'd lived in a block along the outskirts of the city, where people worked for smaller contractors and had apartments that could have fit in her new living room. They were still modern, of course, but the message was clear. The more you suck up to the Government, the more you get in return.

For the good of all, Flit thought to herself, suppressing a derisive snort.

"Walking to work." Chris chuckled, apparently impressed. "You don't get that much around here. Most people catch the tram in hopes of saving a couple of minutes."

Chris and Liana slid onto the empty bench beside her and sat just as closely to each other as she and Scraps did. Flit didn't catch the familiarity at lunch, but they were definitely a couple. Another office romance. Fascinating. She tried to recall what it was that Liana did in the R&D department but couldn't put her finger on it. All she knew was that she had seen the pretty, wispy-haired woman moving from desk to desk for most of the day.

BY THE END OF DINNER, Flit had everyone in stitches with rehearsed stories of times when Ava and Brian were studying at university. Everyone hung on her words, amused by her irreverent observations and well-timed winks. Citizens had a far more reserved sense of humour than the Derivates in the Underground, so she had to stop herself from dropping f-bombs several times. She was rather proud that she managed to go without swearing for the whole night.

Scraps, however, remained quiet at her side. That was his natural state in social situations like this, and it wasn't until Jane pointed it out that she and the others turned their attention to him.

"You're awfully quiet there, Brian. Everything all right?" Jane asked with mild amusement.

"Oh, yes." Scraps snapped to attention. "I've learned not to interrupt Ava when she is on a roll with her stories. She tells them much better than I do." He smiled at Flit, affection warming his gaze. The others cooed appreciatively.

"Smart man." Jack nodded of approval. "Let Ava do the chatting, and you can stay out of the office gossip. Best not to get into that. It's why men invented fishing and golf."

The other males at the table laughed appreciatively. Poor Scraps forced out a scoff with them.

Flit rolled her eyes.

"You invented fishing and golf because you're happy to stare into the distance and do nothing for several hours at a time," Jane said with a dismissive wave.

"Brian! You have to come out with us on our next trip," Chris said, suddenly excited. He leaned forward, peering past Flit to catch Scraps' attention.

Jack perked up and nodded. "I've booked a boat and everything. Can you imagine it? A good stiff drink, and nothing but the quiet lapping of the big old blue?"

"Big old blue? It's just a glorified lake. And can you really call it fishing if you never catch anything?" Jane interrupted.

Jack gave her a look of mock outrage. "What do you mean? We brought home a couple of big ones last month!"

"Bought from the fish market," Liana muttered under her breath, drawing laughs from her colleagues, Flit included.

"I resent that!" Jack slapped his hand down on the table. "Besides, if that were the case—which it isn't—how would you know?"

Liana smirked and leaned back in her seat. Chris shifted uncomfortably beside her.

"Wait!" Jack jabbed an accusatory finger in Chris' direction. "You ratted us out! Again?"

Chris didn't reply. He simply shrugged and became far too interested in the dessert menu.

"That's it you're out of the club. Brian is replacing you. I'm sure he won't tell his wife."

Scraps froze as they tried to rope him into the conversation. Flit was about to chime in, to save him from having to come up with something, when a smile split his lips. "It sounds like a great idea. I would love to come along."

"Great! Ava, that means you are now free to join us at my place while those buffoons are out fishing." Myriel's voice was almost conspiratorial as she leaned in. "Great wine, delicious cheese, and all the best music. You'll love it."

"Oh, I bet I will!" Flit's high-pitched tone was interpreted as over-excitement by her colleagues rather than the sarcasm it was, all thanks to the enthusiastic grin she plastered on her face.

The conversation shifted to other fishing stories and revealed more interpersonal rivalries. The topic of work was not brought up again, which Flit was grateful for. In the Underground, work and leisure were almost synonymous, so the topics where inherently twisted together. It was a nice change, to be able to think past survival and do something just because, although it made Flit resent all the over-the-top finery around her that little bit more.

The main course turned to dessert and then dessert into after-dinner drinks. The conversations circled back around to relationships. Their colleagues asked more about Ava and Brian and their life together, which Flit anticipated. Being asked about their plans to start a family, however, went beyond her expectations. Now that she had a chance to think about it, it was something that her old Hub colleagues used to ask their married friends all the time, as if personal decisions like that were public business.

"Kids?" Flit asked, looking surprised. "Heck, soon you'll be asking about our funeral plans."

The others laughed at her dismissive comment, but when Myriel leaned forward and opened her mouth to speak, Flit knew she wouldn't drop the topic so easily.

Before the inquisition could continue, Liana told the others to mind their own business. It was said casually, but the way that the conversation skidded to a halt and the smiles turned to guilty expressions made Flit wonder if there was something more to the situation.

Flit mused over the change in mood as some people ordered a second round of drinks, and others excused themselves. Beside her, Scraps was still nursing a three-quarters full glass of beer in his hands. She knew he wasn't going to finish it, and from the way he was just staring off into the distance, she figured it was probably time to go home.

"As much as I would love to hang around, it's been a long and exciting day for us, and we've got a strict boss who won't appreciate us being late on our second day," Flit announced in a teasing tone.

"Ha!" Jane gently swatted Flit's arm as she laughed. "Ava, you are hilarious."

Scraps waved at everyone as they got to their feet. "See you all tomorrow." He offered Flit his arm.

The walk home passed in a blur of city lights and yawns. When they finally reached their apartment, it was close to midnight. It wasn't lost on Flit that Scraps had barely spoken a word since they had gotten to dinner. She asked him if he was all right, but he waved off her concern, claiming he was just tired from the long day and said he was going to have a shower.

Flit had a feeling that he was lying to her, but she left him alone while he was in the bathroom to work through is feelings.

When he walked out, towel around his hips, rivulets of water dripping down his carved chest, Flit sighed. She stood and started to undress as he sank onto the edge of the bed, drumming his fingers on his knees.

Flit stilled his hands by covering them with her own and sank down to her knees before him. "What's on your mind?"

His new blue eyes found hers, his expression unreadable. He opened and closed his mouth several times before clearing his throat. "I just… I did not expect that. I did not know what I expected, but it was not that."

Flit tilted her head to the side. "What do you mean?"

Scraps threw his hands up, gesturing around them. "This apartment, dinner tonight, the Citizens… It's all so… so… excessive!"

"Oh." Flit blinked, "You're concerned because it's excessive?"

"Yes! We ordered fancy desserts from holographic menus and discussed fishing. Why do they even need to go fishing? You can buy fish at the supermarket."

Flit understood Scraps' revelation well. She spent her entire life going between the frivolity of the Hub and the survival mindset of the Underground, but while it infuriated her, Scraps almost seemed fascinated by it.

"And the meals were tiny, but the plates were huge. I am hungrier now than when we got there, even though we probably spent a week's worth of wages on a couple of courses!" Scraps stood up, walking over to the window and looking out at the blinking city lights. "Their use of resources makes no sense." Scraps turned around, suddenly worried. "Resources! Oh, I did not even think about that before we ordered our food. Can we afford it? I've never had to pay for anything before, but surely that is not economical decision making."

Flit repressed a sigh at his concern. "Our bank account can handle it," she promised.

Scraps pointed out of the window. "And now, down there, they just do whatever they want. They do not have to take orders. They do not have to look over their shoulders…"

"They don't know how good they've got it." Flit teleported over to his side, resting a hand on his shoulder. "They do whatever they do because they're told to, and they don't look past their own noses. They're so happy to go on with their lives, not even noticing that they are built on the slavery and abuse of others."

"But… why would they know?" Scraps turned to her. "They do not even see us. They do not have to. All they have to do is live within the laws, and they can do whatever they want."

A hint of envy wrapped around Scraps' tone that made Flit's jaw set with near-painful tension. "They're selfish."

"Not selfish…" Scraps stood straighter, squaring his shoulder as a sense of understanding seemed to settle over him. "They just don't know any better."

"Ignorance is no excuse," Flit snapped. "Knowing where your privilege comes from is a moral imperative, not an optional extra."

The words came out with a touch more venom than she intended, but when Scraps looked down at her, he didn't respond. Flit wasn't sure if it was because he was trying to avoid an argument or because he was thinking over what she said. Either way, she was too exhausted to find out.

Flit had spent the entire day trying not to vomit at the sickly, brainwashed environment they worked in. The people were nice enough, sure, but it was all such a façade. She had no doubt that each and every one of them would turn on her and Scraps if they found out who they really were, what they really were, and she was willing to bet they wouldn't even lose a second of sleep over it.

27

SCRAPS

FOLLOWING his rather controversial revelation after dinner, Scraps and Flit reeled their emotions back in. They had both been overwhelmed and exhausted after their first full day as Ava and Brian, and even though they might disagree over how they saw the Citizens, they were allies first and foremost. And they had a job to focus on. Getting caught up in everything else would only distract them from their purpose, so instead of letting the disparities get between them, they threw themselves into their new identities.

The days that followed passed in a flurry of work. Thanks to Flit's naturally sociable personality, the two of them quickly became the talk of the office. Scraps never had to say much, and everyone accepted that he was just the quiet, dedicated husband. It might have been far from the truth, at least in some ways, but it was a convenient cover he embraced.

The morning of the planned fishing trip arrived after a marathon of reports and inspections. When the alarm went off in the morning, it was Scraps who groaned and buried his face into his pillow.

Flit stirred beside him, sliding a leg over his back and pressing her warm body against his side. "You're going on an adventure today. Why so glum?"

Scraps rolled onto his back, staring at the ceiling as the window in their room went from block-out mode to a frosted glass, which let in far more light than he was ready for.

When he didn't answer, Flit popped her head up and narrowed her eyes at him, concern twisting at the corners of her lips. "You've been getting more and more withdrawn over the past two weeks. You've barely said twenty non-work-related words to me over the past three days. What's going on?" Her warm hands massaged slow circles over his skin.

His gut twisted. Was that really the case? He wasn't aware that he was behaving differently, but constantly maintaining their cover and their long work hours was putting a dampener on his desire to communicate about trivial things. Well, at least Scraps assumed it was the work hours, but now he thought on it, he had been doing just as many hours of training and patrols in the Underground. It had been more physically demanding too. His new job just involved sitting at a desk.

Scraps propped himself up on his elbows and looked at Flit. Even with her eyes the wrong colour and her altered hair all mussed up from sleep, she was still incredibly beautiful. "I think I was just looking forward to a relaxing weekend alone with you, but now I have this fishing thing, and I do not really know what to expect."

Flit's eyes dawned with understanding as she pulled herself up his body and kissed him gently. "Just be yourself," she whispered, "Well, personality wise, I mean. They already think you're a sensible, quiet guy, which is the truth. That doesn't have to change."

Sighing, Scraps rubbed his eyes. "I did not think that pretending to be someone else would be so exhausting."

Flit's silky hair brushed against his neck as she nodded. "I know. As much as I am curious to see what tonight is about, it is going to be a long one because I have to pretend to be Ava the whole time."

Scraps ran his hand up and down her back, pressing a kiss against her soft honey-coloured hair. "You don't think we can cancel? Pretend to be unwell or something."

In a sudden movement, Flit rolled over and straddled his hips. She planted her hands on his chest and looked down at him with such mischief in her eyes. "Perhaps we just need to think about it differently," she suggested.

He ran his hands over her stomach, inching them closer to her breasts. "Oh?" He should not have encouraged her to continue, but Scraps was finding himself less and less invested in the idea of leaving the house.

"We are on a covert mission. Our role is to gather intel on the Government. When you are on that boat and they are drinking themselves stupid, who knows what they will let slip?" Flit leaned in, trailing kisses up his neck.

Threading his fingers through her hair, Scraps pulled her closer to him. He slid his hands around her waist and pulled her hips down against his. "You are using your words to inspire me to leave but your body to keep me here. I am confused. What do you want me to do?"

A low chuckle vibrated against his earlobe in the most tantalising way "You have to go, but that doesn't mean we can't have a little fun first."

THEY MIGHT HAVE HAD some fun, but it meant Scraps was running late. He had to race to meet Chris outside his apartment a few blocks away, and Chris pushed the speed limit on his hovercar to get back on track. Chris didn't seem to mind, though. As eager as he was to go fishing, he claimed no one should be made to get out of bed at the same time the sun rose on a weekend.

"So, how are you settling in?" Chris asked as they left the boundaries of the Hub and drove down the highway that led to the lake. The land on this side of the Hub was mostly dedicated to power and agriculture. Windfarms spread as far as the eye could see in one direction, and the others housed a variety of greenhouse rooves shaped like rolling glass hills.

Scraps decided to go with the stock standard approach. "Very well. Everyone in the office is helpful, and our new apar—"

Chris rolled his eyes. "No, no… How is it really?"

Scraps pressed his lips together when his colleague threw his perfectly rehearsed answer out the window. He stole a glance at

Chris out of the corner of his eyes and weighed his options. Flit had explained that relationships like this were often reciprocal. If he wanted Chris to open up to him, he would have to do the same, but how much to tell him?

In the end, Scraps recalled some advice from Newton and Vista. *The easiest lies to sell are those based on a kernel of truth.*

"It is busy and working in Centre One reminds me of how crowded the city is," Scraps conceded.

"Must be a bit of a contrast to Eastbay, huh?" Chris hummed.

There was no honest answer for that because Scraps had never been to Eastbay before, so he picked a different truth. "Ava and I are used to a much quieter life."

"That's one way to put it," Chris scoffed, shaking his head. "You seem to be doing all right at work, though. From what Liana tells me, Jane is impressed with how fast you've both settled in."

That brought a smile to Scraps' face because the assessment was accurate enough. Only the previous day, Jane had called he and Flit into her office to let them know they could drop the buddy work and start their own reviews the following week. She already had a few jobs in mind for them, and it meant that they would be given much more control over their investigations and could spend less time pretending to be people they weren't.

"Do you want to know something I am not enjoying?" Scraps asked, remembering something that had happened at their welcome dinner on their first night of work. The look of annoyance on Liana's face had been clear, even to Scraps, and if they were as close as he and Flit were, Chris would have been annoyed on his fiancée's behalf.

"Hmm?"

"How people constantly ask Ava and I if we want to have children. It is not even remotely related to work or our career aspirations," Scraps said, genuinely indignant. It was something he had barely considered himself. The last thing he wanted to do was discuss it with a bunch of strangers.

Chris looked away from the road for a minute, his blue eyes meeting Scraps'. "Me too."

"They ask you and Liana as well?"

"They used to do it all the time."

Scraps perked up at his use of past tense. "How did you get them to stop?"

"They didn't have much of a choice after we were hit with Regulation Eight-Two-C," Chris muttered, his hands tightening on the control column, his knuckles whitening.

Scraps furrowed his brows as he tried to recall what that code was. "An Eight-Two-C?"

"You know how you have to get compulsory genetic compatibility testing when you want to affirm your status as a couple?"

Scraps nodded, even though it was news to him.

"Well, Liana and I failed the genetic testing."

Failed the genetic testing? Scraps had never really studied the Citizen reproduction rules, but how could they fail genetic testing? He was fairly certain the only way to be considered genetically unfit for anything was by being a Derivate.

"What… Did your DNA refuse to provide the correct answer before the examination ended?" Scraps jested.

Chris snorted in amusement and shared a smile with him. Scraps had to stop himself from patting his own back at a joke well played. "No. Apparently, our genetics are incompatible."

"Hmm." Scraps leaned back in his seat, crossing his arms over his chest as he considered what Chris had said. He didn't realise that the Government had such a personal stake in Citizen's lives. "That must have been very frustrating."

"Frustrating? That's one word for it," Chris muttered, shaking his head.

The two fell silent for a few minutes. Scraps wondered what sort of impact genetic incompatibility would have on a couple, but it was probably something Citizens already knew about, and he did not want to expose his naivety by asking about it.

Chris perked up as the highway curved around the back of a hydroponics farm and the glittering sapphire water of the expansive lake glinted off in the distance. The sight of their destination put a smile back on both of their faces, and as nervous as Scraps was about the whole endeavour, his interactions with Chris had given him a boost of confidence.

SCRAPS AND CHRIS weren't the last to arrive. That honour had gone to Joe, who was the team leader of the R&D Department. He waltzed down the wharf just after they debated what the likely consequences were if they pushed off without him. Joe hadn't been at the welcome dinner, as he seemed to be a less social, more work-oriented sort of character, and Scraps wondered if he was late because he had to motivate himself to get up and join the group as well.

Once Scraps, Chris, Joe, Jack, and two other auditors named Alex and Frank were aboard, they did a final check on all the equipment—mostly alcohol—and were finally underway. Scraps had never been on a boat before. From the movies he had watched in the Underground, he had an ill-informed notion that they would be calming, relaxing vessels to ride. As the sparkling waters of the lake spread out before them, the morning sun warming their windswept skin, Scraps could almost believe that was the case.

Well, he could have, if it weren't the for the nausea simmering through every part of his body. The constant rocking was the very antithesis of relaxing. Instead of feeling like he was being cradled in the loving arms of nature, he could have sworn the damn boat was trying to shake out every meal he had enjoyed over the past two weeks. The urge to spill was so strong he could barely concentrate on what any of his colleagues were saying, let alone actually try and cast out a fishing line.

"Woah, Brian… not good on the water, huh?" Chris joked as he walked over and sat on the bench beside Scraps.

"I have never been motion-sick before. Now I know why I was wise to avoid boats in the past."

Chris patted his back. "Don't worry. All you need is a good distraction. Here, take one of these. It'll set you right."

Chris pushed a bottle of beer into his hand. Scraps knew the effect alcohol could have on the body and was almost certain that it would make no positive difference. Yet, in the spirit of fitting in, he accepted the drink and took a large gulp.

As a Registered Derivate, Scraps had never been permitted to consume any kind of drugs or alcohol, even when off duty. However, in the Underground, he had been given a taste. Being the dubiously created moonshine it was, he had opted to take only a small sample of the bitter-sweet beverage. He couldn't understand why people would voluntarily drink something that tasted like sewer water, but he had seen for himself that alcohol was one of the best social lubricants around.

As such, on this occasion and using his limited skills in deception, Scraps used a grin to hide his disgust. Sway had already prepared him for this eventuality. He had told Scraps that, despite all logic, the more of the throat-burning drink he drank, the less intolerable it would become. Scraps didn't see the sense in that logic, but Sway was an experienced drinker, so it must have been true.

Chris seemed satisfied with Scraps' acceptance and continued talking. He explained that their trip would take them to a special location the group had discovered years ago. Apparently, the fishing wasn't great, but the lake diverged into a still inlet surrounded by tress that was so serene it made the trip worthwhile.

One hour and two beers later, they reached their destination. Chris was right. The water was so calm that Scraps couldn't believe that he was still on a boat. His nausea lessened enough for him to think about something besides not regurgitating his breakfast, and the others set themselves up around the boat while Chris helped Scraps cast a line.

"Ah, this is the life, isn't if, Brian?" Jack exclaimed.

Scraps turned back and gave him the well-accepted thumbs up.

"No work, no women, no worries!" Alex sighed, leaning back in his seat and resting the handle of his fishing rod in a socket on the inside edge of the railing.

"It's not that bad." Chris chuckled.

"You're right. Work is tolerable." Jack winked, and everyone laughed at the joke.

Even Scraps could see the humour in the comment, even if he disagreed with the sentiment.

"Going slow today, Brian?" Frank pointed the lip of his bottle at the half-full can on the ground by Scraps' feet.

Scraps noted the mountain of empty cans beside Frank. Beside everyone, for that matter.

"I'm just pacing myself," Scraps replied, "At the rate Jack is going, I might have to pilot this thing back."

Jack burped loudly upon hearing his name. "I don't know what you're talking about! I always get this good ol' girl and my boys home safe!" He didn't sound completely drunk, but there was a slur in his consonants that made Scraps wonder how much longer he could viably continue at his current pace.

"What, like that time we ended up at the private wharf with that crazy guy who yelled at us for anchoring our boat there? Or the time we almost crossed the restricted zone and the patrol pulled us up and the crew gave us all pat downs? Or that time when you ran us aground on that nudist beach?" Frank scoffed.

"I'll have you know the nudist beach was intentional." Jack gave him a look of mock indignance. "And you'll notice that nobody was ever injured in those circumstances. You can trust me!"

"I think Alex might be injured from the patrol boat incident. I am pretty sure the Derivate was checking for more than weapons down the front of his pants!" Frank laughed, taking another swig of his drink.

Scraps' entire body tensed at the mention of Derivates. The others didn't seem to notice.

"Rubbish. Nobody was hurt in that little incident. You know, I hear Derivates are pretty deprived in that particular department. Poor bastards." Frank shook his head as he pressed the button on his rod and reeled his line back in.

"You don't give your fridge a good night on the town, Frank. Why would you do it for a Derivate?" Joe jested.

Everyone on the boat except for Chris laughed, and Scraps could not force himself to join in either. The joke, most likely not intended to hurt, hit a sore point for him.

"Derivates are humans, not appliances." The words slipped from Scraps before he could stop them. He clamped his lips shut, his fingers aching from how hard he held his fishing rod.

"Yeah, but it isn't like they get horny or have sex," Joe spluttered, shaking his head.

"I wonder why that is," Scraps muttered into his can as he took a long drink to stop himself from saying more. He felt an overwhelming urge to use his telekinesis to fling Joe's drink into the lake. As he visualised how satisfying that would be, he decided that throwing Joe in would be even better.

"What?" Joe asked, brows furrowing as he put his rod on the ground and turned to Scraps.

"Enough bullshit. Let's concentrate on fishing." Chris sliced through the tension and offered Joe another beer. "We have to actually catch something this time. Otherwise, we'll never hear the end of it at work."

Just like that, it was forgotten by everyone except for Scraps. The anger and resentment he felt for the nasty comments were a hard ball that settled in the pit of his gut. While he smiled and joked with the others, he couldn't quite forgive Joe for his unkindness. He made a mental note to be wary of him in the future.

They *fished* for the next few hours. Everyone except for Scraps consumed more alcohol than there was water in the lake around them. His measly three cans were completely overshadowed by the piles littering the boat floor. However, to Scraps' own social credit, he was the only one who managed to catch a fish. When his line bobbed, the rest of them were too drunk to help, yelling out nonsensical advice about how to reel the catch in. Luckily, he had done enough research to know how to resolve the situation successfully.

As the afternoon rolled in, most of the crew had either passed out or were vomiting over the side of the boat. By Scraps' calculations, they would need to leave now if they wanted to return to the city by nightfall.

"I think we should head home," Scraps suggested.

It was no surprise that none of them responded helpfully.

Scraps made his way to the helm of the boat and studied the control system on the steering console. It seemed simple enough, and the GPS already had pre-set locations. He simply set it up for home and started the boat.

Joe woke up upon hearing the hum of engines and stumbled over towards Scraps, having to use the back of the seats to steady himself. However, he fell half-way over and clearly decided getting up required too much effort.

Seeing the commotion, a tipsy Chris joined Scraps at the helm.

"You know what you're doing Brian?" Chris leaned against the control console.

"Seems simple enough."

"You seem like a really good guy. I haven't seen anyone else stand up for Derivates like that before," Chris said, not sounding anywhere near as drunk as Scraps assumed he was.

Scraps measured his next words carefully. "Derivates are under the ownership of the Government, but they're human too." His voice was low as he checked over his shoulder, making sure no one else was listening in.

Chris watched him for the longest while, and Scraps wondered if he had made a mistake.

Finally, Chris nodded. "They are. I think the Government has too much control over people, and Derivates are their way of playing god and getting away with it."

Scraps' hands tightened on the edge of the control panel. He had barely heard Chris' voice above the gentle hum of the electric engine and the rhythmic slapping of water against the hull, but the words felt so loud on a boat with four other Government workers. Scraps kept his lips pressed together, not daring to answer.

"You may think our views are unique but trust me, there are others who feel the same way," Chris said before adding, "About the Government, that is." Chris patted him on the shoulder then he pushed away from the control console and walked back to one of the benches, leaving Scraps alone to his thoughts.

Though Scraps had no problem navigating to the wharf, getting the boat to line up beside it proved to be difficult. The sporadic over and under revving of the engine and the accidental bumps of the hull against the side of the jetty woke the others up. Luckily for him, the sleep had sobered them up enough for them to help him get the boat docked.

Chris didn't speak much on the drive back to the Hub. In fact, Scraps could almost pretend their little exchange did not happen. By the time he dropped Scraps off at home, it was well and truly dark. The apartment was already empty, as Flit had gone out with the ladies. Scraps ate a quick dinner, showered, and then collapsed into bed, his mind too tired to process everything that had happened that day.

WHILE SCRAPS WAS out doing his thing, Flit spent the day pottering about the house. She tidied up a bit, caught some extra sleep, and placed an order for groceries for the week. It had only taken a couple of weeks to fall into a rhythm with the housework. Scraps was a far better cook than her, so he took care of cooking, and she did the dishes. Most other tasks were handled by automated systems in the apartment. It was a far cry fancier than what she had grown up with on the outskirts, and while she resented the disparity, she chose to view it as compensation for having to put up with all the facetious Government bullshit every day.

Throughout the day, she had trouble letting go of her concerns about Scraps. She wasn't exaggerating when she'd said it felt like they had hardly spoken over the past few days. She knew he was still new to understanding his emotions, and she couldn't help but wonder if being back in the Hub was bringing up some old memories he was looking at in a new light. Whatever the reason, she would get to the bottom of it the next day. She hoped he was able to enjoy himself on the fishing trip. Perhaps he just needed some time somewhere different to calm his mind.

When evening arrived, Flit got ready for her own outing. Myriel's place was only a block over from theirs, so she could take her time. She figured a dinner party with cheese and wine probably warranted something at least a little fancy, so she pulled out a dress she had bought after work a few nights before. She found that Ava's fashion sense was, in a word, terrible. The work clothes were understandable as they were a uniform and she had little choice in the matter, but the leisure wear? Flit refused to be seen in it any longer.

Scraps promised she looked good in anything she wore, but even he had been impressed with the dress when she had shown him the previous day. It was a beautiful teal fabric with slight glitter that hugged her curves before floating out at the hips. Comfortable, not impractical, and undeniably pretty. She paired it with some low heels and twisted her hair into a knot at the nape of her neck before heading out.

Flit arrived at Myriel's early, leaving her alone with the office gossip for a good half hour before anyone else arrived, making her regret her punctuality. Myriel brought out the cheese and other finger foods when the others trickled in, with Liana arriving almost an hour late, looking flustered and frustrated. Flit wordlessly handed her a glass of wine as Myriel disappeared into the kitchen to get dinner ready to serve.

The conversation over dinner was light and playful, and when dessert came out, Flit tasted a cheeky hint of alcohol in it. She was only on her second glass of wine, so she was still sober. She was always on the job. She couldn't afford to slip up.

By the end of dessert, the other four women in the apartment were somewhere between tipsy and drunk. They put on some music and moved to the living room to settle down onto the plush couch. Flit took a spot at the edge and stretched her legs out comfortably on the chaise.

"So, how have the kids been, Amy?" Myriel said, leaning forward as Amy let out a deep sigh.

"Benny is good. He's starting school in a few weeks. We tried to get him into North One-East One, but we are just out of zone. He'll have to go to North One-East Five," Amy explained, her nose wrinkling in distaste as she swirled her wine around in her glass.

"But anything more East than three is… Well, I feel bad saying it, but it's going to be a second-rate education. That area's zoned for mostly Government-adjacent employees, isn't it?" Myriel's perfectly plucked brows creased at the idea of being lumped with people who weren't lucky enough to work for the Government.

Flit downed the rest of her drink to keep her mouth occupied. She couldn't believe these women were sitting here moaning about their kids getting into a school in their own zone. None of the kids in the Underground even got to go to a real school, and the Derivates in the Hub… Well, that wasn't education. It was brainwashing. Flit would be thrilled if any child she knew got into North One-East Five without having to risk their lives to do so.

"Are you as over this as I am?"

Flit jumped, heart racing at the unexpected voice right behind her. She turned, letting out a sigh of relief when she saw Liana's amused expression. "Scared the shit outta me," Flit muttered, shaking her head and moving her legs to make room for Liana to sit with her.

Liana flopped back onto the couch with a low *oof.*

"You look like you could use more wine," Flit chuckled, observing her colleague. She didn't get much of a chance to talk to Liana outside of lunch breaks, but when Flit did, she liked what she saw. Liana was opinionated, but kind, with an engaging radiance about her that made most people like her. She was the kind of person Flit would have chosen to be friends with, and she figured it wouldn't hurt if Ava did too.

"Just slice a vein and pour it straight in. I'm done," Liana groaned, sipping from her almost empty glass. She leaned over, looking at the others and seeing that they were still chatting about family stuff. "You know," Liana whispered conspiratorially, beckoning Flit closer. "There is only one thing more frustrating than having to hear all this talk about children."

Flit raised a single eyebrow. "And that is?"

"Being included in it," Liana groaned. "I'm so tired of being asked if Chris and I want kids."

Flit looked at the other woman out of the corner of her eyes and bit her lip, trying not to let curiosity get the better of her… and failing. "I noticed you weren't comfortable with that line of discussion at our welcome dinner."

"That obvious, huh?" Liana's lips twisted into a wry frown. "It is a sore spot for us."

There was a slight slur in Liana's s's. Flit wasn't sure if this was something Liana would be telling her without the liquid confidence, but she wasn't going to interrupt her if she did. Instead, she snatched a wine bottle off the coffee table and refilled her colleague's glass.

"We were denied a Marriage License."

Flit choked on her wine. She covered her mouth, shaking her head in apology. She had never heard of anyone being refused a marriage license before. Then again, she never gave enough of a shit about her Hub colleagues to know that much about their lives.

"But you're still together."

"Yeah, we're still together." Liana laughed. It was a bitter and sardonic sound punctuated by another sip of her drink.

Contraception was mandatory for all Citizens from the onset of puberty to prevent unplanned pregnancies. When the policy had been introduced, well before Flit's birth, it was lauded as the largest single step towards gender equality and early childhood protection. A marriage or relationship license was how people were granted their reproductive rights. Flit had never been too annoyed by it because she was glad for access to the contraception. She had no intention to bring a child into the world the way it was.

"What did the Government say?" Flit kept her tone neutral and non-judgemental, but she couldn't stop a quirk of curiosity from creeping into it.

"An official from the Marriage and Reproduction Department came to our unit to interview us as a couple of months ago. At the end, we were summoned to the twentieth floor of Centre One and given two options: end the relationship or undergo permanent reproductive sterilisation." Liana stared into her drink, eyes glazed.

Flit hid her shock behind her own glass. She had no idea that was something the Government would say to Citizens. She assumed the marriage license was another bureaucratic formality. She and Rook certainly viewed it that way when they had filled one out.

"Well," Flit muttered, her ire rising, "both of those options are shit. Did they tell you what the problem was? Whether it was something you could work around?"

"Nope." Liana broke out of her trance. "And when we asked,

the Official cited some policy number and told us the rest was classified."

"But it is information about you!" Flit hissed.

Myriel glanced over, raising a concerned brow as if to see if everything was ok. Flit waved her off and mimed an apology.

"You know Christine on our floor?" Liana whispered, leaning closer to Flit. "She works in the Medical Procedure Approval department. I sweet-talked her into doing some snooping for me. She managed to link the policy number to something called 'Genetic Code 6B', some kind of genetic incompatibility, before our results were pulled from the system, and we were both given official cease and desist warnings."

Flit shook her head, disgusted. "So, you guys decided to stick it out," she surmised, "but at the cost of never having children?"

Flit couldn't imagine how difficult that must be for them.

"We're putting off the sterilisation as long as we can, but it's a decision we both have to make every damn day." Liana leaned back in her seat and set her drink down. "I can't tell you how many times we've almost broken up because of it. We both want kids, together, but to think we'll never be allowed to have them? It hurts."

There was nothing Flit could say to that, so she drained the rest of her wine to keep her mouth busy. All Citizens were subject to basic restrictions, but what Liana and Chris had to go through was disgusting. Flit wasn't sure what sort of genetic incompatibility could exist that modern medicine couldn't handle. The Government claimed to have eradicated so many health-related issues in society over the past century that she didn't even know what the term genetic incompatibility meant on a practical level.

"Who the hell do they think they are?" Flit muttered under her breath, crossing her arms over her chest and sitting back. "Making decisions about your life like that and not even having the courtesy to tell you why?"

Liana gaped at her.

Flit's heart hammered in her chest, and she set down her wine.

That last sip might have been one too many.

"You mean the Government?" Liana clarified. "Who the hell do the Government think they are?"

Any hope that Flit might have had that Liana hadn't heard her comment died.

Flit shrugged. "I think I've had too much to drink."

Liana shook her head, reaching over to take Flit's hand. "You should drink more often then," she breathed, leaning in close enough for Flit to smell the alcohol on the air between them. "Fuck the Government."

Flit pulled back enough to look into Liana's green eyes. There was so much determined anger in them that Flit suddenly knew what people meant when they talked about the look she got in her own eyes. She had never, not once, heard a Citizen say anything like that before.

"Liana, what we're saying is—"

"Hey, you two!" Myriel crooned, walking over and sliding her arse onto the seat between them, putting a wall of flesh between Flit and the incident. "If you get any closer, I'll have to call Brian and Chris and tell them to watch their backs. Not that I object to some girl on girl, of course, but you're both taken by such wonderful lads. It'd be sad to see their hearts get broken!"

Flit narrowed her eyes at Myriel's verbal diarrhea. She went to say something, but Liana got in first. "You're incorrigible! I was just telling Ava that I think it's time for me to head home. I had my monthly check-up today. You know what the injections can be like. I'm exhausted."

Myriel's expression softened, and she bit her lip. "Liana, sorry… I didn't realise you were dealing with that today."

Liana stood, brushing of her skirt and Myriel's concern. "You weren't to know, but still, I might head off."

Flit got to her feet, too, looking at Liana. "I'll walk with you. I think we're headed the same direction. Safety in numbers and all that, right?"

Amy chuckled. "And here I was thinking I lived in a terrible part of town. Ava, aren't you only a block away? This zone has half a dozen Derivates to every street. What are they there for, if not to make it safe for people to walk home alone?"

Flit's hands balled into fists at her side, her nails digging into her palms so hard pain shot up her arms. She was just about to tell

Amy exactly what Derivates were around for when Liana slipped a hand into the crook of her elbow.

"Come on. I want to get home and see if we'll be having fish for lunch tomorrow," Liana said.

The women laughed and went on to make bets about the severe lack of fish their colleagues would return home with.

Sucking in a shaking breath through her teeth, Flit nodded. "See you all at work," she said by way of farewell, letting herself be led to the door. She wasn't sure if it was the way their conversation had turned or because Liana genuinely was tired, but as they walked home, Flit was thankful for the other woman's timely escape ticket out of that farce.

29

—————

SCRAPS

SCRAPS AND FLIT woke the morning after their outings and shared their findings over breakfast. He couldn't believe the situation Chris and Liana were in. He knew that the Government had rules, but the enforcement of something like that on Citizens was shocking. What he wasn't surprised about, however, was Amy's casual disregard for Derivates. He told Flit about what had happened with Joe.

One thing that stood out to them both was how Chris and Liana had voiced their dissent with Government policies. It was not something either of them expected to encounter from Citizens. After discussing that and what lovely people they seemed to be, Flit and Scraps decided that they would try and befriend them properly.

Getting close to Chris and Liana required little effort. Over the weeks that followed, the four spent time with each other outside of work on a regular basis and became fast friends. At first, it was a double date at the cinema. Then, it turned into dinners or day trips on the weekends. The reality of their situation became even more stark to Scraps when he saw how they were with each other. Their clear affection reminded him of the quiet moments he spent with Flit, and he would have been furious if someone took a personal decision like whether they could have children out of their hands. Not that he was ready to even consider having children, of course, but the power of being able to decide was one he did not wish to relinquish.

Their time in the office continued well. They soon made a name for themselves around the place as a power pair. They worked together on all their projects and always completed them on time and above standard. Jane's trust in them grew, and they went from basic policies in the sanitation or transport departments to more involved reviews in higher clearance areas within weeks.

Scraps felt he had settled in well. In some ways, he found himself wishing that he *was* Brian. Between the simple luxuries afforded to Citizens and his enjoyment of the work, it was a life he could happily live. It helped that Jane approved of him too. He even started up a weekly newsletter focusing some of the more obscure policies and procedures they might come across. Jane enjoyed them so much she made them mandatory reading for all staff. Flit resented him for the extra work, but over time, they found Jane giving them more choice in their assignments than the others had, and Flit admitted it was worth it.

With how smoothly everything was going, he might have forgotten about their mission if he didn't have to walk past the Registereds every day and pretend they were the tools the Government made them out to be. Now that he was on the other side of those reflective visors, he understood why people steered clear of them. It was hard to identify with someone when you couldn't see yourself reflected in their eyes.

It was a good couple of months before something truly interesting crossed their desks. Scraps was sitting and scrolling through the inventory of the Basic Munitions Production team. Even though the weapons in their inventory were standard, there were plenty of smaller components that seemed out of place on the list. Scraps took careful note of the errant items and called Flit over.

As Flit leaned on his shoulder and scanned the document, her eyes widened. "That's concerning. They mustn't be entering their inventory correctly. Not with these discrepancies."

"It looks that way to me, too," Scraps agreed. If he turned to face her, his lips would brush her cheek. With the sweet scent of her perfume filling his senses, it was tempting, but he had to behave at work, particularly given the information they had just found.

"We should pay the BMP team a visit and sort it out. If we don't get an accurate reading, we can't review their procedures appropriately." Flit's tone was laced with mischief.

Scraps frowned. It was out of their normal jurisdiction, and she knew it. Technically, they should turn it over Joe for follow-up. "I don't know, Ava. I think we need to pass this on. It is important to note, for sure, but an audit?" He shook his head.

Flit rolled her eyes as she straightened up. "Send me the file. I'll talk to Jane."

"Ava—"

"Don't 'Ava' me." Flit narrowed her eyes at him. "This job landed into our laps, and we need to follow up. You know, for the good of all."

Flit's use of the Government's motto was just as smarmy as ever, but this time, it made Scraps' gut rear with concern. Their briefing was to gather information and pass it back to Shadow. Their role was reconnaissance, not investigation. He turned his chair to talk to Flit before she left, but she was gone before he could argue. Running after her would only draw more attention, so he sat back, shaking his head as he watched her make her way to Jane through the transparent walls of their pod. Jane seemed to find Flit's lackadaisical personality endearing, so when Flit knocked on her door, it was opened immediately. They talked for a few minutes, Flit's arms flying up in exasperation as Jane shook her head, lips pressed together in a thin line.

Flit walked back to their pod five minutes later with a smug smirk on her lips.

Scraps sighed. "Let me guess. You convinced Jane to let us investigate?" He wished she had waited until they had gotten home to discuss it before jumping in like that.

"Better than that. I convinced her that we needed to do a full audit. As Jane put it: 'Those trigger-happy dunderheads of the BMP are always flaunting policy and procedure.' Well, she didn't call them dunderheads, but you get the idea." Flit winked then, and Scraps pictured those animated hand gestures from earlier being accompanied by complaints about how non-compliant the BMP teams were. "Grab your stuff. We can head there now."

Scraps blinked. "Now?"

"Yep!" Flit walked over to her desk and picked up her work tablet and her bag. "No time like the present."

Letting out frustrated groan, Scraps shot Flit a wary look. Even with the soundproofing in their pod, he couldn't argue with her. There was undoubtedly some sort of surveillance or recording around. They wouldn't even be able to talk on their trip to the facility. The only real safe place for them to discuss matters was in their apartment.

This escapade was a departure from their stated mission. It was an overstep that could potentially put them on the radar of other, less diplomatic departments within the Government, but now that Flit had spoken to Jane, they had no choice but to follow through.

"Come on. Jane's assigned us a vehicle and everything. The day's young. There's still time to go and teach these protocol-flaunting Neanderthals a thing or two." Flit hung her bag over her shoulder and looked at him expectantly.

Scraps forced himself out of his office chair, and he gathered his own things, his mind already racing as he wondered what sort of situation they were getting themselves into.

FLIT AND SCRAPS sat in the hovercar Jane assigned, navigating their way through the clean city streets. Being mid-morning, there was not much traffic to speak of, so their route was easy enough. If it weren't for the radio, Scraps thought the tension growing between them might have been unbearable. In his head, he rehearsed a dozen different things he wanted to say to Flit, but none of them would be covert enough. He could sense the energy in her as she bounced in her seat. She was paying close attention to the news playing on the radio and the interruption to the broadcast reminding Citizens that graffiti would not be tolerated and anyone responsible would be reprimanded accordingly.

Coming from the Underground, Scraps now knew some people considered graffiti to be art rather than vandalism. The leaders in the Underground never discouraged freedom of expression, and it had been one of the things that had surprised Scraps when he'd first arrived there. The vibrant, unique tags were a far cry from the pristine glass and steel of the Hub. Any sort of graffiti on one of the skyscrapers would look out of place. The markings undermined the work of a Government that prided itself on unity and utility.

"Don't they have better things to harp on about?" Flit waved her hand to turn the radio off. She twisted in her seat, looking at Scraps with excitement. Whatever she had to say was almost bursting out of her, and he was surprised she waited this long. "Wanna know how I knew Jane would be ok with it?"

Scraps looked at her through narrowed eyes, his lips pressed together. She ignored his expression and continued anyway.

Apparently, her question was rhetorical.

"Every time Jane gets the tiniest bit of booze into her, she starts ranting about how the outer departments constantly ignore the policies and procedures that make our jobs easier. She was practically itching for a chance to pull them up!" Flit threw up her hands, more animated than she had been in weeks. "If they did their jobs right in the first place, they would save a lot of time all the way up the ladder. Not only do we need to check them out, but we are also doing her a favour by doing so!"

Scraps wasn't sure that he would call it *doing Jane a favour*. Even if they were, it still put them in a position of heightened visibility. Flit was excited to be able to do something more proactive, but her brash approach undermined their partnership. If they were putting themselves in a position of more elevated risk, then they should have talked about it at home that night before running into action. They had so much more to risk in the Hub, and he wasn't sure if she really understood that. At least, he didn't think so, based on the way she was acting.

Finally taking the hint that his answers meant he did not wish to talk, Flit turned the radio back on and slumped into her seat, her hands and feet tapping a much faster beat than the music coming through the speakers.

It took just under an hour to get the hovercar to the Basic Munitions Factory. It was quite a way away from the main city. Many years ago, the Government had to rebuild a fair amount of the Hub due to an explosion in a similar sort of factory and had decided that having a weapons production plant so close to everything they held dear was a bad idea, so they had to go beyond the city limits, and the sizzling blue electrostatic fence, to get there.

The factory was as large and glassy as the other Hub buildings, but the exterior was reflective to make sure no one could see the confidential things going on inside. A monumentally tall electric fence outlined the land, with warning signs posted at regular intervals. Their hovercar route led directly to the largest of several gates looming in the distance.

As they approached, apprehension roiled in the pit of Scraps' stomach. He was acutely aware of the security scans that the Government would run on their identities when they attempted to enter, and he just had to trust that their aliases were well-crafted enough to hold up to the extra scrutiny.

"I hope you're right about this, Ava. I would hate to mess up and upset our new boss," Scraps muttered, glancing at Flit just in time to catch her roll her eyes.

When they reached the gate, their comm screen lit up to reveal a Registered in Government fatigues, visor obscuring their face. "Citizens, state your business."

"Ava Parkes and Brian Parkes from Research and Development," Scraps replied, barely stopping himself from taking on the same robotic tone the Derivate used out of habit. It would sound suspicious coming from him now. "We're here to conduct a policy investigation and review on behalf of Jane White, Supervisor of Research and Development."

"Please hold."

The screen went blank. Flit's lips curled into a reassuring smile as she slowed their hovercar to a stop and awaited further instruction. Scraps leaned closer to the windscreen to get a better view of the factory. It was at least ten stories tall, with a flat roof that likely held an aircraft landing pad. The outer wall that ran parallel to the fence was dotted with two dozen loading bays, all shuttered with reinforced rolling doors.

The Registered returned to the screen. "Your arrival is expected. Please make your way to bay fifteen. Park your hovercar. Exit the vehicle and await further instruction."

The large gates opened before them.

Flit kicked the vehicle back into action, and, in a matter of seconds, they were through.

Scraps took a deep breath as the gate lurched shut behind them. Being out in the city was one thing, but they were now trapped within the confines of a very secure Government compound. It was intimidating, to say the least.

Bay Fifteen was a cavernous space that Scraps imagined was used to holding freighters and other large vehicles. Flit steered their vehicle into the bay and turned it around so that they wouldn't have to reverse out, and they both stepped out just as a harried middle-aged man hustled over to them.

"R&D, huh?" he asked with a bitter laugh. A few strands of his sparse, combed-over hair flopped on his shiny head. "Only you guys could pick such a perfect time for a review. I'm Gareth, the shift supervisor. I'll warn you that we're busy, and we don't have time to mess around."

"Very well," Flit said, apparently unperturbed by the man's obvious discontent. "We'll make this as quick and painless as possible. We don't want to put you and your team out."

Gareth gave her a look of disbelief as he led them through the security scanner, two soft beeps telling them that their scans held up. "My boss tells me that you had issues with our inventory lists?"

Flit pulled her datapad out of her bag and switched it on. "Yes. There are some discrepancies with the stock levels we need to investigate."

"You couldn't have forwarded your concerns for us to deal with?" Exasperation trimmed Gareth's tone.

Tension polluted the air between them and Gareth. Scraps was worried that anything he said might just make it worse.

Flit flashed him a sweet smile. "We know how busy you are." Her tone was sugary sweet and sounded entirely genuine.

If Scraps was the swearing kind, he might have done so in that moment. His girlfriend could get away with murder with a smile like that.

"We're wasting time," Gareth snapped, turning on his heels "This way."

The walk to the storage vaults was short. As they approached, Scraps used the time to recall all he knew about how the stock was supposed to be counted and stored at the facility. Gareth started opening doors for them, one by one, and Flit and Scraps cross-referenced the stock levels and positioning with their own data.

There were some obvious discrepancies, which made Scraps frown with suspicion. "Your data accounted for fourteen vaults, yet you have sixteen. Is that where the missing supplies are?"

"Two of the vaults have been seconded for other purposes," Gareth hedged, not breaking his stride at all.

"Policy Fifteen-C in the Munitions Production Manual requires that all storage facilities are listed in reports, even if they are empty or have been leased to other departments." Scraps recited the policy almost word for word.

"Yes, and you need to have a clearance level of four to even talk about the other vaults." A haughty sneer tugged at Gareth's lips.

"Assuming whatever is in those vaults warrants a clearance level four, then you are right. However, that does not excuse your incorrect counting procedures." Scraps squared his shoulders as Gareth became buoyant in his smugness. It might have been cruel, but Scraps was looking forward to bursting his cocky bubble. "But the point is moot. We have been granted a clearance level two for your department, well above the four that we need."

Gareth's eyes widened. He had most likely assumed he was dealing with lower-level R&D grunts. He walked to the nearest comm screens and pulled up their personnel sheets. When he read over their clearance levels, he pressed his lips together in a thin, disgruntled line.

"Will you give us the information we need? We don't want to waste any more of your time than we already have." Flit didn't even bother trying to hide the sarcasm in her lilted words.

Gareth stomped over, slamming his hand harder than necessary against an access panel and standing back as the doors slid open. "The Advanced Weaponry Factory has run out of room to manufacture one of its latest technologies. They shipped their bulk stock to us in preparation for getting the all-clear for production. The stock level of those items has a higher clearance level and were counted separately and only on internal reports. It is easier this way, too, as we've already started test-production, and stock is fluctuating unpredictably while the team gets used to the new handling requirements." Gareth crossed his arms over his chest. The bored, exasperated look on his face reminded Scraps of the same one Flit got when he went into too much detail about policies and procedures.

"The policy for stock of this nature requires a totalled inventory, regardless of clearance level. The entire list then takes on the highest level required and is dealt with accordingly," Flit said, flipping through her datapad and bringing up the relevant policies. She flashed the screen at Gareth.

Scraps was genuinely impressed. Flit hated this sort of thing, but perhaps the motivation of proving their unhelpful guide wrong was enough to jog her memory.

"That is ridiculous!" Gareth growled. "It's only a couple of lines at a higher level. I am not wasting my time going through more bureaucratic nonsense just because a few items have higher clearance requirements. Besides, that regulation has never been communicated to us."

Flit looked over at Scraps, as if she had run out of arguments. Luckily, Scraps had this one in the bag. He could argue with Gareth about policy and procedure until the sun went down, and, if he was honest with himself, he quite enjoyed the challenge.

"It is this department's job, and no one else's, to make sure you comply with procedure. It wasn't communicated to you, because it was assumed you would have your own compliance obligations sorted. Apparently, you don't," Scraps said, retrieved his own datapad from his bag and fixed Gareth with an unimpressed stare.

"Brian, am I correct in my assessment that the extent of discrepancies and unfamiliarity with policies would warrant a full-scale investigation?" Flit asked in a fake-quiet tone.

Poor Gareth almost choked. His eyes bulged out of their sockets, and his balding head shone with sweat. His mouth flapped open and closed. "Please, there is no need for that," he spluttered, looking between them. "Just let me make the changes and resubmit. I'll have it to you within twenty-four hours."

Scraps opened his mouth to say no, to let the Citizen know that he couldn't get away with not following procedures just because he thought he was above them. Registereds had procedures drilled into them from the time they could talk. They were punished brutally for not following them. There was no way Scraps was willing to let this transgression pass.

An unusual sense of power dawned over Scraps, and he paused, almost giddy with the knowledge. He instinctively knew how satisfying it would be to cut down the smug, caustic man in front of him. Every single part of him that had been growing more and more restless about his past with the Government craved the satisfaction of taking this chance to shut part of it down.

It felt good, but concern gnawed at him. They had a real opportunity here, one they—or any other Underground agent— might never get again. Despite his desire to steer clear of trouble, could he really turn it down?

30

FLIT

"BRIAN?" Flit's brows creased softly as she watched Scraps seize up.

Across from them, Gareth shifted from foot to foot.

"Apologies," Scraps snapped out of it, shaking his head a little. He appeared to collect himself before he turned to the munitions manufacturer. "Ava is correct. The infractions in this facility warrant a full-scale investigation. We will need your superiors to liaise with ours so we can work out the terms of a shutdown until the issues have been quantified and rectified."

Gareth paled. "Please, you can't do that. We're already under a lot of pressure here to get things done. Any halt in progress could set us back months! There must be another way."

Flit and Scraps exchanged glances. Flit was tempted to tell the man that they had no other option, but that would be taking things too far. They just needed a reason to snoop a bit. They didn't want the entire munitions manufacturing department to be out for their blood.

"Look, we can't let this go unaddressed… but there might be something else we can do." Flit spoke hesitantly, hoping she could coax him into negotiating. "If you allow us to carry out a full inspection now, we can do an interim audit. Whatever issues we find, we can help you to address, and we don't need to take this further. Provided we don't find anything completely untoward, that is."

Gareth's shoulders sagged. "What would that involve?"

"We require temporary full access to the entire facility, including the test labs where your staff are handling this equipment. Storage is only part of the problem when you're dealing with a new material. The good thing is that Brian and I both have clearance to write up any policies you are missing. A full review, though? Well, that needs more impartial hands and more bureaucracy." Flit crossed her arms over her chest with a serious, grim expression on her face.

"If that is the fastest way to get this over with, fine. I'll get you the access, but please keep it quiet. I'm already pulling my hair out with all the issues we've already had," Gareth snapped.

Flit bit her lip to stop herself from saying that, judging by the significant lack of hair on Gareth's head, these new materials had to have been incredibly problematic.

Gareth turned back to a wall screen and swiped through several menus before he brought up an administrative screen. He had Flit and Scraps enter their credentials before he approved them, and then he turned back to them. "I don't have time to show you around. I'll get one of my juniors to do it. Please be discreet. You are to do nothing more than observe." Even though Gareth's tone held warning, they all knew that he could do little to enforce it.

"We'll do our best to get this over with with as little fuss as possible," Flit promised, figuring a little ego pandering would help make sure they got their way.

Gareth rolled his eyes, probably sensing her motive. "I'll get Lauren. She'll show you around. Wait here." He walked off without another word.

Flit had to hide her grin at the teamwork they had just displayed. "Thanks for backing me up," she said out of the corner of her mouth.

Scraps gave her a stiff mock salute, but there was a spark of anticipation dancing behind his eyes.

"Let's just hope it's worth it," he whispered so softly that she barely heard it.

It was another five minutes before a young woman wearing a

Government-Issued manufacturing uniform of light grey walked down the corridor to greet them. She was about their age and had a forced smile stretching her lips. "Hello, Gareth sent me to find you. I'm Lauren."

"I'm Ava, and this is Brian." Flit shook the woman's hand.

"So, you two get a tour of the entire facility, huh?"

Flit smiled at her. "Indeed. We need to check that policies and procedures exist and are being followed."

Lauren led them out of the room they were in and into a long corridor. It was well-lit and wide enough to fit their group three times over. The concrete seemed stark and cold in such a long space, but it was clean and functional. Flit supposed that was all it needed to be.

"We've already seen the storage vaults, but we need to get a look at the factory floor and the labs," Scraps supplied as they walked.

"The labs?" Lauren's eyebrows rose into her hair line. "Oh, so you're here because of the incidents?" Her voice softened to a covert murmur, and she looked around as if checking to see if there was anyone standing by the doors they passed.

Scraps looked at Flit. He shook his head, looking like he was about to deny it.

Flit took a gamble and cut him off. "Yes," Flit brought her own voice down to a conspiratorial whisper to match Lauren's, "but we weren't given much information. Whoever wrote the report must have decided details were too much effort."

Lauren let out an exasperated huff. "We're not trained for that sort of thing. The material they have us handling is tempestuous, to say the least. Not that I'm complaining of course—"

"Of course not," Flit reassured her with a dismissive wave.

"It was all just dumped on us. Gareth and the others try their best, they really do, but we have been crazy busy lately and with this new contract..." Lauren trailed off getting lost in her own thoughts.

"Have you been given any instructions or policies on how the new stuff is to be handled?" Flit gently coaxed Lauren out of her reverie.

"There are instructions?" Lauren snorted, her bitterness

creeping from her tone and into her eyes. "If there were, we would have read them. Even though we have a lot to do, some things aren't worth risking."

Before Flit could ask Lauren to clarify what risks they were taking, they turned a corner and arrived at a large set of double doors at the end of the corridor. They were metal, with panels of wire mesh backed with glass at face height. A Registered stood either side. Between how well their uniforms blended with the walls and how still they were standing, Flit almost missed them. With a wave of one of the Registered's hands, there was a low, electric hiss as the doors opened. Without the thick doors between them and the next room, the constant hum of machinery vibrated through the space, punctuated by intermittent staccato tapping and soft whooshes.

Lauren led the way into the factory that was at least four storeys tall and with a footprint almost as large as an entire city block in the Hub. There were machines of all shapes and sizes pouring, cutting, buffing, painting, and assembling. The landing the trio stepped onto was made of clean, polished silver metal grating, with a steel safety rail at the edge. Flit looked down, watching the workers with white safety gear walking between machines and checking various dials or parts that were being produced.

"Welcome to the floor." Lauren gestured to the space beyond. She almost had to yell to be heard over the whirs and groans of the automated machinery.

Flit's lips parted in awe as they moved to the rail. The sheer amount of weaponry being manufactured was flabbergasting. She knew that the Hub made weapons to distribute to all of the Government's cities, but this was something else. She followed the progress of one line from the early 3D printing stage right through to final quality checks and packaging. There were more production lines than she could count from her vantage point.

"Do you want to tour the floor? It will take around two hours to do a proper circuit. What do you need to see for your review?" Lauren asked.

"We might just observe from up here. Seems to be a good view of everything." Scraps took out his datapad, tapped the screen to bring it to life, and started typing notes.

Flit turned to look back at the factory as he worked, taking mental notes of the different types of weapons being produced. Pretty much everything was standard issue for Registered and Citizen Officers alike.

After a few minutes, Scraps asked her to pull up some policies he wanted to double-check. They cross-referenced their observations with the appropriate practices as Lauren leaned against the railing and pretended to be interested in checking some scuff marks on her nails. Flit was certain she was eavesdropping.

"Everything here is in order. The workers appear well versed in relevant operating procedures. Can you please show us to the labs?" Scraps asked as he tucked his datapad under his arm.

"Very well."

Lauren guided them to a nearby elevator at the far end of the platform. The cart took them several stories up, to the levels above the floor. From the elevator, they had to go through another security check and a three-stage decontamination unit before they reached a large, auditorium-like meeting space with dozens of doors spotting each wall.

Excitement fluttered in Flit's stomach as Lauren led them over to a door on the left. Judging by the level of security and decontamination required, this place would be near impossible for an undercover Underground operative to access on any other occasion. She only hoped they were able to find something worthwhile while they were there.

"I'll take you straight to the lab that's working with the new materials," Lauren said.

She opened the doors for them. Beyond was a labyrinth of hallways that she navigated with ease. She stopped at a room right at the end of one corridor, beside a window that gave them a spectacular view that spanned all the way back to the Hub.

The lab itself was separated into four subsections around a central preparation space. There was a table in the middle with trays full of safety gear. Lauren retrieved breathing masks and dark-lensed glassed for each of them. When Flit put them on, she let out a gasp. She couldn't see anything but the core pinpoints of light in the ceiling. Lauren's chuckle floated over, as a soft hand took Flit's elbow. Flit jumped at the sudden touch.

"It takes a bit of getting used to, but you'll need them," Lauren promised as she gently guided Flit across the blacked-out room.

There was a beep of a security scanner and a whoosh of a door sliding aside, and light flared in Flit's field of view. She held a hand up in front of her as her vision adjusted to the startling purple glow. As Flit's eyes reflexively snapped shut, the memory of that mysterious weapon from the tunnels hit her like a hovertruck. She vividly recalled the network of violet sparks sizzling against her skin and turning the blood in her veins to lava. She let out a soft breath and tried to contain her excitement that this gamble had paid off. Whatever this stuff was, it had to have something to do with that dreaded piece of unidentified tech.

"Well, it certainly is bright, whatever this material is," Scraps muttered under his breath.

Flit let her hand drop and realised that the glowing item was inside a cylindrical glass containment unit. It was the only light source in the immediate area, and it was as bright as the midday sun in the room. A pair of robotic arms sat idly at the side of the glass case, and at the base of the containment unit, there was a row of reinforced, capped test-tubes waiting to be filled.

"We call this Vasculum Orani Kintori Zeta—VOKZ for short. This shard is from the second shipment of this material we've had. I'm surprised your team didn't come out here the first time."

"We're new to this R&D department, although, judging by our discussion with Gareth, our team was never notified," Scraps said as he leaned in to get a closer look.

"I'm glad you are here now. The first time we had to deal with this stuff, we had a whole range of problems. You see, the dampening field we use on the containment cylinder to protect us from the VOKZ radiation has to be powered down when we do extractions." As she spoke, Lauren pointed at the control panel on the containment device. She then gestured to the mechanical arms. "During that time, we use radiation suits and operate the mechanical arms, but that stuff is powerful. It turns out that the suits we have aren't protective enough, and the Advanced Munitions Factory didn't send us any of theirs, so we must be quick when we handle it… But being quick can lead to all sorts of accidents."

"I see. What limits have been placed on exposure time?" Scraps asked.

Flit was too busy wondering at just how powerful the VOKZ must be in order to put out that kind of radiation.

"That's the problem. We do not have any protective gear or any safety protocol." Lauren stepped back from the source of the light, her voice wavering. "The first extraction was quick because we did not need much, but the ones after took a lot more time. Some of the other scientists got really sick for a while, but the director was pushing us to keep going. The Advanced Factory wants us to get through this testing ASAP."

"What is the VOKZ used for?" Flit wasn't sure if Lauren would answer, but it was worth a try.

"A power source of some form. I can't tell you what for. My clearance only extends to handling, not what happens to it after." Lauren shrugged. "Once the extraction is complete, we reenergise the field and put the VOKZ into the refinement unit."

Flit looked over at the large roller shutter that covered a quarter of the rear wall. There was a red light at the top of it, and a faint purple glow emanated from the joints in each panel of the cover.

"The problem is, even that short amount of reduced protection seems to cause radiation sickness. Gareth denies it, of course, but that's what it is. We are three technicians down."

Lauren then signalled for them to follow her as she led them to the lab next door. "You can take your glasses off now."

Flit did just that and was startled by the clinical white light of the space compared to the previous eerie glow. The room was lined with cabinets, each one holding a small glass capsule of throbbing purple energy.

"As you can see, the refinement process really helps to dampen the radiation. Those capsules are more than enough to handle it, but getting it to that point is dangerous." Lauren chewed on her lip, watching as Scraps took notes. "I really shouldn't have said so much—"

Flit put her hand on the other woman's shoulder. "Yes, you should have. This substance is a danger to everyone, and your boss and the department are failing their duty to you and your colleagues by not handling it properly," Flit reassured her. "You won't get into trouble, and we'll do our best to make sure this doesn't happen again."

Scraps cleared his throat. "Given that there are no formal procedures in place, we need to take swift action. As inconvenient as it may be to production, there is no item anyone can produce that is worth that level of risk to staff. As such, we will be issuing a temporary cease-work notification for these labs until we can get proper procedures in place."

Lauren's shoulders sagged with relief, and she closed her eyes, taking a slow, deep breath. When she looked back at them, her eyes were filled with a complex twist of relief and anxiety. "I am sure Gareth will be disappointed, but it sounds like it's for the best."

"It is," Flit promised her. "We'll need to finish up the general tour and then speak to Gareth before we go, but I promise we will do our best to make sure that you guys are properly protected against that stuff from now on."

Lauren took a step towards the door.

Flit held out a hand to stop her. "I just have one more question."

"Yes?" Lauren turned around, her hands clasped in front of her so tight that the tips of her fingers were turning white.

"The people who are sick… are they better now?" Flit asked in a quiet tone laced with genuine concern.

Lauren's face softened. "Mostly. I spoke to one of them yesterday. He still gets dizzy, but he is becoming confident enough to carry his toddler again, so that's something, I suppose."

Flit nodded, her teeth gritted behind a genuine smile of compassion. She felt Scraps' hand slide onto the small of her back as Lauren guided them out of the room, and she focused all her energy on that tender point of contact to distract her from the rage coiling around her heart. Even if this was the source of the weapon that had been used against her, these workers were just normal people, too, normal people the Government were failing miserably.

31

———————

SCRAPS

GARETH DID NOT APPRECIATE the news that they were shutting down work with **VOKZ** until compliance could be assured. At first, he looked as though he might argue with them. Scraps had been sure to lace their explanation with enough policy to make their decisions irrefutable. A few of them might have been taken somewhat out of context, but he had worked with people like Gareth before. He wasn't going to deep dive into the complex policies. He was the type that would just complain about it while Flit and Scraps took on the responsibility of doing the hard work to rewrite the protocol.

"Well, I would put that down as a success," Flit announced with a grim smile as he drove the hovercar onto the main highway that would take them back to the Hub.

Scraps pressed his lips together and took a deep breath. "If you mean that we succeeded in testing our limits and possibly putting ourselves on the Government's radar, then yes, it was a success."

The look that Flit gave him would turn ice into steam in two seconds flat. He refused to take his words back, though. From Flit's description of the weapon, Scraps had a strong feeling that they had found what she was looking for. He was glad about it. The weapon was alarming for so many reasons. It was one thing that the Government knew how to control Derivates with inhibitors and chips, but if they started using devices that did not require bodily contact, then it made the world much more dangerous for his kind.

Beside him, Flit sighed. "You're brooding."

"Pardon?" Scraps turned to face her, brows knitting together.

"You. You're brooding. Sure, we made more work for ourselves, but—shit!" She bounced in her seat, her eyes alight with excitement. "This is it—the reason we're here! We found it! I thought you'd at least be a little excited."

"I am excited." Scraps' voice was too flat, even to his own ears.

"You don't sound it."

Scraps scanned the road ahead of them, looking at the towering city that was both their home and their prison. Worry knotted his gut as he thought about what they had just done. "What if we went too far? What if we exposed—" He stopped, shaking his head, knowing there was a high chance their conversation was being recorded by the vehicle's inbuilt security system.

Reaching over, Flit peeled his stiff fingers off the side of the seat and threaded them with hers. "We were just doing our job," she said, as though it was the simplest thing in the world

The problem was, Scraps didn't have her confidence. Even though he knew that everything they had done was in the parameters of their job description, he couldn't shake the shadow of danger hanging over them. Scraps was under no illusion about what the Government did to deserters and rebels, and the idea of that happening to Flit if they got captured was seeming less and less like an acceptable risk.

"I just don't want you to get hurt," Scraps admitted, voice catching in his throat. He kept his eyes schooled on the road ahead and tried to not let emotion get the better of him as the adrenaline of the investigation wore off. It was a drop he was familiar with, and he was used to dealing with it. He could keep himself under control.

"We face dozens of risks every day, but now? Now, we get to pick which dangers are worth risking our lives for." Flit lifted his hands to her lips and brushed a kiss over his knuckles. A warm sigh fluttered against his skin. "And for me? This is worth it."

All Scraps could do was nod. She was right. So long as the status quo remained intact, just being alive was a dangerous pastime for Derivates. If this weapon was part of some new plan, and they had just uncovered information that could help the Underground, then it would be worth the cost.

Scraps was about to agree with Flit, to tell her that it was worth it, when something caught his eye near a building they were driving past.

"Flit, look," Scraps said, tapping her shoulder and pointing at the side street as they stopped at a set of lights. A crew of Registereds were working to clean what looked like splatters of red paint of the side of a shop. He thought back to earlier their trip that morning. "Do you think that is some of the graffiti they were talking about?"

"It certainly isn't Government-approved advertising." Flit tilted her head to the side and peered at it.

Scraps chuckled. The traffic lights changed and he continued to drive them deeper into the heart of the Hub. When he was a Registered, the graffiti would have annoyed him, especially if he was the one who had to clean it up. Now, though? Well, he found it reassuring. He and Flit were not the only one breaking the rules today.

THE MOMENT FLIT and Scraps returned to Centre One, Jane called them into her office. Any sense of achievement Scraps felt was swallowed by dread. Flit must have sensed it, too, but she looked over and gave him a firm nod as she led the charge.

The instant they stepped into the pod, Jane looked up. "I heard you two shut down some of the labs at the factory?" She glanced between them with disbelief.

"The issues with their inventory management were more extreme than anticipated, and then, we saw their labs." Flit shook her head for dramatic effect. "Jane, they had no procedures in place, and they were dealing with materials that made their workers violently ill after an ho—"

"Ava, calm down," Jane whistled, raising her hands in the air.

Scraps stood closer to Flit. She could be passionate when she felt there was something going wrong, but she was entirely right about this. He would support her, no matter what.

"I'm not angry. I'm impressed. Gareth is an obnoxious loaf of a person. We've been trying to nail him for his laziness for years. Hopefully now, his superiors will get out of their comfortable offices upstairs and head out there to see what is really going on!"

Scraps' eyes widened in surprise. "You are not upset we shut down production?"

Jane let out a snort of laughter. "Please! The fact you got the evidence to trip him up is a massive win for our department. The Munitions Manufacturing Team is the worst with their compliance." She rolled her eyes "They act like we owe them our undying gratitude because they make the weapons that help maintain peace."

Flit, much closer to Jane because of their numerous social outings, laughed along with her. Scraps didn't feel that comfortable, so he chose to remain professional and pressed his lips together while standing at attention.

"That's good," Flit said, smiling at Jane. "Because when he comes for our arses, we know you've got our back."

Scraps was amazed that Flit got away with swearing like that in front of their superior. In the Underground, it seemed like every second word was profanity. His time in the Hub had taught him that the Citizens were much more careful with their language. Even so, there was something about Flit's expert use of the curses that had everyone more amused by her than offended. It was yet another example of how some Citizens were exempt from the rules that Derivates were punished harshly for.

"We'll do our best to get those policies and procedures up to scratch ASAP," Scraps promised, drawing attention away from Flit's casual banter, just in case.

"There's no rush." The seriousness returned to the office at that point. "But thank you, Brian. You and Ava have been a real asset to this office," Jane said with a kind smile in his direction. "I'll make sure you both have a light load of new cases until it is done." She turned and looked over her shoulder. Behind her, through the full-wall glass window, the pinks and lilacs of late afternoon were starting to reflect off the building across from them. "Look, you two have done enough. Why don't you head off for the day? Start fresh tomorrow."

An early mark? Not only had they shut down weapons production, but they were being rewarded for it? He looked at Flit, incredulity marring his features.

"Well, I don't need to be told twice." Flit's small smile stretched into a wide grin as she hooked her hand through the crook of his elbow. "Thanks! See you tomorrow, Jane." Flit turned and dragged him out of the office before he could say his own farewell.

"Woah, slow down Ava," Scraps muttered.

Flit chuckled. "Are you kidding? We're getting out of here before she changes her mind!"

They made their way back to their pod and started to pack up. Scraps' mind was buzzing with conflicting thoughts and concerns about the day. He was just about to put his datapad in his briefcase when there was a knock on the door of their pod.

"What's going on?" Liana whispered, leaning in through the door. "Is there some sort of evacuation or something? What's the rush?"

Flit laughed as she slipped the strap of her handbag over her shoulder. "Jane gave us an early-mark. We're getting out of here before she realises what she's done and recants it."

Liana smiled. "Well, before you go, Chris and I wanted to invite you over for dinner tonight. We've got some friends coming by, and we thought you guys would get along with them. How does that sound?"

Flit looked over to Scraps as if to see what he thought. He was exhausted, but they didn't have plans. Spending time with Chris and Liana was always worth it, so he nodded.

"It sounds great. Can you please send us the details?"

"Sure. See you then." And with that, Liana was off.

WHEN THEY GOT HOME, Flit and Scraps were finally able to debrief with each other. Optimistically hopeful that they had gotten away with their investigation, they contacted the Underground for the first time since starting their mission. As directed,

Scraps opened Brian's e-mails and sent a message to 'Aunt Edna'. It said they were enjoying their new job but missing family and friends. It was a code that Shadow had taught them, so they could let the Underground know when they found critical information and needed to meet.

"How long do think they'll take to reply?" Flit asked, biting her lip as she read the message over his shoulder.

Hitting send, Scraps pressed a soft kiss against her cheek and shrugged. "I'm not sure. Hopefully some time before production starts again."

Things had gone well enough that he decided the tension of the day was enough. He did not wish to fight about it anymore.

"I wonder how things are going there." Flit's tone was wistful as she slumped back against the comfortable couch and put her hands behind her head.

"I'm sure everything is fine," Scraps said, even though he wondered the same thing.

Scraps had only spent a year in the Underground, but it felt more like home to him than the Hub ever had. They had figured out who was behind the explosions before they left, but that didn't mean the Underground was safe. He missed being down there—the Blue Team and their training sessions, the easy patrols where he and Flit could just be themselves, being able to use his powers without fear. Really, though, he felt for Flit. She had left behind a mother, a father, and a best friend. He couldn't imagine how difficult it must be for her.

Flit let out a long, tired sigh. "Do you regret it?"

Scraps looked over at Flit, his brows furrowing at her question. "Regret what?"

"Coming up here. This." She gestured towards the window.

Settling onto the couch beside her, Scraps took her hand in his. "No. I don't. If I had stayed, you would have been up here, and I would be down there. I cannot say for certain, but I have a feeling that missing you would take more of a toll on me than missing everything else does."

Flit's face softened, her hand squeezing his a little tighter. Her eyes started to shine with emotion, and he gave her a gentle kiss.

When they pulled apart, she started to whisper, "I lov—" but then seized up, pressing her lips shut.

Scraps was thrown back to the night she'd told him about the mission and then again when they found the wedding rings on the table. He knew what she wanted to say, and he could see that flicker of fear in her eyes as she realised she had almost done it again. Flit did not like making herself vulnerable, but it seemed she could not help it around him.

The look on Flit's face told him the conversation had become painful for her, and he was overwhelmed with the urge to fix it.

"I mean, after you introduced me to the joys of forty-two, what else was I to do?" he said in a teasing tone.

Flit's amused chuckle spluttered between them as she leaned back and gave him a playful poke in the ribs. "You're terrible."

Shrugging, Scraps said, "No, just honest."

Flit rolled her eyes. "Pfft, I'm sure you'd have done fine without me down there. Swipe would've snatched you up the second I left. If you were interested in exploring guys, I know Tweak was definitely interested."

"I don't want them. I only want you," Scraps argued.

He wrapped his arms around her. She turned and curled up against his chest, pressing her lips to his and moaning softly against them as she deepened the kiss.

Scraps gave into it for as long as he could before he felt his body reacting too strongly. "We should stop, otherwise we won't be able to make it to dinner tonight."

Flit's face scrunched up in an endearing mix of desire and petulance, strands of honey brown hair falling over her flushed cheeks. "Is that really such a bad thing?"

Despite her protest, she flopped back in her seat and opened a quick tactical ops VR game they both liked to play together when they had spare time. The time they spent together like this had to be one of Scraps' favourite things about their relationship. He enjoyed the sex and kissing, of course, but when he and Flit had a chance to just be themselves and have fun around each other, it unlocked a different part of him that only she had ever been able to access.

32

———

FLIT

FLIT AND SCRAPS arrived at Chris and Liana's apartment with a bottle of wine and the usual tension that came with meeting new people they would have to explain their cover story to. The front door didn't do much to dull the music and conversation from inside. Just as Flit wondered whether they would need to ring the doorbell for a second time, the door opened to reveal Liana in a sleek red dress, holding a glass of wine.

"Already into the good stuff?" Flit teased, nodding towards the glass. She offered Liana the bottle she was holding, "Lucky I brought reinforcements.

Liana laughed as she took the bottle and pulled Flit into a one-armed hug. "You guys are just in time. Chris has got the entrees ready to go."

Flit slipped past her friend. Liana hugged Scraps on the way through as well. Scraps was still a little stiff when accepting affection from others, but no one ever commented on it.

"Brian! Thank goodness you're here. These guys are ravenous, and there's no way I was going head-to-head with them to protect your share!" Chris called out as he walked out from the open-plan kitchen and into the lounge room.

Like Flit and Scraps' apartment, the exterior walls of Chris and Liana's place was floor-to-ceiling windows. Being a little further away from Centre One, their view wasn't quite as expansive. The apartment was lovely, though, and there were pictures of the two of them on the various screens around the room.

There were three people in the lounge room as Liana ushered them in. Two women sat on the lounge near the window. One was probably around five years older than Flit and had gorgeous dark skin and eyes, and a broad, welcoming smile. The other was slightly younger, with hair a shockingly brilliant shade of teal and curious glint in her eyes. On the armchair beside them sat a man who was dressed in very expensive clothes, well-styled brown hair, and a posture only naturally charismatic people could muster.

"Ava, Brian, meet Andy." She gestured to the teal-haired woman first. "Petra, and Trey," she finished.

Petra, the older woman, gave Flit a small wave, and Trey nodded in greeting.

Liana walked into the dining area, grabbed two chairs, and dragged them into the lounge room. "Brian and Ava recently joined the R&D team. Transferred from Eastbay."

Flit smiled at the others. "Hi!"

"Nice to meet you all," Scraps said with a firm nod.

Flit took his hand and guided him over to the chairs Liana had set up for them.

"So, how are you enjoying the Hub?" Petra asked, the warmth in her smile radiating into her smooth voice.

Flit plastered a smile on her lips. She'd answered that question so many times she wished she could ban it from conversations. "Not all that much, to be honest. We've been too busy to really explore. This place is just as full-on as everyone at Eastbay warned us it would be!"

The others laughed. If there was one thing that the Citizens of the Hub liked to hear, it was that they were far busier and more important than people who lived in the other cities.

"So, you know we are in R&D. What do you guys do?" Flit asked, knowing that would ease them into conversation.

"I am lead developer for a VR game corporation," Andy, the teal-haired woman, said.

"I love VR Games!" Scraps blurted, seeming pleased to have something in common with the people they were spending time with.

"What's your favourite?" Andy asked, leaning in.

Scraps sat back and shook his head. "I cannot pick just one."

Andy laughed at that. "Seems like you and I are kindred spirits then," she said with a wink.

Flit looked at Petra and Trey. "How about you two?"

Petra sat up taller in her seat. "We own Nightmix, a club in North Four-East Three."

Positioned in the border blocks between the Government and the outer corporate buildings, it was an interesting location to have a club.

"I suppose you'd get all sorts of people there," Flit hummed. Most of her other colleagues in the R&D department refused to go further than a three-block radius from Centre One.

"We do, indeed. It's quite the melting pot. That's what makes it more interesting than a lot of the central joints," Trey explained.

"So, a good mix of Government workers who are too stiff to have fun and the corporate types who know just how to party?" Flit asked.

"Ooh, I like you already," Andy announced with a smirk.

The others laughed, and Flit smiled at Scraps. She had a feeling that Chris and Liana wouldn't hang around with anyone who took themselves too seriously, and at the very least, if they hadn't appreciated her comment, she could've played it of as a self-depreciating joke.

AFTER AN HOUR OF LIGHT CONVERSATION, Chris and Liana moved the group over to the dining table. They took their seats, and Liana carried plate after plate of delicious food over. For a while, the chatter was replaced by enthusiastic dining. It was a far cry better than anything Flit and Scraps would have cooked for themselves at home.

"Well, I don't think I've enjoyed a meal this much since the last time you guys cooked for us." Flit sighed in contentment, slumping back in her chair.

"We are more than happy to share our recipes with you, you

know that," Liana teased. There was a mischievous glint in her eyes.

"Yeah, but Ava does not know how to follow instructions," Scraps chimed in, right on cue.

Flit rolled her eyes.

"Sometimes, that's a good thing. If we all follow the same rules, there would be no spice or diversity in life," Petra said, raising her glass in Flit's direction.

"You say that, but you have not tried her cooking," Scraps insisted.

"Yeah, no one needs Ava's kind of diversity in the kitchen," Chris agreed, giving Scraps a look of commiseration. Clearly, Flit's poor skills in the kitchen were an amusing point of conversation for them. She didn't mind so much if it helped Scraps deepen his friendship.

"Well, at least she nails life outside of the kitchen." Liana raised her glass towards Flit. "Did we mention what Ava and Brian achieved at work today?"

The others leaned in, curious. Flit didn't know why anyone would want to hear about the boring exploits of their job in the R&D department. If she wasn't an undercover Underground operative, she wouldn't have cared.

"They shut down some of the labs at the Munitions Production factory!" Chris blurted.

"You mean the one that you guys have been trying to nail for years?" Trey asked, resting his elbows against the table and steepling his fingers.

"Yeah. They spent a few hours there today and shut them down. Just like that!" Liana confirmed.

"It was only a couple of the labs. Not like we managed to shut the whole plant down or anything. Now that would have been an achievement worth bragging about." Beneath the table, Scraps' hand gently squeezed Flit's thigh, probably an attempt to remind her about the confidentiality that their job and mission required. Flit ignored him.

Andy and Trey looked more interested.

"My brother died because in an accident at a similar factory a few years ago," Petra said, her default warm expression flickering with grief.

"It's how we met," Liana explained. "I was called in as part of the investigation, but the manager cut me off at every avenue. We never did get justice for Jacob."

Flit looked at Petra, her face softening. "That makes me wish we could have done more today."

"It's amazing you got that far," Andy reassured her, shaking her head. "Takes guts to do what you did. Not many people like to ruffle the Government's feathers. I imagine you've made yourselves a few enemies by shutting down whatever they were working on."

With a shrug, Flit said, "It's not hard to get on the Government's bad side. One original thought and—bam! You're done for."

"Ava…" Scrap's voice was low and filled with wariness.

"Bah, don't worry. You're amongst friends here." Trey waved his hand dismissively. "We are all good for a little bit of creative anarchy."

Flit looked at Scraps. His worry was etched into his face. She slid her hand into his under the table and squeezed it gently, begging him silently to trust her.

"Speaking of creative anarchy," Petra said, leaning back in her chair and picking up her wine glass, swilling the deep crimson liquid around slowly. "Have you guys seen the graffiti around town?"

"We saw some being removed from the side of a shop today," Scraps said, sounding unimpressed with the continued blasphemous direction of the conversation.

"What time was that?" Andy asked.

Scraps looked at Flit as he tried to figure it out. "Late afternoon?"

Flit nodded in confirmation.

"Damn… took them a while to clean it up then. I saw some this morning on my way to work," Andy explained. "It was a good tag too. Big enough to be seen from the street."

Flit rested her chin on her hands and leaned her elbows on the table. "The one we saw was mostly cleaned off. Do you think it's all the same thing? What did you see?"

Andy looked at the others. Something silent passed between them before she spoke. "It's a stylised image of people and flames. Free Citizens logo."

"Free Citizens? Is that a record label or something?" Flit asked, imagining that only some sort of big corporation with the clout to protect itself would dare with a publicity stunt like that.

"No!" Trey scoffed. "They are a group of Citizens who are unhappy with the Government. Apparently."

"Ha, cute!" Flit snorted out a laugh. "So, they go around graffitiing their logo on stuff? What's that going to achieve?"

The others looked at Flit like she had grown a second head. Scraps included.

"The Government hates it. The second someone reports it, they scramble to remove it!" Trey said it as though he was impressed by it.

"The Government does hate wasting their resources on things like that," Scraps added, clearly trying to ease the tension from Flit's comment.

"Yeah… but it's paint. They just clean it off. Game over. It barely made it onto the radio as a warning." Flit shrugged. "I'm just saying if I was leading a group of *Citizens unhappy with the Government*, I'd want to do more than paint some pretty pictures."

Scraps grasped at Flit's hand and looked like he might faint. "Ava, can I speak to you, please?" Scraps got to his feet. "Outside?"

Flit tugged her hand back and glared at him.

"No! Stay," Liana said quickly, putting her hand on Flit's shoulder. "I was just about to serve dessert. After that, Chris wanted to play a game."

Scraps looked between Flit and Liana, but with all the eyes on the table at him, he backed down. "Dessert would be nice. Thank you." He settled back into his seat but not before giving Flit a pointed look.

CHOCOLATE AND ICE CREAM, was there anything they couldn't fix?

By the time dessert was over, the tension from the conversation about the Free Citizens had dissipated. Everyone was laughing and joking about a recent movie that had been released. Flit and Scraps hadn't seen it yet, but from what the others said, the plot was so bad that it turned what was supposed to be a romance into one of the best comedies ever released.

Taking the discussion to the lounge room, everyone settled down facing the window. Chris tapped the glass and brought up the entertainment screen as Flit curled up against Scraps' side, ready to pass out after the great meal.

"Liana and I found this new module and thought it would be fun to play, seeing as how we're all in relationships," Chris explained. The screen lit up with a generic logo of two linked question marks, and then that faded as a question appeared on the screen.

Flit looked over at Petra, Andy, and Trey, understanding dawning on her. They all seemed very close, but she kept getting mixed signs about who was with who. With what Chris just said, she guessed they were all together. The Underground was home to all types of relationships—committed, open, polyamorous, and more… Flit always figured it had to do with their reduced numbers and more liberal approach to life. During her time growing up on the outskirts of the Hub, she had never seen anything like it with Citizens. She assumed it was another thing outlawed by the Government.

Chris read out the first question, ready to start the game. "Tell the group about your worst shared holiday memory."

This time, Scraps was unable to hide his confusion. "I thought this was a game. How do you play it? What are the rules?"

With a laugh, Chris said, "It's a game, just not one you win or lose. You just answer the questions."

"We figured it would be a nice way for everyone to get to know each other better," Liana explained. "Sorry. I know you guys like your competitions. This will be fun, though."

Flit frowned. What the hell was the point of a game if it had no rules? No winning condition? And what was the point if all they were going to do was exchange stories? After a moment, she shrugged, figuring it must have been some sort of Citizen trend they were unfamiliar with.

"Fair enough. I can answer that," Flit offered. The others smiled at her. She thought back to the picture on the wall of their apartment, the edited image of Ava and Brian on a beach. "A few years back, we took some time off for a beach holiday. We were so excited. We checked into the hotel and hit the sand. We put our towels down, kicked off our sandals… and then it started pouring. It was a torrential low system that threatened to turn into a cyclone but didn't. We were stuck inside all week, and on the day that we check out, the sun showed up again. Holiday totally ruined."

The others groaned and sympathised about their terrible luck. Scraps smiled at Flit as she spouted out a nonsense story for the both of them. Improvising like that would be difficult for him, so she was only too happy to fill in the void.

"We'll go next!" Petra called out excitedly. "So, Andy, Trey, and I went to the mountains for a ski trip—"

"Oh no, not this one again," Andy groaned, flopping back on the couch.

"Shush." Chris waved away her complaint. "I want to hear it."

Petra went on to explain about how three of them were skiing when Trey's pole snapped half-way down a huge hill. He had stumbled and broken his ankle, and they had to stay in their resort because they were refused a refund. Trey disagreed, saying that it wasn't until the end of their holiday, and it wasn't that big a deal. Somehow, the disagreement about what happened just made the group laugh more.

The game continued. Flit and Scraps were able to provide picture-perfect answers without disagreeing, but the others told real stories, stories with laughter and tears, borne from conflicting memories and amusing disagreements that made them all the richer. The Citizens spoke of their shared histories in a way that made Flit's stomach clench with frustration. She couldn't imagine what it was like to be able to have lazy sunny afternoons at the beach or nights spent dancing away drunkenly in a club without fearing discovery. She couldn't relate to the ease with which they shared their past, either. To be able to share sensitive details with the others, without reserve…

Even with Rook, she could count on two hands the number of times they had been able to take a night off and just be together.

And with Scraps... Well, she needed only a couple of fingers. She looked over at him, at his altered hair and eyes and with that familiar jawline, and she felt as if they had been cheated.

Flit and Scraps had spent the start of their relationship bonding over life-threatening situations, with adrenaline and cortisol playing more of a role in their bonding than the usual oxytocin hit of a new fling. The most passionate discussions they had were about how they wished they could just be themselves. They didn't have arguments over where they wanted their children to go to school, like Andy, Petra, and Trey, and they hadn't even considered what they wanted to do when they retired, like Chris and Liana did over their final drinks. If things remained the way they were, Flit and Scraps would never retire. They would spend every moment up to and including their dying breath, fighting for the freedom of their kind.

As much as Flit knew she needed to fight, she realised then it wasn't something she wanted to do. She just didn't see sitting in the dark tunnels forever as a viable alternative. She did what she did because they had been backed into a corner, and fighting was the only way out.

When it came time for Flit and Scraps to make their exit, Flit's mind was racing. Far from being just a fun night, their dinner party had highlighted all the things wrong with the way their world worked.

For once, Flit was silent on the trip home. She slipped her hand into Scraps' as she tried to figure out how to give them a chance to experience what a normal, simple relationship would feel like.

33

SCRAPS

SCRAPS DIDN'T UNDERSTAND why Flit was so quiet when they left Chris and Liana's place. If the game had been the kind one could win, they would have taken first place with ease. The others had fumbled over and argued about their answers with laughter and teasing, but Flit and Scraps had answered every question perfectly.

Their success didn't detract from Flit saying way more than she should have. He had been meaning to talk to her about it when they got home, but she was still quiet and sullen, walking around with her hands balled into fists and a storm brewing behind her eyes. As much as he wanted to bring it up, one thing that he had learned in their relationship was that it was better to give her some space while she worked through whatever was worrying her.

The next evening, after a stand-offish day at work, Scraps decided the time for waiting had passed. It was probably the longest he had seen Flit go without some sort of shift in her mood. He hadn't even seen a single smile from her since the night before.

So, as Flit angrily butchered some vegetables and he mixed the seasoning for their dinner, Scraps used his telekinesis to gently take the knife from her. He set it down on the chopping board.

"Flit, what's wrong?" He looked down at her as she stood there, face puckered by her grievance.

"Nothing. I'm fine."

Scraps pressed his lips together. That was a red flag if ever he saw one. As Hawkeye had graciously pointed out months earlier, if Flit said she was *fine*, the situation had to be dire.

"No, you're not. Something happened last night. Was it because I said something when you were talking about the graffiti?"

Flit shrugged. "I was only telling them the truth."

"A truth we—"

"I know. I know!" She threw her hands up in the air. "I get it, ok?" She took the knife back and resumed chopping, going even harder at the poor greens.

Scraps figured he must have missed the mark. He changed track. "Was it because we did not win that game?"

The knife clattered against the chopping board, and Flit rounded on him. There was a fire in her eyes, one that he knew all too well. Instead of being intimidated by the look, like most would be, he relished it. It was preferable to the sullenness.

"Because we didn't win the game?" Flit blurted, shaking her head. "Scraps, we weren't even playing the damn game!"

Head tilting to the side, Scraps looked at her. "I am pretty sure we were at the same dinner…"

The glare Flit shot him could turn molten lava to ice in two seconds flat. After a moment, her narrowed-eye gaze softened, and she leaned forward, shaking her head as an exasperated huff tumbled from her lips. "Yes, we played theme but not really. Not like the others. Our answers were bullshit, nothing more than perfectly manicured stories to make it look like we've actually had a life."

"Well, they are part of our cover story," Scraps said slowly, unsure of what it was that was bothering her.

She slammed her palms down on the smooth stainless-steel bench. "Exactly, a cover story." She stopped, turning to him. "Scraps, I want more with you than some stupid cover story. I want a real relationship. I want the chance to go on adventures that don't put our lives at risk, to skip work without fear of blowing our cover so we can spend all day in bed, or going to visit the beach, or… something, anything!"

He had been about to argue that they did have a real relationship, but then his mind snagged on the last thing she'd said. He imagined what that would be like, being able to relax on the beach and not worry about their cover, or their powers, or anything other than each other. As nice as it sounded, it just wasn't possible.

"That isn't our life, Flit. We chose to do this."

"Did we?" she asked, her cheeks flushed, "Or were we left with no other option? Scraps, what we have in the Underground isn't a life. It's survival. And… I'm over it. Survival isn't enough. I want to really live!"

Just as he was about to pull her in for a hug, Flit teleported away. She reappeared by the wall in their living room, her arm thrown out in the direction of the pictures projected onto the wall. "This! This is what we should have had, Scraps! The real moments behind these photos, not some fucking doctored images to make it look like we actually got to do anything fun or relaxing!"

With every ounce of frustration Flit shared, Scraps found his own growing faster. He pushed the vegetables they had been prepping aside and rested both of his hands onto the bench, his fingertips white as he pressed hard against it. "You're right. I know what you are saying, but there is nothing we can do to get those moments back. They will never be ours. No amount of cursing the Government will change that."

Chest heaving, Flit looked over at him. "I know we can't change the past, but we sure as hell can change the future."

Scraps' brows furrowed when Flit teleported over to the communication panel on the wall. "What are you doing?" he asked.

"Messaging *Aunt Edna*," Flit grumbled as swiped through the menu to get to their inbox.

Scraps frowned and walked over. "We already sent *her* a message." He put a hand on her shoulder.

"Yeah, well, clearly *she* didn't understand how important it was!" Flit tapped at the screen, her fingers trembling.

Scraps gently put his hand on Flit's hips and turned her to face him. He cupped her cheek and guided her face so that she had to look up at him. "I'm sure we'll hear from them as soon as they can get back to us." He leaned down and pressed a soft, reassuring kiss against her lips. "But for now? Let's focus on what we can control."

Flit rolled her eyes. "You mean nothing?"

Scraps smiled before he kissed her again. "That is not true. We can control us. While we wait to hear from *Aunt Edna*, let's work on our new mission—making good memories together."

This time, when Scraps followed his words with a kiss, Flit's pout dropped away, and she melted against him.

TWO MORNINGS LATER, Scraps and Flit woke at the crack of dawn, donned some exercise attire, and made their way out of their apartment building. On any other day, Flit would have bemoaned their early rising, making comments under her breath about the madness of people getting up before the sun to exercise, but this morning, she was wearing her best activewear as they took a brisk walk through the empty streets. She had her hand slipped into the crook of his elbow as she almost vibrated with excitement beside him.

Scraps leaned down. "What did *Aunt Edna* say in that message she sent you last night?"

"*She* said it had been too long since we caught up."

"That's it?"

Flit nodded. "Yep, that's all there was to it. Apart from where she wanted to meet, of course."

Scraps did not like the sound of that. He kept silent until they skirted past a café with a line of construction workers waiting outside to get their coffees before their early morning starts. "So, she got our message but didn't say anything about what we told her? She just wanted to see us? That does not sound positive."

Flit rolled her eyes as she tucked her hand into the crook of his elbow. "Don't be so worried. We did exactly what we promised we would do. Maybe our message gave her some new ideas, or she has thought of new places for us to visit while we're here."

It wasn't worth debating. They would find out the purpose of their meeting soon enough. Flit had sworn the VOKZ was the source of the energy the weapon had, and even Scraps felt a little queasy in that room despite the radiation shields. Whether it was because of the substance being related to the weapon or just because it was clearly so dangerous, he wasn't sure.

Regardless of his own theories, it was a relief to know they would be handing the intelligence over to people who could better analyse it.

Scraps looked up at the archway of the train station they had entered. They followed the tunnels down one level and boarded the first train that came by. It took them all the way to the outskirts of the city. The train was almost empty by the time they reached their stop, and when they got off, they made their way back above ground, and their surroundings were quite different.

"Wow, this café must be good if we're going all this way. You can see the fence from here," Scraps muttered.

True to his word, the blue electrostatic fence glowed off in the distance. It was close enough that they could hear the occasional zapping as freight trucks and Government vehicles slipped through it. As far as the Hub went, they were on the very outskirts, in the parts people tried to avoid.

"Well, you know me. Anything to get some good waffles," Flit said with a shrug as she took his arm and tugged him down the street.

The café was only a block from the station. Nestled between a tech repair store and a medical clinic, it wasn't busy. Unlike the ones they passed in the city, no one in these parts really seemed to be wanting coffee at this time of the day. All the same, Flit rubbed her hands together and said something about looking forward to breakfast as they walked through the automatic doors.

The interior was no less disappointing than the facade. All the screens on the walls had distinct flickers, and there were more posters and old-fashioned artworks nailed to the walls rather than holographic advertising. The barista didn't even look up as they entered.

Movement in the back of the café, at a table and chairs behind a screen, drew their attention. Scraps' eyes widened as they fell upon Shadow and Acumen standing by a closed door. Shadow waved to them. Before they could say anything, Shadow put a finger to his lips and opened the door, waving them through. They walked past a dingy kitchen, into a small staff area with lockers, aprons, and some screens flashing workplace health and safety notices. Given the state of the building, Scraps had to resist his now inbuilt urge to check their policies and procedures for compliance, having a feeling any inspector would be in their right mind to shut this place down.

Shadow, seemingly unperturbed by the rundown appearance of the room, tapped the control panel by the door a few times and retrieved a RFID chip from his pocket. The moment he scanned it, a low, electrical static buzzed in the room around him. Scraps' eyes widened, surprised that a place like this would have high-tech and tightly controlled anti-listening technology. Acumen smirked as the realisation swept over them.

"What is this place?" The question spluttered from Flit the moment Shadow waved the all-clear.

"It is one of the very few safehouses we have in the Hub," Shadow told her.

Scraps was not confident that any public space in the Hub could secured against the Government's extreme surveillance. How could they be sure it was safe?

"It's safe, I promise," Acumen supplied, snatching the concern straight from Scraps' mind. "At least, it is while Francesca is on shift."

Scraps thought back to the disinterested woman at the counter. Was it safe because she didn't pay attention or because she was one of them? He was tempted to ask, but that wasn't why they were here.

"Did the file transfer properly?" he asked instead.

"Yes, it did." Shadow's voice was sharp enough that it made Scraps' body tense up. "What do you think you were doing?"

Scraps' stomach fell. Flit's grip on his arm became painfully tight, and he looked at her. She was never good at hiding her feelings, and right now, he could read her anger by the set of her jaw and her narrow-eyed glare.

She jutted her chin out defiantly before saying, "What you asked us to."

"We asked you to wait for information that crossed your desk, not to infiltrate a highly secure munitions factory and demand information on their most classified materials." Shadow stood.

Unlike Flit, who became more animated as she got more emotional, Shadow was dead still, his voice low and cold.

"If we did that, you would never get anything. Our job is as boring as batshit and just about as mundane," Flit muttered.

Shadow looked utterly unimpressed by Flit's reasoning. "You went too far to get the information. Do you think that the heads of that facility are going to take that lying down? You know that our protection can go only so far. If this leads to an investigation, we can't be caught up in it."

The words landed like a punch to Scraps' gut. Even Flit's tense-shouldered stance sagged. "We did our best to back up all of our decisions with policies and procedures. If they do investigate, I am sure they will find that our case is water-tight," Scraps said, squaring his posture. He hadn't been happy about the way they had gone about the investigation, but they had made sure there were no holes in their approach.

"I expected this from her but not you, Brian." Shadow turned his cold glare on Scraps.

If Scraps had been defensive before, he was angry now. The way Shadow had referred to Flit was both disrespectful and unprofessional. "We might have gone beyond the boundaries of our initial mission briefing, but we did our job. I do not believe that our behaviour will warrant any undue suspicion of our motives," Scraps replied, not backing away from that steely grey stare.

"Was the information useful?" Flit asked.

For the first time in the meeting, Shadow's expression faltered.

"We are still assessing it," Acumen supplied, earning him a warning glance from Shadow.

Flit rolled her eyes. "Any delay on weapon development and production will be a welcome reprieve when push comes to shove. You're welcome, by the way."

Shadow's hands twisted by his side, and Scraps could imagine him leaning forward and strangling Flit at any moment. "One more escapade like this and we will be forced to recall you. Right now, you're more of a liability than an asset. Don't make me regret giving you this opportunity."

Flit flinched at his use of the word asset. "We're not asse—"

"We chose a course of action, and we will bear the consequences." Scraps put what he hoped was a reassuring arm around Flit's waist. "We will keep your warning in mind."

Flit was shaking with so much frustration that Scraps was concerned she would spontaneously teleport into a million pieces. He held her a little closer.

Shadow rose to his feet, his chair sliding out screeching against the floor. Scraps winced at the high-pitched whine. "Good. We wanted Intelligence Agents, not loose ends." Shadow gave them both meaningful looks. "Now, is there anything else?"

Flit crossed her arms over her chest, narrowing her eyes at him.

"No," Scraps said, tone stiff. "We have nothing left to say."

"Very well. Stay out of the places you're not supposed to be in. Keep sending us relevant information, and don't get too involved," Shadow said.

Acumen gave them an apologetic smile. "And stay safe."

Then, Shadow draped an arm around Acumen's shoulder, and they were both gone.

34

———

FLIT

THE TRIP HOME only served to intensify Flit's fury. She kept her lips pressed together so tight that her face ached from the strain. She was counting down the minutes until she could shut the front door behind them and unleash a torrent of frustration about how ridiculous Shadow was.

However, Scraps spoke first. "Shadow is just doing his job." The words were apprehensive, and as Flit rounded on Scraps, he squared his shoulders, clearly preparing for her to unleash.

She stopped at that look on his face and crossed her arms over her chest. "So, what? You think he's right and we should just hang around like brainwashed little Citizens and do nothing?"

"He is following protocol—"

Flit groaned.

Scraps held up a hand to indicate he wasn't finished. "Shadow is following protocol… but I don't think that is the right thing to do in this instance. The information we got is important, and if we are in a position to get more, we should take it."

Flit blinked. "What?"

"You were right. You have been all along."

"What are you talking about?" Flit's brows furrowed. In any other circumstance, she wouldn't stop someone from telling her she was right, but in this instance, she needed more clarity.

Scraps took her hand. He ran his thumb along the wedding

band she wore on her finger, the symbol of a relationship they had never really lived. "The Government has denied us too much. The Underground has had over a century to take action, and they haven't. If we can help fix things, then we need to do that, and that means taking calculated risks."

The surging tide of rage within Flit refused to be calmed, but as Scraps spoke, the emotion morphed into a swelling mix of gratitude and love. She gently tugged on Scrap's hand, pulling him closer. She looked up at him, searching his blue eyes and hoping to find the truth. "Do you really mean that?"

Scraps nodded. "I do. You and I aren't reckless. We're not going to run out and expose ourselves, but we are also not going to sit idly by. If you want a world where we can have a real relationship, where we don't have to hide… then I want to help you make that world."

"Scraps," Flit breathed, her fingers caressing his stubbly jawline. She gulped, throat aching with emotion. "Thank you, Scraps. I lo…"

Flit stopped. Once more, she had been about to let the words 'I love you' tumble from her lips. Her cheeks heated at the memory of how well that had gone, so she swallowed them back down.

"I really appreciate that," she finally said.

Scraps, oblivious, beamed. "Good. Now, let's get ready for work. We have a difference to make."

He leaned down and kissed her, and Flit's head spun. The morning had been such a rollercoaster of emotion, so she focused on what was real. Even though she didn't voice her true feelings, that didn't stop her from feeling them. She kissed Scraps with all the emotion she felt, and he responded with a fiery passion that made them both get carried away enough to be late for work.

WHILST THEIR ENTHUSIASM WAS HIGH, no amount of drive to make a difference could make the mundane aspects of their job go any faster. Luckily, they only had to wait another week before a new opportunity fell into their laps.

Flit looked at the file on her screen and spun around in her chair, poking Scraps' leg with the tip of her shoe. "Hey! Did you see the message from Jane?"

Scraps jumped. He turned, rubbing his face. "Uh, what message?"

Flit rolled her eyes. Judging by the tiny lines of text on his screen, he had gotten too absorbed in one of the policy reviews they had due the following week. She bit her lip to stop herself from making a playful remark about his eagerness to get a head start on the most boring work. Instead, she got up and walked across the work pod. She sat on the edge of his desk and tapped his screen, opening his inbox. Sure enough, Jane's e-mail was there.

Leaning forward again, Scraps read through it. "Another on-site review?" he asked, his brows furrowing. He flicked the screen back to their work log. It was already full enough that they would be coming in early every day the following week to try and catch up. "Surely there is another team with better availability."

Flicking back to the email screen, Flit pointed at the top field. "She sent it to us and us alone," Flit said pointedly.

Normally, Jane would either assign a job to a pair, or she would send out extra work requests to the team, giving people an opportunity to volunteer. Putting your hand up for extra, last-minute reviews was a great way to score schmooze points with the boss. The fact she had asked if Flit and Scraps were interested was new. There had to be more to the review than met the eye.

"Do you think we can get more information about it first?" Scraps rocked back in his seat and looked at Flit. "I can send her a message."

Flit stood, stretching her limbs as she looked out of their pod. At the far end of the office, she could see Jane typing away at her screen. There wasn't anyone in the office with her, and she didn't seem to be on a conference call. "Don't bother. We'll just pop over."

"There is a protocol to follow," Scraps reminded her.

Rolling her eyes, Flit stepped over to the door of their pod and put her hand against it. "Yeah, but that's so cold and impersonal. She doesn't look busy. Let's be social and drop in."

Sighing, Scraps got to his feet. Flit beamed at him, knowing she had won.

On their way across the office Flit stopped and chatted to various colleagues. Scraps, as usual, just smiled and made small talk where he could. Their coworkers relished the chance to chat or share a bit of gossip, and Flit figured it was an excellent way to ensure that they were well-liked.

When they got to Jane's office, Flit knocked on the glass door. Jane looked up and waved her hand, and the door slid open. "Ah, my prodigies. I take it you got my email?" She gestured for them to come in.

Flit smirked. *Prodigies?* If Jane was sweet-talking them, whatever she had was going to be particularly painful.

Flit walked over, plonking into the chair opposite of Jane's and leaning forward, resting her elbows on the edge of her desk. Scraps followed suit but sat with his back straight and expression far stiffer and more formal. "So, what is this wonderful task you have for your favourite employees?" Flit waggled her eyebrows, letting Jane know she was onto her.

Jane chuckled and turned her screen around so that Scraps and Flit could see it. She tapped a file, and some notes for a facility cascaded onto the screen, along with a map and a history of reviews.

"We have an annual assessment of one of our more… controversial facilities," Jane explained. "Last year, Jack and Michael handled the review, and it didn't go to well, to say the least. There were a few philosophical differences between them and the facilities workers, and things turned ugly. I would be willing to give them a second chance at it this year, but I think they would refuse. You two handled the weapons processing plant with tact, logic, and an admirable amount of initiative. I think you could handle this one too."

"Ah, and that is why you are buttering us up," Flit said, leaning back in her seat and smiling at Jane. "Please tell us more about what you meant when you said *philosophical differences*."

Jane tapped the screen and brought up an image of a building a few blocks away. It always had a contingent of Registereds guarding the door, and Flit had never really seen many people going in or out. She'd seen plenty getting turned away from the doors, though.

"This is the Department of Advanced Human Research," Jane explained. "It's so classified that the staff who work there are kept in the dark about the lunch menu."

Flit was already in. The idea of getting into such a highly classified building was why she was on the surface, but she didn't let Jane in on her eagerness. "Jane, this isn't about lunch menus…" Flit said in a singsong voice.

Jane sighed. "You're right. However, this facility has chewed up and spat out even my most experienced assessors. I can't actually give you more details until you agree, and I promote you both to improve your clearance rating, but suffice to say that when the department is called Advanced Human Research… you can safely assume that Human Research also equates to Human Experimentation."

A promotion?

Flit looked over at Scraps, who leaned in closer. His lips were still pressed together in that broody way of his, but there was a flicker of something in his eyes as he caught her gaze. Advanced Human Research wasn't anywhere near their mission objective, but Jane was practically begging them to do it, and knowledge was power. If push came to shove, any bit of information about the Government had the potential to be used as a weapon.

Flit turned back to Jane and gave her a determined nod. "We're in."

THE DOCUMENTS for the new review came through, with notification of a promotion in Flit's and Scraps' clearance levels. Flit knew immediately from how small the file was that they were onto something interesting. They were given little more than a list of policies numbers they would need to review and a date and address for their visit. Everything else, the file said, was on-site access only. They wouldn't really be finding out what they were looking at until they were there, and they would be required to work remotely on that site until their reports were compiled. If Flit had thought the Government was secretive about their weapons development, it was nothing compared to how tight they kept their human experiments to their chest.

Flit was about to tell Scraps that there was little to do to prepare when she turned around to find him working on a checklist and some notes to take with them. She could already tell from the set of his shoulders that he wasn't dealing well with the uncertainties the review presented, so she left him to it while she finished up their outstanding reports.

They received a message from the Department of Advanced Human Research, confirming their presence for the first two workdays of the next week, so any prep work Scraps could do would be helpful.

When the end of the day came, Flit and Scraps packed up and said farewell to the others. Flit was eager to get home and discuss the new review with Scraps. However, their attempt at a swift exit was interrupted as they walked out of the main office, towards the elevator, and got stopped by Liana as she leaned back against Chris' desk at reception.

"Hey, you two! Just the couple I was waiting for," Liana said, smiling as she got up.

Chris spun around in his chair and gave them both a playful salute in greeting.

"Oh no. That means trouble," Flit tutted with a wink.

Liana smirked. "What fun would we be if we didn't get into a little trouble?"

"Probably a lot. Whenever we spend time together, we get to bed way too late. I like my sleep," Scraps supplied, not entirely sarcastic.

Everyone laughed.

Flit shook her head and hitched her bag up on her shoulder. "So, what can we do for you?"

Chris looked at Liana, and she nodded before he turned back to them. "You remember Petra and Trey, right?" he asked.

Flit nodded. "Of course."

"Well, they own that club, Nightmix, in the basement of North Four-East Three. They have given us some VIP entries for tomorrow night and asked if you two would like to come along?" Chris looked between Flit and Scraps.

Scraps shifted beside Flit, and she already knew what he was going to say before he opened his mouth. "We've got a huge review next week. We need to prepare."

Chris groaned. "Oh, come on! You know what they say about all work and no fun…"

"No." Scraps shook his head. "Who are 'they', and what do they say?"

Chris and Liana laughed, taking Scraps' comment as a sign of a dry sense of humour rather than genuine naivety. A lot of the people they had met in the Hub saw it that way. Flit thought of it as an unexpected blessing.

Flit waved off Scraps' concern. "Brian's right. We do have a lot of work to do. But… I suppose it wouldn't hurt to pop by."

Liana's emerald eyes lit up. "Awesome. We'll forward you the invites. Just skip the line and flash them at the bouncers. No cover charge."

"Nice," Flit said, perking up. "See you there."

Flit and Scraps said their farewells to Chris and Liana and made their way down to the street.

When they were walking home, Scraps leaned closer to Flit. "Nightmix… That is a nightclub, isn't it?"

Flit nodded, excitement buzzing through her. When she lived in the Hub with her parents, she never had the time nor inclination to explore the nightclubs. She had been either in the Underground or purposefully avoiding those kinds of places to maintain her closely held cover. She was excited now, though, eager for an opportunity for her and Scraps to let their hair loose for a night.

"Ava?"

"Hmm?"

"What exactly does one do at a nightclub?" Scraps whispered.

Flit stopped walking and looked at him. Of course. Nightclubs wouldn't have been part of his experience, either.

"They drink. They socialise. They dance," Flit explained.

"Oh." Scraps paled. "Dancing…" Dread dripped off every syllable of his response.

Flit just chuckled and shook her head. "It'll be fine. We'll have a good night. At the very least, it will be an interesting diversion from our everyday life."

Scraps didn't look convinced, but when Flit reminded him that they were trying to make their own memories, he gulped, but his expression became resolute. Flit's heart warmed. He was consistently proving his open-mindedness and bravery when it came to new experiences, and she was so proud of how far he had come since she had rescued him from those rats.

35

———

SCRAPS

WHAT FLIT THOUGHT WOULD BE an interesting diversion was Scraps' idea of a nightmare.

He never understood the purpose of dancing. Music, he liked, but the odd undulations of the human body in time to the beat was something he had never attempted nor wanted to. As excited as Flit was, he just couldn't summon the enthusiasm. Combining their secret identities, dancing, loud music, and alcohol seemed like a terrible idea to Scraps. All the same, Flit had committed to it, and backing out would probably take more social finesse than just putting in a short appearance.

The following day after lunch, when Scraps was absorbed in his twenty-eighth 'How to Dance' tutorial on his datapad, he felt thoroughly unprepared. As he sat on the sleek but comfortable couch in their living room, he wondered how they had managed to wind up in such a predicament. From his understanding, professional dancers usually started in their early childhood and had years of vigorous training. All he would have to try and blend in was one afternoon with some vague video instruction.

"Scraps, hey… take a break. You've made all the lists and packed our bags. There is nothing else you could possibly do to make our review go smoother." Flit's voice came from behind Scraps, startling him.

Face flushing with embarrassment, he quickly minimised the

video. "Er, yeah. You're right. I should just leave the work stuff alone," he said as he got to his feet and shoved the datapad onto its holder on the side table.

"I'm gonna head out for a walk to grab a few things for tonight. Want to come?" Flit asked, rolling a hair elastic off her wrist and cajoling her honey brown hair into a high ponytail.

"Like what?" Scraps asked, unsure of what supplies they would need to go clubbing.

Flit shrugged. "A new dress, probably. Maybe some new lingerie too."

Scraps bit his lip at the mention of lingerie. In the past few months, he had discovered that what the Hub had to offer was far superior to any of the standard-issue stuff Flit defaulted to in the Underground. He wasn't sure what Flit would get this time, but he wanted to be surprised. He also wanted some time to try the dance moves he had been watching for the past couple of hours.

"No, I'll be fine. Thanks. I might just stick around here. Catch up on news and stuff." Scraps pointed back to the datapad.

"Suit yourself. Send me a message if you think of anything we need while I'm gone." Flit teleported over and kissed him before making for the door.

The moment she was gone, Scraps got to work. He had spent too long making excuses for his inability to do the most mundane things that the Citizens or Underground Derivates did. This time, he wanted to impress Flit with some smooth skills, however basic. He had mastered complex telekinetic abilities and was a strong in hand-to-hand combatant.

How hard could dancing possibly be?

"THAT IS NOT DANCING," Scraps claimed, dumbfounded, as he and Flit stepped through the doors of Nightmix.

It was like the entire morning commute had squeezed themselves inside the club. It was mostly dark, with a dizzying rainbow of strobe lights flashing in time with music so loud Scraps could barely hear himself think.

Flit grabbed his arm and pulled him down to her level. "What did you say?" She yelled the words right into his ear, but instead of hurting, it made it possible to hear her over the throbbing music.

Scraps pointed to the dance floor in the middle of the room, with people writhing and undulating against each other. It looked less like the dancing tutorials he had seen on his datapad and more like the content that came with adults-only warnings in the Underground.

"That—" Scraps said, this time close to Flit's ear, "—is not dancing!"

Flit smirked up at him. He bit his lip as he let his eyes wander farther down her body to the beautiful dress she was wearing. Made of mercurial silver fabric, the neckline sank low into the valley between her breasts, and the dress clung to every dip and curve of her body. When he had first seen it before they'd left the house, he'd done a double take. He had seen Flit in dresses before, but the veritable scrap of fabric she slipped on was something else entirely. It made him feel simultaneously over- and underdressed in a sleek pair of black pants and a black collared shirt.

"Come on. Let's find the others." Flit looped an arm through his and led him farther into the club.

He balked at first, not sure how they would make their way through the wall of humanity around the dance floor. Flit, however, had no such problem. Being smaller, it was much easier for her to wedge herself between the loosely formed groups and weave a zig-zagged path towards the bar. Scraps, clinging tightly to Flit, did his best to follow the path she blazed, apologising as he brushed against person after person.

The club, like most places in the Hub, was an impressive mix of technology and sleek design. The bar featured an interactive benchtop where you could order. It freed the staff up to make the drinks, and the line moved quickly. A series of dark metallic standing height tables lined a wall that overlooked the dance floor, ending at a set of stairs that wound up to the mezzanine level. Scraps perked up as he saw a head of familiar teal hair at one of the tables. He nudged Flit and then pointed in Andy's direction. Flit didn't bother verbalising a response. She just nodded and led the way over.

The tables to the side were out of the main blasting radius of the speakers. Still, as they approached, they had to lean in close to be able to talk to Andy.

"It's good to see you two again!" Andy called out over the music, her lips stretching in a wide smile as the multi-coloured lights of the club flashed in her eyes. "Chris and Liana are just getting a drink. Go help yourself. Tell them you're with me. It's on the house."

Scraps looked between Flit and the bar. He could just see Chris and Liana at the back of the line. "Are you drinking tonight?" he asked Flit, wishing they had discussed the practicality of it before.

Flit shook her head and turned around, pressing her hands against his chest and getting to her toes so she could reach his ear. "No, but we need to get something. Order anything called a mocktail. It will be non-alcoholic."

Scraps nodded before he disappeared, leaving Flit to make small talk with Andy while he approached Chris and Liana. He gently tapped their shoulders and was greeted with a warm hug from Liana.

"Glad you could make it!"

Scraps would have liked to talk to his friends, but the pounding music made it impossible to communicate with any efficiency, so he stood behind Chris and Liana in the line and looked around. Flit was not the only one wearing the barest hint of fabric for a dress. Scraps noticed, with a blush, that many of the women in the club wore outfits that might pass for sleepwear in another setting. The men seemed to be more covered, like him, but there were a few in outfits with sheer panels or fabrics that clung to them in revealing places.

When they got to the bar, Chris and Liana ushered Scraps forward to put an order in with them. He surfed the menu, ordering the first 'mocktail' he could find for Flit and some water for himself.

As they stepped to the side to wait for their order, Chris leaned in. "You look bewildered. Were the clubs in Eastbay not as lively as this?"

Scraps froze for a moment, trying to figure out what the right answer was. His study didn't account for the nightlife in Eastbay. He shook his head. "Not the ones I went to."

Chris laughed. "Well, Petra and Trey run a great place. They're busy dealing with management type things now, but we'll see them later tonight."

All Scraps could do was nod in reply. There was no use shouting to be heard over the music.

It was only a minute before the bartender slipped a tray onto the bar with their drinks. Scraps gulped. He had no idea how he could pick that up and get it back to the table without spilling it all down his front and making a fool out of himself. If he could use his abilities, perhaps he could manage. He was saved from trying to figure it out as Chris slipped the tray off the countertop and carried it in one hand.

Scraps followed along, watching his friend with awe. As he fell along beside Liana, he leaned over. "Did Chris work as a waiter in the past?" he asked as the other man danced around drunken Citizens who were gyrating about like they were the only ones in the room.

Liana snorted an amused laugh. "Hardly. He just loves his drinks. If he spills a single drop, he'll be devastated for weeks."

That sounded right to Scraps. He remembered some of the banter about not spilling drinks on the first boat trip he had gone on with his colleagues. However, that had only seemed to apply when they had still been sober. He wondered if Chris would be less concerned about spilling his beverages if he was more inebriated later in the night. He would have to come up with a contingency plan in case he had to carry the next tray of drinks.

Andy and Flit cheered as the trio arrived at the table. Chris distributed the drinks, and Scraps slid in beside Flit.

Andy leaned past her and said, "I heard a congratulations is in order. A clearance promotion at work? How did you score that so fast? Jane must really like you."

Flit's laughter pealed above the music, and Scraps settled a hand on her hip as he watched her carefully, wary of what she was saying about their work in a place like this.

"I am surprised too," Flit said with a shrug. "After the ruckus we caused with the last inspection, I thought she might bench us for a while. Most departments don't like having their feathers ruffled."

Andy smirked. "And you feel like ruffling some feathers, huh?"

"Of course not!" Scraps said quickly, shaking his head.

"I'm not ruffling feathers," Flit said innocently. "I am performing my duty. You know, for the good of all." She scoffed and then added with a dismissive wave, "And all that shit."

Heart thundering in his chest, Scraps looked between Flit and Andy, wondering if his girlfriend had finally pushed things too far. He adored Flit, but it was moments like this that he wished she was a little more careful.

"Yes, Ava, for the good of all." The teal-haired woman gave a lackadaisical salute, and then she and Flit burst into giggles.

Scraps let out a breath of relief and shook his head as he leaned back.

"She's trouble, your wife."

Scraps looked to his left to see Chris smirking back at him. He sighed and nodded. "Oh, you don't know the half of it…"

AFTER SOME MORE CASUAL BANTER, the group took to the dance floor. Well, Scraps thought of it as more of a stand-and-gyrate floor. All the practice he had done while Flit had been out of the apartment had left him thoroughly unprepared for the evening's activities. Flit didn't seem apprehensive, though. She took his hands, settled them around her waist, and then draped her own arms around his neck. Standing so close to her like that, Scraps could hardly find it within himself to care much about what the other people packed onto the dance floor were doing.

While Scraps could concede that dancing would never be a strength of his, he did enjoy it. It became just another opportunity to hold Flit's soft, warm body in his arms. Once he got used to the sheer amount of people around them, he let them fade away. His hands settled over her lower back, gently rubbing his thumbs along the dangerous amount of skin exposed by the drape of her dress. He leaned closer, letting the music throb against him as he breathed her in. The strangest feeling of freedom overwhelmed him in that moment. He was just one person amongst a sea of others, doing something so simple and instinctive. There was no one to hide from, no one to run from, no one trying to tell him what to do.

The music was still playing when someone tapped on Scraps' shoulder. Jolted out of the moment, he turned back to see Andy and Liana. He looked at the two women curiously, wondering where Chris had disappeared too. Andy either didn't sense or didn't care about his confusion as she offered Flit her hand, and Liana reached out for his. As much as he wanted to keep dancing with Flit, she accepted Andy's offer with a smirk and draped her arms around the taller woman's neck, and Scraps was left with no choice but to dance with Liana or head for their table and sit on his own.

Sensing his resignation, Liana smiled broadly and took both of his hands. She didn't get nearly as close to him as Andy did to Flit, but he didn't mind. She leaned in only enough so that she could speak and be heard over the music. "It's good to see you and Ava out here, you know," she started.

Scraps nodded. "We're not really the clubbing types, but it has made for an interesting night out."

"Chris and I aren't really the clubbing types either. There's another reason we come here," Liana admitted.

Standing so close to her, he caught a whiff of the rather lovely perfume she always wore and took in for the first time just how pretty she was. "Why else would you come here?"

"It is a good place to meet likeminded people," Liana confessed, leaning in close enough that her warm breath brushed against Scraps' cheek. "I can see Ava has a rebellious spirit… but do you?"

Freezing on the spot, Scraps drew back to look at the friend he was dancing with. Her green eyes took on a searing intensity. He shifted under her gaze and looked over to Flit, hoping she would jump in to rescue him, but she and Andy were dancing far too close and having far too much fun to even look his way. He might have been jealous if he didn't appreciate the sight so much.

He turned back to Liana and cleared his throat. "Er, well, Ava and I agree on many things…" Scraps trailed off as he slipped a finger into his collar and tugged it out a little. Was it getting hot in the room, or was it just him?

His non-answer seemed to be enough to make Liana smile. She grabbed his hand, winked past him at Andy, and dragged him off the dance floor. Scraps wasn't sure where she was taking him, but once he looked over his shoulder and noted that Andy and Flit were only a few footsteps behind, he gave in and let himself be led away.

36

———

FLIT

ONE MOMENT, Flit was having a bit too much fun dancing with Andy, and the next, the teal-haired beauty was leading her towards a door at the back of the club, quite discretely disguised behind two potted plants. Flit caught Scraps' gaze as Liana dragged him ahead of her and Andy, and he just gave her a helpless shrug.

The corridor was sparsely lit and free of décor and other fussiness. There were two doors on the right-hand wall and one at the end of the corridor. They passed a side door before Liana pushed the end one open, and clean, bright light spilled out. Flit snatched her arm back and covered her eyes with her arm. She guessed that the hallway was dim to keep the light from this new room from flooding into the club every time the door was opened.

Flit lowered her arm and blinked enough for her eyes to adjust. They were standing in a modern sitting room with two sleek couches and a holographic-projector topped coffee table. Chris was sitting opposite of Petra and Trey. Flit was a little surprised that she hadn't even noticed Chris leave the dance floor. Then again, she and Scraps had been in their own little world for quite some time.

When their eyes met, Chris gave her a bright smile, full of mischief before turning to Andy and raising a single eyebrow at her in.

"You were right," Andy conceded.

Liana let go of Scraps and picked up a cocktail off a tray on the table. She took a sip before saying smugly, "Told you so."

Andy left Flit's side and walked over to stand behind the couch, settling one hand on Trey's shoulder and another on Petra's.

Flit pressed her lips together impatiently. She felt like she was back in the Mess, waiting for Sway and Acumen to let her in on some wager they had made between themselves. "Told you what?"

Petra rose from her seat and smiled at Flit. "Just that you'd fit in well here." She set her drink down. "We've got someone we'd like you both to meet."

Flit looked over at Scraps, whose lips were pressed together, brows furrowed. She could see the concern in his eyes, and she let out a soft sigh and shrugged. She had no idea what was going on, but if the others thought it was important enough to draw them off the dance floor, she was willing to hear them out.

"Sure. Why not?" Flit walked over to Scraps and slipped her hand into his. Her ears were still ringing from the relative silence in this room, but she made a resolution to remain on her guard. She trusted Chris and Liana, but this situation was getting more suspicious by the second.

The others got to their feet.

"Come on," Petra urged them, walking to the back of the room.

Flit frowned as they followed, skirting around the sleek couches towards the blank rear wall. Just as Flit was about to ask what was going on, Petra slid her hand up behind an ordinary holoscreen and looked at Flit and Scraps over her shoulder.

"I take it you two can keep a secret?" Petra asked.

Flit snorted.

Squeezing her hand, Scraps cleared his throat. "Yes. Confidentiality is an important part of our job. It always has been."

Looking uncertain, Petra turned to Chris and Liana.

"It's fine. I swear," Chris promised.

With a sigh, Petra ran her fingers over the wall behind the screen. There was a low hiss, and two creases that looked like normal gaps between panels deepened as part of the wall slid back and then to the side, revealing a dark, downward passage that was cut from the concrete that had to be the foundations of the levels around them.

Petra and Trey led the way, with Andy and Liana following them. Scraps' grip tightened on Flit's hand as a warning flashed in his eyes. Flit could tell he was about to turn and walk away when Chris stepped closer to them.

"I know this seems a little crazy, but… we trust you guys so much. Please trust us too. Just give it a go, ok?" Chris said in a low tone as the others disappeared around the curved, downward ramp.

"Ava?" Scraps' tone wavered with obvious uncertainty.

Flit levelled a serious glance at Chris. "What's down there?"

"Just someone we'd like you to meet. I'd say more, but we need to be careful. If you want to leave at any time, just let me know, and I'll show you out. Promise."

Flit wished she was a telepath. She would love to know what Scraps was thinking.

Actually, she probably already did. She was sure some lines of the Covert Operations Manual were running through his head, as well as Shadow's demand that they keep out of trouble. Flit wasn't sure if it was the prospect of something new and secretive that drew her towards the opening in the back of the room or her frustration at Shadow's lack of trust in them, but she started walking, dragging Scraps along with her.

The passageway was narrow, with the rough concrete walls sporadically lined with pipes, wires, and exposed steel supports. Flit suspected that whoever cut this passage had no idea what they were doing. She was at least grateful that they had taped off or re-joined any live wires along the way. Looking over her shoulder, Flit kept track of how many steps they had taken from the door and the various line of sight angles in the curved descent. If something bad happened, she and Scraps would be able to teleport away, and he could blast through the door faster than the others would be able to understand what was happening.

The passageway eventually opened into a bunker. Thanks to the internal compass she had developed during her years spent traversing subterranean labyrinths, Flit figured they were now below the main dance floor of the club. Various-sized crates and stacks of chairs were lined up along the outskirts of the room in neat rows. In the corner, there was a large L-shaped desk with several monitors on it. The light from them fell on the face of a handsome but sharp-featured man in his mid-forties. Hearing the arrival of the group, he turned around, his black eyebrows raising in question.

"Adam, this is the couple we told you about," Chris said, stepping forward with a wide smile on his face.

Adam got out of his seat and walked towards them, running his eyes up and down Flit and Scraps appraisingly as the others stepped back in almost reverential silence. Flit hated that kind of cool assessment in his gaze, almost as if he thought he could see right through them. She stood straighter, and Scraps stepped that little bit closer to her side.

"Have you told them?" Adam asked.

Chris shook his head. "I figured you would want to meet them first."

Flit took that moment of Adam's distraction to peer past him. On the desk he just left, there were several different spray cans with dried red drips drizzled from the nozzles. There was also a metal sheet with something cut out of it tucked between the edge of the desk and the wall.

Adam cleared his throat. Flit wanted to keep looking around, but she decided to play nice and let the stranger speak. For now.

"If these wonderful people have brought you down here to meet me, I can only assume you hold a certain level of… dissatisfaction with the way that our society is currently being run."

Scraps stiffened beside her. "I wouldn't say that," he informed Adam, shifting uncomfortably on the spot as all eyes fell on them.

"None of us would. Openly, at least," Adam conceded with a shrug, "but whether we say it or not, it is what we feel."

Scraps didn't bother arguing with that.

Flit tilted her head to the side to get a better look at the graceful curves that were cut out of the metal sheet, and her eyes widened.

"If you've been brought here, it also means that Chris and Liana thought you both had not only the attitude but the ability to do something to help our cause," Adam continued, straightening up and stepping closer again. He reached out, offering Scraps his hand to shake. "So, please, allow me to introduce myself. My name is Adam, leader of the—"

"Wait, wait!" Flit waved her hands excitedly and bounced on the balls of her feet. If she'd been in the Underground, she would have teleported around in several animated hops as she spoke. "Let me guess."

Adam's face contorted with disparagement at her sudden interruption.

Scraps grabbed her hand and squeezed it. "Ava, sweetie… Why don't you let Adam talk?"

Flit rolled her eyes impatiently and continued, unperturbed. "If you're down here, in a rough-hewn bunker beneath a thumping nightclub, you're trying to hide something. You've already said you don't like the way the city is run. Those spray paint cans over there look like they've seen a bit of use recently, and, if I'm not mistaken, that metal sheet in the corner would make a great template for a bit of recreational graffiti!"

Out of the corner of her eye, Flit saw Chris and Liana smirking. Petra, Trey, and Andy seemed a little more surprised but no less impressed.

"Now, I'm no detective, but I'm willing to bet a big haul of chocolate bars that you guys are the Free Citizens," Flit finished triumphantly.

Scraps looked at Flit, eyes wide as he connected the dots. He pressed his lips together and straightened his shoulders as he regained his composure. "That's a big assumption to make, Ava," he said, clearly trying to give them an out.

Flit shrugged and turned to Adam. "So, am I right?"

Adam looked over at Chris and Liana. "Is this the woman who thought that spreading our logo around was… cute?"

Liana choked back a laugh and covered it as she cleared her throat. "Er, yes. That was Ava," she said, giving Flit an apologetic look.

"And ineffective," Flit added. If he had to know what she said, he might as well know all of it. Her opinion still stood. She didn't care who she was talking to.

Scraps' hand tightened around hers. "Ava…"

Adam gestured to the stack of chairs. Trey started to unpack them and spread them around. He set one down for Adam first and then for Flit and Scraps.

"Please, sit," Adam urged them.

Flit sank into her chair, but Scraps frowned and stood at her side, resting a hand on her shoulder as he remained vigilant.

"I understand that you believe that our acts of resistance have been ineffective, but we are spreading the seeds of dissent among the Citizens of the Hub," Adam said slowly, as if he was explaining it all to a person much younger than Flit.

"Sure, you pissed the Government off a bit," Flit scoffed. "But at this point, they are catching the paintings and covering them up before anyone gets to see them. Given that you're getting almost no media attention for it all, what are you actually achieving?"

Adam narrowed his eyes at her. "Oh?"

Bristling at her comment, Trey leaned in closer as he sat down. "Ava, give us at least a little bit of credit. We're starting an underground movement here—"

"Like, literally underground," Petra added, pointing at the concrete ceiling above their head, seeming impressed with herself.

Flit burst into laughter.

Everyone looked at her like she had grown a second head. Scraps' grip on her shoulders was so tight that it almost hurt. He leaned down. "Ava… please," he pleaded.

Catching her breath, Flit rubbed some amused tears out of her eyes and cleared her throat, doing her best to look contrite. It wasn't an expression that sat naturally on her face. "Sorry… I just…. Look, honestly, I appreciate what you guys are getting at, but if all you ever do is paint some symbols on the walls, you're never going to get anywhere. If the Government catch you, you'll wind up in prison, and for what? A bit of unlawful graffiti? If you're going to put yourselves at risk, at least do it for something worthwhile."

When she finished speaking, Adam looked at her the same way her sparring partners did when she was training in the Underground. Flit crossed her arms over her chest. He sized her up, refusing to back down.

"If our current methods are ineffective, what would you suggest?" he asked evenly as he watched her.

Flit knew a test when she saw one. "If you really want to shake the Government? I'd say you need to—"

"Okay, Ava darling. I think you've had a little too much to drink." Scrap stepped around the chair and stood between Flit and Adam.

Flit frowned up at him. "But I've only had mockta—"

Scraps ignored her and turned back to Adam. "As much as we appreciate the trust you have put in us, Ava and I really must go. We have an early morning, and—"

"Early? It's the weekend!" Flit argued.

"We really must go." Scraps grabbed Flit's hand and helped her stand. She looked at him, the corner of her lips curling into a frown.

Getting to his feet too, Adam walked over. "You two clearly need to talk about this. When you decide if you want to tell us whatever it is you think we need to know to improve our processes, please reach out. Chris and Liana will be your contacts."

Scraps nodded. "Thank you, Adam. It was... nice to meet you."

Wrapping an arm around Flit's shoulder, Scraps led her away before she could say anything else that he clearly feared would get them into trouble.

37

SCRAPS

IT WAS a quiet and hurried trip home. Judging by the disgruntled pout on Flit's face and the way she muttered at the smallest inconveniences on the walk back, she was frustrated. Scraps understood why. He wished he had found a better way to remind her of their purpose in the Hub, but with so many people around, he had little choice but to cut her short. He wanted to hear what Adam had to say, but he and Flit needed to discuss how to best portray themselves.

Scraps was still in a state of shock at the revelation that their closest friends in the Hub were involved in a Citizen-resistance movement. Chris and Liana were good people, and had spoken several times of their frustration at the Government, but he never pictured them actively flouting the rules, especially not when they worked in a department focused on compliance!

When they got back to their apartment, Flit shut the door behind them and walked over to the dining table, unceremoniously dumping her clutch onto it as she sat down and unbuckled the straps on her heels.

Scraps undid the buttons on his cuffs. "I just thought we should talk about it, alone, before you said much more."

Flit kicked off her shoes before leaning back in her seat, sighing and looking up at him. "We could have gotten some really good intel off them tonight." She shook her hair out of the low, messy bun at the nape of her neck.

"I understand that, but we don't know the Free Citizens. We have to be careful." Scraps leaned against the kitchen island bench, watching her warily. "We need to watch what we say around them."

"What is that supposed to mean?" Flit snapped.

"When Adam asked what you thought would be more effective, what were you going to say?" Scraps looked at her seriously.

Tearing her eyes away from him, Flit leaned farther back in her seat and crossed one leg over the other. "What else was I supposed do?" She raked a hand through her hair. "I couldn't deny the comment, and it's not like we could scold them for being rebels and walk away. Who knows what they would have done to us? We were fucked the minute we walked into that bunker. Now they know who we are. If we don't go along with it, we'll be making some potentially dangerous enemies."

Scraps blinked. He hadn't thought of that. It was a good point. What would Adam and the others have done if he and Flit had shown open disagreement with their reveal? Surely, after letting them in on such a secret, they would have had to have some insurance against them telling the Government.

Scraps groaned and walked over, sinking onto the couch beside Flit. "Well, there is a difference between not showing outrage and giving them ideas. We don't know what they will do with any suggestions you give them."

"So, what do we do, then?" Flit threw her hands up in the air, exasperated.

After taking a few moments to consider it, Scraps finally said, "We will not reach out to them, but we won't reject them if they contact us. I also think we should inform Shadow and see what he would like us to do, as this is not part of our briefing. The Underground might already have agents investigating the Free Citizens."

Flit's knees bounced up and down so rapidly that they looked like they were vibrating. "Yeah, because it worked out so well the last time we gave Shadow bonus information."

Scraps settled his hand gently on her leg to stop the increasing agitation. "We didn't go looking for this. We made friends. They dragged us into it. I'll send Shadow a message, let him know, and maybe he can give us some ideas about the appropriate protocol for this situation."

In the blink of an eye, Flit had teleported from the couch to stand in the middle of the living room. Scraps' hand fell to the warm cushion, and he looked up at her as she crossed her arms and her hip popped out to the side.

"If you're convinced that writing the message is the right way to go about this, then go for it. I'm not so sure. Honestly, I wouldn't be surprised if Shadow pulls the plug on this whole thing because of it. If he was pissed last time, he will be utterly furious now."

There was no point arguing. Instead, Scraps levitated the datapad from the side table over to settle it onto his knees. He went through the log-in screens to open up his messages, and he started typing out something to Shadow, being sure to stress that he and Flit accidentally stumbled across this one, and they would like guidance on how to proceed. Each full stop he typed was punctuated by a cabinet door slamming shut as Flit moved about the open-plan kitchen and poured herself some water. Scraps winced at the sound, but he finished the message and sent it before she could change her mind.

When he was done, Scraps floated the datapad back over to its charger and got up, turning and walking into the kitchen. He leaned against the bench as Flit finished her water. "Please do not be angry with me."

Flit froze, her hand tight around the cup. She swallowed the water she had in her mouth, set the cup down with a heavy sigh, and shook her head. "I'm not pissed off with you," she said with a shrug. "I mean, I may not agree with the fact we didn't get more information, but you're right. It isn't our briefing."

That had been far too easy.

"You are clearly still upset about something." Scraps gestured warily to where her hands were gripping onto the edge of the bench so tight that her fingertips were turning white.

She looked down, frowned, and then crossed her arms and shoved her hands under her armpits so she couldn't see them.

"I just wanted one night, Scraps!" She threw her momentarily tucked hands into the air in frustration. "One damn night where you and I could go out with our friends, dance, relax, have some fun… maybe come home and tangle into bed! You know, one night to feel—" Flit turned around and slammed her palms on the counter "—normal! Scraps, I wanted one night with you to feel normal!"

All of Flit's anger melted as her shoulders hunched, and she hung her head. Those words, that posture, it was like a punch to Scraps' gut. His own shoulders sagged as he walked over to her and wrapped his arms around her from behind. He held her tight and pressed a kiss against that soft, sweet-smelling spot behind her ear.

Leaning into him, Flit cupped the back of his head and held him to her. "It was nice being on the dance floor with you. There were so many people around us, and for a little while, I forgot about all the shit we've got going on."

Scraps took hold of Flit's hips and spun her around to face him. "Nightmix is not the only place we can dance."

Stepping back from Flit, Scraps summoned the datapad into his waiting palms. He turned all the lights off and deactivated the electrochromatic function on the windows so that the lights from the city beyond shone in like stars. With another tap of his finger, one of the songs from the club starting playing through the sound system.

Flit looked up at him, her head tilted to the side. "Scraps?"

"I was sad the dancing ended too." He held a hand out to her in a silent offer.

"Really?" Flit seemed surprised.

Scraps swiped at the datapad screen and brought up the dance tutorial he had watched earlier that day. He let it play for a few seconds while Flit looked between his face and the video, her smile growing wider with every passing moment. "I studied for the dancing because I wanted to impress you," he confessed, "but I much preferred just holding you close without all of the complex steps."

A small, joyous laugh bubbled from Flit. Finally, she took the hand he offered and stepped closer. "Scraps, you are such a dork," she said fondly, nothing but endearment behind her words.

Scraps placed the datapad on the bench and led her to their private dance floor. Despite his concern about the situation they were wound up in, he found that his worries floated away once Flit was in his arms, her head resting against his chest. He leaned down, kissing her hair and breathing her in. She was right. Life would be so much better if they could have continued their night without interruption. One day, he hoped he could give her that.

THE MESSAGE from Shadow came through bright and early the next morning. Scraps and Flit didn't get it until they finally tumbled out of bed around midday. Scraps read it aloud while Flit got breakfast ready. He was not surprised when Shadow told them to retreat from further meetings carefully and in a way that would not arouse suspicion. They were not to show outright disagreement with the Free Citizens, but they had to do their best to step back. They couldn't be caught fraternising with them, and their agenda had nothing to do with their mission or the Underground's purpose.

Upon hearing the message, Flit sighed, shook her head, and muttered something about Shadow under her breath that Scraps was glad he couldn't hear. She didn't argue, though, and Scraps was pleased about that. Instead of lingering over the Free Citizens issue, the pair spent their weekend doing bits of research for their next assignment and catching up on some movies that Flit swore were 'classics'. Scraps wasn't a fan of the manufactured drama and terribly inaccurate historical costuming of a lot of them, but he did enjoy the opportunity to sit on the couch and hold Flit to his side without interruption, so he just went with it.

38

FLIT

AFTER THE ROCKY start to the weekend, the rest of it went by smoothly. It was a lovely chance for Flit and Scraps to relax and spend some time together before what was going to be a big week at work. The frustration of the situation with the Free Citizens was a niggling presence in the back of her mind, and when Chris and Liana messaged casually asking how they were after *a big night at the club*, Flit responded with a generic thumbs-up character and ignored the follow-up texts. She didn't like it, but she and Scraps needed to play it cool. The problem was, once she opened her mouth, she didn't trust herself to close it again.

In some ways, the impending, yet controversial, assignment at the Department of Advanced Human Research was a relief. They wouldn't be going back to their office on floor ninety-eight until they were done, so they could avoid any difficult questions from their Citizen friends until then.

As usual, it was difficult for Flit to summon the motivation to get out of bed on the first day of the week. Scraps, however, was already up and ready by the time she managed it. She dragged her sleepy self into the shower and made the water a little colder than was comfortable so she wouldn't linger. It was invigorating enough that she was able to get dressed and think about breakfast as she made her way back into the kitchen. Scraps sat on a stool on one side of their island counter, buried in a text-heavy file on his datapad.

"I still do not like the idea of going into the building without any sort of intel," Scraps said by way of morning greeting.

Flit didn't hold the lack of real salutation against him. She could tell by just how his eyebrows had furrowed into one straight, thick, furry line that he was stressed out, so she walked over, slipped her arm around his shoulder, and kissed his cheek.

With a sigh, Scraps set the datapad down on the counter and slid it towards her. She looked down at the non-disclosure agreement they had been told to sign in preparation and snorted. "Yeah, sure. Ava won't say a thing about this facility. I promise," Flit muttered to herself as she entered in her cover's credentials and then confirmed it with her fingerprint. "But you can bet your arse Flit will."

That was enough to make Scraps chuckle as he took the datapad back and opened their case briefing. "Are you having breakfast?"

Flit looked at the time. "How about we stop by that new café they opened up in North-Two West-One on the way? I think a nice hearty breakfast will be a good start to the day."

Scraps perked up at the idea. "That would be a great start, indeed!"

"Then it's a date," Flit gave him another kiss on the cheek before she stepped back. "Let me get my stuff together, and we'll head out. If we don't take too long to eat, we should be able to walk. It'll be good to work off some of this energy before diving into it."

WITH FULL BELLIES and well-stretched legs, Flit and Scraps came to a stop across the road from the Department of Advanced Human Research and looked up at the towering glass monolith before them. Even though every surface was covered in windows, they were all electrochromatic and impossible to see through. The building was curved but came to a sharp point at the front. It made the whole façade feel more like a giant, impeccably polished scalpel than an actual building.

The front door, as she remembered, was guarded by a team of Registereds who stood in their crisp uniforms, visors opaque, shoulders stiff. Flit bit her lip. She wanted to reach out and hug them then drag them all back to the Underground. She hated that she couldn't do anything to help them.

"Flit…" Scraps' voice was low as his hand wrapped around the fists she balled at her side.

Startled, Flit looked at him. She didn't realise she'd been squeezing her hands so tight. She let out a soft breath and relaxed them then threaded her fingers through Scraps'. "Mmm?"

"Promise me that, no matter what you see in there, you won't lash out."

Flit almost choked. "You're asking me to behave?"

A cool shadow fell over her in the reflected morning light as Scraps stepped between her and the view of the Registereds across the street. He gently took her chin in his hand and leaned down to kiss her. When he pulled back, his eyes were full of affection and concern. "I am serious. This department, being so classified, will have the best monitoring systems around. No matter how hard it is, we cannot afford to slip up. When we get home, you can rant and rave all you like. But in there?" Scraps stopped, looking back over his shoulder to take in the building before he turned back to her. "In there, please… be safe."

Even though she was frustrated that he'd asked her to behave, Flit's shoulders sagged. Scraps' voice was so full of genuine concern and affection that she couldn't deny him. Besides, he made a good point. A building like that was no place to run her mouth unless she had a death wish. Before Flit was able to reconcile the fact that this was a terrible idea because she could never keep her mouth shut, she grabbed Scraps' hand and dragged him across the road to join the people trickling into the building.

One of the Registereds held up a scanner as they approached. "Citizens, please halt for authentication," he intoned. After a moment, the scanner beeped. "Cleared. You may enter."

Flit gave him a winning smile. "Thanks! Have a great day."

Beside her, Scraps tightened his grip on her hand and dragged her through the doors with a frustrated huff.

If Flit and Scraps thought a team of Registereds guarding a single front door was excessive security, it was nothing compared to what was waiting for them inside. The measures there were far more stringent than even Centre One.

Flit looked around with awe as the sleek, black-marble floored lobby led to a glowing blue forcefield in front of a bank of elevators. At strategically placed gaps in the forcefields, Registereds in all black uniforms stood and inspected the people filtering through. The other workers who walked in ahead of and behind Flit and Scraps approached as if it was nothing. The Registereds held their identity scanners and watched the passersby with intense concentration.

She subtly tugged on Scraps' hand. When he looked down at her, she tapped her head in question, and he nodded. He brushed off the chest-area of his shirt with a wink, and Flit frowned. He tilted his head towards the row of Registereds, and she realised they all had small tags affixed to their shirts. The letters were a deep red, and she couldn't read them, but as Scraps started guiding their approach the words were clear. 'Mandatory Mental Screening Agent' with a small, predictable 'For the Good of All' written beneath it.

Well, that confirmed it. Flit tried to clear her mind as they approached and wiped her sweaty palms on her trousers. Instead of focusing on her nerves, she decided to think about something else.

"Just scanning your Identification, Citizen," the Registered said in a rigid tone as he held the scanner out behind her, parallel to her neck.

The Registered watched Flit closely, and she conjured the most consuming recent memory she had, the one of what she and Scraps did up against the apartment window after they finished dancing.

There was a soft beep as the identity scanner approved her chip.

"H-Have a good day, Citizen," the Registered stumbled over

his words, and Flit had a feeling that, if she could see behind his visor, he would be blushing at what he'd found in her mind.

When it was Scraps' turn, the Registered must have recognised him from Flit's thoughts, and he cleared his throat and spluttered out a warning he would scan Scraps. After a beep of confirmation, the Registered told them to head to level four, and Flit gave him a thanks and a smile before she and Scraps made for the nearest elevator.

"What was that about?" Scraps muttered under his breath.

"What was what?" she returned, feigning confusion.

Scraps shook his head but didn't say more as the elevator arrived, and they stepped in.

The ride up was quick, and when they got out, they found themselves in another large waiting area. They had to walk through a second set of scanners, manned by a team of two Registereds, before they made their way across a white marble floor and spoke to the receptionist. She told them that their contact would be advised of their arrival and to take a seat.

As much as Flit wanted to get this job over and done with, she took the chance to inspect the space seriously. This level was as cold and clinical as any of the Government's other buildings. With an underwhelming colour pallet of white, black, and brushed steel, there was nothing even remotely inviting about the waiting space. The benches themselves were lined up against the wall underneath a large, metal cutting of the Government's logo. Flit shifted uncomfortably in her seat as she thought about what they might encounter.

While they were waiting, several people walked past and through the secure door behind the reception desk. It was the standard start-of-the-work-day influx. When it started to dwindle, Flit looked at Scraps and then at the screen of the datapad in her bag, and she frowned. She was just about to get up and ask the receptionist if she had informed their contact of their arrival, but the door slid open and a middle-aged man with a dour, prematurely frown-lined face and sharp chestnut eyes strode over.

Scraps and Flit got to their feet as the man looked between them with impatience tugging at his forced smile. "You must be Ava and Brian? I'm Doctor McNeill."

"You got it," Flit chimed in.

As Dr. McNeill turned to her, his eyebrow twitched with irritation. "I'm one of the sub-directors here at the Department of Advanced Human Research." He pulled out a datapad that he had tucked under his arm and tapped the screen a few times before looking up at them. "Have you been briefed about what you will be doing here?"

"Yes, well, as much as we could have been," Flit said with an easy smile, "but there were so many classified areas in our data that I thought you guys were creating a new shade of red. "

Doctor McNeill's facial expression was one of utter contempt.

"We will be doing a standard annual review on compliance to policies and procedures," Scraps supplied, stepping in before Flit throttled the smug doctor.

McNeill rolled his eyes. "I do not know why they insist on sending you people over here. It's a waste of our time and yours. Compliance to policy and procedure is written into our operation. We conduct our own reviews on a fortnightly basis."

Without another word, McNeill turned around and strode towards the lone door that was opposite the elevator. There was a slight beep as the chip reader recognised his permissions, and the door slid open smoothly. The room beyond was all bright clinical lights and security. To the right, there was a set of lockers, all numbered and with chip scanners to operate the locks. The left side of the room held a set of glass-walled decontamination cubicles.

McNeill talked them through the decontamination process which, to Flit's dismay, involved stripping off completely and putting their belongings in a locker before getting into a decontamination cubicle and coming out on the other side to don a boxy, sterilised jumpsuit. It involved showing far more skin than she was comfortable with, and there was a look on the doctor's face when she stepped out that made Flit cringe and hold her suit tighter around herself.

"So, do you guys normally do this in big groups, or do you aim for a bit of privacy?" Flit snapped, annoyed that they had not been told about this part of the process, although it could have been something Scraps warned her about that she had just forgotten.

"A naked body is a naked body," McNeill replied in a flat tone that was at complete odds with the way he ran his eyes up and down Flit's white-clad form. "You'll see plenty of them inside. Here in the AHR department, we have become quite desensitised to nudity."

"And we have become desensitised to attempts to intimidate us." Scraps stepped out of his decontamination booth and adjusted the collar of his jumpsuit, fixing the doctor with a derisive narrow-eyed glare. He walked over and slipped his arm around Flit's waist.

Flit was surprised by the familiar contact. Scraps was never really one for public displays of affection at work, but she decided not to say anything with McNeill watching, especially after the way he had looked at her.

Flit stood a little straighter. "So, what do you say Doctor? Why don't you let my wife and I get started so we can get this audit over and done with and be out of your way?"

The doctor looked as though someone had dumped foul-smelling sewage down the front of his shirt, but still, he nodded. "Follow me."

He pivoted on his heel and led them deeper into the level, not waiting to see if they were on his tail.

Flit was not sure if she should be excited or intimidated by the thought of what they might find in a place like this.

39

SCRAPS

SCRAPS WAS NOT sure what he was expecting from a doctor in this department, but it seemed everyone he and Flit were assigned to assess believed their presence was an inconvenience. He could not understand why. Policies and procedures were what kept everything running smoothly and safely. They were a safety net provided by the Government in an otherwise unpredictable world. Then again, judging by the way the man treated Flit, he was not the reasonable or respectful sort. When he had looked at Flit so lecherously, Scraps had wanted to treat the man to a hard punch. Still, Scraps had made Flit promise to behave, so he could hardly go out on a whim and rearrange that smug, derisive look on Dr. McNeill's face.

With a deep breath and a considerable amount of control, Scraps walked with Flit and followed Doctor McNeill deeper into level four. McNeill rattled off a string of information relevant for their audit as they went along. From what Scraps could see out of the corner of his eye, Flit was too busy looking around to pay much attention to what the man was saying. For person his age, Doctor McNeill walked and talked very quickly and didn't seem to make breathing a priority.

Scraps, however, was leaning over ever so slightly as they went along, listening to the doctor's explanations with unabashed interest. He asked occasional, simple questions about various compliance aspects, and the doctor would answer sufficiently without giving away more than he needed to. The doctor did not seem pleased about the interruptions when Scraps spoke up, but Scraps was doing his job and thus refused to capitulate.

As they made their way past lab after lab, the small windows on the doors were barely enough for Scraps to see staff members in the room, looking at datapads and conducting chemical analyses or having quiet, very serious-looking discussions. Everything seemed far more normal than Scraps had been expecting. At least, it did, until—

"Doctor McNeill, can you please explain the procedure over here, in Lab Twenty-Two?" Flit asked, stopping in her tracks and taking a few steps back to look into one window.

McNeill looked between Flit and the door, his expression dour as he clung his datapad tighter. "That is not your concern. The only thing you need to know is that it is being conducted within the given guidelines."

Flit gritted her teeth and awarded Doctor McNeill with an overly enthusiastic smile. "Forgive me, Doctor, my professionalism means I must seek evidence for myself rather than taking information at face value. Please, explain."

Concerned that steam would start whistling out of the infuriated doctor's ears, Scraps cleared his throat. "My colleague is correct, Doctor. According to departmental guideline Five-A, we are required to *personally* inspect and audit any practical procedures to determine they are implemented and documented correctly."

With people like McNeill, rules held more weight than appeals to good-nature or reason. To make his point, Scraps stepped closer to Flit and peered into the small window for himself. When he did, he had to hold back a wave of disgust.

In the middle of the room, strapped to a gurney, was a naked man with all sorts of tubes and devices twisting out from his body. The monitor on the wall was taking all sorts of readings, but the man appeared to be unconscious, the sickly pallor of his skin and the way it almost hung off his bones indicated he was not faring well.

McNeill strode over and slipped his hand between Flit's and Scraps' faces and the glass. He tapped the window twice, and it frosted over, blocking their view. He cleared his throat and turned his glare on them. "Mr Parkes, Mrs Parkes, you are new to this facility and clearly don't know how things have been done in the past," he said slowly, his tone dripping with contempt. "Allow me to illuminate the situation for you. I take you for a brief tour of the facilities and assure you that all policies and procedures have been adhered to. You spend no more than half a day wasting my time. Then, you use one of the empty labs for the rest of the afternoon to write up your report stating that all is well, and then you are off on your way."

Flit let out a long sigh, defeat tugging her mouth into a frown. Scraps pressed his lips together, confused, as Flit spoke. "You're right, Doctor McNeill. Look, why don't you just show us where the computers are, and we'll get this sorted out without wasting any more of your time?"

Looking victorious, McNeill nodded and turned on his heel, walking back the way they came and leading them into one of the smaller labs near the front door. He unlocked it for them and led them over to the consoles. Scraps looked at Flit, not sure what she was playing at.

"Your log-ins should work on these consoles," McNeill informed them curtly, "and don't even bother trying to snoop around. We track everything. When you're done, knock on the door of the lab next door, and Alfred will see you out." He walked towards the door.

"Wait!" Flit called out.

The doctor let out an audible sigh. "What is it, Mrs. Parkes?"

Flit turned around and started tapping at her screen, logging in and bringing up one of their standard proforma servers. She opened a form and started filling it in. "I just want your approval before I send this."

Flit typed up a short message as McNeill walked over. She turned around, pointing back at the screen as she met his eye. "This form, in case you're unaware, is what we call an E-Thirty-One. In our department, we use these to report misconduct while we're on duty. In this case, if you look at this line here…" Flit ran her finger along the screen under a row of text. "You can see that I have highlighted your noncompliance and hostility in regards to our review. Brian, darling, would you care to tell the lovely Doctor McNeill what happens if I file this report and Jane approves it? Because she will approve it, you know."

Scraps had to hide a smirk as McNeill turned to him. "I am afraid that a high level of noncompliance with reporting and investigation would warrant a full-operation shutdown until the policy and procedure adherence can be confirmed."

McNeill looked between Flit and Scraps with fury burning in his eyes.

"So, Doctor," Flit said, her voice quiet, sharp, "what will it be?" She held her finger above the *send* button.

Taking a deep breath, McNeill glared at Flit. Scraps took a step closer to him, worried he would lash out at her.

"I will never know how your department got such a high concentration of insolent—"

"There, there, Doctor. No need for name calling," Flit tutted, patting his forearm gently. "We have a job to do, just like you. Now, the sooner you let us do our reports properly, the sooner we'll be out of your hair." Her tone might have sounded soothing to an outsider, but it was laced with condescension. "For the good of all, of course."

Scraps had never heard Flit say those words with such genuine gusto.

"For the good of all," Doctor McNeill muttered before turning and walking out.

When he was gone, Scraps turned to Flit and gave her a broad smile. "Here I was thinking you wouldn't remember E-Thirty-One." He gently squeezed her hand in approval.

Flit blinked. "Oh… so, it can be used like that?" she asked, a smirk on her lips and a sparkle in her eyes.

Scraps laughed out loud as he shook his head. Flit just winked at him as she turned back to the console she had been working on and started to pull up the various policies and procedures they were unable to access from outside the building.

THE DAY WENT by faster than Scraps anticipated. It was all a bit of a blur as he and Flit learned why the Department of Advanced Human Research was so controversial. It turned out that, on this level, at least, Human Research really was synonymous with Human Experimentation.

Having never given much thought to how the Government created new medicines and made ground-breaking leaps in biotechnology, it was a shock for Scraps. As a Registered, he had been controlled, but never like that. Seeing so many people strapped into machines and in all sorts of horrid conditions was enough to taint his view of the advances the Government had made. He might have warned Flit to behave herself earlier that morning, but even he was having trouble controlling himself when they walked into the labs where human subjects were being kept.

Their last stop for the afternoon was one such lab. Flit and Scraps followed their scrubs-clad attendant into the large room. Easily double the size of Tinker's medbay, it had six beds and four separate workstations. The walls the beds were lined up along had screens almost from floor to ceiling, reeling off a constant stream of biodata. Two of the beds had curtains pulled around them, shielding the occupants from view.

"So, who are these people?" Flit asked.

The attendant, frustrated at Flit's refusal to use the appropriate terms for the individuals they were seeing, turned to her. "These *subjects* whose identity—yet again—I am unable to divulge for confidentiality reasons, are involuntary and were brought in through the Department of Corrections."

Scraps did a double take as he observed the people on the bed. When he had been working for the Government, it had been his job to apprehend lawbreakers in the city. His responsibility for them ended when he handed them over to the custody of the Department of Corrections. He couldn't help but wonder if any of the people he had captured were subjected to this fate.

Guilt and horror sizzled through him as he looked at the people on the beds. Covered in nothing but thin white sheets, they lacked muscle tone and were pale and gaunt. He wondered how long it had been since they had seen the sun.

"What procedure manuals are relevant to this lab?" he asked, redirecting the line of discussion to the task at hand.

The attendant gestured for them to follow her. She flicked open a menu on one of the workstations and selected procedures for DNA splicing and involuntary patients. Scraps leaned against Flit's back ever so slightly as he read the information over her shoulder.

Just as he had suspected, these people were never allowed outside. They weren't even brought into a conscious state unless they required a mental status examination for experimental purpose. Flit shuddered against his chest, and he gently squeezed her shoulder.

"Questions?" the attendant asked as she waited somewhat impatiently for them to read through the information.

"So, in lieu of informed consent documents for these people, you have court orders. Do you have those recorded somewhere?" Flit asked.

The woman nodded. "Yes. All of that information is in their individual subject dossiers." She reached past Flit and opened four separate files. The names of the people were replaced with a string of letters and numbers, but their 'crimes' remained visible.

Scraps read the infractions out loud. "Defrauding a Government Department, third and final account of civil disobedience, ignoring a Government-issued genetic incompatibility warning."

Flit straightened and turned her narrowed eyes on the attendant at that last one. Scraps could feel Flit shaking against his chest. "Those aren't crimes. They are fre—"

Scraps tightened his hold on her shoulder, and she pressed her lips shut.

"I don't make orders or the procedures," she huffed.

Scraps slid his palm down Flit's arm and wrapped his hand around the fist she'd formed at her side, holding it in place for fear she might hit someone or something.

The woman stepped back and checked the clock on her data-pad. It was already past the time most offices closed business for the day. "Will you both be returning tomorrow? My shift is ending."

"We can continue this tomorrow," Scraps said. The break would be good for all of them.

Just as they were about to leave, Flit stopped. "You only showed us four files."

Quick as a flash, even without teleporting, Flit dashed to the closed curtains around the two final beds and tore them back.

Scraps choked back a gasp, and his head spun.

Lying there, unconscious and being kept alive by countless tubes and pumps, were two Registered Derivates. Both were just as gaunt as the others. The solid black of their tattoos stood out like dark voids against the pronounced chords of their necks. Scraps reached up, unconsciously brushing his fingers over the spot where his tattoo used to be.

Flit turned around, face flushed with rage. "And what about these two?" she snapped.

The attendant pinched the bridge of her nose. "They are Derivates." She shook her frustration off and continued in a tone of utter exasperation. "They are not subject to the same procedures as Citizens. And these ones?" Her lips curled in distaste. "They were found guilty various malfunctions. Excessive individuality, improper use of their abilities, disobeying direct orders, unauthorised behaviour, and the like. Once their convictions are signed, their registrations are assigned to our inventory and are therefore exempt from the same requirements for recreational and physiological breaks."

They were convicted, Scraps realised, for being the humans they were rather than the machines the Government wanted them to be.

Flit whipped around, pointing a finger at the woman. Before she could open her mouth, Scraps rushed over, gently taking her hand and holding it to his chest.

He looked back at the woman over his shoulder. "It's been a long day. We don't usually work late. We will return tomorrow."

Flit's entire body shook as he led her out of the lab and into the hallway.

"Let me go. I need to go back there," Flit hissed under her breath, trying to squirm out of his grip.

"No. We need to go home, *Ava*." He put emphasis on her cover name.

She stopped walking and looked at him. He could see she was ready to argue. She was probably just one thought away from teleporting back into that room to free the people there.

Scraps lowered his voice, concern for Flit's safety coursing through him. "Please."

Flit took a long, shuddering breath, all the muscles in her face tight. She didn't answer. She just turned around and walked away so fast that even Scraps, with his longer legs, had to run to keep pace.

40

————

FLIT

IT TOOK every single ounce of control that Flit had within her to keep walking. The trip back to their apartment was a stream of muted sound and blurred motion. She put one foot in front of another, paying no attention to where she was going and trusting Scraps to guide them. At one point, she swore she left her body and was looking back down at herself as she rode the train that would get them home fastest. She heard Scraps attempt to make conversation with her on a few occasions, but being so far away from herself, she was unable to respond.

That terrifying, pervasive numbness kept her away from the miasma of fury growing in the pit of her belly. In fact, it wasn't until they reached their apartment and Scraps quietly closed the door behind them that she slammed back into herself.

"Fuck!" The word exploded from Flit's mouth as she took her bag off her shoulder and threw it into the ground so hard that the datapad inside smashed with a definitive crack.

"Flit!" Scraps was at her side in an instant, wrapping his arms around her as her body shook so hard it hurt.

She teleported out of his arms to stand beside him and turned, slamming her fist into the wall. There was a loud thud, and pain lanced through her arm. When Scraps reached out and grabbed her, pulling her against him again, she saw that there was no damage at all on the wall. Blood dripped down from her knuckles, and Scraps held her wrists tight enough that she knew she couldn't get away, not without teleporting again.

"Please, Flit. Stop," Scraps begged, putting himself between her and the wall. "There was nothing we could do."

"Yes, there was!" she snapped, eyes burning. "We could have knocked that bitch out and taken all of those people away from there, away from this fucking nightmare of a city. We should have freed them, Scraps. We should have done something—anything!"

Tears spilled from her eyes hard and fast. Each word felt like a razor blade as it clawed its way out of her throat.

"You know there was nothing we could do today," he said, voice far too calm and collected.

The truth and conviction in his words was Flit's undoing. When she collapsed to her knees, Scraps fell with her. He held her tight against his chest as she sobbed, soaking through his shirt until her head ached and her throat was parched and sore.

"There was nothing we could do today, Flit," Scraps whispered, pressing a kiss against her hair so tenderly. "But we will do something soon, I promise."

Flit put her hands on her chest as she looked up at him. He reached out with shaking fingers to wipe the sheen of tears off her cheeks.

"We cannot risk our cover when we still have so much to investigate. We will get every bit of information we can tomorrow, and we will send it back to the Underground. If what we found last time wasn't enough to get them moving, this will be. It has to be," he said earnestly. "And if not? We will find a way to fix it together."

Flit took a deep breath and nodded as she looked into his eyes. The desperation she felt to set things right was reflected in his gaze.

Scraps was right. If this was the sort of thing the Government was doing to Citizens and Derivates in one department, there had to be more going on. If Scraps had let Flit do what she wanted to, she would have ruined everything. They had to be smart. They had to get enough information to convince the Underground to rise and put an end to the madness.

FLIT DID NOT GET any sleep that night. After Scraps tended to the grazes on her knuckle and bandaged her hand, they cleaned up and went to bed. She had several messages from Liana, asking how their first day on the case went. Flit couldn't bring herself to answer and spent the night tossing and turning. Images of the people lying so lifelessly on those beds haunted her.

When their alarm went off, she was out of bed and ready to go within half an hour. She wasn't sure if it was adrenaline or some sort of second wind, but she was determined to get back to that lab and get every single bit of information she could squeeze from the bastards.

Before they left the apartment, Scraps pulled her into a tight embrace. "Remember, Flit… No matter what we see today, we can't react. We will take notes, and then we will do everything we can to bring them down together. Got it?"

Flit looked up at him. "Yes. I've never looked forward to anything more in my life."

Unfortunately, no amount of sleep or resolve could make the sight of that same lab any less enraging. Still, Flit stuck to her promise. She kept her questions smart and pointed, and she took down every little detail she could. They still had the whole other half of the floor to explore, and the horror and depravity of the lab from the previous afternoon was repeated so often that she wasn't surprised the so-called doctors had become desensitised to it. None of the people on beds were people anymore. Registereds and Citizens alike had all been stripped of the life they had lived before. They were nothing more than their name, their sex, and— in the case of the involuntary subjects—their criminal record.

During their lunch break, Flit excused herself to use the restroom and vomited up her breakfast. She kept heaving until there was nothing but bile left, but she washed out her mouth, cleaned herself up, and got back to work as the hard edge of fury inside of her turned to a molten core.

Just when Flit had thought there couldn't possibly be any more surprises, they were led towards a lab that had no window in the door.

The man showing them around for the after-lunch shift paused and looked at them warily. "My colleagues explained that some of the labs you saw today and yesterday were confronting for you," he started slowly. He looked between Flit and Scraps. "This one will be even more so, but I assure you that we are following all appropriate directives. In previous years, we have kept the curtains drawn around the patients to preserve the objectivity of the assessment process."

Flit looked at Scraps out of the corner of her eyes and saw that his lips were pressed into a thin line.

"We are not amateurs. We will remain objective," Scraps said so evenly that even Flit was convinced.

The man sighed and shrugged. He pulled a separate RFID tag off his belt and swiped it against the door. The reader beeped, and he pushed the door before holding it open for them.

The room was small, not much larger than Flit and Scraps' bedroom. It was divided into two sections by separate sets of curtains, with a console at the end of the narrow walkway. Flit felt the world closing in around her as she followed the man through the narrow alley of swaying fabric. The weight of the man's warning settled on Flit's shoulders, and she shoved her hands into her pockets to stop herself from tearing the curtains open.

The man tapped the screen on the console between the two beds and opened up the documentation for the procedures they were carrying out in this lab and then the two patient files. There was so much information that Flit couldn't decide what to look at first, but after a moment of wide-eyed staring, one part stood out, blazing into her retinas like the midday sun.

Code 6B.

Flit's mind whirled back to the patient in the bed the previous afternoon, the one who had gone against Government-Issued Genetic Incompatibility Warning.

But this patient was not listed as voluntary or involuntary. There was no sentence under their name. There was nothing other than a note that they were female and—

"Eight years old?" Flit snapped, wheeling on the man.

Something the man saw in her eyes made him back up a step.

"Your test subject is eight fucking years old?" Flit pushed the man aside and tore the curtain open.

Sure enough, on the bed, was a young girl with ghostly pale

skin and matted, dark red ringlets that fell against her shoulders. There were oxygen lines taped under her nose and IV tubes in her left arm. She, like the other subjects, was fast asleep.

When she looked at the girl, all Flit could think about was Kindling and Seeker. She thought conditions for the children were bad in those tunnels, but this child? Flit had made a promise to Scraps, but this was so far beyond what she had imagined she would find that it no longer applied.

"Where are the policies covering the treatment of this subject? According to your own department's regulations, they should be clearly displayed at all times," Scraps said. Flit could tell he was already searching for a legitimate way to rescue the poor child.

"Everything is on the console," the man explained, exasperated. Scraps went straight over and started flicking through the files.

Flit was about to teleport to the bed and tear those tubes out of the poor child when a shift in Scraps' tone made her pause.

"What is this policy about? Determining Derivacy Status?"

When Flit seized up, the man took the opportunity to step between her and the child as he answered. "That is, as you can imagine, a highly classified and department-specific document."

"Yes," Scraps said slowly, "but… one is either a Derivate or they are not. What relevance does it have, and which protocol applies to these chil—patients? They are not listed as voluntary or involuntary, and nor are they classified as Citizen or Derivate," he asked, confusion lacing his tone.

Flit flinched as Scraps pulled his words, as he tried in his own way to distance himself from repulsive reality of the situation.

"Those protocol aren't relevant in this situation. If you keep reading the Derivacy Status Procedure, you'll see an exemption from other compliance requirements," the man said. He watched Flit warily as he stepped aside and scrolled to the relevant section for Scraps to see. "And as you will note in the patient files, they are being given adequate vitamins, minerals, and physical care."

Scraps scrolled through the documentation and let out a low sigh as he looked back up at the man. "Everything seems to be in order here." His voice was stiff as he turned and made to walk out.

The man went to follow but stopped when he realised Flit hadn't moved. Instead, she reached out for the other curtain.

"Please leave the curtain, Ma'am. The doctors here prefer to keep them drawn."

Flit looked up at the man, disgust making her stomach churn. "Of course they bloody well do. It means they can forget these patients are human, that they are children."

Stepping around them, Flit tore the curtain open to reveal the second child, a twin, a carbon copy of the first, except for the small brown freckle on her chin. Flit walked over, brushing a tender finger over the poor girl's cheek as she made her a silent promise. Flit would not rest until these girls, and all the other patients in this department, were freed.

And then, she would make the Government pay for what they had done.

THE TOUR of the lab concluded in the mid-afternoon with a final review of the Department's plans to move some of their operations to a newer, larger facility just outside the electrostatic barrier surrounding the Hub and away from prying eyes. There wasn't much information about it in their files, but they planned for it to be fully operational within two months. It was enough for Flit to realise that they couldn't just let this Department slide, not if they had plans to expand.

Much to Flit's dismay, Doctor McNeill was right when he had told them the previous day that the Department of Advanced Human Research followed their policies and procedures to the letter. It meant that, when Flit and Scraps wrote their reports, there was absolutely nothing they could use to hang the bastards. Even the inhumane and unethical experiments going on were not enough to warrant a shut-down, not when it was the Government who sanctioned them in the first place. After seeing their repulsion, the doctors had made a point of elucidating all the critical medical discoveries their labs had made thanks to their grisly work.

That was one of the problems, Flit thought, with having a Government overseen by an anonymous, internally elected council.

If someone had a problem with what they were doing, there was no one for the general populace to hold accountable. No human facet to question. It was all just one big, unstoppable wall of bureaucracy that was impossible to pin down.

The Department of Advanced Human Research was the worst illustration Flit had seen of the atrocities of the Government. So much evil was disguised in the name of human betterment. Flit wanted to copy all their evidence and the policies and procedures into a message and send it to every news outlet possible, but she doubted that would do anything. The outlets were in the pocket of the Government. Then, Flit realised that, even if she did get word out, it was unlikely anyone in the city apart from the Free Citizens would care. So long as the regular Citizens were free to enjoy their top tier medical service, would they even give a damn about the things being done to innocent children 'For the good of all'?

As much as Flit wanted to shout the injustice from the rooftops, they had to be smart about it.

That night, when Flit got home, she didn't break down. With a single-minded focus, she went straight to their comms unit and demanded an emergency meeting with Shadow. She knew he might not see it with the same urgency she did, but once they handed the information over, there was no way the Underground could just leave it be.

41

____

SCRAPS

SCRAPS HAD NEVER FELT SO NUMB BEFORE, not even when he was under the influence of the control chip. Seeing the adult test subjects the previous day, humans and Derivates alike, was horrifying, but it had given him a new sense of purpose and determination, a sense of determination that went into overdrive when Flit pulled the curtain back on those two poor children.

Seeing those young girls strapped to the bed should have made him furious. He should have felt that gnawing, gnashing heat in the pit of his stomach. Every single muscle in his body should have been clenched with rage.

But it wasn't there. Other than a distant sense of horror, the only thing in his mind and heart was that he had to find a way to make it right.

Thinking back to his early days in the Underground, Scraps had been certain the Government was doing the best thing for their people. He had believed in the rules, in the regulations, even in the sacrifice, but what he had seen in those labs? There was absolutely no justification in the world that would make what he saw right.

And when he had seen those children?

It was only his concern for Flit that made him keep his own resolve. Well, barely. If she had turned around in that moment and given him *the look*, he would have helped her rescue those children without a second thought.

As soon as they walked in the door, Flit teleported over to the communication screen and sent a message to Shadow. Scraps didn't try to stop her.

Once the message was sent, some of the tension in Flit seemed to ease. Scraps made them dinner, but he barely picked at it, and Flit seemed to have no stomach for it at all. After pushing food around on her plate for almost an hour, Flit finally spoke.

"Did you see the code on the children's records? Six B. That is the same code—"

"Chris and Liana were given for their genetic incompatibility," Scraps finished Flit's sentence with a serious nod.

"And the person in the first lab we saw was put in as an involuntary patient for—"

"Disobeying the Government's direct orders about genetic compatibility testing."

Flit looked at Scraps as he finished her sentence again. "Liana has sent me almost a dozen messages, asking if we found anything. I know Ava and Brian are our just covers, but she has been a lovely friend, and it would feel wrong keeping this from her."

Scraps pressed his lips together in concentration as he considered the information they had. "While the conviction and the code are concerning, I am still wondering what on earth they were doing with the Determining Derivacy Status policy." Scraps met Flit's gaze as his words slowed. "It should be simple. Yes or no. But…"

Flit leaned in closer. "Combined with the genetic incompatibilities and the code, there has to be more to it than that."

Scraps nodded and drummed his fingers on the table as he thought it through. "We cannot tell Chris and Liana the truth. Not if we are giving the information to Shadow. If we do, we may give away possible ammunition for the Underground's arsenal. It needs to be brought to light, yes, but at the right time, when it can help the most people."

From the way Flit sighed and slumped back in her seat, he knew she could tell he was right. He squeezed her hand gently.

"I think I'm going to head to bed early. I didn't get any sleep last—"

The pinging tone of a new message bounced around the apartment. The next instant, she was by the commscreen in the living room, standing straight and looking alert as she opened the message.

"It's Aunt Edna," Flit said, using their code name for Shadow. "She wants to meet tomorrow morning before we go to work, at the same café as last time."

Scraps' eyes widened. "Gee, that was fast."

"Well, I said it was urgent," Flit said with a faux-innocent shrug.

According to the Intelligence Field Agent Manual, this information, while hideous, was not the sort of finding that warranted an urgent tag. However, Scraps understood why Flit had done it, and he was not about to argue with her. Not when he hoped, perhaps a little too optimistically, that the faster they told the Underground, the faster they would do something about it.

"Then bed sounds like a good idea." Scraps got to his feet, levitating their dishes over to the kitchen bench.

"Can we deal with the dishes tomorrow? Right now, I just want you to hold me." Flit bit her lip as she made the soft plea.

Her sweet words softened every bit of frustration Scraps held. "Of course. They'll still be there in the morning," Scraps conceded, reaching out his hand for her.

Flit teleported over, but instead of taking his hand, she threw her arms around his neck. Scraps wrapped his arms around her, and she teleported them into the bedroom.

It turned out that Flit had made a good call. It became easy to block away the horrors of the outside world when she was in his arms.

WITH A SENSE OF DÉJÀ VU, Scraps and Flit got ready for their early morning rendezvous at the café safe house. Flit spent the entire trip with her hands shoved in her pockets and her jaw clenched shut. Scraps attempted to make conversation on several occasions, but from the look on her face, the truth of their discovery was balled up inside of her, and if she opened her mouth, it might just tumble out. Scraps didn't push her. He could see how hard she was trying to stay calm.

When they got to the café, they slipped past the modest crowd of trade workers and outer-city Citizens. They were both wearing standard morning exercise clothing, with Scraps carrying a bag over his shoulder containing their work uniforms. Looking up from her coffee machine, the woman at the front counter gave them a subtle nod and jutted her head towards the back.

Flit and Scraps went through the door at the back of the café and then through the dingy kitchen to see two figures seated at the table in the small back room. Both people were facing away from them. One was unmistakably Shadow, with his smooth salt-and-pepper hair and permanently rigid posture. The other had lighter, sandy-coloured hair that was all sorts of messy.

"Hawk?" Flit blurted, bursting into a run as she dashed past the table and skidded to a stop. When she turned to face the man at the table, her eyes went wide, and she launched herself across the space to pull him into a back-breaking hug.

"Shit, Ava! Go easy, will you?" Hawkeye grunted, patting her back.

Scraps walked over to join them. He nodded respectfully at Shadow and gave Hawkeye a broad smile of greeting. Scraps was not sure how he was here, given the injury he had when they'd left the Underground, but Scraps was unprepared for how heart-warming it was to see his friend.

Flit pulled back from the hug and held Hawkeye at arm's length, looking him up and down with a frown on her face. "Are you… are you ok?"

Hawkeye shrugged. "As ok as I can be. Still in pain, but not enough to stop me from joining Aunt Edna." He smirked at the leader of Intelligence.

Shadow got up and scanned his RFID chip against the panel by the door to activate the anti-listening tech. "Sorry to break up the reunion, but you sent a message claiming you had urgent information."

Scraps gestured for Flit to sit before he settled into the chair beside her. Under the table, he slipped his hand onto her thigh and squeezed it, hoping it was reassuring. She reached down her top, pulled out a datastick, and slid it across the table. Shadow picked it up and tucked it into his pocket as he settled back in his seat.

"We were given a job to assess procedures at the Department of Advanced Human Research," Flit begun, voice barely above a whisper. Hawkeye and Shadow had to lean closer to hear her. "While we were there, we found evidence that they are experimenting on Citizens and Derivates."

Shadow sat back and looked between Flit and Scraps. "It's the Government. Of course, they are," he said so smoothly that it was glaringly obvious he was already aware of the fact.

Flit flinched.

Scraps patted her leg and continued for her, "They are planning to open a newer, bigger facility, another place for them to experiment on people. They are also experimenting on children too. The girls we saw were only eight years old."

Hawkeye's shoulders stiffened, his lips parting in surprise.

Shadow didn't even react. "And?"

"And?" Flit scoffed, leaning forward with her elbows on the table. "Children, Shadow! They were strapped to a bed with all sorts of tubes going in and out of them. Their files said they've been at that facility for two years! Two fucking years!"

Shadow took a deep breath before he continued, "Is that all?"

Flit jerked forward, probably to reach across and strangle Shadow, so Scraps put a hand on her shoulder to hold her back. For her own good, of course. Not because Shadow didn't deserve it.

"One of the procedures we saw there was called 'Determining Derivacy Status'," Scraps said evenly.

Hawkeye scrunched his face up in confusion. "But that doesn't make sense. You are, or you aren't. There's no *determining* about it."

Flit nodded, shaking Scraps' hand off and leaning in again. "Apparently not."

"Is all of the information and your related observations on the drive?" Shadow asked, cutting off further discussion.

"Yes," Flit and Scraps said at the same time.

"Good." The man patted the drive in his top pocket. "I don't want to hear about this again. Do not go poking around."

Scraps furrowed his brow. "Do you already have operatives looking into this?"

"You don't have enough clearance for me to confirm or deny that," Shadow replied.

Flit pointed a finger at him. "You already knew this, didn't you?"

"I said—"

Flit waved an angry hand at his attempt to brush her off. "I heard what you said, but it didn't surprise you, and you don't look like you give the slightest of fucks. I know that we're taking things slowly, but there are people up here being treated worse than lab rats! We can't just—"

"We are done here." Shadow stood up abruptly. His tone turned callous as he said, "Your job is to find information that will help with the protection of the Underground, not to go around freeing prisoners." He turned to Hawkeye. "I'll meet you outside. You've got five minutes."

Before Scraps registered what was happening, Shadow turned and strode out of the shielded area. Flit jumped to her feet and pushed past Scraps to follow him. Hawkeye snatched up her hand and pulled her back.

Flit yelped and turned to glare at him. "Let me go!"

"We need to talk."

Scraps frowned, looking between his girlfriend and her best friend. Flit looked like she might tug her arm out of his grip and walk away, but there was something in his tone that gave her pause. She looked back at Scraps, and he gave her a small, uncertain shrug in reply.

"What is it?" Flit sat rigidly on the edge of the seat Shadow vacated.

Hawkeye sighed and reached back, rubbing the back of his neck. "Guys, you have to know that this is not how I wanted our reunion to go…"

Flit's expression hardened in an instant. "Get to the point, Hawk."

"You two need to watch yourselves," Hawkeye whispered, looking at Flit with a plea in his eyes. "You're getting into places you shouldn't be, and that is putting your actual operation at risk."

Scraps frowned. "How so?"

Hawkeye glanced over his shoulder, but Shadow was long gone. He leaned in. "Shadow asked me to give you a friendly reminder of your role up here... but I know you need more than that." Hawkeye looked at Flit, his expression a little lighter as he took her in. "I'm not meant to tell you this part, but that information you found earlier, about the weapon? They are following some leads there, and they need you two both to calm down for a bit and wait until they send you some new orders. They will need you in your positions, uncompromised, when the time comes."

Sitting back in his seat, a little surprised by Hawkeye's revelations, Scraps nodded. "So, they are doing something..." he said, more to himself than the others. It was reassuring to hear it from someone he trusted.

"Something about the weapon, maybe," Flit said, not backing down. "What about the kids, though? We just need to forget about them?"

Hakweye took Flit's hand. "You need to trust that Shadow and the others are on top of the situation, Flit. While I've been recovering, I have been training in deeper levels of Intelligence. There are so many things going on that no one else knows about."

Rubbing her eyes with her free hand, Flit shook her head. "Hawkeye, we can't just ignore information because it doesn't fit our mission brief. If we find something, we need to share it."

"Do you want to be recalled?" Hawkeye snapped.

"No," Flit and Scraps said at the same time.

"Then please, sit tight and keep your noses clean. Don't take extra assignments at work. Don't go out of your way to get new info. Just wait, ok?"

Scrap knew by the sharpness in Flit's gaze that she was not ok with that. Not even in the slightest.

He wasn't really, either.

"I need to go. Despite how this went, I'm so glad to see you both. The only reason they let me up here is because they figured I'm the only one you'd listen to, so I can't push my luck." Hawkeye pulled Flit into a hug. Scraps heard him murmur, "Is there anything you want me to tell your folks?"

"Just that I love the and miss them," Flit whispered.

"And you still have your bracelet?"

Flit rolled up the sleeve of her long, fitted shirt to show Hawkeye. He smiled and nodded with approval.

He reached out to shake Scraps' hand. "I need to get going. I wish I could stay longer, but there is so much work to be done."

With that, Hawkeye turned in his seat, stood up, and stepped into the thoroughfare. Scraps' eyes widened as he took in the shiny metal brace frames that ran up the full length of both of Hawkeye's legs.

Sensing the surprise, Hawkeye looked down and blushed, scratching the back of his neck uncomfortably. "Oh… Yeah, I guess you guys haven't seen these yet. I'm healing well, but I'll need to wear them until I'm strong enough to walk on my own. It might be a while, yet."

"Hawk, I'm so, so sorry," Flit whispered.

The sandy-haired remote viewer waved his hand dismissively. "That's old news. I'm dealing with it, and I've got a new position with Intelligence. It may not be what I planned to do, but I'm damn good at it. No getting all apologetic on me now, Flit."

He gave her a playful salute and walked off, his gait so smooth that Scraps' wouldn't have known about the braces if he hadn't seen them for himself.

Scraps and Flit sat at the table together in silence, both lost in their own thoughts. After what they had seen in the Department of Advanced Research and Shadow's response, Scraps' mind was all muddled up. They had been given their orders, but it didn't feel right just leaving those people in that facility. He assumed Shadow already knew about it… but how long had they been waiting to move? The Underground was good at taking its time but not so good at following up on its promises. There was no way Flit was going to let it go, but as Scraps sat in the café, he had no idea what they could do about it.

Still, they had a cover to maintain.

"Ava, we need to leave now if we are to get to work on time." He stood up, offering Flit his hand. When she took it, he brought it up to his lips to brush a kiss against her cool skin.

"We can't just leave them there, Scraps," she whispered, looking up into his eyes.

He nodded. "I know. But right now, if we do not go to work, we will just draw suspicion. If our cover is blown, and we are not here to help them, who will?"

Flit leaned in, resting her head on his chest for a tender moment, and he stroked her hair. They stood there for a few precious seconds before Flit pulled away, took a deep breath, and straightened her shoulders. "All right, let's get to work and turn this stupid report in. The sooner we get things sorted there, the sooner we can go home."

For the first time since coming to the Hub, Scraps found himself really missing the simplicity of life in the Underground.

42

FLIT

JANE WAS PLEASED with the speed and efficiency of Flit and Scraps' review of the Department of Advanced Human Research. She also thanked them profusely getting through it without making a fuss. At that praise, Flit bit her tongue so hard it bled, but at least she managed to keep her mouth shut.

As a result, Jane allowed them to maintain their enhanced clearance rating and promised to let them in on some of the more high-profile reviews and information. Flit was grateful to be at work, as it was a time when Chris and Liana couldn't ask them for information about what they had found. Even though the copious amount of surveillance devices often got forgotten by ordinary Citizens, anyone who had anything to hide from the Government knew full well that almost nowhere in public was safe from some level of monitoring.

It was only a short reprieve, though, as Liana sent Flit a message that night, asking her and Scraps over for dinner the following day.

As Scraps finished cooking their meal, Flit walked into the open plan kitchen and leaned back against the smooth bench, holding her datapad close to her chest. She watched him, his face scrunched in concentration as he tried to get the sear on the chicken perfect. She smiled, affection warming in her as she wondered if she would ever get tired of loving just how much effort he put into even the most mundane things.

"Scraps?"

He didn't look up. "Mmm?"

"Liana messaged. I don't think they're going to stop unless we tell them something," Flit said slowly.

After flipping the chicken and nodding in approval at the golden-brown coating of herbs on the outside, Scraps stepped back and gave her his full attention. "We can't tell them what we found."

"Well," Flit started with a sigh and an innocent shrug.

Scraps set the tongs down on the bench. "Flit…"

Flit raised her hands defensively. "You said you wished you could do something just as much as I did. You saw Shadow this morning. He has no intention to do anything about it. We can't just leave those people there. Those poor kids, Scraps." Anger rippled through her. She clutched the datapad closer to her chest. "Can you imagine if that was Kindling and Seeker?"

Scraps pressed his lips together at the comparison. Flit could admit she was possibly taking the emotional blackmail a little far, but it was true. Just because they didn't know the children didn't mean they were any less worthy of saving.

"Shadow was furious. Hawkeye said we need to sit tight for our next mission, not go poking around anymore."

Flit rolled her eyes. "We're not poking our noses anywhere. We're just… redistributing information as we see fit."

"Section One of the Intelligence Operative Training Manual states—"

Flit threw her hands up in the air. "Seriously?"

Scraps let out a huff. "Chris and Liana cannot do anything with the information. There is nothing to gain from telling them."

"True." Flit teleported so that she was sitting on the edge of the bench, swinging her legs back and forth. "But the Free Citizens can."

The expression on Scraps' face was enough to tell Flit that he thought her idea was preposterous. He just stared at her, not even bothering to grace her suggestion with a response.

"Now, hear me out—"

"It is a terrible idea. We are already playing with fire," Scraps warned.

Flit shook her head. "We were born to play with fire. Even the act of breathing is dangerous for our kind."

"Ok," Scraps conceded. "Then we are not playing with fire. We are dousing ourselves in gasoline and running headfirst into an inferno."

Flit laughed. "When did you get so dramatic?"

Scraps took a deep breath an closed his eyes for a moment before he looked back at her. "You said the Free Citizens were useless. What are they going to do? Spread graffiti about the department? That will only link it all to us. It is too dangerous."

"Maybe the reality of what is happening in these facilities will be enough to convince them to do something real about it. Even if they can't do anything about the one in the city, we might be able to convince them to do something about the new facility."

"I fail to see how they can help."

Flit rested her elbows against the bench as she watched him. Luckily, she'd spent plenty of time thinking about it. "Did you ever wonder where the Underground gets a lot of its supplies?"

Narrowing his eyes, Scraps nodded. "It crossed my mind, but we always seemed to have enough, so I did not question it."

"The Government is wasteful, the bastards," Flit begun, voice hushed. "The second they get newer, better, shinier products, they put everything they have into producing those, and whatever was left in the old facilities is… well, left. For every new factory that opens, there is an old one the Underground can raid. Weapons, tech, everyday supplies—the amount of stuff we get without having to make it for ourselves is pretty impressive. Whenever Intelligence gets hold of a new place, they send crews out. We take what we need, which is never too much, and there is always something left behind in case the Government come back and get suspicious."

Scraps leaned down, resting his elbows on the bench as he looked at her too. "You want to give the Free Citizens the locations of these facilities?" Scraps asked, putting two and two together as he always did.

Flit nodded. "We can give them more than spray paint to work with."

"We cannot just give them weapons. They are untrained. Office workers, club owners…" Scraps trailed off.

Flit waved her hand dismissively. "We won't be throwing rifles at them. Maybe just a few EMP devices. You know, get in there, mess shit up a bit. Make it so they can expand their operation to buy some time until someone can actually do something real about it."

As always, Scraps took in her wild plan with genuine consideration. His eyebrows knitted together in that serious, broody way of his. A few times, he looked like he might say something, but he would press his lips back together and shake his head a little as he considered it more. Flit bounced on the balls of her feet as she waited to see what he would say.

Finally, Scraps straightened up. Just as he opened his mouth to speak he froze, sniffed twice, and then his eyes widened. "Oh, no!" He turned on heels and dashed to the stove.

Flit scrunched up her nose, not sure what the problem was, but then she saw the black smoke billowing from the frying pan. Scraps used his telekinesis to lift the meat out and settle it on the bench, but it was a lost cause. He grumbled something under his breath. Flit winced at the frustration in his tone.

"I'll order a delivery." Flit teleported over to the commscreen and brought up the menu for their favourite restaurant. As she ordered, she waited for Scraps to come over and tell her what he had been thinking before the untimely demise of their dinner, but he didn't.

Their replacement dinner arrived within fifteen minutes, and Scraps was quiet throughout the meal. When the kitchen was clean, Scraps spent a short time on the couch catching up on the news and excused himself to go to bed early.

Flit spent the next hour or so looking at the satellite images to find the factories she remembered hearing about and wondered if Scraps would agree to her plan. When her eyes grew heavy and started to sting, she put her datapad aside, showered, and climbed into bed. She did her best to stay quiet as she slid between the sheets and curled up against his chest. As she always did when she went to sleep after him, she pressed a soft kiss against his bare chest and rested her head on his shoulder.

"Flit?" His voice broke through the darkness, sounding more alert than it should have given he had been in bed for a few hours.

"Yes?"

"We should contact Adam."

Flit smiled, relief flooding through her at his words. "I will do that in the morning," she said firmly.

She squirmed further up the bed and cupped his cheek, bringing his face closer so she could kiss him gently. She moaned softly at the reassuring taste of his lips on hers and breathed a sigh of relief at the knowledge she had his support yet again.

"Thank you, Scraps. I lo—"

Flit froze. The words almost slipped out. She hated how many times she almost lost control and how easily the words were coming these days. Not that she had a problem with them, the feelings had become undeniable, but after his reaction the first time she'd said it, she wanted to leave those kinds of commitments in his hands.

And, if she was honest with herself, she didn't want to go through the heartache of not having her sentiments reciprocated again.

"Yes?" Scraps propped himself up on his elbows a little.

Flit shook her head. "Nothing."

She rested her head back on his shoulder, and he settled back onto the bed, his hand running in slow, comforting lines up and down her back. She yawned, letting her eyes flutter closed, secure in the knowledge that they had a plan.

A FEW DAYS LATER, Flit and Scraps made their way to Nightmix with a renewed sense of resolve. They spent the past few nights researching the various facilities that had been abandoned around the Hub and avoiding questions from Chris and Liana by promising to give them more information at the club.

"Are you sure you do not want to borrow my jacket?" Scraps asked in a hushed tone as they skirted past the line snaking outside of the busy nightclub.

Flit chuckled. "No thanks. I'm good."

Scraps twisted his lips together as he dragged his gaze over her. Flit cocked an eyebrow at him as he couldn't seem to tear his attention away from where the hem of her silver dress sat on her upper thighs.

"Are you concerned about me being cold or you being distracted? You still seem to like this dress as much as you did the first time I wore it," Flit said easily, loving how Scraps squirmed at her words.

She had no doubt he remembered just how much he appreciated the dress that night after their first visit to Nightmix, enough, in fact, for him to ask her to leave it on well beyond when she would have normally torn it off.

A blush bloomed on Scraps' cheeks as he straightened up. "Perhaps a bit of both," he conceded in a gruff, begrudging tone.

Flit laughed, taking his arm and wrapping it around her waist as they flashed their credentials at the bouncers and were waved through. "Don't worry. I'll make sure I leave it on for as long as you like once we get home tonight."

Her teasing only served to intensify his blush, but she revelled in his obvious appreciation.

Stepping into Nightmix again remind Flit just how much of an assault it was to her senses. She wasn't sure if she would ever get used to the loud, thrumming, heart-shaking bass of the club music. Combined with the humid, sweat-laden air, Nightmix was a world unto itself. Even in the very core of the Hub, the pulse of the place made it intoxicating, disorienting, and enchanting in its own way. The way she had started to dance so freely weeks ago still played on her mind. She never quite understood the allure of a packed place like this, having avoided clubs and similar places when she had lived in the Hub with her folks. Now, though? She was just disappointed that they weren't there to dance. Not really. Just like last time, she would have to cut that sense of utterly consuming freedom to deal with the Government's bullshit.

"Ava! Brian!"

A hand settled on Flit's shoulder, and she tensed up at the sudden contact to avoid the instinct to teleport away. She whipped around, sagging with relief as she came face to face with Chris and

Liana. She hugged them both in greeting as Scraps performed one of his awkward little greeting waves.

"Here for business or pleasure?" Chris peered between them with a glimmer of suspicion in his eyes.

"Business, I am afraid," Scraps said, voice solemn even over the music.

The group skirted around the dance floor to find a quiet corner to continue talking.

"I told you they found something!" Chris said to Liana. Even though he shouted, Flit barely heard it.

Liana did, and she poked him in the ribs. "Not here!" she snapped. Then, she smirked. "Ava, let's leave these buffoons to get some drinks. I want to dance before we head downstairs!"

Liana snatched up Flit's hand and started to drag her away. Flit turned back to give Scraps an apologetic smile as she let herself be whisked away, but from the look in his and Chris' eyes, neither of them minded so much.

Flit chose to spend as much time as she could on the dance floor. The constant stream of thoughts and frustrations that had bothered her over the past week took a backseat as she let herself sink into the music, the bass replacing her own heartbeat and sweeping her way to somewhere different, somewhere she could just be herself.

At some point, Chris and Scraps came to join her and Liana on the dance floor. Flit was unsure of how long it took them. Chris leaned in and explained that they were safe to go downstairs in ten minutes. He then stole Liana from Flit.

Flit gladly turned to Scraps. After the private tuition at home, he seemed more comfortable with the nightclub style moves. He was still wary of the people around them, but he got in close enough that they could enjoy the intimacy of the situation for the short time they had.

When the time came, the four of them weaved their way out of the throng and took the route through the back passage of the club. Petra and Trey were waiting for them in the office. Apparently, Andy was busy tonight, but Flit figured it was fine. They were only really there to speak to Adam.

Down in the bunker, there were more crates of supplies around the place than last time.

Adam stood up from his makeshift desk as they walked in, his eyes alighting on Flit and Scraps with amusement. "So, you decided to return to us?" His tone was smug, as if he knew they would.

Flit nodded towards the crates. "More spray paint? Hopefully you ditched the red in favour of something a little less… melodramatic."

Adam snorted and shook his head. He gestured for them to walk back over to a corner that was now set up with several seats and gestured for everyone to settle in. "I was told you had some more information for us."

Flit looked at Scraps, and he straightened up. "That is correct. We were wondering how the Free Citizens feel about forced human experimentation."

Several conflicted cries went up around the room. Adam held up his hand, and silence fell immediately. All eyes were now on Flit and Scraps.

"We are against all forms of non-consensual experimentation on Citizens," Adam said in a slow, firm tone. The others muttered their assent.

"Good. Because the Department of Advanced Human Research has involuntary test subjects," Flit said. The others looked upset but not terribly surprised. "Amongst them were some children. We saw two—twin girls, only eight years old. They had been in that facility for at two years, strapped to a bed, not able to move or sit. I'm not sure how long they have been in Government custody for."

Their initial reveal might not have garnered much attention, but the mention of children got everyone fired up.

After letting a heated discussion full of disgust and outrage go on for a few minutes, Adam held up his hand again. "So, what do you think we can do about it?" he asked, watching Flit carefully.

"Honestly?" Flit shrugged as she sat straighter in her seat to let Adam know that she wasn't the type to back down. "Nothing right now but we might have found a way for you to change that."

The challenge in Flit's tone was clear, and Adam fell right into the trap.

"What are you proposing?"

Flit looked at Scraps, giving him the opportunity to speak, hoping it would help him feel more control over what they revealed. "When the Government makes new leaps in technology, it is often cheaper for them to build a new factory from scratch to produce it, rather than renovating an old one. In a recent assignment, we happened across the details of one such facilities."

Everyone in the room hung on Scraps' words. Flit smiled to herself. That certainly got their attention.

Scraps continued, "The facility we found was used to make the old electromagnetic pulse devices. While it will not do much against the building we investigated—it is far too closely guarded—we found evidence they are nearing completion on a new facility just outside of the electrostatic barrier around the Hub, between here and Old City." Scraps let that settle as the others looked at him with eyes wide.

"Brian and I figure we should go in and retrieve some EMPs. Then, we hit the new facility. Do as much damage as we can. We may not be able to stop the experimentation completely, but we can sure as shit make it harder for them to expand their operations." Flit leaned in, looking at the others and wondering if they would take this opportunity to make something of their movement.

The silence in the room was so deep Flit could hear the vibrating thuds from the dance music in the club above them. Chris and Liana looked at each other, visibly concerned, but Petra and Trey nodded firmly at Adam.

The leader of the Free Citizens got up and walked over to his desk to retrieve his datapad. When he sat back down, he opened a note-taking app and looked at Flit and Scraps. "Give me all the information you've got."

SCRAPS

SCRAPS AND FLIT spent a good hour telling Adam and the Free Citizens everything they could without jeopardising themselves or the Underground. The gave specific details about the abandoned factory that had left over EMPs, the extent of human experimentation in the Department of Advanced Human Research, and the new facility that was being built and just how huge it was. The expected completion date was two months away, but it gave them time to get supplies and get organised. Adam agreed to see who would be interested in raiding the factory and then get back to them with details the following week.

Having spent almost the whole night before awake, discussing whether to tell Chris and Liana about Code 6B, Scraps assumed that Flit would want to head straight home and sleep.

She didn't.

Instead, after they left the bunker, she took his hand and dragged him to the dance floor. Well, dragged was too strong a word. Once she had a hold of him and was walking ahead, his eyes were glued to her, and he was in a trance. As tired as he was, he did not think he would ever be unable or unwilling to hold his girlfriend in his arms and dance with her, especially when dancing, in this instance, amounted to swaying and grinding their bodies together.

Countless hours later, when Flit was finally tired, they went home. After a shower and some much-needed physical intimacy, they fell asleep. That weekend, they 'took it easy', as Flit would say. They spent some time catching up on their favourite VR games and going for long walks. Flit even allowed Scraps to take her to a museum. He picked one on the outskirts of the city because he knew better than to try and take her to anything closer to Centre One and more Government oriented. This one was dedicated to different artefacts that had survived from times well before the war. Having never had a chance to explore venues like this as a child, Scraps enjoyed it. Flit even cracked a smile for him, although she maintained it was because she enjoyed seeing him so happy.

The rest of the week dragged by under a mounting pile of new reviews at work. Still pleased with their achievement so far, Jane made sure to send them the more complex or challenging tasks. While Flit muttered about their 'stupid decision to overachieve', Scraps was loving it. He had always found entertainment and refuge in work.

When the week ended, Flit and Scraps left work and went home to get dressed for Nightmix. This time, Flit had a new dress. It wasn't the barely-there silver outfit Scraps had grown to love. If anything, it was potentially even more distracting. Tightly fitted to the body he knew so well, the red fabric hugged every single curve she had. It was short, short enough that he doubted she could bend over in it, and there were no straps holding the top part of it up. He was sure to walk either close to her side or behind her so he could enjoy the view as they made their way to the club. When they got inside and found their usual table, he spent the whole time thinking that it would take nothing more than the smallest flick of his finger to telekinetically tug Flit's dress down—

"Brian?"

Hearing his cover name, Scraps snapped out of his daydreaming. "Yes?" He smiled politely at Petra and tried to focus.

"Are you and Ava ready? *He* is waiting for us in the office."

Scraps put his drink down on the tall table he was standing next to with Chris and looked over to where Flit and Liana were dancing. Both were holding each other far closer than they had the previous week.

"It seems such a shame to interrupt them when they're having so much fun." Chris winked at Scraps.

A smile tugged at Scraps' lips, but it was quickly wiped away by the disapproving look Petra gave them both.

Scraps cleared his throat. "Sorry. I will go and let them know he is ready."

Peeling away from the table, Scraps made his way onto the dance floor, weaving confidently through the writing bodies. Flit was facing away from him, but Liana smiled as he approached. He put his hand on Flit's shoulder. Instead of flinching, she reached up, holding his palm against her warm, smooth shoulder.

He leaned in and kissed her neck before saying, "Adam is ready for us now."

Flit's shoulders sagged, and she turned around, pressing her body up against his as she looked up into his eyes. She pulled him down for a kiss that made his blood rush to one spot.

When Flit pulled away, she winked at him before gesturing for Liana to follow them.

Adam was waiting for them when they got to the bunker. It was far fuller than it had been the last time, with all sorts of wooden and metal crates stacked up around the place. The instant the door was shut behind them, he smirked at Flit.

"Ava," Adam said, gesturing to the crates, "we have more red, some orange… and a whole lot of other pretty colours that might tickle your fancy. Why don't you take a look?"

The haughty challenge in his tone was enough to have Flit walking over to the nearest crate. It was a thick-walled metal storage chest often used by the Government. Even though the lid was heavy, Flit pushed it open with ease.

She narrowed her eyes at what she saw in there and turned back to Adam. "You got them already? You said you would tell us when you had a team."

Surprised, Scraps walked over to stand beside her and peered into the crate. Rows and rows of EMP devices were nestled into protective foam padding.

"You doubted what we could achieve, Ava. We are far more competent than you give us credit for." Adam nodded pointedly at the rest of the cases.

Scraps took that as permission to open the next and the one after that and the one after that. He went around the room with Flit, calling out the contents so Petra, Trey, Chris, and Liana would know what was in there. "Body armour… medical kits… security chips… rifles—"

"Rifles?" Liana snapped, breaking away from Chris and walking over to peer down into the crate Scraps had just opened. "What are we supposed to be doing with these?"

Flit frowned at the crate. "The only thing you do with rifles is shoot people," she snapped, glaring at Adam with accusation in her gaze.

Scraps let the lid fall shut and turned around. "The facility we told you about should have only had the EMPs and maybe some security chips… Where did these come from?"

Adam crossed his arms and smirked. "Well, you mentioned one facility, so it got me wondering what other resources the Government had abandoned. I had a small team do a bit of good, old-fashioned exploring, and it was very, very well worth our while."

Scraps watched as Flit balled her hands up into fists at her side. They had hoped that by giving the Free Citizens the location of one factory, they would accept it, and the rest would still be safe stockpiles for the Underground. Now, they had inadvertently given some of the resources that their people might need to the Free Citizens.

"What are you planning to do with them? The raid on the experimental facility is just about messing with the Government's progress. We are not going in there to kill people," Flit said slowly.

Adam shrugged. "Guns aren't always for killing. Let's think of them as insurance."

Scraps caught Flit's eye. He wished he had a chance to discuss the situation with her. This was not what they had planned.

"What's the big deal?" Trey asked, sounding bored. "It's not like there will be anyone at the facility, right? You said it was still going through internal fit-out."

Scraps pressed his lips together.

Flit nodded in response to that statement. "Well, if we are going to do this, we need to make a plan so we are in and out before the Government show up."

"Agreed," Chris said, looking at Liana as he stepped forward. "If we get caught, this movement ends. We need to be smart about it."

Adam's lips split into a wicked smile. "Excellent. Let's get planning."

SCRAPS CHECKED the contents of his pack and Flit's for the sixth time that evening.

Flit chuckled. "The same stuff will be in there no matter how many times you check it." She walked over to stand beside him.

He frowned as he looked down at her. It had been a long time since he had seen her in more practical clothes. She had chosen to don a pair of black tights and a thin body-armour vest that the Underground left for them in their apartment. It was different from the Underground fatigues she used to wear but spoke to their purpose enough to remind him of what they were walking into.

"One can never be too prepared." Scraps ran his hands down her sides, checking to ensure that all of the buckles on her vest were firmly tightened.

"I know." She shrugged as she reached past him and pulled two small pistols from a box on their bench. Adam might have offered them weapons, but they wanted to keep their own concealed, just in case. "But we've both checked it. We have medical kits, EMPs, flame grenades, daggers, and we will also get more stuff from Adam on site. I think this is a little less about the supplies and a little more about your concerns about the raid itself."

Scraps' shoulders sagged. Flit read him so well. She had gotten good at that. "I do not think Shadow would approve of this."

"Fuck Shadow."

Scraps shook his head.

"What? We're not messing with anything in the Hub. The Free Citizens will do most of the work. We're just doing a little something to make sure the Government can't hurt more people. It was something the Underground could do if they gave a damn, but they don't." Flit threw her hands up in the air. She picked up a black jacket and shrugged it on as she muttered, disgruntled.

Given the location of the facility, it would take minimal effort to send a couple of skilled operatives in to destroy it, but the Underground either didn't see it as an issue, or their priorities were out of line. He did not know what they were doing to get themselves back up to the Hub, but from what he gathered, it might not even be a goal anymore.

As much as Scraps had put his trust into the leaders in the Underground, Flit was right. Entire generations had come and gone, waiting to live their lives freely. Every new cohort of Underground Derivates who refused to make a move was another cohort who failed the one who would follow. He didn't know about the others, but he would not be satisfied letting wonderful children like Seeker and Kindling spend their lives in those dark tunnels.

Scraps smoothed his hand over Flit's neatly braided hair and leaned down to press a kiss against her forehead. He took a deep breath of her and nodded. "Please do not forget the plan. We stick together. If something goes wrong, you teleport us out of there."

Flit pulled him down for a passionate kiss. When it ended, she nodded. "I don't normally like plans, but that one is as good as it gets. I'm not leaving your side," she promised.

"Then let's get this over with," Scraps replied firmly.

Together, they shouldered their packs and made their way out.

Flit and Scraps met Chris and Liana in the garage of their apartment building so they could go together. The rendezvous point for the operation was at the very edge of town. Apparently, Andy was capable of far more than game development. She had used some rather skilful hacking to locate a trio of barrier posts that were losing efficiency in the electrostatic fence. As the small convoy of vehicles joined together and turned their lights off upon approach, Andy dropped that part of the barrier long enough for their hovercars to get through without trouble. Apparently, Andy was travelling with Adam in the first car, Petra and Trey were together in the middle one, and Flit, Scraps, Chris, and Liana were at the tail end.

They had to take the trek slow without their lights on, using only the moonlight to guide them, but the ground between the fence and the factories outside of the Hub was relatively flat and made for a smooth and easy trip. Off in the distance, the shadow of Old City loomed over them. The cracked buildings split the night, shooting straight up and piercing the dark thunderclouds brewing overhead.

It was only five minutes before the vehicles pulled to a stop in a copse of evergreens that stood by a laser fence surrounding the new, ten-story research facility.

Scraps cut the engine and looked over at Chris and Liana. "If things go badly in there, you both need to get out, back to the car, and then return to the city as quickly as safely as you can," he warned them.

Liana screwed her face up in concern. "What about you and Ava? We can't leave you."

Flit pulled Liana into a warm hug. "Don't worry. Brian and I can take care of ourselves, but not if you guys are waiting for us, ok?" Flit said as she let her go. When Liana pulled back, Flit's expression turned serious. "Why do you think Brian and I insist on going for regular walks? Lady, these legs can get us far. We'll be fine."

Liana laughed, and the tension that had been growing as they got farther away from the Hub settled. She tucked a strand of loose raven hair behind her ear.

Flit reached into her pocket and pulled out a small metal jar. She opened it up to reveal a gooey silver substance that shifted colours in the light, then showed the others. "Interference paint," she explained. "It contains special pigments that mess with techno-logical identity confirmation."

Flit dipped her fingers into the goop and then swiped three horizontal lines across Liana's cheeks. She did the same to Scraps, Chris, and then herself.

"Does that stuff really work?" Chris asked, scrunching his nose up in disgust at the cold wetness.

"Well enough." Flit wiped her fingers clean on her black tights. "Nothing can entirely protect your identity from their anti-interfer-ence software or microkinetics, but instead of identifying you straight away, the interference pigments will blur any images enough to ensure that you are just one of hundreds of possible matches that come up."

Scraps sat back in his seat and looked at the others, a sense of protectiveness surging in him. "No matter what happens in there, do not allow yourselves to get split up," he warned Chris and Liana sternly. His friends were new to all of this, and he did not want them to get hurt.

Liana smiled at him, reaching over to pat his hand. "We'll be fine, Brian. This has all been planned out."

Scraps unlocked the doors of the vehicle and got out, the dewy grass crunching under the soles of their boots as they walked over to where Adam was waiting for them.

"Evening." Adam nodded towards them, a small but satisfied grin on his lips.

Behind him, Trey, Petra, and Andy greeted them too.

"We are approaching go time. Have you got access to the nodes for the security field and surveillance?" Scraps asked, looking between Adam and Andy.

Andy nodded, teal hair fluttering in the late night breeze. "Yes, but we're just waiting on confirmation from the others before I bring down the right panels."

"Wait, what?" Flit snapped, narrowing her eyes at Andy.

Adam's smirk widened. "We want to make sure we do this right, so I called in reinforcements. There are four more teams entering from other locations. The more damage, the better, right?"

Scraps looked at Flit, hiding his concern behind a grimace.

"Adam, that was not what we discussed." Flit stepped closer to him and put her hands on her hips.

"What? Surprised I can plan something without your input?" Adam teased her.

Flit balled up her fists.

Scraps stepped up beside her. "Who is on these other teams, and what are you planning to have them do?"

"I've got other cells of Free Citizens around the city. Did you really think this was the only one?" Adam frowned between Flit and Scraps.

Scraps didn't answer because it would make him seem far more naive than he wanted to appear.

Adam pulled a handful of earpieces from his pocket and threw one to each of them. "I'll be busy managing things from here.

Brian, you're in charge of this team. You and the other teams will take down the security doors closest to your entry points. Once you're inside, you'll have two floors each to clear."

Scraps was not happy about the surprise teams joining them, but at least it meant they would all be in and out of there faster. "Who goes where?" he asked.

With a shrug, Adam said, "Up to you. You are all to meet in the foyer. Since you and Ava have the best idea of the layout, I will need you to split up and take the teams to their levels then give them a rundown of what they will find on each one."

There were so many things wrong with Adam's logic that Scraps didn't know where to begin.

Flit, however, did not have that issue. "Brian and I are not splitting up."

"What is this, high school?" Adam shook his head. "You both have the best grasp of the floorplan. We need you to guide the teams separately so you can get in and out before the Government realises their security has been breached."

"I said Brian and I are not splitting up," Flit replied through gritted teeth.

Adam stepped closer to Flit, using his height to stand over her. Flit didn't even flinch at the obvious intimidation technique. Scraps was about to step closer when Flit pulled out the earpiece she had just fitted to her ear.

"We're done here. Brian, let's go," Flit snapped, throwing the earpiece back at Adam and turning on her heel. She stalked off to the hovercar, leaving Scraps scrambling to follow.

Scraps wasn't sure if abandoning the Free Citizens now was a wise idea, but he was not about to let Flit leave on her own or go into the facility separately.

44

———

FLIT

THE RELATIONSHIP between Flit and Adam had become a pissing contest. He might be the leader of the Free Citizens, but she wasn't about to let some office-softened arsehole of a Citizen tell her what to do on a mission, so she called his bluff. She kept on walking, smiling at the sound of Scraps' boots crunching on the grass behind her, until she reached the door of the car.

"Fine. Stay together," Adam yelled after them.

Flit stopped suddenly, and Scraps stumbled to the side to stop from crashing into her back.

Adam's voice got softer as he approached them. "But you will still need to brief the others once you are in there. They are expecting it, and you can't let them down. If they fail, it will be on your heads." When he stopped in front of Flit, Adam was whispering so only she and Scraps could hear the last part.

Flit whirled around and jabbed her finger in his direction. "They won't fail," she snapped, glaring at him. "But if they do, it will be because you neglected to bring all of the information to the table in planning." She was about to say more when Scraps shook his head and put a hand on her shoulder.

"Ava… remember why we are doing this," he whispered.

Flit covered Scraps' hand with her own and took a deep breath as she nodded. "Let's do it," she told him.

The two turned and walked back to the others, who were all

gaping in surprise at the drama.

Flit looked at Andy. "How long until you get that barrier down?"

"Umm… two minutes?"

Flit leaned over and plucked the earpiece she had thrown at Adam off the grass. She wiped off the dew on her tights and nestled the tech into her ear. "Good. We should get started. The longer we are out here, the more exposed we are."

Adam nodded at Andy. She took a small datapad from her back pocket tapped at the screen so quickly her fingers were a blur. Scraps came up to stand beside Flit as he looked at the others while Andy worked. He shifted to stand taller, and Flit recognised from the set of his shoulders and expression that he had gone into mission-command mode.

"The moment the fence is down, we run over to our entry point. Ava will put the EMP on the door sensor, and once it is off, we go in, keeping our eyes open, and—"

"Rendezvous with the others in the foyer," Adam interrupted.

Scraps rolled his shoulders, shooting Adam a glance before continuing, "We rendezvous with the others. We will drop a team off every two floors and take the top two levels ourselves. Do not use your weapons unless you need to. Placing the EMPs on their equipment will do enough damage without putting us at risk."

Scraps plucked an EMP device from his pocket and held it up for the others to see. It was a small silver disc no larger than an almond, with a single, concave button on top.

"Set the device in place, hold the button down for three seconds, and get out of the room within fifteen seconds. If you get stuck in there, you will fry the circuit in your earpieces and personal datapads, if you have them on you. Make sure you retrieve them after use, too. We cannot leave them lying around for the Government to find." He passed the EMP around for everyone to familiarise themselves with. "I know you have weapons, and it will be tempting to do more physical damage, but you are not trained in their use, and we do not want any injuries tonight. Do you copy?" he asked.

"Copy that," Flit replied instinctively.

The others gaped at Scraps.

"Gee, Brian… have you done this before?" Chris said with a weak smile, trying to break the tension. "Or is that just what you pull out sometimes to remind Ava why she's with you?"

Andy snorted a laugh, and Petra and Trey were smirking also.

Scraps looked at Flit, disgruntled. She would have laughed, too, if the situation wasn't so concerning. Did these Citizens do not understand the risk and danger they were in?

"I don't need any reminders to know why I'm with Brian," Flit said, "but we do need to remember the stakes of this situation, and right now? We need to get this over with before we're caught."

Adam picked up a black duffel bag off the ground by his feet. He reached in, pulling out bits of pieces of equipment that he had gathered and distributed them to the group.

"So, you will be commanding the operation, but Ava and I will be the field captains?" Scraps confirmed as Adam handed him a pistol. Scraps checked the charge on it before tucking it into his belt.

"You will be the field captain," Adam corrected.

Flit rolled her eyes at Adam's attempted slight and decided to be the bigger person. They did not have time to deal with his shit, and Scraps was more than capable of leading a mission like this. She was just relieved Adam would be hanging back. She didn't like his overzealous approach and would rather not be in a high-stakes situation with him if she could avoid it.

"Adam, can you please tell the other teams to get ready to go and give us a countdown from ten on Andy's mark?" Scraps asked.

Andy looked up from her datapad and nodded. "This is ready to go."

"Very well." Adam pressed his finger against the earpiece he was wearing, and Flit motioned for everyone to make sure their earpieces were on too. "Is everyone in place?"

A chorus of "Yes!" chirped through the channel. Scraps stepped forward, and Flit stood by his side. The others milled about loosely behind them.

"Good. Everyone, go on the count of ten. When you are in there, meet Ava and Brian at the elevator bank, and they will make sure you know where you're going." Adam let that sink in for a moment before starting the count. "Ten… nine… eight…"

Scraps looked down at Flit, his face set in unwavering concentration. When he was on a mission, he was entirely dedicated. This would be no difference. Flit gave him a small smile before returning her attention to the building.

"This is so exciting!" Petra whispered.

Flit rolled her eyes, able to get away with it because everyone else was behind them.

"I hope I don't have to shoot anyone… I can't shoot anyone," Liana blurted, suddenly sounding very concerned.

"Don't worry. The facility is empty at night. You won't need to shoot anyone," Flit promised, confident in their research.

"Four… three… two…"

"Ready?" Flit whispered, turning to Andy.

Andy's finger hovered above her datapad. She squinted at the screen, as if worried that touching it might cause it to explode. Still, she took a deep breath.

"One… Go!"

There was an audible fizzling as the fence lost power. Andy, Trey, and Petra cheered.

"Let's move!" Scraps barked, leading a headlong sprint towards their entrance door.

Flit gasped as a rush of adrenaline hit her. She might have been wary about the mission, but it was exhilarating to be doing something other than paperwork.

Her feet pounded against the grass as she ran. She reached into her pocket and pulled out an EMP device. "I've got the door," she called out. She flicked off the safety.

Scraps stopped running and held his arm out. The others skidded to a stop, swearing when they almost slipped on the damp grass. Flit covered the final twenty metres alone and looked at the door. The bioreader for the lock was just below the handle. She tore off some backing paper on the adhesive foam, stuck the EMP device to the reader, activated it, and then ran back to the others.

Flit reached the safety-zone just in time to hear a loud click from the EMP. The light on the screen of the bio-reader sparked and then fizzled, and a green indicator on the EMP device let them know it was done.

"Got it. Let's move." Flit now took the lead. She ran to the door, tugging the device off the panel and shoving it in her back pocket. "Don't forget, we need to make sure we get these all back. The fewer clues left behind, the better," she reminded the others, holding the door open for them.

They all acknowledged her reminder as they filed in, and she ran in, leaving the door ajar. The group made their way past some security screening stations that were still not operational. Flit fell in behind them. She kept her hand on her pistol while she took in their surroundings. The main lobby was as modern and spacious as any Government building's, with towering steel and glass structures all around them. The reserve lights were on, casting the silver décor in an eerie red hue. Flit wasn't too bothered by it, though. In some ways, being in the reserve lighting felt like being home.

She missed the Underground.

She didn't have time to dwell on her homesickness as Scraps led them to the elevator bank in the middle and urged everyone into a small group.

Once they were there, he scanned over them and did a head-count. "All six present and accounted for," he said, more to Flit than the others.

Flit nodded then whirled around at the sound of footsteps. "And more incoming."

Small groups of people emerged from the shadows, ambling along and chatting in conspiratorial whispers. It was like they were a bunch of gagglers discussing some sort of sordid art exhibition. Their eyes were alight with amusement but with little sense of urgency.

"Double time!" Scraps barked.

The authority in his tone made Flit stand straighter, and the newcomers walked a little faster, but there were a few giggles amongst them.

When they got closer and Flit was able to see their faces, she frowned. "Where is your interference paint?"

One of the women, someone younger than her with a look of apathy on her pretty face, shrugged. "It felt gross."

The others murmured their agreement.

Flit rolled her eyes, reaching into her pocket to retrieve the cannister. "You know what feels gross? Being strapped into the

Government's sick experiments because you got caught," she said in a terse tone. "Quit your whining and put the paint on. If you get caught, it puts everyone else at risk. Put it on, or get the fuck out."

"Who do you think—"

Scraps stepped forward, putting a hand on Flit's shoulder. "This is Ava, and I am Brian," Scraps interrupted the woman. Flit threw her the cannister, and she was too busy trying to catch it to argue. "Adam has put us in charge of this incursion. The interference paint is compulsory." He looked around, narrowing his eyes at anyone who dared to protest. "While you are putting that on, you need to listen to me. We will be taking this building in the teams we entered in. Ava and I will lead the way to the top floor, dropping one team off every two storeys. You are to clear the floor we leave you at and the one below it, and then you are to get out."

"Shouldn't we wait? You know, make sure everyone is fine?" a middle-aged man at the back of one of the teams asked.

"No. Nobody is to loiter. You check out of the building through the comms and then once more when you reach your getaway vehicles. Is that understood?"

At the determination and firmness in Scraps' tone, everyone seemed to pay more attention. They were all passing the interference powder around, and Flit did her own headcount. Each team had about four people in it.

"Does everyone know what the mission objective is?" Flit asked.

"Er…. destroy shit?" a woman near the front said with a shrug.

On any other day, Flit might have been the one saying something similar, but not today. "Get into any room with a computer or electronic tech, place your EMP charge, find shelter outside the radius, and then remove it once it has worked its magic. Don't leave any behind if you can help it," Flit explained, looking at them all seriously.

"Why don't we just smash stuff?" a younger man asked, looking disgruntled. He had a metal bar strapped to his back.

"Because we do not want to risk injuries, and we do not need to *smash* stuff." Scraps scowled at him. "If we hit the right servers, we destroy months of their work without them even knowing we were here. We have to fight smart, not hard."

"Who put that killjoy in charge?" the man muttered.

"I did." Adam's voice came through the comms. "And he's right. Do what he says, or you'll answer to me. Remember, Free Citizens, this is but the first skirmish in the battle for our freedom. There will be time for more satisfying anarchy later."

Scraps frowned at the last part, but Adam's interjection settled the group. When the final person finished with the interference paint, Flit took the empty tin to put into her pocket.

"Everyone, stand in your teams, please," Scraps said. People rearranged themselves, and he spoke to Andy through the comms. "How much time do we have?"

"System should be out for another… hour," she replied.

"All right, everyone. If you have a timepiece, synch it for forty-five minutes. That is when you need to be heading for the doors, regardless of the amount of EMPs you've set off."

Flit looked around at the sea of blank stares looking back at Scraps. "Brian meant to set an alarm. Set an alarm on your devices for forty-five minutes."

"Oh!" A woman at the front chuckled as she looked at her watch.

Scraps took a deep breath, and Flit marvelled at how this bunch of ordinary Citizens managed to frustrate him like that when she never had.

When people stopped shuffling and tapping their wrist devices, Scraps straightened up. "I'll take point. Ava, you cover the rear."

"Copy." Flit waited for the group to follow him towards the fire-escape stairs door that was neatly nestled at the core of the bank of elevators. As the Free Citizens jogged to keep up, Flit heard some muttering about how ridiculous it was to be using the stairs when there were perfectly good elevators available.

The sound of footsteps echoed up the emergency stairwell shaft, sounding just like the heavy rain that started to fall outside of the building. Flit couldn't help but think the weather was a good omen for them. Any evidence of them being outside of the building would be washed away if the rain kept up. The world itself was helping them hide their tracks.

45

SCRAPS

THE GROUP REACHED the landing on the second floor, and Scraps looked back at the full team as they stood on the stairs below him. "First team going in, you are to cover the second and first floor in that order. You will be Alpha team. Remember the mission: use the EMPs to frazzle as much tech as you can and then get out. If you come across unexpected resistance, retreat."

"Unexpected resistance?" A woman at the front looked shocked at the idea.

"Our intel and research led us to believe that this facility should be vacant, but you always need to be prepared." Scraps pushed the door open to the second floor and motioned for the first group to head in. "Once you're done, check in with Adam via comms and then leave immediately."

"And don't use the elevator! Stairs only!" Flit's yell echoed from farther down the stairwell.

As Alpha team filed past him, someone from the next team looked disgruntled. "I wasn't told we'd have to use the stairs."

Not for the first time that night, Scraps was reminded that he was working with a team of utter amateurs. He looked at the dissenter sternly. "If something happens and you get caught in the elevator, you can consider yourself the Government's newest experimental subject," he told them, tone brokering no argument. "Use the stairs."

The surprise in the eyes that blinked back at him was enough to reassure Scraps they would heed his advice.

He turned around and started to climb the stairs again two at a time. At the fourth floor, he reissued the instructions to Bravo team then kept climbing. They repeated the process every second floor, dropping off Charlie and Delta teams. When they finally reached the landing at the top of the fire stairs, all the Free Citizens were out of breath. Flit, panting but still full of energy, bounced over to his side. He smiled at her, unable to remain serious when faced with her flushed cheeks and that flash of determination in her eyes.

"Are you getting the door or covering?" Flit asked, resting her hand on the pouch on her belt that held a mix of flash and fire grenades.

"You stick on tail and cover." Scraps reached for the door handle and looked at Liana, Chris, Petra, and Trey. "We are Echo team. What I said to the others stands true. We get in and get out. No messing around." Scraps looked at Flit. "And no hotshotting."

Flit pretended to look outraged at the insinuation, but Scraps knew her flaws too well to play dumb.

With a firm nod, Scraps pushed the door opened and hurried the team through. The area immediately around the elevator bank was a large reception zone for the rows and rows of doorways that shot out of the space. Almost completely bare of furniture, the level reeked of the adhesive they used for the sterile panelling. The only furniture in place were the computers and datascreens, as they all had to be wired in.

"Split into pairs. Stick with your partner. Report back here when you are finished or if I give the order early. Remember to stay out the range of the EMP pulse. You don't want to fry your communicators." Scraps retrieved an EMP device from his pocket.

Everyone acknowledged the orders and turned to take a corridor. Flit stepped up to his side, and they both turned and jogged down the corridor just to their right.

Thanks to the fact that this facility was not yet operational, the Government was relying on their security fence and external doors to keep intruders out. All the office and lab spaces on these levels were unlocked and clear.

It was almost too easy to get into the rooms, set the EMP

charge, run out, and move to the next room. Flit lagged just enough to retrieve the wasted charges and then run out. The pattern served them well, as they were the first to return to the lobby of level ten. There wasn't much else to see or do, so they stood together as the others started to trickle back. Fifteen minutes after getting to level ten and twenty-five minutes after entering the facility, the group was back together.

They were joined first by Chris and Liana, and then Petra skidded to a halt as she and Trey were the last to come in. "Shit… you guys are fast," she panted, leaning over and putting her hands on her knees, sweat plastering her dark hair to her face.

"Brian went in, set the charge, and then left. After he left, I collected it, and he moved on. We didn't stop moving, no need to wait," Flit informed them then looked at Scraps. "I've got twenty minutes on my clock. Twenty minutes until alarm, thirty until hard out. We need to keep moving."

"Ava's right." Scraps nodded. "Let's try and get the next floor completed in ten minutes. Use the strategy Ava and I did, and you should be fine."

Without checking to see if they were following, Scraps turned and ran for the stairwell, knowing Flit would keep an eye on the rest of the team between them.

As he ran, he pressed a finger to his earpiece. "All teams, twenty minutes until your alarms go off. When that happens, evacuate, regardless of mission objective. Understood?"

There were a couple of harried acknowledgements through the comms. Scraps wanted to ask which teams had spoken, but it would just be a waste of time at this point. They were not trained to respond properly to field orders over the radio, and now was not the time to correct that oversight. He would have to bring it up with Adam later. That, and several other concerns.

Level nine was, thankfully, a carbon copy of ten. Flit and Scraps made short work of the offices and labs like they had before, all just as empty as the ones above. Every comm screen or data terminal they saw got destroyed indiscriminately, and even though there would be back up of the data on the Government's servers, replacing the infrastructure and making sure the networks played together nicely would be a gargantuan task for them.

They had just about finished when a loud boom shook the building and screaming vibrated through the earpiece. Scraps stopped, hand on the door of the next office he was going into, and looked at Flit as she came out of a room with an EMP in hand.

"All teams, report! What was that?" Scraps snapped, pressing his finger against his earpiece.

"Third floor!" a frazzled female voice said.

"We found a gas tap. Decided to have some fun," another voice added.

"But Kiara got hurt. She's bleeding," the first female voice trembled through the radio.

"Fucking idiots," Flit groaned, shaking her head. She pressed the comms again. "Can she walk?"

"Yes."

It sounded like something Flit might do in another situation, but Scraps chose not to bring that up right now. It wouldn't help.

"Someone take off their jacket and wad it up against the wound. Put pressure on it and retreat," he ordered.

"We haven't finished the mission," the woman argued.

"Every drop of blood Kiara loses is a drop that could lead the Government to us. Get her out immediately. You have done enough. Beta team, retreat immediately," Scraps snapped, looking over at Flit, who sighed and shook her head. "That's an order."

"If the Government picked that up somehow, we should probably all retreat," Flit hissed in a low voice.

Scraps looked down the row of unfinished offices and then back at his wrist device. He frowned. "All teams, retreat now."

There was a chorus of disagreement, but Adam's voice cut through it. "Brian's right. I saw that out here. Everyone, get out, now! Brian, Ava, can you go down to level three and clean up as much blood as you can find?"

Flit let out a huff at that command. "If one person gets caught, we're all at risk…"

"Yes, but we need two team members to remain there to show us where to go. We are not wasting time searching for ourselves," Scraps told Adam and the others.

"We'll wait in the lobby," the woman who called it in volunteered.

Scraps turned around to see the rest of Echo team running towards them. He ensured that his friends were safe and accounted for as they made for the stairs. Once more, the emergency stairwell was filled with the drumming of racing feet. The downstairs scramble was much faster than the ascent, and by the time Flit and Scraps broke off on the third floor, they had seen all of Delta and Charlie teams evacuating. The two remaining members of Bravo team were waiting by the fire escape door for them, looking somewhat nervous now that the order to evacuate had been given and they were left behind.

"Show us to the room," Flit demanded as they made it into the foyers. She looked over at Scraps. "You go with them. I'm going to follow after and clean up any splatters on the way." Flit reached into her pocket and took out a torch they had both brought with them, courtesy of the Underground's supplies back in their unit. She flicked through various light settings until she reached an ultraviolet beam and pointed it around the lobby.

"Good thinking." Scraps retrieved his own torch and gestured to the Citizens. "Lead the way."

Flit took her jacket off and used it to wipe up at some of the spots of blood that were glowing white in the ultraviolet rays. They would have been impossible to see in the reserve lighting of the building.

Scraps hated leaving her behind, but he hoped he would not have to go far. He let the Free Citizens lead him to the lab that was still smoking. He pulled up the collar of his T-shirt to cover his nose at the burning tang and frowned as he looked inside, eyes watering. The room was destroyed. At least, destroyed enough that going in would be foolish, so, he turned to the two women with him.

"Take off your jackets. Get cleaning. Hurry. We don't have much time." He used his torch to point out splatters of blood around the corridor, and they all got to work.

Kiera must not have been injured badly enough to leave too much blood around. They couldn't be sure that they got it all, but they could not linger, so they did their best.

"Adam, we are leaving level three now. What is the situation outside?" Scraps asked as he led the group through the lobby and towards the stairs.

"All clear so far. Andy's working some of her technomagic, and it doesn't seem the Government have been alerted to our presence. Yet. Just get back as fast as you can. Not long left before the system reboots and kicks us out of security," Adam informed Scraps.

"Copy that. Is everyone else out?" Scraps asked.

"Yes, all others present and accounted for."

Scraps breathed a sigh of relief. That had to count for something. They just needed to keep moving, and they would be fine.

"Wait… what's that sound?" Flit asked as the group turned the corner and raced down the final flight of stairs that led to the ground floor.

Making a concerted attempt to control his panting so he could hear whatever Flit did, Scraps looked at her as he settled his hand over his weapon. "What sound?"

Flit jumped down, overtaking the other two and landing on her feet with a slight *oof* as she skipped four stairs. Scraps could only imagine that it must have been a jarring impact, but Flit was used to sticking her landings. She held up a hand, gesturing for the others to stop. They did, and the only sound in the stairwell was their laboured breathing.

Several tense seconds passed. Scraps was about to suggest moving on when a loud banging came from a panel at the back of the stairs. Flit looked at him and unclipped her pistol from her belt. She held up a finger to her lips as she jutted her chin at the two women with them and then towards the door. "Go!"

The women looked at each other, but in the end, their fear won out over any possible desire to stay and fight. When they fled, Scraps took out his own weapon and gestured for Flit to follow him towards the door that led to the stairwell. They held it open as they waited. Another round of frantic knocking shook the panel before it exploded to the side.

Scraps raised an arm to shield his face from a blast, but there was none. Instead of the fire and smoke that would come from a grenade or the laser-guides from weapons blasting the panel aside, a woman and a man stood in a dark corridor that had been hidden by the panel. The man, gaunt and hunched over, wheezed and let his arm fall to his side.

"Good work," the woman beside him whispered in a gentle tone, slipping her hands under his armpits to hold him up.

"Who are you?" Flit demanded.

The woman held the man tighter to her side as she eyed Flit and Scraps warily. Everyone in the group wore Government-issued grey scrubs that reminded Scraps of the patients in the AHR facility. The woman's left arm was wrapped from wrist to mid-bicep in a bandage. Her red hair was tied in a messy plait, but her green eyes were alert. She didn't say anything, but she did not need to as Scraps peered closer at the man beside her and saw red irises peering back at him in the darkness. There was an old, faded tattoo on the side of his neck that made Scraps' own skin crawl in that area.

"Are you Derivates?" Scraps lowered his weapon slightly.

The man nodded. "We are."

"Who are you?" The woman asked, as the people behind her shifted uncomfortably.

"Friends," Flit said, putting her hand on Scraps' arm and pushing it down all the way. "We can get you to safety." She looked up at him, and Scraps nodded at the unspoken request in her eyes.

"How long have you been here?" Scraps asked.

"A couple of months? They moved us from another facility." The woman's voice was wary as the people behind her moved in closer to one another.

They did not know they would find other Derivates here, but there was no way they were going to leave them behind to be recaptured by the Government. They all looked so tired and scared; he was not sure if they would survive it.

"Are there any more of you?" Scraps asked the woman as he started counting how many people were in the group.

The woman cast a glance over her shoulder before confirming, "Two more. We have to leave one behind, but the other will be here soon."

"We're just north of the electrostatic fence, in the dead zone between the Hub and Old City. If you continue through the trees for two kilometres, you should come across an abandoned train shed. There is a safehouse in the basement with food, water, and blankets," Flit explained, reaching down and taking her gun out of her holster. She offered it to the woman, but the woman shook her head and pushed it back towards her. "The people we are with made a bit of a mess, so you need to get out now and move fast. We will come by tomorrow afternoon, and we'll get you somewhere safer, ok?"

The woman nodded and straightened up, seemingly strengthened by a renewed sense of purpose.

Just as Scraps was about to suggest they leave immediately, a middle-aged woman with dark brown hair that was greying at the temples ran up to the group from farther down the passage. She dashed a stream of tears off her flushed cheeks as she said, "Sorry, Layla."

"Don't you dare apologise," the red-headed woman, Layla, said in a surprisingly fierce tone. "Are you ready to—"

"Fortune?" Flit launched herself towards the newcomer.

Panic seized at Scraps, and he wrapped an arm around Flit's waist to hold her back. She teleported out of his hold and the next instant, she was standing before the brunette, her shoulders shaking.

The brunette woman squinted as she reached out with trembling fingers to trace the lines of Flit's face. "It can't be…" she whispered, awe suffusing every syllable. She tilted her head to the side and then her deep brown eyes went wide. "Oh my goodness."

The older woman pulled Flit into a fierce grapple hold and Scraps raised his gun. The other people in the group gasped and cowered back, but Flit turned to look at him over her shoulder. "Put it down, Scraps!" she snapped, clinging tighter to the woman. "This is Fortune, Rook's mother."

Scraps took out his torch and shone it towards her. Sure enough, her deep caramel complexion and carved cheekbones reminded him of the pictures he'd seen of Rook. He remembered Flit saying that Rook and Fortune had been taken at the same time.

Scraps gulped. If she was here, did that mean Rook was too?

46

———

FLIT

FLIT STOOD, heart beating all the way up in her throat, leaning into Fortune's emaciated form as the woman looked at her with wonder. Flit felt like she was floating, as though she had gone from the hard reality of the mission that had gone awry and fallen head-long into some sort of dream.

Or nightmare.

She wasn't sure yet.

What she was sure of, though, was that this was Fortune. The woman who had been taken away from her. Around two years had passed, but the poor telecoercionist had aged a decade. The subtle crow's feet that had just been starting to form in the corners of her eyes were a prominent fixture, and her dark, glossy brown hair was grey and thin in so many places.

Regardless of how much she had aged, she was a sight for sore eyes and a broken heart. It took a great deal of effort for Flit to shake herself out of her stupor, but there was one thing on her mind that helped her push through.

"Rook?"

If Fortune was alive, maybe Rook had survived too.

The smile on Fortune's face fell, her eyes shimmering with tears as she straightened her shoulders.

Flit's throat became so tight that she could hardly breathe.

"He can't leave," Fortune whispered, voice shaking.

Flit blinked. The world tilted on its axis. "H-he's alive?" She pressed her hand against the wall to keep herself upright. "Where is he? We can't leave him behind. We can't—"

"I would move the earth to bring him with us, but it is impossible." Fortune shook her head as she captured both of Flit's hands, grasping them in her own and holding them against her chest. "He wants us to leave."

"I'll talk to him." Lips set in a stubborn line, Flit asked, "Where is he?"

Fortune pointed back over her shoulder. Flit nodded and went to move past her, but Fortune pulled her back. "I'll take you."

"No, you have to get to safety," Flit said firmly. "We're two kilometres south of the trainshed on the outskirts of Old City that the Underground converted into a safehouse. I gave the others directions, but you actually know what you're looking for. They need your help more than I do."

"It's a maze back there," Fortune argued.

A voice piped up from behind Flit, "I'll show her where to go." Layla stepped towards them.

Fortune winced. "Layla, you don't have to—"

Layla pulled Fortune into a hug and then held her at arm's length. "I'll catch up. You know the way, lead them to safety."

Flit kissed Fortune's cheek. "Go. I'll see you soon," she promised, hating the idea of leaving her. A tear slid down her cheek, but she sniffed back her emotions. She still had work to do.

There was the slightest hesitation before Fortune complied. All it took was a wave, and everyone followed her out of the stairwell, leaving Flit, Layla, and Scraps alone.

"How long do we have?" Layla asked, looking between Scraps and Flit. Flit tried to place the woman's face but couldn't. Without the red eyes and tattoo, she had to assume she came from one of the Underground's outposts that had been discovered a few years ago.

"Max, ten minutes. Ideally less," Scraps said, voice stiff. "Really, we should just leave now."

Flit teleported over to him and placed her hands on his chest. "Rook is in there, Scraps. I have to see him."

His stern expression was unreadable, but he examined her

teary-eyed desperation and nodded almost imperceptibly. "Then let's make this quick." He gestured to Layla. "Please, lead the way."

Layla led them down the narrow corridor. It was made of raw, unfinished concrete and ended in a security door that had been blasted open to reveal another staircase. This one went down, and after one flight, they found themselves at a second unhinged door which opened onto a foyer with dozens of glass-walled labs. All of them had been completely trashed. There was another checkpoint and what looked like a series of single-room cells towards the end of the space. Flit was just about to ask where Rook was when movement in a lab caught her eyes.

Flit teleported over in the space between heartbeats and pressed her face to the glass. Her heart sank as she saw an unfamiliar man behind the door. He had bedraggled blond hair and eyes that darted around the room warily. When he saw Flit through the window, the straps holding him to the bed disintegrated, and he slid off and got to his feet.

"Give me a minute. I'll let you out!" Flit called to him.

"No!" Layla cried.

Flit froze.

"Leave him. He's dangerous!" Layla's footsteps thundered through the space, and she grabbed Flit by the shoulder, pulling her back. "Rook's over here, come on."

Disgust roiled through Flit, and her braid cracked like a whip as she snapped around to glare at Layla. "I will not leave anyone behind."

"You don't understand—"

Flit held a hand up. "Is he a Derivate?"

"Yes, but—"

Flit interrupted again. "Is he a prisoner of the Government?"

Layla groaned. "Yes, but he's dangerous. The report said he killed two do—"

"Do always believe what Government says?" The man's rough, deep voice was muffled through the window.

"Let him out, now. And then take him with you to join the others!"

Layla muttered something under her breath and pressed her hand against the locking mechanism on the door. It clicked open, and the man stepped out. Layla stepped back and frowned at him. "Keep up and we may make it out of here alive," she said. She offered Flit and Scraps a final wave before running out of the room with the man on her heels.

"Flit? Flit!"

Rook.

The voice was croaky, parched, pained… but there was no mistaking that smooth molasses baritone.

Flit teleported to the door of the next cell over. It was already ajar, and as she pushed it open, her sweet, loving fiancé sat up in the bed. He couldn't move far, though. All sorts of wires and tubes ran from various parts of his body and into the wall behind him. His previously solid, stocky physique had almost withered away to nothing but skin and bones. His once-chiselled jawline had morphed from striking to gaunt. The artful ruffle of his deep brown hair was now more of a wild tangle that hung past his ears and covered his eyes. *But those eyes…*

They still held that spark of mystery and mischief that had made her fall in love with him.

Flit gasped, her body wracked with sobs.

Rook's thick eyebrows furrowed as he looked at her and sucked in a breath. "Flit?" he whispered as though he didn't dare believe it. "Bloody hell… Flit!"

With a teleport that was entirely instinct, Flit appeared at his side. "Rook!" His name trebled from her lips, her fingers itched to pull out all the tubes that kept him tied to the bed. "We need to get you out of here."

Before Flit could do anything, Rook reached out and pulled her into a hug. He pressed a kiss against the top of her head as he murmured a torrent of disbelief and wonder. Flit let herself sink against his solid chest as it rose and fell with his breath.

He was breathing.

He was alive.

And she was in his arms.

Flit pulled back enough to look up at him, guilt flooding through her. "The file said you were terminated," she whimpered. "I'm so sorry. Rook, I thought you were dead… I thought you were gone. I would have come to find you. I swear I wanted to. I'm sorry. I'm so—"

Rook silenced her with a kiss that tasted of desperation and heartbreak.

But a new sort of guilt flooded Flit, and she pulled back, her breath catching in her throat as she realised Scraps was standing in the doorway. Her cheeks flushed with panic.

"Scraps, shit… I—"

Scraps shook his head, his mouth opening and closing uselessly.

When Flit turned back to look at Rook, understanding dawned in his eyes, but instead of looking heartbroken, Flit saw… relief?

"Scraps, was it?" Rook asked, holding Flit close against his chest and looking over her shoulder.

"Yes." Scraps' reply was sharp. Clipped.

Flit didn't know how to process the situation, but she did know they had to get a move on. She turned to Rook, unable to stop herself from tracing her fingers along his jawline, just like she used to. "Tell me what I need to do to get you out of here."

Something odd flashed behind Rook's eyes, but it was gone in an instant. Flit thought she might have imagined it. The emergency lighting and the emotions of finding Rook were doing weird things to her mind.

"We need to bring this building down," Rook said slowly. "Can you help me with that?"

Flit snorted. "Of course." She pulled the hem of her jacket back to reveal the flame grenades secured to her belt.

With a mix of a cough and laugh, Rook smiled at her. "That's my girl." He cupped her cheek again. "Each lab has a gas tap. Turn them all on full, and then get back here, quick."

When the Free Citizens had exploded a lab upstairs, Flit had been furious, but now? Witnessing what she had in the past five minutes, Flit was ready to burn the entire fucking facility down.

A grim sense of determination settled over her, and she straightened up. "Come on, Scraps. Let's do this."

Scraps looked like he was about to argue, but he stopped himself after glancing at Rook. Instead, he and Flit spent the next two minutes going from lab to lab, flicking all the gas taps fully open. They had quite a high flow rate, and the air was already smelling painfully sharp by the time they returned to Rook's room. Flit teleported over to him.

"Right. What do I do next?" she asked, sizing up all the wires and tubes attached to him.

"You leave."

"No." Flit's heart turned to stone and dread leached all the warmth from her body. "I am getting you out of here."

Rook exhaled shakily. "You've already given me a way out."

The room spun, and Flit would have fallen if it were not for the strong hand that slipped under her arm and held her up. She would know the feel of Scraps' embrace anywhere, and she leaned back into his firm body as she narrowed her eyes at Rook. "This isn't how it ends."

With a bitter laugh, Rook shook his head. "Sorry, beautiful, but no amount of stubbornness will change this. I won't last more than a minute without these life support systems."

"I will not lose you again!" Flit stepped forward, grasping Rook's shoulders as tears sprung to her eyes.

"If it could be any other way, I would be leaving with you, I promise," Rook whispered, brushing a tear off her cheek with shaking fingertips. "The thought of seeing you again is what kept me alive through all of this. I love you, Flit, but I cannot come with you."

Without thinking, Flit leaned in and kissed him. It was a hard, desperate thing that left her breathless and flushed. If the thought of her kept Rook alive, then she planned to wipe away any doubts about his survival by reminding him that she was still there.

Behind Flit, Scraps coughed. When she pulled back, she scented the increased dispersion of gas creeping into the room, and it felt like a dagger stabbing through her frontal lobe every time she breathed.

"You need to leave before the gas poisons you," Rook said with an expression of complete and utter resolve.

"Rook—"

"Could you do me one last favour, gorgeous?" Rook asked with a weak attempt at a smile. "Let me have one of your flame grenades. I'll give you five minutes to get out of here, and then I'll make sure they can't use this place to hurt anyone else."

Flit clutched at the grenades on her belt and shook her head.

Rook combed his fingers through her hair as he pulled her close and pressed a rough kiss against her lips. "Damn it, woman! Let me be the hero for once," he begged, resting his forehead against hers.

A moment later, a warm, solid hand settled on Flit's shoulder.

"Are you sure there is nothing we can do to save you?" Scraps asked, his voice taking on that robotic, mission-commander tone.

Flit stared at Rook, desperately hoping this was some sick joke, that he was just tricking her, that he had an answer, and they could get him out alive.

"I've seen what happens when people are taken off life support. I'd much rather go out in a blaze of glory than gasping for air."

"No!" Flit's pained, furious cry filled the room.

Rook took her by the shoulders, his fingers digging into her skin through her top. "When we started dating, I promised I would never use telecoercion on you. Don't make me break that promise."

A whimper slipped from Flit's lips, and she dashed a stream of hot tears off her cheek, smearing her entire face with interference powder. "Are you sure?"

"The only thing I'm more sure of is how much I love you," Rook confirmed. "Now get out of here. Let me show these fuckers what happens when they mess with the Underground."

With tears streaming down her cheeks, Flit pressed a flame grenade into Rook's hand.

Rook leaned to the side slightly, catching Scraps' eyes and nodding. A silent understanding seemed to pass between them and Scraps wrapped his arm around Flit's waist. "It's time to go."

When Scraps turned Flit around and guided her to the door, she didn't argue. She stopped in the threshold and looked back over her shoulder at Rook, a shadow of his former self, lying in the bed and cradling the flame grenade like it was the most precious gift in the world.

The injustice of it all turned the blood in Flit's veins to ice. "Rook?"

He looked up from the grenade, as if surprised that she was still there. "Yes?"

"I will love you until my bones turn to dust and our names are nothing more than an insignificant scribble in the history books," Flit said, needing him to know that, needing to tell him how much he meant to her while she had the chance.

"Just a scribble?" His smile was bright enough to light up the room. "Bring these bastards down and make sure you get an entire damn chapter named after us."

"I will, I promise."

With a new sense of resolve, she turned to Scraps and wrapped her arms around him. She placed one hand on the small of his back and the other at the base of his neck. "Let's get out of here."

Then, without further delay, they were on the move.

They traversed the secret tunnel and the lobby in a series of quick flashes, making up for lost time. When they got to the fire escape, their watches started beeping and the radio pieces in their ears crackled.

"Ava, Brian, where are you?" Adam barked.

Scraps used telekinesis to push the exit door open. They ran through it, no longer able to teleport in case the Free Citizens were watching. While they were in the facility, the night skies had opened up, and the scent of the heavy rain washed away the acrid tang of the gas in Flit's nostrils.

"Coming now," Scraps replied as they raced towards the gap in the fence.

The posts of the segments Andy had deactivated started to crack and pop as they approached.

"Guys, hurry, please!" Andy begged, panic in her tone.

As the cars came into view, Andy was standing on the bonnet of one, datapad in her hands, looking around desperately as the rain poured down. Adam ran around the cars, throwing all of the doors open and ushering the others in. As Flit and Scraps crossed the threshold of the fence, the others got in the vehicles and switched the engines on. While they were in the facility, someone had turned them around to face the road, which had been a sound idea.

Just as Flit and Scraps skidded to a stop beside the cars, the entire horizon behind them exploded with a roar of flames that consumed the facility and shook the ground beneath their feet.

The Free Citizens cried out in shock. Flit turned around and watched as the fire licked the land clean of the sins of the Government.

"Rest well, Rook," Flit whispered, pressing a hand against her thundering heart.

As the rain pelted her, it washed away her all fears, all her regrets, all her hesitation. It stripped away the rage and the indignation, leaving only a cool indomitable sense of purpose.

She would hold the Government accountable for their atrocities and nothing, or no one, would get in her way.

47

———————

SCRAPS

THE WORLD RUMBLED AROUND SCRAPS, but after the events of the night, he was too numb to take it in. What was supposed to have been a simple mission had turned into something he wasn't quite able or ready to process.

"Brian!" Adam's voice snapped Scraps back to reality. "What the hell happened?"

Scraps opened and closed his mouth several times, feeling more and more at a loss for what to say each time he tried.

Flit slipped between him and the leader of the Free Citizens. She held her shoulders back, all signs of the sobbing wreck she had been when they left was gone, replaced by a more focused version of his girlfriend than he had ever seen before.

"You wanted to bring the Government down?" she asked, gesturing to the burning building. "This is how it begins."

Then, without another word, Flit took Scraps' hand and dragged him over to Chris and Liana's car. The decommissioned panels of the fence sizzled back into place as all of the vehicle doors slammed and the cars sped off into the night.

A clap of thunder boomed. Lightning splintered through the night, showing the silhouettes of Government drones in the distance as the hovercar convoy slipped into the shelter of the trees. The road was slick, and visibility decreased as the deluge intensified. The hammering of the rain on the roof of the car was so heavy Scraps couldn't hear himself think. When he looked up, he caught sight of matching expressions of concern on Chris' and Liana's faces as they peered back at him and Flit.

Liana went to say something, but Scraps subtly shook his head. She bit her lip and reached for Chris' hand as he steered their vehicle towards the city.

THERE WAS a reason the Government held as much power as they did. They were smart, and they knew how to work their population. Scraps had always known it, but when he woke up the morning after the assault on the facility, the reality of the extent they went to hit him. It was hard for him to comprehend the true horror of it, and the sheer danger of the risks they had taken the night before were startlingly clear.

He rolled over in bed, reaching for Flit and craving the warm comfort of her body against his.

But she wasn't there.

The cold sheet against his skin was a jarring reminder of how strange things had been when they got home after the raid. He had been preparing for Flit to break down, expecting to be up until the early morning comforting her and trying to help her sleep. But when they'd walked in the door, she'd teleported straight over to the couch and pulled out a datapad. When he'd asked what she was doing, all she'd said was 'research'. He went to probe further, but the look she had given him had chilled him to his bones.

In the end, Scraps had gone to bed alone. The fear they might be discovered was a visceral thing that singed every thought in his head, but the image of Flit kissing Rook, of her passionate declaration of love for him… that haunted him far more than the prospect of getting caught.

Until that moment, he hadn't understood what true love meant.

He had no sense of the scope of the sacrifice one had to prepare to take to give themselves so fully to another.

Months ago, Flit had let it slip that she loved him. Back then, Scraps was not sure if he was ready to say it back. Now, he knew he wasn't. If he had been in Rook's shoes, he didn't know that he would have been able to let go of Flit again, to imagine her living a happy life without him in it. It occurred to him the moment he had seen them kiss. An ugly, immature surge of jealousy gripped him and made him forget about everything else. So much had changed since he had been willing to let her go on a mission with Hawkeye months ago. She had become his constant companion, his sole confidante, the direction in his life.

Slipping out of bed, Scraps rubbed his face as he walked into the lounge room. Flit was still in the same place she had been when he'd left her. Her beautiful olive skin was pale, dark purple crescents underscoring her eyes. She was still wearing the clothes from the night before, but they had dried with creases, confirming just how long she had been sitting in the same position.

Scraps sank on the couch beside her and turned in his seat, crossing one leg in front of him so he could look at her. He reached out, smoothing strands of her messy hair out of her eyes. He let out a breath as he tried to figure out what to say.

She spared him the trouble of speaking first. "There's nothing here," she said, scrolling back up the feed. "Just a small shitty article about a fire in an abandoned facility outside of the barrier and another article further down saying they are tightening checkpoint requirements to leave the city."

Scraps levitated the datapad away from her and set it on the floor beside their feet. He took her hands in his own and threaded their fingers together. "That *is* something," he promised her. "It is a sign that they cannot ignore what happened last night. Enough people must have noticed it if they were forced to make a report."

Flit shook her head. "No, it's how they keep the Citizens happy and dumb. They filter every piece of information to within an inch of its life, and unless the Free Citizens hack the news outlets and spread the truth, no one will ever bloody know what is going on right under their stupid noses."

"They are tightening the barrier protocol," Scraps said slowly, "which means they are worried it won't be an isolated incident. They will not be pleased that they had to report it at all, Flit. As much of a mess as last night was, it was the first step. We cannot expect results immediately."

Flit rubbed her eyes as a yawn slipped from her lips.

"Did you get any sleep at all?" Scraps asked, gently squeezing her hand.

"No," Flit turned away from him. "My mind wouldn't switch off."

Scraps reclined back against the couch and wrapped an arm around her shoulder. He tried to pull her closer, but she resisted, shaking her head and pressing her lips together.

"What is it?" he asked, concerned.

"Why are you hugging me?" She wouldn't meet his eyes. "I kissed Rook last night. I told him I loved him—"

Scraps winced. "You don't have to apologise for that," he interrupted despite the way jealousy reignited in the depths of his thundering heart.

"I'm not," Flit said firmly, her grip on his hand getting painfully tight. "That's the problem. I did all of that in front of you, and I can't be sorry for it. I am sorry that you had to see and hear it, but… I wouldn't take it back for anything in the world."

Scraps closed his eyes and took a deep breath. Flit was nothing if not sure of herself. She always meant what she said, for better or for worse. Part of him instinctively knew she would never take back what she had done.

And he wasn't sure that he wanted her to.

When Scraps opened his eyes, he met her appraising gaze without hesitation. "You told me months ago that a part of you would always love him."

He did not blame or resent her. Nor did he envy the situation she was in. All it took was one look at Flit to see she had been shaken to her core, that the fire in her had turned to ice. He marvelled at the strength it must have taken to do what she had done.

To say goodbye again.

"Having Rook back in my life, even for a few moments, made me think and feel so many things," Flit whispered, looking up at him, her tired eyes flickering with something more than determination. "Do you want to know what was at the forefront of my mind when I got home?"

Scraps nodded mutely, not wanting to say anything in case he interrupted whatever she was building to.

"Terror."

That was not what Scraps expected to hear. He kept quiet as he waited for her to elaborate.

Flit bit her lip for a moment before continuing, "I was terrified, Scraps… because if I can lose Rook like that, twice, what is there to guarantee that I won't lose you, too?" She reached out, brushing her icy fingertips over his cheek. He shivered at her cool touch, at the tenderness in it. "And I realised that I could never let you go. Living a life without you would be no life at all."

Scraps could not believe what he was hearing.

She slid closer to him, her legs pressing against his as she leaned in. She was near enough that her breath ticked his cheek when she spoke. "It taught me that I can no longer leave things unsaid. Life is too short. Too unpredictable." Taking his hand, Flit sat straighter and squared her shoulders. She held her chin up high and the intensity of her gaze made his heart skip a beat. "So… I'm just going to say it. You don't have to say it back, and you don't even have to acknowledge it—"

"Flit…" he breathed. He had a feeling he knew what was coming, and he wasn't sure if he was ready for it.

"I love you, Scraps. I said it a few months ago, and when you didn't say it back, I freaked out," she said slowly. He went to talk, but she let go of his hand to press two fingers against his lips. "But whether or not you say it back doesn't change how I feel. I love you, and I don't want to have to say goodbye to you. Ever."

Scraps' mind went from nervously quiet to conflictingly cacophonous. His limbs were so light and tingly that he worried he might float away.

Flit leaned in, pressing a chaste kiss against his lips.

"I am going to get some sleep," she said as she pulled back.

She teleported to her feet and looked down at him, halting in that moment, as if giving him a chance to reply.

He wanted to. He wanted to say it to make her happy, to give her something to hold onto in the midst of this storm.

But he couldn't.

He was still trying to figure out the words and their true meaning. Saying them now would be like sitting for a test he hadn't studied for. He would just be guessing at the answers, and Flit deserved better than that. When they first started dating, he thought that loving someone meant holding onto them at all costs, but after seeing Rook and Flit together, he realised that sometimes love required an even greater sacrifice. Sometimes love meant letting go. It was confusing, and he was not sure where it left him, but he was certain of one thing: if that was love, then he wasn't there yet.

Flit teleported to the hallway before going into their room and quietly shutting the door behind her.

He jumped to his feet, wondering if he was supposed to chase after her.

But even if he did, he had nothing to offer.

In some ways, her silent retreat was worse than any shouting could have been.

Scraps knew how to deal with an angry Flit. He knew how to deal with a frustrated Flit.

But he did not know how to deal with a broken Flit.

With a heavy conscience, Scraps made his way to the kitchen. It was already late. He had slept in well past the time he normally would on the weekend. On any other day, he would have gone for a run in the morning while Flit slept in. He could do that now, better late than never, but it didn't feel right leaving her alone in the house, so he wrote that part of his routine off for the day and moved on to his next task—planning and ordering the ingredients for their meals for the next week.

They might have had a difficult night, but they still needed to eat.

Scraps spent the next few hours trying his best to get their home in order. He purchased groceries, did the washing, cleaned the apartment by hand instead of using the automated systems, and scrolled through the news feed to search for updates.

When Flit finally emerged from her nap, she walked over to him. "We need to go out," she said slowly, looking up at him but not quite meeting his eyes.

Scraps frowned. "Why?"

"We told Fortune we'd help get her and the others to the

Underground." Flit held up her hand and pulled the sleeve of her jacket back, revealing the bracelet that Hawkeye had given her. "We can't take them back ourselves, but if I give them this, Hawkeye will come and get them."

"Hawkeye gave that to you for an emergency," Scraps said gently, taking her hand and holding it against his chest. "You do have a habit of getting yourself into trouble, you know."

His attempt at a joke was met by a stony expression. "This an emergency. Who knows what condition those people are in? They may need urgent medical attention."

Scraps let go of her hand and gently cupped her cheek. Even though she didn't lean into his touch like she usually did, she didn't pull away. That had to count for something.

"Very well," he conceded, knowing it was pointless to argue. The last thing he wanted was for her to go alone. "When did you want to go?"

"Maybe give me an hour to get ready?" Flit suggested with a shrug, looking back towards the bathroom.

"I may go for a run, then. I did not go for one this morning. I don't want to leave you alone tonight to do it, but now you're awake and moving around, it should be ok," he told her.

Flit nodded and murmured something that sounded like agreement.

Scraps kissed the top of her head and skirted around her to go to their room and get changed for his run. His routine was a source of comfort for him. It provided a sense of stability in an otherwise unpredictable world. It reminded him of the things that were in his control, the things he could focus on. Right now, he needed it more than ever to keep him from floundering. Only a hard run would help him clear his head, and he needed to be at the top of his game to make sure they got the people they rescued to safety.

48

FLIT

FLIT POTTERED around the immaculately clean living room while Scraps got changed for his run. Even though she'd tried to sleep, her attempt had been fitful, and she'd gotten up feeling more tired than when she'd laid down. Exhaustion pulled at her limbs, and her mind replayed the events of the previous night on a relentless loop.

She had spent over a year wishing she had a chance to say goodbye to Rook, and now that she had, it didn't make it any easier. Instead, it tore open a new wound and reminded her of why it hurt so bad the first time she'd lost him.

As Scraps emerged from the bedroom, she couldn't muster a wave of farewell. Instead, she just nodded. His expression was grim, but he forced the corners of his lips into a smile that reeked of tension. She knew it might have been unfair to spring her confession on him, but she was over dancing around the truth.

Flit was done living with regrets.

When Scraps pulled the front door shut behind himself, she let out a breath of relief and rushed over to the screen in the living room. She turned it on and immediately started scrolling through the news again to see if there were any updates. She wanted to see some frustration from the Government, some sort of anger. They had literally burned one of their newest facilities to the ground.

Some terrible, dangerous part of her wanted them to get angry and retaliate so she could fight back.

But nothing had changed. If anything, the articles on the destroyed facility and the increased barrier protocols had all but disappeared from the prime news feed. It frustrated Flit to no end. After everything she had been through, she wanted some reaction from the Government. She wanted some sign that what they had done had gotten under their skin.

In the absence of any sense of success with that mission, Flit focused on creating her own. She started researching the barrier restrictions and how they could get around them. If they couldn't piss off the Government, the least they could do was get the escapees safely back to the Underground.

WHEN SCRAPS GOT BACK from his run, Flit told him the plan to get to the emergency shelter in Old City. Given the barrier restrictions and the lockdown which, thankfully, did not include their part of the city, he was nervous about going, but they both agreed they couldn't leave Fortune and the others hanging around for too long. Scraps had a quick shower, and they got ready to leave. Flit packed her work datapad in a bag, and the couple made their way down towards the subway station.

Being in public meant they did not have to talk, and Flit was glad for it. She wasn't sure how Scraps felt about the previous night or her declaration, and she did not think she had the mental or emotional capacity to deal with that kind of conversation.

They continued in silence as they got onto a train that went all the way out of the city. They were taking the train to the end of the line, so far that the tracks emerged from the well-lit underground tunnels and sped over the expanse between the Hub and the electrostatic barrier. The glow of the fence faded quite well against the deep blue of the late afternoon sky. The only reason Flit could see it at all was because the hexagonal grids that formed the projection contrasted with the crumbling rectangular shapes of Old City, and the blue did not blend well with the vibrant emeralds of the plants that had reclaimed the once thriving metropolis.

Usually, their destination station had a simple security check-in process. If people were coming out this way, to the Memorial Forest, then they were grieving, and extended security procedures would have been over the top. The train slowed to a stop and the automated voice announced the end of the line. They joined a small contingent of people visiting the venue as they stood up. A rustle of voices sounded through the carriage at the sight of a dozen armed Government vehicles surrounding the platform.

"Are you sure this will work?" Scraps whispered. He and Flit walked over to the doors together.

"No, but we have to try." Flit didn't even have to summon a deep frown and weary eyes. That expression hadn't left her face since the previous night.

When they disembarked, a Registered walked over to them and held up a hand. Around them, others were being halted and questioned.

"Citizens, the Government has enforced tighter entry and exit requirements for the Hub. Please state your names and purpose." The woman's face was shielded by the visor, but her voice was firm.

Stealing a glance at the patch on her uniform, Flit saw the designation *KB-1599*. A pretty highly powered macrokinetic for this kind of thing. The Government must have been more shaken by the hit on the facility than she assumed.

She shared a curious glance with Scraps before saying, "We are Ava and Brian Parkes. We work in the R&D Department in Centre One. We… we're not here for work, though," Flit unlocked the vault of her heart and unleashed a little of the pain from last night, letting tears spring to her eyes. "A man on our floor died last month. We used to see him in the lunchroom. We… we wanted to pay our respects."

The best thing was, it was mostly true. They had overheard that an older man had passed away, and they had seen him once or twice in the shared food spaces.

"What was your colleague's name, Citizen?" the Registered asked.

Flit wouldn't have known the man from a bar of soap, but she found his name while Scraps had been out for a run. "Rafe Allsop."

"Please hold while I crosscheck this information."

The Registered stood perfectly still, and Scraps sidled closer to Flit, putting an arm around her waist. Flit had never seen the inside of one of the Registered's visors, but from what Scraps had told her, they had access to a lot of information on there.

"All clear. Rafe Allsop was laid to rest in the far northern quarter of the forest. If you take one of the buggies, I will transfer the data to its mapping system," the Registered offered, gesturing behind herself. Flit peered around the woman, seeing the welcome building and lot of buggies that was partially obscured by the Government security vehicles. "The maximum time allotment available is four hours. You must return by then, or drones will be sent out to ensure your safe recall."

Stopping herself from rolling her eyes at the euphemistic *safe recall*, Flit nodded. "Thank you. Have a lovely afternoon."

The woman took a step back. Flit linked her arm with Scraps', and they walked over to the welcome kiosk. It was easy enough to speak to the attendant, buy some flowers, and sign out a buggy. As soon as they entered, the location of Rafe's memorial tree pinged on the screen, and Flit frowned. It wasn't the exact right bearing, but they could travel part of the way and leave the buggy there, then claim they wanted to walk the rest.

Once they were in the buggy and heading in the right direction, Flit turned to Scraps. "I think this is working well so far."

He didn't take his eyes off the path as they left the busy station behind. After a few moments, they drove into a lush, perfectly planted forest. It had a variety of trees towering overhead, all with small plaques at the bases of their trunks. Sometime after the Government had taken over, they had decided that standard cemeteries were an inefficient use of space. Instead of horizontal graves with stones on top in a sea of wasted land, they decreed that Citizens must either be cremated or buried in vertical, biodegradable pods with a tree seed. It put some much needed greenery in the devastated landscape and created a beautiful, albeit haunting, reminder of the fragility of life.

"Won't there be cameras in the forest?" Scraps asked, his grip tight on the buggy controls.

"Once a cremation pod is planted, people make one obligatory visit, two tops. Citizens are far too busy and important to come out of their way to visit some trees." Flit let out a bitter laugh. "I checked our work databases for the traffic and visitation stats. It's not worth much more than the occasional drone sweep. I mean, even if it all burned down, the Government wouldn't give a shit. I think the only real reason they've kept it going instead of forcing cremation is because they hope the trees grow tall enough to shelter the Hub from some of the visual pollution of Old City."

"Oh." The disgruntled sound was enough to let Flit know that he believed her, even if he didn't agree with her cynical view.

Leaning back into the seat, Flit watched the scenery outsize zoom past. The past twenty-four hours started to catch up on her, and despite the thoughts racing through her mind, she found herself being woken by a gentle shake of her shoulder.

"Flit, we are here."

Yawning, she straightened up and looked around. They were parked between a couple of trees, off a small path that was a good distance away from the main road.

"Right." Flit rubbed her eyes and saw they had already lost almost half an hour. The forest was far bigger than she had anticipated. "Let's go. We can't waste any more time." When she got out of the buggy, Flit stretched her arms and legs as she looked around. "This was a good spot to park," she said with approval. She pointed down the long row of perfectly spaced trees to her left. "Apparently, part of this area was a traditional graveyard in Old City days. They used to use their train line to transport the caskets out here, so if we head that way until we see the end, it should be a relatively straight shot down the line to the train shed."

Fallen leaves crunched under foot, releasing a fresh, invigorating aroma as Flit and Scraps passed by. Thanks to the orderly planting, they were able to see up and down each row without obstruction. Flit might have thought it beautiful, if the Government hadn't been so pedantic about the planning. It was ordered in a way that no true bastion of nature would be. It made her long for the deeper caves in the Underground, the ones that twisted and turned upon their own whims, the ones that existed long before she was born and would still be there long after she passed on.

"Is this far enough?"

Flit broke out of her musings and looked back over her shoulder to determine that they were a good distance away from the buggy and the main roads. "Yeah, this should do." She stepped in closer to him, wrapping her arms around him and holding him close. "This is going to be a lot of long, fast jumps, and I'm rusty so it might get a little rough. If it gets too much, let me know."

Reaching out and brushing a strand of hair off her cheek with startling tenderness, Scraps nodded. "Of course."

He settled his arms around her. Flit waited for him to nod one more time before she started their journey.

While Scraps would likely be feeling nauseous from the rapid-fire teleports, Flit found it exhilarating. It was even better than that first full body stretch after rolling out of bed in the morning. Every single part of her was alive with the energy of the fast-paced, instinctive movements. The environment was well suited for it, too. The way between the trees was straight and wide enough for her to really let loose. When they reached the end, the tracks were right in front of them. They took a five-minute break before continuing, following the splintered, grass-covered rails and traversing the distance at a breakneck pace.

The train shed came to view from quite far way, and they approached it in fits and starts. When they got there, Flit let go of Scraps and wiped a sheen of sweat off her forehead with the back of her arm. Her heart was racing, her body tingling with the expenditure of so much energy when she was so rundown, but she didn't care about that. All she could feel was the growing ball of dread that sat low in her throat.

She turned to Scraps. "What do I say to Fortune?"

"She already knows, Flit." Scraps stopped and put his closed fist against his mouth for a moment, looking rather green in the face, before continuing, "She knew last night when she left him there."

Flit closed her eyes and gathered her thoughts. Scraps was right, of course, but that didn't stop her from thinking she should have done more to save Rook. A reassuring hand settled on her shoulder, and Flit covered it with her own as she looked at Scraps. They didn't have time to waste.

Flit pulled off the bracelet Hawkeye had given her, squatted down, and set it against one of the railway sleepers. She picked up a nearby rock and, with a hard strike, shattered the protective glass and activated the emergency tracker. She tucked the tatters of the crushed bracelet into her pocket and clutched the tiny, grain-of-rice-sized device in her closed fist as she led the way to the train shed.

The large, warped timber doors were boarded shut with decrepit planks and rusty nails. There was no sense trying to open them, as she did not want to ruin the small amount of protection they afforded anyone seeking shelter within. Instead, she got to her toes and looked through one of the rot holes in the door. It was all still inside, but that didn't mean much. The main shelter was in the storage holds beneath the warehouse itself.

Just in case Fortune had set up guards, Flit leaned closer to the hole and called out, "No need to panic. Just Flit out here. We've come to speak to Fortune and to get you guys to safety."

Without looking away, Flit gestured for Scraps to come closer. He stepped up beside her, and she wrapped an arm around him. She kept her eyes plastered to the view through the hole to use as reference and teleported them into the shed.

Inside, shafts of light pierced the darkness, setting clouds of dancing dust motes alight and giving the whole place an almost dream-like quality.

"Don't come any closer!" a woman called, stepping out of the shadows with her hands raised. Towards the rear of the room, obscured by shadows, there was a tall, stocky framed person who stepped forward too.

Flit blinked, letting her vision readjust to the low lighting and then sighed as she recognised the red hair and bandaged arm. "Oh, Layla." She approached the other woman slowly. "It's Flit. From last night."

"Joel!" Layla called out, still wary. "Tell Fortune that Flit is here."

"Ok." The person in the corner backed away slowly.

With a slight frown, Flit wondered why they wouldn't just let them through, but Layla's pose was taut with anxiety, so she didn't push. "We'll wait right here until Fortune comes up, if you like," Flit told the woman in her calmest voice.

Everyone stood, rooted to the spot and waiting. A few minutes passed before Fortune emerged from behind a stack of crates. Her entire body sagged with relief as she saw Flit, and Flit teleported over to her and threw her arms around the older woman in a tight embrace.

"My sweet girl, I am so glad to see you again," Fortune whispered into Flit's ear.

"I'm sorry…" Flit squeezed her tighter, wanting to know she was real. "I'm so sorry," Flit whimpered.

"You have nothing to apologise for." Fortune took Flit's face gently in both of her hands. "Rook was so tired of suffering, but he refused to let go while I was there." Fortune shook her head. "I wish there was another way, too. I… I want my son, but there was nothing we could do. If we tried to bring him with us, he would have died gasping for breath in our arms."

Flit winced at the thought, at the confirmation of just how reliant Rook's survival was on those horrible Government systems. She hated them for it, hated them for taking away the life and vitality that was the very core of him.

"But we saw those flames," Fortune whispered, tears streaking down her cheeks. "He brought that place down, just like he wanted to, and he is beyond their reach. They cannot hurt him anymore."

Another layer of ice froze around Flit's heart. No mother should ever have to feel that way about her son's death.

Fortune sighed. "But this is not a good place to talk. Why don't you come into the shelter, and we can discuss more there?" She didn't wait to see if they were following before she turned and disappeared between the musty rows of broken pallets and crates.

49

———

SCRAPS

SCRAPS FOLLOWED Flit and Fortune past the crates, through a door at the back of the warehouse, and down an old metal staircase. The level underneath was a large storage space in the middle, with rooms off to the side. Fortune led them over to one of the rooms, knocked quickly three times, and then twice slowly.

The door slid open to reveal a group of tired, dishevelled people scattered around the room, sitting on the various stretcher beds and sharing unidentifiable meat from old tins. Scraps wasn't sure if the food was still good, but they must have been hungry enough to eat anything. He was well versed in the procedures for restocking emergency shelters in the Underground, but he had never come across any such manuals for safe houses like this.

The people watched them warily as they passed, and Fortune took them to an old, mostly empty storeroom at the rear of the space. Scraps shut the door behind them, assuming Flit and Fortune would want privacy. He stood by the entry, back straight, trying to remain alert for possible threats.

"Before we start," Flit said, holding her hand up and showing Fortune the tiny flashing piece of technology in her palm, "I activated a beacon for Hawkeye, so he can come and get you. Hopefully, he'll be here soon. I want to wait around until he gets arrives, but we're operating on borrowed time."

"Ah, they finally decided to give their Intelligence agents beacons," Fortune said with a hint of approval.

Scraps cleared his throat. "Uh, no. That is not a sanctioned beacon. It was a gift from Hawkeye, and it is probably better for everyone if you do not to mention it when you return to the Underground."

Fortune chuckled. "Of course you brought contraband on a mission, Flit." She sighed, reaching out, closing Flit's hand over the device, and smiling at her fondly. "It's good to know I'll have Hawkeye there to help get this lot out. There are quite a few of us, and so many are injured. His skills will be helpful to get us to the nearest Underground entrance safely."

"When you go down there, please try to avoid letting the others know we had anything to do with this," Flit said quietly, looking over at Scraps as she bit her lip. "Shadow is just waiting for a reason to kick our arses, but we have a few more things to do up here before we're ready to go back."

"You are like a daughter to me. There's no way I'm turning you over to Shadow."

Scraps' shoulders sagged with relief, but they didn't have time to relax. "Just in case Hawkeye gets up here sooner rather than later, may we ask you a few questions, ma'am?"

"Please, Fortune is fine. I am happy to give you whatever information you need…" Fortune stopped then, looking at Scraps a little more closely. "Sorry, I don't think I have met you before?"

"My name is Scraps." He reached out to shake her hand. "I arrived in the Underground about a year ago. Flit saved me when my team tried to enter the Nest. I used to be Registered, but I chose to join the Underground."

Fortune let out a low hum of understanding. "You must have made a good impression if they let you come back here on a mission so soon."

"I was not their first choice. Hawkeye was supposed to come up, but he got injured, and they figured that I was the only one who would be able to keep Flit in line," he said, not thinking anything of it.

He realised his mistake when Fortune narrowed her eyes a little and looked between them. He glanced at Flit, wondering if he had messed up, and saw a rare blush on her cheeks.

"He's selling himself short," Flit said with a nonchalant wave, "but that isn't important right now. What were they doing in that facility?"

Fortune leaned back against the wall and sighed. "Experimenting on us," she admitted. "There were so many different things going on it was hard to keep track of them all. Drugs, DNA manipulation, stress testing…"

"I knew pretty much everyone in the Underground," Flit jumped in quickly. "I don't know anyone else out there. Only a couple of them are ex-Registereds. Where are the rest from?"

"You've always been too sharp for your own good." Fortune chuckled. "There are some undercover Intelligence operatives there that you wouldn't have met. They have been in the Government's system now for decades, and you're right about the ex-Registereds. The others are Citizen Derivates."

Scraps blinked. "Pardon?" He was certain he misheard Fortune. Citizens were Citizens, and Derivates were Derivates. It was as simple as that. The term she used was entirely foreign to him.

"I felt the same way too, when I first found out." Fortune shook her head. "I learned a lot in that facility. I wish I had time to tell you everything, but I don't. The most important thing is that the Government has been lying to everyone."

Scraps expected to hear a snort and some smug comment from Flit, but she didn't say anything. She just sat in silence and waited for Fortune to continue.

"Derivacy isn't exclusively hereditary. There's a chance some Citizen couplings will result in a spontaneous mutation, giving rise to Derivate children. They have studied this and found the most likely combinations. It is one of the reasons they brought in mandatory DNA approval for those wanting to marry or have children. It isn't only about preventing genetic diseases… It is about preventing the spontaneous birth of Derivate babies. They refer to it by some code. I can't quite—"

"Code 6B," Flit interjected, her voice an unsurprised monotone.

All the parts of the puzzle clicked into place in Scraps' mind. "That explains the procedures to determine Derivacy status," Scraps said, looking over at his girlfriend.

"It does. So, these spontaneous Derivates are born to Citizen families, and then… what?" Flit asked.

Fortune shrugged. "It's impossible to tell how many there are, but the ones they find? They bring them in and study them. Layla was working in that department and trying to give people the drop before the Government discovered her powers and brought her in."

Scraps though back to the woman guarding the door. Her willingness to help them and her understanding of the man they had freed made more sense now. As someone who had brought his own kind in and turned them over to Government custody for a living, Scraps was in awe of the fact that Layla had actively put herself into a risky position to help give others a fighting chance of evasion. The familiar sense of guilt at his previous role in ruining people's lives started to crawl up Scraps' spine, but he couldn't linger on it. They didn't have long, and there were more questions to ask.

He straightened his shoulders and leaned forward. "We are up here, looking for information on a weapon. It emits a charge that disables a Derivate's ability. Have you heard anything about something like that?"

Fortune's smile fell, and she winced. "Yes. It is one of the things they were testing on us."

"Ah, do you know any more about it?"

Fortune looked at the ground and shook her head. "No. Just that they started testing the early radiation on us around six months ago."

"Well, somehow a stupid bunch of Citizen thugs got hold of the weaponised version and decided to use it on us," Flit said. She looked at Scraps. "I wonder where they got the weapons from if they belonged to the Government? The emails we saw said that they weren't affiliated with them."

"Some Citizens got into the Underground?" Fortune asked, looking genuinely shocked.

"Yes." Scraps spoke up so Flit didn't have to. "Well, they did not make it all the way down. They managed to use some old comms lines to communicate with someone who betrayed us, and Flit and I were in the wrong place at the wrong time."

Fortune's frown was solemn enough to cause deep lines to appear on her friendly face. "So, it is a fully functioning prototype now?"

"Yeah. It knocked me out of action for weeks. It will be devastating if they start using it properly," Flit explained, crossing her arms.

"Wait… there was a traitor?" Fortune rubbed her face, as if it was too much.

"It was Heft. Do you remember him?" Flit asked, her voice short. "The tunnel collapses he caused killed people."

Fortune pressed a hand against her chest and let out a soft curse. "He was rough around the edges, but I never would have pegged him for a traitor."

"I agree, it did not sit right with me," Scraps said, the words slipping from him before he could stop them.

Fortune turned to him. "What do you mean?"

Scraps squared his shoulders. He didn't know why the information came back in this moment, but he needed to share it. It felt important, somehow.

"When I was trying to convince him to give up, he tried to blame me. He tried to say something, but one of the dying thugs shot him. He seemed… confused?"

Silence fell between them.

Flit leaned in, seemingly sensing something in Fortune's expression that Scraps didn't see himself. "What is it?"

"Nothing." Fortune's smile was forced.

Even Scraps could tell she was lying.

But Flit didn't press her on it. The conversation paused for a beat before a new question exploded from Flit. "What happened that night?"

Scraps felt like he'd missed an important segue, but Fortune's eyes shuttered over, and she let out a soft breath, apparently knowing what Flit wanted to talk about without further clarification.

"What do you already know?" Fortune asked.

"I came to see you after I filed the paperwork. The apartment had already been raided. I saw Vector—"

"They just left him there?" Fortune's voice caught on her last word.

"They sectioned the apartment off, and I found him where he fell. I went back to the Underground, and they tried to track you and Rook as much as they could. It was a while before I got called in. Your record was lost in obscurity, but Rook's stated he had been terminated. Irredeemable, apparently."

Fortune managed a small chuckle. "Oh, he gave them hell."

The corner of Flit's lips curled the tiniest bit, the first show of anything close to an emotional expression Scraps had seen all day.

"That was why we got pulled out to the covert facilities. They figured Rook would make a good test subject for some of the projects they were working on."

"And that was where you met the others and learned about the spontaneous Derivacy mutation?" Scraps asked.

"Yes." Fortune turned to face him. "I tried to be as compliant as possible. Eventually, they trusted me enough to help with some tasks around the place, taking meals into the others and the like. The fewer external workers they needed to maintain the facility, the tighter they could keep their secrets."

As repulsive as it was, Scraps had to admire the efficiency of the Government and the cleverness of Fortune's plan.

Fortune continued speaking, telling them about life in the lab. She seemed to skim over the worst of the details, but the more she spoke about the horrific treatment of herself, Rook, and the others, the more Flit's eyes filled with cold determination. The detached fury was so different from Flit's usual burning rage that he stepped closer and took her hand, concerned.

After Fortune stopped speaking, Scraps had one question that seemed more important than all of the others. "How did they find you?"

Flit winced, and he wondered if she had avoided asking this for a reason.

Even if she didn't want to hear it, he had to know. It sounded like Fortune, her husband, and Rook had been mostly minding their own business. Scraps and Flit, however? They were actively putting themselves into high-risk situations. If the Government had some enhanced way of finding Derivates, he had to know so he could keep Flit safe.

"To be completely honest, I'm not sure." Fortune looked at him, taking a heartbeat to think over her answer before continuing. "I have some suspicions, though. Maybe we were flagged on their system before we moved over from Longbeach. The Underground should have scrubbed the data, though, so I don't think that was it."

"They recalled the other half-halfers from Longbeach after you guys were taken," Flit informed her.

Fortune shrugged. "It isn't like our roles were particularly critical. We weren't even working for the Government; just a contracted organisation."

"Perhaps it was the marriage application?" Flit asked, her voice small and shaky.

Her tone was enough to tell Scraps why she hadn't asked the question herself, and now he hated himself for doing it. If Fortune said yes, Flit would blame herself for everything more than she already did.

Knowing that she must be hurting, Scraps pulled her closer and wrapped his arm around her waist, holding her warm body to his side. Fortune looked between them, and Scraps realised that this is the woman whose son was going to marry Flit. Perhaps it was inappropriate of him to show signs of physical intimacy with Flit in front of her. He let his arm fall from around Flit's waist but did not step away.

"No. They would have had to get the information, process it, and come down on us in a matter of an hour. They are good but not that good," Fortune said firmly. She leaned closer to Flit. "Do not blame yourself for this. Do you hear me?"

Flit nodded mutely.

"So, if not work, your past in Longbeach, or the marriage application…" Scraps trailed off.

"Sometimes, when looking outward fails, you need to look in."

Screams and the unmistakeable sounds of fighting from outside ruined the moment.

The door flew open. "Fortune, there's someone out there!" a

gaunt, elderly woman panted. "Layla and Joel are holding him off —barely!"

Fortune, Flit, and Scraps raced past the woman. Scraps snatched up Flit's hand so she wouldn't teleport ahead, and they ran through the room and then up the stairs together.

Yelling interspersed the sounds of splintering crates and pained grunts.

"I know she's here. Let me see her!" a familiar voice demanded.

Scraps and Flit rounded the corner just in time to see Hawkeye pinning Layla to the ground. At their arrival, he turned, but the redhead took advantage of the distraction to snatch her wrist from his grasp and slam her fist against his cheek.

Hawkeye's head snapped to the side with a groan as he tumbled onto his back.

Layla jumped up, holding her hands out towards him. "Make one more move, and I'll turn your brains to mush!"

From the look in her eyes, she was dead serious.

"Don't bother, Layla," Flit called out, working her hand from Scraps' hold and jogging over. "There's nothing in that thick head to mess with."

"It's fine. He's one of us," Fortune called over, breathless from the run up the stairs.

"Oh!" Layla blushed and cleared her throat as she got to her feet. She shook out the fist she'd socked him with. "Er… sorry, I guess?"

Hawkeye scoffed at the apology. Wincing, Layla offered him a hand. He glared at it for several strained seconds before taking it and letting her help him up. "You've got a good arm on you. Most people can't get a hit in on me," he muttered with begrudging appreciation. The braces on his legs whined, potentially damaged in the scramble. He cast a narrow-eyed glare at Flit. "Would you care to tell me what the fuck is going on here?" He looked like he was ready to strangle her.

With a wary look at Layla and Joel, Scraps cut in. "Perhaps we should go somewhere more private."

"I agree," Fortune said.

Then, Hawekeye looked at Fortune properly for the first time.

His knees buckled, and he grasped Flit's arm. "Fortune!" He looked around, searching for someone. "If you're here, where's Roo—"

"Don't," Flit begged.

The word was so small, so broken, that Hawkeye shut his mouth without argument.

Scraps walked over, wanting to help ease the tension. "We can explain, I promise. Just give us a chance."

After an uneasy hesitation, Hawkeye nodded. He approached Fortune and rested his hands on both of her shoulders gently as he assessed her condition. "Fortune, it's so good to see you again."

"You, too, Hawkeye." She pointed to his legs. "What happened there?"

Hawkeye glanced in Flit's direction before saying in a stiff tone, "Accident."

Fortune didn't push him further. Instead, she patted his hand and led them to the stairs.

Hawkeye rubbed his cheek and moved his jaw from side to side, shaking his head. "That woman of yours packs a bloody good punch."

Fortune smiled but kept quiet. They walked down the stairs and through the room of escapees. Hawkeye looked around, seeming startled by the amount of people who blinked back at him, terrified, undoubtedly hoping he wasn't there to turn them in.

When the door was closed behind them once more, Flit launched into an explanation. "We stumbled across Fortune and the others in a facility as they were making their escape. I told them to come here and used the bracelet so you could lead them home. Some of them are injured, so they need your help."

"You just happened to run into them?" Hawkeye's voice was deadpan as he gave Flit a disparaging look.

"Yes, it was quite the coincidence," Scraps agreed, slipping his arm around Flit's waist.

"Quite," Hawkeye scoffed before grumbling something under his breath that Scraps did not want to hear. "I don't know how the hell you expect me to explain this when I get them back to base."

Flit shrugged. "What does it matter? They're alive, and we always have room for new people."

Hawkeye sighed in resignation and ran a hand through his hair. "Rook's really not here?"

"No." Flit's voice cracked.

Scraps wrapped his arm around her shoulder.

Hawkeye paled and bowed his head. "Fortune, Flit, I'm so—"

Flit turned away from him.

"He went out fighting," Fortune said softly.

Hawkeye looked as though he might ask for more details, but Scraps shook his head to discourage more questions. Scraps could not fathom the pain Fortune must be feeling, nor the strength it took for Flit to let go of Rook. All he knew was that he would fight with everything he had to keep Flit safe. When those thugs had tried to abduct her, he had torn them limb from limb without even thinking.

Maybe blowing up the facility was not so crazy after all.

Flit grasped Scraps' wrist and looked at the time on his watch. She turned to Hawkeye. "I would love to stay and chat, but these guys need to get somewhere safe before dark, and Scraps and I are on a curfew. Before you go, though, I need to talk to you." Flit looked back up at Scraps. "Alone."

"Oh," Scraps blurted.

Flit's dismissal stung more than it should have.

"Come on. Let's give them the room." Fortune took Scraps by the elbow and guided him out. When the door shut behind them, she looked up at him. "So, while we're waiting, why don't you tell me a little bit more about Heft's confusion?"

50

FLIT

"WHAT THE HELL IS GOING ON?" Hawkeye asked the moment the door shut behind Scraps and Fortune.

Leaning against a stack of dusty boxes, Flit crossed her arms over her chest. "We told you. Scraps and I ran into them at a facility. They were already making an escape. That is all you need to know."

Hawkeye ran a hand though his hair. "They are going to kick my arse for this. The least you can do is—"

"I didn't ask to talk to you privately so we could fight. Just roll with it and give yourself some sense of plausible deniability, ok?" Flit snapped, her usually short patience far too frayed to mince words. "There is something else, something more important."

"Well, fuck me. This just gets worse." Hawkeye turned his back to her and leaned against the wall, shaking his head. He sighed heavily. "What is it? What else could you possibly add to this situation to make it any bigger?"

Too tired to respond with the same kind of exasperation, Flit laid out the facts. "Some of those people out there are ex-Registered. Some are undercover Underground Agents. But… most of them are Derivates who were born to Citizen parents."

Hawkeye snorted as he looked at her over his shoulder.

Flit stared at him, deadpan.

At first, Hawkeye's posture stiffened. His hackles rose, and all the years of reading his body language in their friendship told Flit he was one wrong word away from letting loose on her for messing around.

When Flit did not capitulate, Hawkeye's irritation turned to incredulity. "That's not possible."

"It shouldn't be," Flit agreed, pushing up to stand as she tele-port-paced across the room. "But it is."

"If they were born to Citizen parents, then it means—"

"Derivacy is a spontaneous genetic mutation," Flit supplied.

The Government's history was based on the premise that Derivacy was an aberration, a genetic evolution triggered by some unethical testing in a lab over a hundred years ago. They got it under control, apparently, by taking custody of all the Derivates and ensuring the only offspring was a direct result of their breeding program. Or at least, that was what they told everyone. If the people in the shelter, the ones Flit and Scraps had rescued from the facility, were telling the truth, it meant that the Government had lied. Derivacy was an inevitable, spontaneous evolution of human DNA.

They were not freaks. They were not an affront to nature. They were part of a normal variation of the human species.

An inevitable variation of the human species.

"Who knows about this?" Hawkeye asked quietly. All the fight in him fizzled as he tried to come to terms with the shift in his reality.

"Apart from those guys out there and the Government arse-holes torturing them?" Flit shrugged. "I'm not sure. You're in Intelligence now. Maybe you can figure it out?"

It was a lot to ask. From the way that Hawkeye's shoulders buckled, she wondered just how much pressure he was under right now. "Speaking of the people out there, what the hell am I supposed to do with them?" he asked with a heavy sigh.

That was a good question, especially because Flit was running out of time. "Actually, I have an idea that may work." She tele-ported over to the door and tugged it open. Scraps and Fortune, who were both caught in a deep conversation as they sat on the end of one of the beds in the larger room, looked over.

"Is everything ok?" Fortune asked.

"Everything's fine," Flit lied. "Can we get you both back in here for a minute before Scraps and I go?"

The four of them crammed into the space probably not even designed for two and shut the door. Flit caught Scraps glancing at the time on his watch.

"Scraps and I are onto something big up here," Flit admitted, more determined than ever to stick to their resolution to take an active role in bringing the Government down. "So, if we get recalled, it would be pretty bad for everyone."

"We need to keep the fact that you found us a secret?" Fortune surmised. When Flit and Scraps indicated their assent, Fortune drummed her fingers against a nearby crate as she considered her options. "If the others will let me use telecoercion on them, I can convince them to forget a few details of the escape."

Scraps cleared his throat, observing Fortune with a new, wary expression. "You can do that? That's a—"

"AA ability, yes," Flit confirmed. A part of her buried deep beneath the developing permafrost around her heart was amused that he still used the Government's classifications. "Rook and Fortune were two of the most powerful telecoercionists in the Underground."

"Apart from Harmony," Hawkeye amended.

Flit waved her hand dismissively and returned her attention to Fortune. "If you could, it would save us all a lot of trouble."

"Don't worry, I'll make sure everything seems genuine."

"Thank you." A grim smile tugged at Flit's lips. "We'd appreciate any time you can buy us. I promise, it'll be worth it. We've got plans to—"

Hawkeye held both hands up. "Nuh-uh! Flit, if you reveal one more thing today, I'll knock you out and drag you back home myself."

Flit and Hawkeye's relationship was based on good-natured taunting and empty threats, but Flit was confident that one was entirely genuine.

Scraps cleared his throat. "Flit, as much as I hate to remind you, we need to leave."

Despite every part of her wanting to get back to their mission, a sharp pang of loss stabbed through Flit at the reality of having to say goodbye to her friends.

Fortune pulled Flit into a tight embrace.

Flit rested her head against Fortune's shoulder. "Please stay safe," she whispered.

"Don't you worry about me. I'll be fine." Fortune chuckled. She gave Flit an extra squeeze. "You just take care of yourself and this lovely boyfriend of yours, darling, and don't worry. I'll send your parents your love."

When Fortune released her, Flit teleported over to hug Hawkeye.

"I don't have another beacon, Flit," Hawkeye breathed in her ear. "Please, for the love of everything good in this world, don't do anything stupid."

"I never do stupid things," Flit replied as Scraps came over, resting a hand on the small of her back and offering the other to Hawkeye to shake in farewell. "Make sure you guys leave soon. There is an increase of surveillance out there, and you don't want to get caught up in that."

With Scraps' strong arms around her shoulder, the pair walked back out through the main area of the shelter. Flit took a final look around at the people they had saved. Something good had come out of the situation. Those people, at least, now had a fighting chance.

They made their way up the stairs and waved their thanks to Layla and Joel. Before they could go any further, Layla caught Flit's hand. "Can we speak for a moment, please?"

Flit agreed and Layla led her off to the side, between a row of crates. "Is everything ok?" Flit asked.

"I'm not sure." Layla crossed her arms, looking far more tired than she had moments ago. "You know the man we released from that cell?"

"Yeah?" Flit shifted on her feet as her stomach started to churn.

"I lost him on the run to catch up with Fortune. Thanks to that explosion, I didn't have time to look for him. He just… disappeared," Layla informed her.

"Of course he did." Flit closed her eyes and took a deep breath. When she opened them again, concern twisted Layla's delicate features. "Thanks for letting me know. I'm sure everything will be fine. You just focus on getting to the Underground safely."

Before Layla could say anything else, Flit teleported over to Scraps' side and dragged him out of the train shed, her mind racing a million miles a minute.

When they made it to the train tracks, Flit let every part of her conscious mind sink into the familiar, instinctual comfort of teleporting. She pushed herself to jump farther and faster, and by the time they arrived back at their spot in between the row of memorial trees, she let go of Scraps and doubled over, panting hard as her heart jackhammered against her rib cage so hard she swore it was trying to escape.

Without a word, Scraps scooped her up into his arms and carried her towards the buggy. She wanted to fight, to insist that she could walk, but all her limbs were shaking, and her head was spinning. She should have been worried. The Underground had drilled the signs of over-exertion into her ever since she was tiny, but anything, even the physical agony of hyperextending her powers, was better than the numbness growing inside of her.

THAT EVENING, when they got home, Flit couldn't bring herself to do anything. Scraps helped her to bed, and she lay in the darkness, eyes closed, wondering how one single night could stretch out into an eternity. When Scraps joined her, his steady breathing and warm body lulled her into a restless sleep.

Flit woke the next morning well before her alarm and checked the news straight away. There wasn't anything about the man from the facility. Although, she wasn't sure what she was expecting. If he was one of these new, non-Underground and non-Registered Derivates, he was probably very good at hiding. She put her datapad aside just as the alarm woke Scraps, and they got out of bed in silence.

After breakfast, the couple got ready for work as they always did. In some ways, the events of the weekend were all just one bad dream. It was so easy to imagine they didn't even happen, but there was a new coating of steely resolve encasing every part of her, one that made her more determined to get to work, to find something, anything, that would help her destroy the Government.

Flit's newfound resolve helped her get to work that day, but she was so tired that she felt like she was viewing the world through a curtain of numbness.

Her time in the office dragged. The new maglev train security procedures they had been asked to review were the most boring things Flit had ever read in her life. By midday, she could have sworn it was time to head home. When she settled down to eat in a quiet corner of the lunchroom with Scraps, she decided to check the news again. At this point she was just about ready to give up hope that the Government would react to the facility raid, but one of the new headlines caught her attention.

Twenty-five found dead in gas leak.

It was rare for accidents like that to happen in the Hub, so Flit opened the article and gasped at the picture on the screen. A man and woman lay strewn across a couch, blood cascading out of their eyes, ears, and nose. Their lips were blue, and their gaze was unfocused and distant.

Alarm bells rung in Flit's mind.

She thought back to the micro she had freed, the one Layla had said killed some Citizens. In her work in for the R&D Department, she had read policies and procedures about plenty of different chemicals, and none of them had any sort of effects like that or, at least, nothing that should be in a residential apartment building. What Flit was aware of, however, were all the different ways a micro could kill a person if they wanted to, ways that matched those pictures far too perfectly.

Flit bit her lip as she read and discovered the true extent of the devastation. The Government maintained the gas leak story, but instead of just dealing with it, they had cordoned all buildings within a ten-block radius and told people to remain indoors. Those restrictions were totally out of proportion to the event.

"Ava?"

Startled, Fit dropped the datapad on the table. The concern in Scraps' tone was etched into his features.

"What is it?" he asked. She pushed the datapad over to him

and pointed at the screen. He scanned it several times before frowning. "I do not understand."

"It's the…" She paused, the low drone of chatter and clinking utensils reminding her where they were. "The man. From the place. The one who our new red-headed friend said to leave. He… he wasn't with them yesterday."

Scraps picked the datapad up and read the article again. Then, he closed the page. "It's a gas leak, Ava."

"No… I don't think it w—"

Before she could finish, Scraps reached across the table and took her hands. The expression he wore was full of fatigue. "It's been a long couple of days. You're reading too much into this." His voice dipped to a whisper. "We need to lay low right now."

Flit wanted to argue. Perhaps, a few days ago, she might have, but the new determination within her was something smarter, more calculated. Instead of fighting Scraps, she just nodded and focused on finishing her food.

That afternoon, Flit approached Liana while she was alone at her desk and suggested they go over for dinner. Flit offered to bring a nice bottle of wine if Liana cooked some of her famous chicken. Her friend was so eager for a debriefing after the facility that she agreed immediately.

When they got home from work, Flit feigned a headache. She told Scraps what type of wine Liana would like and urged him to go to dinner without her. He wanted to cancel, but she told him that it was better to stick to their plans and not raise suspicion from Chris and Liana. Besides, she had said, she just needed to catch up on some sleep.

It was with a great sense of reluctance that Scraps left, but if Flit was honest with herself, things between them had been tense ever since she had said she loved him. She wouldn't be surprised if he was glad for the reprieve, for some respite from having to watch her glide around the place as distant and detached as a ghost.

As soon as Scraps left the house, Flit walked over to the comms system in the living area. She tapped a few options on the screen and made a call. It answered almost immediately, and Andy's friendly, teal-hair-framed face came into the frame.

"Ava! What a surprise," Andy said, sounding genuinely excited.

She smiled wide enough that the dimples in her cheeks stood out. "What can I do for you?"

"I need a favour," Flit said seriously, cutting straight to the chase.

Andy's expression set. "Petra and Trey are out tonight dealing with some stuff at the club, but if you want to catch up tomorrow—"

"No," Flit said it so sharply that even she winced at her own tone. Andy tilted her head to the side, interest glinting in her eyes. "No. It's only you I need, and it has to be tonight."

Silence reigned between them for several long, drawn out moments before Andy nodded. "I'll send my address through."

"Thanks."

51

FLIT

FLIT FOLLOWED the directions to Andy's, Petra's, and Trey's apartment. It was in a swanky building just on the opposite side of Centre One from where she and Scraps lived. When she got to the front door, Andy buzzed in her right away. Flit took the elevator almost all the way to the top. Andy opened the door and gestured for Flit to come in, greeting her with a tight embrace.

As Flit waited for Andy to shut the door, she looked around the apartment with great interest. The inside of Andy's home showed her just how lucrative owning a nightclub and working for one of the most popular game development companies was. Top tech lined the walls, and the furniture in the apartment was sleek, neat, and expensive. Just as she was about to turn around and say something to her friend about the apartment, the teal-haired woman held a finger to her lips.

With a flick of her fingers, Andy activated a menu on the screen by the door. A low buzz filled the apartment. Something about the frequency or incessantness made Flit edgy, but she had heard the sound before. It was an anti-interference frequency.

"Now," Andy said with a wide-armed gesture, "you can talk. Sorry. We can never be too careful."

"You've got some impressive tech around," Flit said appreciatively.

Andy shrugged. "It'd be pretty embarrassing for me if I didn't."

The woman walked over to her. "How are you holding up? What happened over the weekend was—"

Flit waved her hand to dismiss Andy's concern. She didn't want to talk about what went *wrong* at the facility, or why it got blown up, or why she hadn't contacted any of the Free Citizens since. "That's part of the reason I'm here," Flit said, forcing a smile that probably looked more like a sneer, and straightened up. "I saw how good you were with your tech. When you said you were a game designer, I didn't realise that *game designer* was synonymous with *super hacker*. What sort of systems can you access?"

"Eh." Andy shrugged. "Security and communication networks are the easiest, but I dabble in a lot of things. I worked on a project two years ago where we used the Government's mapping and camera system to create a great immersive game where—" Andy paused and rubbed her hands together. "Heh, sorry. You don't need to know the details. Long story short, I kept access I probably shouldn't have. Left a few backdoors open for myself."

"Good. A back door is what I need right now," Flit confessed.

The amused, almost expectant energy that had been radiating from Andy settled into something more wary. "Oh?"

"I need you to help me save some lives… but I need you to promise you won't tell anyone else about it. Can you do that?" Flit asked.

There was a flicker of concern in Andy's eyes, but it was gone almost before Flit could worry about it. Ever since the night they had met, Flit had thought of Andy as a kindred spirit of sorts. Just like her, the Citizen had a healthy disregard for the Government, and, if her relationships were anything to go by, she played by her own rules. She could see the love between Petra, Andy, and Trey, but if Flit had hedged her bets right, Andy wouldn't be able to resist the temptation.

"You need my help to save some lives?" Andy asked.

Flit nodded.

"Then count me in."

That was all Flit needed to hear. From there, she asked if she could use Andy's computer to access the news. She showed Andy the article about the gas leak, as well as the fact no gas would be able to cause that kind of damage. She couldn't tell Andy the full truth, that she suspected a Derivate was behind it, but she didn't need to. All Andy needed to know was that the Government was callously lying about the demise of over two dozen Citizens, and she was ready to do what needed to be done.

The back doors Andy had open startled Flit. She knew that the Underground microkinetics were good, but it was utterly mesmerising to watch Andy work. She navigated her way through the Government's network as if it was a part of her, and she managed to access security recordings from the buildings in question, not long before they had exploded. They didn't even have to scour the footage. All Flit had to do was give her a description of the *person of interest*, and Andy set up a bot to scan the recordings.

Andy and Flit stopped for a drink break while the bot worked, but it didn't take long for the program to find valid evidence that the escaped Derivate had, in fact, been at the scene of the *gas leak* in the minutes before the time mentioned in the article. With that solid information, Andy cast a wider net to track the man's movements through the city. There was evidence the Government had tried, but, Andy explained, it was almost as if someone had put detours in the code that led them around all the main clues. Andy was good. She pushed past the detours and managed to follow the breadcrumbs through the network. As she worked, Andy asked Flit about the man, about whether he was a new recruit for the Free Citizens, but Flit shrugged off the questions until they found what they were looking for.

"Right here." Andy sighed, exhausted, as she flopped back onto the couch.

The escaped Derivate's face filled the screen, and Flit's breath caught in her throat. He was eleven blocks away, hiding on the twelfth floor a building. Or, at least, he should be. They had seen him enter the level, and no cameras had picked him up on him leaving. Unless he went out a window, but Flit figured that would have made the news.

"Andy, you're a fucking genius," Flit said, picking up her jacket and shrugging it on. "Thank you so much." She turned to make for the door.

"Wait, Ava!" Andy jumped back up, any sense of tiredness

scrubbed away by that split-second respite. "What are you going to do?"

"I just need to have a quick word with him." Flit reached for the panel to open the door, but it locked in front of her with a low beep.

Andy's frown was as deep as it was disapproving. "What if you get caught on Government footage?"

That gave Flit pause. "What do you mean?"

"Well, if something happens and they manage to get around the mess that is their own network…" She gestured to the screen, still running a program to watch and alert them if the man's face reappeared on any new cameras. "Then you're done for."

"I appreciate the warning," Flit said slowly, "but I can be sneaky."

Crossing her arms over her chest, Andy frowned. "Like you were in that facility?"

Flit's lips curled into a grimace. "This is different."

"How so?" Andy watched her closely, not showing any sign of backing down.

Deciding it was better to change tact, Flit said, "I don't really have any other option here. I'm going in there tonight. Unless you can follow along and turn me into a ghost on the cameras, then there isn't much else I can do."

Andy went from worried to excited in a split second. She straightened up, eyes widening and face setting in a grin. "Give me five minutes, and I'll be ready to go."

Flit's eyebrows shot up. "Wait, what?"

The look of confusion on Andy's face deepened Flit's own. "You asked if I was willing to follow along. I am."

"But—" Flit gestured to the screens around the room, pointing to the tools of Andy's craft.

Andy rolled her eyes. "That building is private property, so the backdoor I have to the Government's network won't work. I need to be closer to get onto their network. I can hack in and view from a distance, but it will only accept edits and changes from an internal IP."

Not a word of that made sense beyond the fact that Andy had to go along with her. "What if you get caught?"

"Um, Ava…" Andy pointed to herself. "Hacker, remember? If I can hide you on the cameras, I can ghost myself as well. I just need to be there."

It was not the best idea, but Flit needed the anonymity. Besides, she could go and deal with the Derivate while Andy stayed in the foyer or something. She didn't have to be anywhere near the guy. Their secret would still be safe.

"Fine," Flit conceded, stepping back. "I would appreciate your help, but I need to speak to him alone."

Andy's eyes sparkled with anticipation as she looked Flit up and down. "Oh, don't worry. I have no intention of going anywhere near him. Besides, I have a feeling you can handle yourself."

Without further discussion, Andy disappeared into a room down the hall and returned dressed in drab greys and blacks that the more boring Citizens favoured. It was cool enough outside that she was able to pull up a hood to cover her teal hair and not look too conspicuous. Just before they walked out of the door, she slipped on a pair of digital glasses, the likes of which only the rich or well-connected Citizens used as part of their everyday outfit. Like the Derivate's visors, the glasses had their own interface and connectivity, but Flit had a feeling Andy's were fitted more with hacking tools than games or social apps.

"All right," Andy said, rolling her shoulders. "Let's do this."

Outside, darkness had fallen in the towering glass city, and the lights of the buildings shone all around them in all shades. In some ways, the Hub was even more impressive at night. Without a beautiful sky to distract from it, the architectural feats and sheer scale of it all took precedence. It was easy to feel complacent in a place like that, Flit thought, as if you were just one of an infinite number of people, as if it the Government would never pay attention to you.

But Andy and Flit knew better. The Government used technology and Derivates to ensure the Citizens were well controlled, and they were careful not to rouse suspicion by lingering too long anywhere. They caught the subway to the closest station to the building in question and then followed a twisting route that saw them stopping to get a drink along the way. They didn't want the drinks, of course, but Andy maintained that the building was the only one so close to the Hub that sold the old-fashioned beverage. It gave them an excuse to be there.

The building was a standard commercial/residential split. The bottom three levels contained a supermarket and a range of clothing and lifestyle stores. The next few had other services, such as allied health or aesthetic therapy offices. It was easy enough for them to step into the elevator that would take them up to the residential floors, but they needed access. If Flit had been on her own, she would have just swiped her finger over a range of apartment numbers and hope someone was distracted enough to let her in. Her hand twitched, about to do just that, but Andy captured it in her own.

Andy shook her head subtly, and, a moment later, the panel by the door lit up with access to level twelve. The hacker was distracted the whole ride up, and Flit didn't interrupt her.

When they alighted the elevator, Flit looked around. It was nowhere near as nice as the apartment building she or Andy lived in, but there was a functional foyer with a few common seating areas. Flit gestured for Andy to take a seat on the clean but well-loved furniture.

"Are you sure?" Andy asked, peering around, her voice shaking with… nerves? Excitement? Fear?

"Yes, I'm sure. I'll be back in a few minutes. I'll let you know if I need anything."

Before Andy could argue, Flit disappeared down one of the hallways that led out of the foyer. The doors were clearly numbered, which made it easy to find her mark. She took a deep breath and then rapped on it smartly, not wanting to alert the intercom system to her presence and make more work for Andy to undo.

For the next minute, there was nothing but silence behind the door.

She sighed and knocked again, looking back over her shoulder to make sure there was still no one else in the hall.

Still nothing.

Flit leaned against the door, pressing her lip against the crack. "It's not the Government," she stage-whispered.

There was an unmistakable chuckle from inside. "Obviously.

Your friend's not the only one who can hack into the cameras, you know."

The voice, though muffled, was familiar. Despite the intervening days, it still held the same dry, gravelly tone.

"It's the person from the other night… at the place… the one who told the woman to let you out? Please, we need to talk," she whispered. Really, she just wanted to yell at him to open the bloody door, but that would get her nowhere real fast.

After a full minute of silence during which Flit tried to figure out just where she would need to kick the door to knock it in, there was an electronic his and the door opened. The man from the facility reached out and grasped her by the shirt. The only reason she didn't teleport away was because Andy would be watching the hallway footage. She let the man yank her into the apartment and then slam the door shut behind them.

"What are you doing here?" he snapped, narrowing his midnight blue eyes at her.

Straight to the point. Flit was fine with that.

"You were supposed to follow the others to safety." Flit crossed her arms as she watched him.

Like most people, the man was a good two heads taller than her. Unfortunately, his time in the facility had turned what might have once been well-built muscles to ropy sinew and stretched skin. His hair was still a straw-like bird nest. His face was covered in a thick splattering of stubble, and the bags under his eyes made him look as exhausted as Flit felt.

"Safety?" he muttered, shaking his head. "I don't want safety. I want revenge."

That was the dumbest excuse Flit had ever heard. "We all want to get back at the Government."

The man shook his head, in much the same way a dog would shake water from its coat. "I'm talking real poetic justice, not blowing up some stupid, empty facility. What did that achieve, huh? It was barely even on the news."

Bristling under his criticism, Flit squared her shoulders. "You didn't get revenge, you killed innocent people. You're lucky I found you before the Government did."

Understanding flashed in the man's eyes. "Oh, let me guess. You're here to save me. Again."

"I'm here to offer you a path to safety. You have killed people, yes, but so have I. I know what it feels like to be so backed into a corner that the only way out is to fight," she said, looking up into his eyes and willing him to listen.

It was the man's turn to laugh. He spun around, unlocking the electronic locks on the door with a wave of his hand. "Leave me alone, girl."

Frustration sizzled through Flit. "If you're not going to let me show you where to go, then maybe we can work together. We can find a good way to get back at the Government that doesn't involve hurting more people."

The man's laughter was even louder this time. "Are you kidding?" he asked. "I spent my whole life hiding and behaving myself. Then, some nosy neighbour turned me in, and the Government tortured me. No one tried to help, so I am going to show them their mistake. I have powers, girl, and I intend to use them."

"If you keep this up, you'll give us all away!" Flit's stomach roiled, and she swallowed her repulsion at the callous disregard in his tone. "I have powers, too, and I will bring the Government down, but not by killing innocent people."

"Innocent?" The man slammed a fist against the door. "They turned me in like some kind of stray dog!"

"They didn't know any better! They are just as brainwashed as the rest of us," Flit argued, needing him to see it.

"No, they had all the resources in the world. The best education, the best jobs… freedom! They chose to remain blind, soaking up their privileges like overstuffed cows at a feed lot, but not anymore. Not on my watch."

Months ago, Flit would have said the same thing. Word for word.

She wasn't sure when her opinion had changed. Whether it was getting to know her colleagues or becoming close friends with Chris and Liana, meeting the Free Citizens or seeing the poor people being experimented on in Government facilities… but somewhere along the way, her own views had changed.

Was she still pissed at the Citizens for being blind sheep?

Yes.

Did she want to hurt them?

No.

They were suffering too. They needed freedom almost as much as the Derivates did.

"I promise there's another way!" Flit stepped closer.

The man held his hand out, sending a pulse of power in her direction. Flit's head exploded with a flash of agony, and she had to reach out to steady herself against the wall. "Come with me, it's not too late to fix this." Flit looked up at him as a drop of blood slithered out of her nose and over her lips. She dashed it away with the back of her hand.

"No, I'm not going anywhere." He closed the distance between them and leaned over her, close enough that his hot breath blasted across her face. "I'll kill anyone and everyone who gets in my way. Even you."

This time, when the man reached out, Flit was ready. She teleported farther into the lounge room and squatted down, retrieving her dagger. Her hand shook as she pointed it at him. She had killed Citizen Officers before, yes, but never another Derivate.

"A teleporter, hey? If I can't catch you, maybe I'll show that little hacker friend of yours who she's messing with."

With a wave of the man's hand, the screens on the wall lit up. So much of it was code that went beyond Flit's understanding, but nestled amongst the lines was an image of Andy sitting in the foyer.

His threat knocked the wind out of Flit. "Don't you fucking dare."

The man paused, smirking at her. "Oh? That touched a nerve, did it?"

Flit didn't answer. She was too busy trying to figure out how to turn this around, what to say to convince him that he didn't have to live like this.

A message application interface popped up over Andy's image. "I knew you were coming after me the moment your friend started following my tracks," the man explained, "so I did my own research before you arrived. Her firewalls are good, but... I'm better." He swiped to a log-in page where he had an account set up with Flit's image as the profile picture and her cover name as the sender.

Need some help in here, ASAP!

The message was typed and sent before Flit could yell, "No!"

The man laughed and waved a hand at Flit. Another wave of brain-rendering pain sizzled through her, and she stumbled back. Her vision exploded with spots of bright white light. She didn't understand why he was doing this. She had been angry too, but that didn't make what he was doing ok.

"Stop!" Flit spluttered, "It's not too late."

"For you? I'm afraid it is." He reached out again, but Flit teleported over to the door and then into a far corner of the room in rapid succession. He turned around just as the door to the apartment behind his back slid open, and Andy stumbled in.

"Andy, no!" Flit was too far away to push her friend out of the man's way, so she launched herself at him instead.

She was too slow, and Andy crumpled to the floor as the man laughed. It was cut short as Flit slammed an abrupt strike to the top of his head with the butt of her dagger. She teleported as he staggered away and slammed the door shut then turned back to him, dagger raised as she stood over Andy. She could barely register the rise and fall of Andy's chest.

"She's not even a Derivate, is she?" the man spat, disgusted, straw-like hair knotting as he shook his head from side to side. "How dare you protect one of them?"

This time, Flit was fast enough to evade his strike. She teleported behind him and grasped his shoulder with one hand as she held the dagger to his throat with the other. "Please… just stop," she begged as the sharp edge of the blade bit into his skin and drew blood.

He held a palm towards Andy.

"Don't!" Flit begged

He curled his fingers into a fist, and Andy started to convulse.

Flit closed her eyes and jerked the dagger back, slicing through the man's throat and jumping to the opposite side of the room as he collapsed. He held his hands to the gushing slice as he tried to heal himself, but the wound was too deep, and his gurgled breaths spurted out in time with his failing heartbeat.

Falling to her knees beside Andy, Flit leaned over the woman and checked her pulse. It was still strong, but they had to get out of there. She didn't know how to get Andy out by herself. All she knew was that they had to be careful.

One of the arms of the glasses Andy wore had snapped, but as Flit took them off her and slipped them over her own eyes, the interface was still running. It took a few moments to figure out how to access the call function, but when she did, she scrolled down the contacts until she found Brian Parkes. The ring tone sounded directly into Flit's ear, and she shook, hoping Scraps would answer.

"Good evening, Andy. What can I—"

"Scraps, it's me," Flit panted. "I need your help."

52

SCRAPS

THE INSTANT SCRAPS heard Flit's voice, he frowned at the watch he was wearing.

Chris and Liana, who were still talking over glasses of wine, paused their conversation to peer at him.

"Uh, excuse me for a moment." Scraps stood and walked down the hallway, shutting the bathroom door behind himself and holding his wrist closer to his face so he could turn the volume down on the call. "Ava, what is it?"

Her words come out in a torrent of sobs and splutters, but Scraps was able to make out an address and the fact that someone —thankfully not Flit—was injured. It was all he needed to know before ending the call and heading back out to the living room. Chris and Liana stopped talking immediately.

"Could I borrow your vehicle, please?" Scraps asked, his heart thundering in his chest. He had no idea how Flit had gotten to that part of town or why. All he knew was that he had to get her.

Chris slipped off the couch and walked over. "Is everything ok?" he asked, voice low with concern.

"I…" Scraps stopped, not sure how to answer.

Before he could figure it out, Liana was at Chris' side. She placed a gentle hand on his shoulder. "Of course, Brian. You head down to the garage. I'll approve the access now. It's yours for as long as you need."

"Thank you." Scraps was touched by her immediate concession. He strode to the door as Chris called out after him, asking if there was anything else they could do. "No, but I appreciate the offer."

Scraps didn't stick around after that. He made his way to the elevator and then down to the basement parking lot. The door of the vehicle popped open as he approached, and he was grateful once more for Liana's quick reactions. He slipped inside, started it up, and relied on his own memory to navigate to the address Flit had given him, not wanting to put it into the GPS system.

The trip to the building took too long for Scraps' comfort. He wondered if it would have been wiser to take public transport, but he didn't know what condition Flit was in, so the car was the better option, despite the delay. His mind kept veering, trying to figure out how or why she was there, but he reeled it back in. It wasn't important and getting stuck in that line of thinking would only be a distraction. What was done was done. He just needed to get her somewhere safe.

When Scraps arrived, he was pleased that the building was a mixed purpose one. It meant there was public parking available in the basement that he could slide into. He sent Flit a message to let her know he was there and again when he stepped into the elevator. There were a few other people riding up with him, but he kept to himself as the approval for floor twelve blinked on the control panel.

Scraps had worked hard on the trip to avoid coming up with stories of what he would find in his head, but he could safely say that what greeted him when he opened the door was the farthest from his mind.

The small apartment was an absolute mess. A man lay on the floor, pale and lifeless, in a shining pool of blood. His throat was sliced open in a gory mess of red tissue and ligaments, and Scraps turned away as Flit jumped up from where she was on the floor, cuddling Andy, and threw her arms around him. He held her close and looked down at her, brushing a strand of crusted hair from her face. Her eyes were puffy, face streaked with tears and blood.

"What do we need to do?" he asked.

Business first. He could get answers later when they were safe.

"Andy's unconscious. I think she's ok. We need to g-get her home" Flit sniffed, dashing at the tearstains with the back of her hand.

"I'll deal with all this. You need to find the bathroom, clean up a little before we go. Make sure you wipe down anything you touch, ok?"

Flit started to nod but teleported away mid-movement.

A cursory glance at Andy told Scraps she was breathing regularly, so he focused on the dead man instead. Part of Scraps' and Flit's training with Shadow had included in-depth information about how to avoid detection by postcogs. Luckily, the Government's own ability capping practice put them at a disadvantage in this area. If their postcogs had access to a live subject, they could search up to a couple of days in the past, but they could only manage a few hours off inanimate objects and general locations. Scraps wasn't sure if the Government was likely to raid this apartment any time soon, but that was out of his control. What he could manage, however, was what genetic information they could get off the body.

Turning towards the kitchen in the open-plan living space, Scraps used his telekinesis to open all the cupboard doors and rifle through them. It wasn't long before he found a bottle of cleaning chemicals. Thanks to his time with the Law Enforcement Department, he knew that certain substances could degrade the quality of DNA. So, he used his powers to spread the noxious smelling liquid over as many surfaces as he could.

Once he was satisfied that any trace DNA from Flit and Andy would be useless, Scraps sank to his knees beside the teal-haired Citizen. He frowned as he noticed the dried blood coming out of her nose and ears. He shrugged his jacket off and pulled the back of his shirt around then tore a strip off. He dabbed away the blood and combed some of Andy's hair back to make her look more presentable before tucking the rag into his pocket. He pulled his jacket into place and slipped his arm around Andy. With a mix of muscular and telekinetic strength, he got her standing upright as Flit came back out.

"If anyone asks, she had a little too much to drink and we are taking her home," Scraps said, thinking ahead.

Flit's gaze was skittish as she looked between Andy and the man on the floor. Scraps peered at him too. He was familiar for some reason, but he couldn't remember where he had seen him before.

"Let's go," Flit whispered. She slipped her arm under Andy's other armpit and then put a pair of broken glasses on their friend. "How did you get here?"

"Chris' and Liana's vehicle. It's in the basement."

"You're incredible.'

Scraps was not in the mood to receive the compliment, so he let it fall between them as they walked out of the apartment. When they got into the elevator, a couple who were already in there seemed amused by the predicament. Flit muttered something about one too many shots of vodka, and the couple enthused about the pitfalls of too much alcohol before getting off at ground floor.

The rest of the trip was quiet. Flit suggested heading back to Petra's, Trey's, and Andy's apartment. Scraps let Flit give him the directions, finding it much easier to just drive than to look at the back seat and see the injured woman passed out there.

Just as he pulled into a guest parking spot, there was a groan from the back seat. Scraps killed the engine and turned around to see Andy coming back to consciousness. She held her head in both hands and massaged her temples with her thumbs.

"Andy? How do you feel?" Flit clambered over to the back seat and took Andy's hands in her own, looking at her. Scraps could tell from the dilation in Andy's eyes that she wasn't quite able to focus yet.

"Ava? What happened?"

Just as Scraps was about to claim she had too much to drink, Flit jumped in with, "You hit your head after I asked for your help."

Eyes widening with what seemed like recognition, Andy took Flit's hands. "Are you ok?"

"Me?" Flit laughed, the irreverent, nervous sound spluttering between them. "You wake up after being passed out in the back seat of a car and you ask about me?"

Andy gave Flit a weak smile and shrugged.

"I'm fine. I needed your help with some tech stuff, but a vase fell off a shelf when you walked in the door and knocked you out. It's all sorted, though. Thanks for your help," Flit said quickly, dismissively, as if it was no big deal.

Even though he had seen it several times before, Scraps was alarmed by how smoothly Flit could lie when she really wanted to.

"Here, let us help you get back to your apartment, and you can have your home assistant run a medical scan to make sure you were not injured too badly," Scraps said. He got out of the car and walked around to the back door to help Andy out.

The three made their way up to Andy's apartment and got Andy settled in bed. They ran the scan of Andy's vitals and found that everything was normal.

"Just a splitting headache, then." Andy chuckled. "Next time we go on one of our little adventures, please protect me from our own clumsiness, Ava."

Scrap shot Flit a narrow-eyed glare. "Adventure?"

Flit winced. "No more adventures, Andy. This was a one-off. I swear."

Andy closed her eyes. "I hope not. It was the first time I've felt so alive in years."

"Just get some rest. Call me if you need anything, no matter the time… I'll check on you tomorrow." Flit gently squeezed Andy's shoulder before turning and leaving the room, turning the lights off behind them.

Every part of Scraps was buzzing with curiosity as he drove home, but he did not know what kind of recording settings Chris and Liana had in their vehicle, so he kept his questions to himself. Flit, for once, did not seem to be volunteering any information. When they parked under their own building, he walked around and helped her out of the car, holding her small frame close to his side as they made their way to their apartment. He held the door open for Flit and ushered her in. He was just about to ask her questions when she teleported over to the full-window screen in their room and brought up the news article from earlier that day.

"The gas leak?" Scraps asked, rubbing his chin as he walked over. He scanned it, but there was nothing there that he hadn't seen before. "I thought we discussed this at lunch and decided to leave it alone."

Flit crossed her arms, but instead of being the frustrated pose he was used to seeing, this looked different, almost like she was hugging herself.

"You decided to leave it alone," she corrected.

He went to argue, but he thought back to the conversation and realised she had not conceded. She had just fallen silent.

"But it was him? The man from the facility?" Scraps asked, trying to match the pale, bloodless face to the snatches of the man he had seen through the small cell window.

Flit nodded.

If the micro was responsible for all those deaths, he was incredibly dangerous.

"We could have gone together. Why didn't you tell me, Flit?" Scraps asked, caught between disappointment and betrayal. The last few days had been so odd, so intense, that he was struggling to figure out what to make of them.

Tears streamed down Flit's cheeks thick and fast. "Because I… It was my fault. My responsibility. I thought I could handle it. I went there to talk to him. I figured it would be an easy conversation. I thought he might be like us, you know, that he just wanted freedom. Layla was right, he was dangerous. He was u-unhinged." Flit stopped, putting a hand on her flushed forehead.

In the blink of an eye, she was standing in front of him. She fell against his chest, gripping his shirt with both hands as she sobbed. "I begged him to r-reconsider. I told him there w-was another way." She had balled his shirt up so tightly in her hands that his chest hurt. "B-but he tried to kill Andy, and I couldn't let him. I didn't even think. When I saw her c-convulsing, I just… I just did it. And there was so much blood, Scraps. Fuck, there was blood everywhere."

Flit dissolved into a mess of emotion, and Scraps closed his eyes as he took several deep, steadying breaths. He could not believe Flit hadn't told him about her plan beforehand.

"I do not care who was responsible, you should not have gone alone."

They were partners. They were supposed to work together, and he had been there for her time and time again.

"I just thought this was one thing I could do, one thing I could f-fix on my own!" Flit muttered, burying her face into his chest. "Everything has been so fucked up. I just wanted to make it right."

Flit didn't say anything else after that. She just leaned against his chest and soaked his shirt with her sorrows. Eventually, Scraps convinced her to move over to the lounge with him. He levitated a blanket over from a nearby armchair and settled it over them.

He hadn't been completely honest when he said he was not angry with her. In one way, he was. He was angry because she had thrown herself into that situation with so little regard for her own safety. She believed the best in everyone, and what happened in that apartment was bound to be a shocking way for her to learn that some people were beyond saving. But any negative emotions he felt about what she had done were washed away by an overwhelming sense of relief that it was the man lying on the floor with his throat cut and not her.

"Flit?"

She turned her shining face up to look into his eyes as she croaked, "Yes?"

"Please promise me something."

"Anything."

Normally, Flit was wary of making promises like that. Even though she rattled off comebacks and insults like they were her first language, Scraps had come to learn that she was very careful with her words when it came to the commitments she made in their relationship.

"Please promise me you will never do something like that again without telling me first," he whispered. He leaned in, brushing a soft kiss over her lips. "We are partners, and if something had happened to you…" Scraps stopped, closing his eyes as he pushed his own fears away. "I just… I could not bear it."

Flit rested her forehead against his and cupped his cheek with her soft, warm palms. "I promise," she told him.

And when he heard the rawness in her tone, Scraps was certain she meant it.

Silence fell between them for a few minutes before Flit sat back and watched him. The tears had dried, and the sadness was gone, replaced by confusion. "Why?" she whispered.

Eyebrows furrowed, Scraps asked, "Why, what?"

"Why are you taking this so well? I kissed another man in front of you. Then, I killed him. I set another one free, and then I killed him, too. I put one of our new friends in danger. Why are you taking this so calmly? I'm a hot mess right now."

"You are not a 'hot mess'," Scraps insisted. "You are a passionate, loving, brave woman who has found herself in several unusual situations in a short space of time."

Flit didn't look convinced.

"We all have lapses in judgement," Scraps said earnestly, pushing a stray strand of hair behind her ear. "Given your track record for excellent hunches, I figure this is just the natural order playing catch up."

Despite her misery, Flit let out a soft snort of laughter.

"There is no such thing as a mistake if we learn from our experiences. If we can take something from the mess of the last few days, that will be enough." Scraps wrapped his arm around her shoulder and guided her to stand with him. It was late, and they had both had an eventful night. They needed to get to bed so they could go to work in the morning.

"Speaking of learning…" Flit sniffed. "I think I know what we can do about our situation with the Free Citizens."

Relief flooded through Scraps at those words. The forward thinking was a far cry from the cold, distant Flit he had been dealing with for the past few days. She was still fragile, he knew that much, but if she was plotting and planning, she would be able to fall back into herself in time.

53

———

FLIT

DESPITE HOW POORLY things had gone that night, working with Andy had opened Flit's mind to a whole new set of vulnerabilities that the Government had, vulnerabilities they could exploit. Combined with the information they had access to from their maglev rail reviews, they had an opportunity to make an impact that the Government could not ignore. She explained her new ideas to Scraps. He listened to her just as well as he always did, and she was glad he did not dismiss her concerns as part of her mourning. When she thought he would argue about going beyond the purpose of their mission, all it took was a soft word about the suffering they had seen to remind him of what was important. It no longer mattered who acted, only that someone did. If the Underground would not work to fight the horrors the Government were inflicting on innocent people, they both knew a group that would.

The Free Citizens.

Both Flit and Scraps agreed that they wanted to continue to help the Free Citizens. They had just as much right to rebel against the Government as the Underground did, but they had to find a way to do it that would ensure the Citizens wouldn't get themselves killed and Flit and Scraps wouldn't get captured. It meant that Flit and Scraps had to assess where they would be the most effective but also the safest. The protections that the Underground had given them, biologically and technologically speaking, would not withstand the intense scrutiny that they would receive if the Government brought them in. There was a reason they were supposed to blend in.

Instead of putting themselves on the front line of the fight, they decided to use their training, knowledge, and positions to become integral parts of the planning process. If it helped improve the Free Citizen's efficiency and kept some of them safe from Adam's wilder, less practical plans, then they would consider it a job well done.

In the days that followed, Scraps checked in with Flit regularly, wanting to make sure she was dealing with everything that had happened with a tenderness that stole her breath away. It took Flit a while to reassure him that she had come to terms with Rook's death. She had spent a whole year wishing she could have said goodbye. Of course, she would have preferred not to, but Fortune was right. Rook had looked so tired. That level of constant agony and exhaustion stole away everything that had made Rook the man he was. During their time together, they would spend hours in the dark at night, talking about all the hypothetical situations they could wind up in in the future. When the topic of being captured came up, both had agreed, without reservation, that it would be better to be dead than to be property of the Government.

As morbid as it was, Flit was honoured she could be part of granting Rook that relief. That she could give him some sense of dignity the Government had deprived him of in those final moments.

Killing the microkinetic had been a different matter. After Scraps' initial dismissal of her concerns, she had done what she always did. She'd acted on her instincts. This time, instead of helping her bring a new, wonderful Derivate to the Underground, it would up with her killing a man. It had gone wrong just as quickly, and just as spectacularly, as the mission to Old City months earlier. Between injuring her best friend and taking the life of a misguided Derivate, Flit had come to realise that she had to be smarter about things if she wanted them to go right. She would not make any more mistakes.

When the week ended, Scraps and Flit decided they had enough information to take their plan to Adam. To gain a reprieve from the constant tension in their lives, they decided to invite Chris and Liana to dinner before heading to Nightmix. They had hardly spoken to the pair since the night Scraps borrowed their vehicle.

"Flit, can you set the table, please? Chris and Liana should be here soon," Scraps called out from the kitchen while he prepared dinner.

Flit looked up from the schematics for the maglev subway network on her datapad. "Sure." She set the device aside and teleported into the kitchen to get things ready. She had only just started taking items over to their dining table when the doorbell rang.

"They are a full ten minutes early," Scraps muttered, checking the timer on the oven.

"They must be eager. Between the facility raid, and you borrowing their car last week, I'm surprised they didn't try and pester information out of us all week at work." Flit teleported to the door and opened it.

Liana launched herself into the apartment and pulled Flit into a tight embrace that knocked the air from her lungs.

"Gee, we only just saw each other a couple of hours ago," Flit wheezed, trying to catch her breath.

Liana rolled her eyes as she pulled away from Flit. "Yeah, because work is a great place to spend time with your friends."

"And now we have dinner and a night out at Nightmix planned. That sounds much better than work," Chris said, hugging Flit as Liana walked into the kitchen to greet Scraps.

"Brian! This place smells amazing. Can I swap you for Chris for a week? I could do with a good-looking, live-in chef," Liana teased.

Scraps blushed as he turned off the heat on the stove and settled the spatula down so that he could shake hands with Chris.

"If you're that desperate for a husband swap, you should have just said. I'm sure Ava and I would have plenty of fun gaming all night. You never do that with me," Chris told Liana, playfully elbowing Flit.

"Ha, you'd be crying into your coffee after fifteen minutes of me kicking your arse," Flit said, entirely certain she could wipe the floor with him.

Liana shook her head as she stood beside Scraps. "I'll never understand why they are so competitive."

Scraps stage-whispered, "Ava is bad enough on her own. I believe Chris just feeds into it."

Flit narrowed her eyes at Scraps, but a small smile tugged at her lips. "Are you two just gonna stand there and insult us, or should we get this dinner sorted so we can hit the club?"

Liana stepped back and motioned zipping her lips.

With a laugh, Chris walked over and put an arm around her shoulder, pulling her close and kissing her cheek. "I love you."

Hearing those words made Flit flinch. When she looked up, Scraps seemed far too interested in making sure he had every single drop of the dinner sauce scraped out of the pot. Restraining the urge to sigh, she walked over, getting the plates and glasses out of the cupboard and starting to set up with help from their friends.

Five minutes later, Scraps set the food down onto the table. Flit made sure her friends had some wine and water, and they fell into silence as they started their meal.

"This is delicious, Brian. Thank you," Liana said, breaking the hush that had fallen over them.

Scraps puffed up with pride. "You're far too kind."

"It's not half bad," Chris agreed, his own teasing compliment hidden in those words.

Just as that silence was about to return, Liana put her fork down. "Right. What's going on?"

Flit tilted her head in question.

Scraps swallowed. "What do you mean?"

Liana rolled her eyes. "Did we walk in after a fight or something? You guys are never this quiet. Especially you, Ava. I know things went awry at the facility, and you haven't been the same since. If you want to talk—"

"We are going to propose a new plan to Adam tonight," Flit blurted, figuring it was easier to give them a preview of the night ahead than an insight into her own losses.

Chris set his fork down on the table and leaned back in his seat. "What sort of plan?" The wariness in his tone was understandable. He and Liana were lovely people who had just jumped straight out of the frying pan and into the fire. At this stage, they had to be questioning whether the risk and danger were worth it.

"A smarter one," Flit said with a wicked smile. "No more potshots. They are too good at hiding the small skirmishes. We're thinking something bigger. Something far more visible. Something that will make every Citizen in the city sit up and take notice."

Liana looked down at the table. "Is it… dangerous?"

"There will be risks involved," Scraps admitted, voice matter-of-fact. "But there are parts to play on the sidelines that do not require direct physical danger."

"Brian and I are going to step back from the more active roles and focus on planning and coordination. You can join us, if you like," Flit offered, reaching across the table and gently squeezing Liana's hand.

Chris looked at his wife, an unspoken question in his gaze. Whatever Liana saw there made her nod, and Chris asked, "What will it involve?"

"You'll find that out when we tell Adam later," Flit promised. "But for now, we should eat dinner and enjoy each other's company."

Liana's frown morphed into a smirk. "Ava, I think that is the wisest thing you've ever said."

54

SCRAPS

IN THE PAST, and quite despite himself, Scraps had enjoyed their trips to Nightmix. After the initial dread of being forced to spend time in an overly loud environment with far too many drunken people wore off, the place had grown on him. The music was loud enough to wash out any thoughts or need for conversation, and any excuse to hold Flit close was a win in his books.

With the week they had endured, Scraps thought the club might be enough to help Flit clear her mind, but the dancing and socialisation did not to improve her mood this time. Although she played her part well, holding a smile on her face even as her gaze darted between the dance floor and the door at the back of the club that led to the bunker.

When Scraps, Flit, Chris, and Liana finally got permission to speak with Adam, Flit walked so fast the others had to jog to catch up with her. Down in the bunker, Adam was sitting alone at the desk that had been set up for him. His face split with a smile as they walked in, and he got up, coming over to shake their hands.

"It's nice to see you all again. I was concerned last week's raid turned you off the cause," Adam said.

"Quite the contrary," Flit replied, bristling at the condescension in his tone. "We've got more intel for you."

Adam cocked an eyebrow at them. "Oh?"

"Before we share it, we need some reassurances from you," Scraps said, looking at Adam seriously.

Adam straightened up. "What sort of reassurances?"

"That we won't have a repeat of the facility raid." Liana clung tighter to Chris as she spoke up.

"I wasn't the one who burned the building down," Adam reminded her before smirking at Flit and Scraps. "Nice move, by the way."

"The whole raid was destined for the shitter the moment we got out of the vehicles." Flit dismissed his praise with a wave of her hand.

Immediately, Adam's mirth turned to annoyance. Scraps did not think Adam and Flit would ever be able to get along.

They were far too alike.

"What Ava means to say is that, when you make a plan, you cannot go and change it on a whim," Scraps supplied, squeezing Flit's shoulder to remind her to stay calm.

"I didn't change the plan on a whim. I made that plan the day before the raid, after careful consideration." Adam kicked his feet up and rested his heels on the desk.

"Then perhaps you should have bloody told someone!" Flit snapped.

Adam rolled his eyes.

"Ava has a point." Chris crossed his arms. "Sure, you had a plan, but we were working off different information. Quite frankly, if you had told us the truth, we probably would not have participated."

"You came to me because you wanted to make a difference. I gave you a way to do that." Adam raised his hands, as if to pacify Chris' frustration. "I'm just trying to do my best with what I've got. This isn't a militia with a tactical ops team, or mission planners." Adam let that sit, and then turned his attention to Flit and Scraps, his gaze narrowing. "Speaking of which, how on earth did you two get so good at covert operations? What else are you holding back on us?"

Scraps' stomach tightened at the implication, and the new spark of curiosity in Chris' and Liana's eyes.

"We came here because have some information for you," Flit said before Scraps could ask what Adam was talking about.

The leader of the Free Citizens chuckled and tipped his head at Flit. "Nice deflection, Ava."

"It isn't a deflection, it's the truth." Flit's voice was icier than Scraps had ever heard it. He put a hand on the small of her back, a reminder that they needed Adam just as much as he needed them. "As long as you say you won't go changing things on us anymore, we have a plan that will really set the Hub on fire."

Scraps was not afraid to admit that his social perception skills were lacking, but even he could feel the shift in the tension in the room. The amused derision on Adam's face turned into something sharper and more dangerous.

Adam let his feet fall to the ground with a heavy stomp, and he leaned forward in his chair, resting his elbows against the desk as he observed them. "Fine," he conceded when it became clear that they would not reveal any more until he agreed. "What have you got for me?"

THREE DAYS LATER, Flit and Scraps sat in their office bubble, going over the emergency maglock subway shutdown protocol. The review for those particular procedures should have only lasted a day at most, but they wanted to get as much information as they could for the Free Citizens while Adam pulled all their resources together.

"I'm really pleased we took this transfer," Flit said idly as she stared at the subway network map and ran her fingers along the junctions that held the traffic control centres. "I wasn't sure if it would give us any new challenges, but we are getting everything we need out of it."

Scraps looked over at her and forced a smile. "You're right. It has been good for us."

A soft ping sounded through their bubble, and Scraps looked down at the mail notification that popped up on the screen. He ignored it, though, as it was a whole-team message. He would get to it when he wasn't concentrating so hard on trying to memorise the most important waypoints. Behind him, Flit muttered something about, "Bloody useless whole-team mail notifications." That was her usual response, so Scraps would have ignored it if it wasn't followed by an "Oh!"

Turning, Scraps looked over Flit's shoulder at the message she had opened. It was a standard review allocation notification.

"Looks like the next month will be a crack-down on all Government-operated training facilities." Flit's voice was hushed as she followed a link in the email to the spreadsheet. She scrolled down the list of facilities that would need to be visited. "Yes, that's the jackpot!"

Derivate Education and Training Facility.

Scraps' heart thudded against his ribs when he read those words. That was where he had grown up, the very same place that had brainwashed him into thinking he was a lesser being.

"That is not assigned to us."

It was only a few blocks away from their apartment and Centre One, but he had made sure they steered well clear of it on all their walks and outings.

Flit turned, cocking an eyebrow at him. "What isn't?" She tapped the screen and, with a swipe of her finger, reassigned the task from Frank and Joe to their own load.

"You can't do that," Scraps said, lips twisting into a frown.

"Do what?" Flit asked in a faux-innocent tone as she saved the document and closed it.

Thanks to the increased clearance Jane had given them, they were able to make certain changes to important documents. It was necessary for them in the higher-profile cases. The privilege certainly was not meant to be used to undermine Jane's authority and decision-making.

"Ava… I think you saved that document incorrectly. Just go back and check it. I would hate for Jane to think we messed up her allocations," Scraps warned in a low tone, looking around the office to see where Jane was.

Flit tapped the screen and brought the subway map back up. "I have no idea what you're talking about, Brian. Those allocations looked fine to me."

Scraps wanted to warn her that she was flirting dangerously

with the rules, but he kept his mouth shut, not wanting anything recorded by their pod.

He wondered whether he would have been as pleased as Flit was if he hadn't grown up there. It was most likely a useless adventure. The Derivate Training Facility's adherence to protocol and procedure was as strict as it got. There was nothing to be gained but more frustration about things they were not yet able to change. He wished he could explain that to Flit, but it would have to wait.

When they finally got home that evening, Scraps tried his best to convince Flit to change her mind about the assignment. As always, she had a one-track mind and a few convincing points. Regardless of whether they could find an excuse to shut the place down, they would be able to gather more intel. At some point in the future, the Underground might need to rely on the people living in the facility to bolster their own numbers, and any updated information Flit and Scraps could get about it would help their cause.

In the end, Scraps agreed they should keep the assignment. He did not *want* to see the facility again, but he *needed* to.

Instead of dwelling on it, he and Flit turned their datapads on and started drawing out the maps they had been memorising all day, cross-referencing their work as they went to ensure it was accurate. By the time they retired for the night, they had completed their last contribution to the Free Citizen's next strike. Adam would now have all the information he needed to bring the Hub grinding to a halt for an entire morning at the very least.

If that didn't get the Citizen's attention, Scraps didn't know what would.

THE NEXT MORNING, a subtle sense of unease settled in Scraps' gut. He wasn't sure if it was because they planned to go to Nightmix to share their findings that night or because he was still concerned about Flit getting them into trouble. He did not have to sit with it for long, though. When they got to work, there was an email from Jane waiting for them. Scraps read over it, dread running down his spine like drips of icy water.

To: Ava Parkes; Brian Parkes
From: Jane White
Subject: Review Allocations
Dear Ava and Brian,
Frank has brought it to my attention that you took it upon yourself to change the next lot of review allocations. I would like to give you both the benefit of the doubt and assume this was a simple mistake… but you would have had to enter your clearance details, so I am not sure how it happened.
Either way, it is important that it is remedied immediately, as I am the only one who is allowed to assign or alter these allocations.
Please see me once you have gotten yourselves settled in for the day.
For the good of all,
Jane

SCRAPS PRESSED his lips together as he read the email and restrained the urge to say, "I told you so." Instead, he turned to Flit. "So, do we insist it was a mistake?"

Flit rolled her eyes and shook her head. "No, I'm going to fight for it."

"Ava…" Scraps grew more concerned. "Jane is our boss. We do not want to push this."

"So, we let Frank and Joe go in there, with their bigoted opinions, and overlook whatever policy violations are there?" Flit stood up.

"It is not like we can change any more than they can," Scraps reminded her.

"Yes, but at the very least we need the—" Flit stopped herself short of damning them. "We need to get the job done properly. Look, Jane likes me. It'll be fine. You wait here." Flit fled their bubble before he could stop her.

Scraps watched as Flit approached Jane's office and was invited in. At first, the conversational appeared amiable enough from the outside. As it went on, Flit's shoulders stiffened, and she seemed to grow more frustrated, her gesticulations increasingly exaggerated.

From Jane's expression, whatever Flit was saying was not convincing her of the purpose of the reassignments.

With a decisive tap, Scraps opened a folder on his desktop named 'Household Chores Timetable' and pressed his whole hand against the screen to unlock it, although he did not intend to find any timetables there. He had only called the folder that so Flit would never bother trying to open it. She would be suspicious if she saw something locked that she couldn't get into, especially if she thought it contained something exciting. Scraps used it to store documents containing his emergency plans. He leaned forward, reading the list of file names closely. He scrolled down until he saw something that would suit the moment, attached it to a whole-team message, and titled it 'Weekly Policy Spotlight: Conflict of Interest'. He sent it off and sat back, pretending to work as he looked between his screen and Jane's office.

It was a full minute before Jane stopped talking and frowned at her screen. She then looked back up at Flit and crossed her arms. Flit was gesturing about wildly with her hands. When she stopped, Jane nodded. Flit got up and left Jane's office with a smug smile on her face.

When Flit arrived back in their pod, she flopped into her seat and declared, "That went well."

"It did not look that way from here," Scraps said quietly.

Flit shrugged. "I convinced her to let us have the job."

"Actually, I believe it was Emergency Contingency Plan Echo that convinced her."

Flit stared at Scraps like he had grown a new head. "Emergency Contingency what now?"

Scraps opened a copy of the email he sent to the team. "Conflict of interest. It is the only logical and valid excuse for you to take the review off Frank and Joe. I think everyone is aware of their personal feelings about Derivates, so it was the Emergency Contingency Plan that saved you."

"Why have I not heard of this plan before?" Flit crossed her arms over her chest, balling her fists under her armpits as she glared at him.

"Because it was on a need-to-know basis—"

"Says who?"

"Me," Scraps told her firmly. "I'm just glad I left that particular policy out of the weekly reviews until now."

"Woah, hold on." Flit swung around in her chair to face him. "What do you mean until now? Have you been holding certain things back?"

Cheeks heating at the realisation he had incriminated himself, Scraps shrugged. "I kept aside policies covering the transgressions you were most likely to make at some point."

"How do you know what transgressions I am likely to make?"

"I made a formula based on the—"

"Stop. Stop!" Flit commanded with a laugh. "Forget it, ok? I don't need to hear the formula. All that matters now is we got the job, so we can start researching and prepping for that while we finish this one."

Flit opened the policies and procedures for the Derivate Training Facility. Scraps turned away from her screen and back to his own, letting out a sigh of relief that the fight was already over.

"You get started on the new tasks," he suggested. "I will complete the current one. We need to finish up on time. We should not be late for our outing tonight."

55

FLIT

FLIT DIDN'T CARE whether it was her own cunning or Scraps'
policy review that landed them the Derivate Training Facility job.
She was just pleased they got it. It was going to be emotionally
trying because it would take them straight into the belly of the
beast, but it was a gold mine. It fell perfectly into the kind of plan
she and Scraps wanted to make—something longer term, something smarter, something that would work.

Instead of feeling excited about their night, a sense of calm
resolution had settled over Flit. It was so different to how she
normally felt, but she liked it better in some ways. There was an
alluring quality to the level-headedness of her new approach. She
was so used to instinctive reactivity that it took the events of the
past few weeks to show her why it was so important to be careful,
to make calculated moves. She still wanted to tear the Government
down, but instead of going in guns blazing, she planned to build an
inferno under them that they couldn't escape.

When they got to Nightmix, they skipped the dancing and went
straight into the bunker. It was fuller than Flit had ever seen it, and
that made the whole thing feel more dangerous, more real. The
people in the club above were so drunk and high on the beat that
they were unlikely to have noticed the twenty people who slipped
through the rear door in dribs and drabs. At least, she hoped they
were.

Regardless of whether the people above noticed the stirrings of an uprising beneath their feet, the group was busy planning the next endeavour. Flit and Scraps used a large screen on Adam's desk to pull up the maps of the subway system and communication network they had acquired from work as Flit explained the plan.

"So, once we take out the maglev subway system, the ensuing chaos will act as a distraction, and we can send our insurgents in through the underground access tunnels to slip our bugs into the media broadcast servers." Flit was feeling a little breathless by the end of her explanation.

Instead of arguing like Flit thought he might, Adam scanned the room with a serious expression. "Any questions?" There was a general mutter and a shaking of heads. "Then we will put this into action in two days, at the start of the new work week."

The faces of the people in the room set with a sense of wonder and anticipation as they processed what would happen. They would not only bring the entire Hub subway system to a grinding halt at peak hour, but they would also be leaking the information they had found about the Government's transmissions on every communication channel available in the city.

Flit straightened up as she stood beside Scraps. She settled her hand in the crook of his elbow and let out a soft breath, pleased their plan had been so well received. The mood in the bunker was electric as everyone realised just how much they were now capable of. It was a far cry from spray-painting logos on the outside of cafes.

"Brian, are you leading us again?" one of the Citizens, a woman who had been at the raid on the medical facility, called out.

Scraps shook his head. "Ava and I will be helping Adam coordinate the attack remotely."

A few of the Citizens' expressions turned from attentive to concerned.

The woman frowned. "But… we need you. You and Ava got us through that last raid safely."

Flit and Scraps had discussed the likelihood of that objection, so Flit leaned against Scraps' more heavily, and he slipped an arm around her waist. "Brian and I have other priorities at the moment that mean we can help, but we cannot take any physical risks."

Some of the brows that were furrowed in concern rose, pushed higher by knowing smiles. Flit hadn't given them any explicit information, but everyone would jump to conclusions about why a young married couple might want to steer clear of physical danger. From the look in their eyes, that was exactly the conclusion they had come to. Flit was glad she was right, but she only hoped that it was not too difficult to explain later when it became clear she was not pregnant.

But that was something they would deal with when the time came.

Their real priority was making sure they had a solid plan to keep the Free Citizens safe on their next mission and to get the information they gathered about the Government's abuse of Citizen's medical rights onto screens all around the city.

"Does everyone understand their roles in this?" Adam asked, bringing the discussion back to the issue at hand. "Good. I'll go over it one last time, and then you can start leaving slowly. Any supplies you need will be delivered to you before the end of the weekend. When you get them, please make sure you hide them somewhere safe. Now… the plan. Alpha, Bravo, and Charlie team leaders, what are your positions at oh-eight-hundred hours?"

Flit took a deep breath and leaned her cheek against Scraps' chest. He gently kissed her hair before whispering, "Everything ok?"

"Yes," Flit said decisively, looking around at the group of Citizens who were going above and beyond to fight for the freedom of people who didn't even know they existed. It was inspiring, really, and something she wished the Underground was better at. "For the first time in weeks, I'm feeling good."

The final run through showed Flit and Scraps that the Free Citizens had been listening, as they had a good grasp of how things needed to unfold. The plan was designed to operate like old mechanical clockwork. It would only succeed if everyone was where they needed to be, doing their part at the right time, in the right way. There was no room for error, no room for the kind of improvisation Adam had tried during the last raid.

With everything firmly in place, people started to trickle out. Flit and Scraps were eager to head home, but Adam asked them to stay back. Chris and Liana tried to hang back with them, but Adam dismissed them.

As they left, Flit grew wary. She was not fond of Adam, and she didn't know what more he could possibly want from them.

"What can we do for you?" Flit asked, following the man as he returned to his desk and sat down.

"I wasn't sure if you two were serious about the cause or not at first, but you have both shown yourselves to be indispensable." Adam looked between Flit and Scraps. "And, Ava, I have to admit your ideas are turning this outfit into quite a resistance."

"Rebellion," Flit corrected immediately.

Adam rolled his eyes. "Same thing."

The leader of the Free Citizens went to continue, but Flit shook her head. "They're different."

With an impatient sigh, Adam crossed his arms. "And I suppose you're going to tell me why."

Ignoring the snark in his tone, Flit delineated the terms for him. "Desperation fuels resistance. Hope sparks rebellion."

Adam opened his mouth but paused, pressing his lips together as he considered what she said.

"This has gone beyond a desperate need to survive," Scraps explained, pulling Flit closer. She leaned back against his steady, solid strength. "Ava and I are doing this because we have hope for the future, for the ways things can be if we stick with this fight."

"Ah, I see what you mean." The amusement behind Adam's eyes set into something almost akin to respect. "I am glad we have you both. While I would prefer to have you out on the field, I will not put you at that risk if you have special reasons to request otherwise."

"Thank you," Scraps said in a gruff tone, gently rubbing his hand up and down Flit's side.

"Our numbers are growing, though. I have been able to handle the swelling ranks and satellite sites until now, but with this upcoming attack we have planned, I anticipate people will flock to our banner." Adam picked up his datapad and showed them a map of the city with several glowing pinpoints on it. "Therefore, I am going to need to have more of the right kind of people up top to help me organise things."

Flit blinked. "You want us in leadership roles?"

"What? Not up for the responsibility?" Adam smirked.

"Of course we are," Flit snapped. "I'm just surprised you want to hand over some of the control."

Scraps squeezed Flit closer to his side and shot her a warning look.

Instead of getting angry at her, Adam just laughed. "As much as I hate to admit it, you two are the change we needed to go from idealists to proper rebels or, as you so eloquently pointed out, to take us from a resistance movement to a proper rebellion. That is the kind of passion and wit we need leading us. So, as of now, you are my right-hand man and woman."

Flit looked up at Scraps, and it was hard to ignore the mix of wariness and pride that flashed in his blue eyes before he spoke. "Thank you, Adam. We appreciate this honour."

Adam stood up, stretching over the table so he could shake both of their hands. "You're welcome. I am looking forward to whatever you cook up for us next."

With an unmistakable sense of irony, Flit realised that their attempt to step back had inadvertently thrust them forward. Still, if it meant they had more say in the direction and planning of the Free Citizens, then it would be worth it.

The Underground might be happy to sit in the dark and let the Government abuse their people, but Flit would make sure the Free Citizens didn't let themselves get that complacent.

THE MORNING of the attack came after two nights of restless sleep.

Flit and Scraps spent the darkest hours in each other's arms, sharing their fears and anticipation about the following day. They went over everything together, feeling a deep sense of responsibility for the people involved. As far as they could tell, there were no flaws in their plan, but that didn't mean they weren't there. It just meant they were too close to see them.

Still, when it came time to rise, just before dawn, they were ready to roll out of bed.

"I'll get breakfast sorted while you set up the tech," Scraps said, leaning over and giving Flit a gentle, lingering kiss.

She pressed a hand against his bare chest. "Thank you."

Flit turned back to their closet and pulled up the false floor that the Government had installed. She retrieved the two datapads and tactical headsets Adam had supplied them with, and she went over them with the Underground's security scanners to double check there was nothing extra fishy about them. Thankfully, it all seemed legitimate.

Just as Flit was about to put the panel back down, she remembered the last time they had prepared for a mission. She had no idea what they were walking into or that she would see Rook again. She paused, resting her head against the door of the closet as emotion welled up inside her.

"This one is for you, Rook," she whispered.

Flit set the false floor back into place. As she stood, she let out a slow, soft breath and welcomed the cool sense of purpose and calculation settling over her.

Flit walked out into the living room and set the datapads up on the table. She connected the headsets and tested them before she teleported over to the floor-to-ceiling wall of windows and deactivated the electrochromatic function.

The deep orange sunrise cast the sleek, shining buildings of the Hub in an undeniably ethereal light. The beauty of it felt like a farce. The city concealed far more ills than any place should. It did not deserve to have the warm, inviting light of sunset making it look more wonderful than it was.

"Flit, are you ok?" Scraps asked.

Hearing his voice, she turned and smiled. "Not yet, but I will be."

Scraps nodded grimly, but he appeared to shake off the lingering concern in his expression after a moment. He held up the bowls of cereal for her to see as he carried them to the table. Flit teleported over and sat down.

They watched the datapads as they ate. One by one, the different teams involved in the attack logged on and checked in. They slipped their headsets on and connected the digital check-ins to their network map.

"Good morning, everyone." Adam's voice came through the connection, clear and alert.

Being so early in the morning, Flit could barely find the energy to talk.

"We have a big day ahead, and judging by the check-ins, everyone is on track. Remember, today is the first real step we are taking to show the rest of the city the horrors that the Government are committing. Every ounce of disappointment, frustration, and outrage you feel needs to go into this. Let it light the fire under you, a fire of hope for the future, for what your actions today will achieve in the weeks to come. Remember, now is our time to rise."

"Thank you, Adam," Flit said, cutting in after a few people cheered through their comms. "Before we begin sending everyone out to their starting posts, we will be doing comms checks. If at any point your comm stops working, you report to your team leader. If theirs stop working, carry out your part of the plan then retreat to safety immediately."

"Yep."

"Copy that."

"Sure."

"Sounds good."

The responses weren't the ideal format, but they were an improvement on radio silence.

"Comms systems look good. Go time has arrived for Alpha and Bravo teams. Good luck, guys. Stay safe," Flit announced.

After two acknowledgements, the teams departed to set their parts in motion.

Flit had never been one for sitting back and watching others do the real work. She had wanted to try out for the leader of the Blue Team because it meant she could still go out on patrols while taking on more responsibility. Aside from getting into Intelligence, that was the kind of goal she had been willing to work towards. While higher positions came with more authority, there was nothing quite like making calls in the heat of action, and Flit was much better at instinct than planning and trying to use people like chess pieces, but it was a skill she needed to learn if she was going to help get her people back to the surface.

One thing Flit had never considered was just how frustrating it would be to sit back at base while others were out. She kept picking up the datapad and looking at it closer, wondering if she had missed any notifications.

After the sixth time in twenty minutes, Scraps gently patted her hand. "They will radio in when they need to. The comms are operational. We have tested them. I know you hate waiting, but they need to maintain operational silence while they work."

He was right, but it didn't make Flit feel any less impatient, so instead of checking the datapad repeatedly, she tele-paced around the room. It was a nice distraction, using her powers like that. At one point, she teleported into their room to get changed out of her pyjamas.

The first call came in just as Flit tugged a T-shirt over her head. "Alpha team reporting. In place, devices armed, ready to detonate on command."

Flit was back in the living room in a heartbeat.

"Good work, Alpha team. Charlie team, that means you're up. Get into place, set the device, and wait for detonation cue," Scraps commanded.

"Copy that, Control."

Scraps sat a little straighter, nodding with approval. Flit chuckled at his expression, and she slid her arms around his shoulders and rested her cheek against his.

"Bravo team, you've got five minutes to cross that track before the next train comes through. Hussle," Flit called through comms, checking her watch.

There was no answer, but that was probably because the team were trying to make their way through the start of the morning crowd incognito.

As part of the plan, the first three teams had the job of getting into key transport conductor locations and using EMPs to take out the systems. With those down, the maglev rail network wouldn't work, and the Government would be too busy scrambling to fix it in the morning rush to notice the team sneaking into the communications hub.

It was another two drawn-out minutes before the next report came in. "Bravo team in place. Ready to detonate."

"Good work." Scraps' shoulders sagged with relief.

Flit squeezed his hand. "I can't wait for the Citizens to find out what their precious Government have been doing. 'For the good of all', my arse'."

"It is about time their corruption is uncovered," Scraps agreed.

Flit looked down at the plan they had on their datapads. "Delta and Echo teams, prepare to move out in two minutes."

The next ten minutes were a tense wait while their key players got into place. Thankfully, everyone radioed in and let Flit and Scraps know they were ready to go. They were a couple of minutes early, but they had assigned extra time to make sure people didn't get caught in the wrong places. Just as Scraps was about to signal the next stage of the plan, detonation of the EMPs, Adam's voice came through the comms.

"All right, teams, fantastic work. Each and every one of you is playing your part perfectly. Now, can ancillary team members please retreat," Adam said.

Flit looked at Scraps, suddenly wary. That was not part of the plan.

Adam continued. "Primary team members, thank you for your service. You will be remembered as heroes for our cause. Your ten-second countdown to detonation starts now."

Bile rose in Flit's throat. She swiped her comms channel to command-members only. "What the fuck is going on?"

An automated voice continued the countdown through the main comms. "Ten."

"We weren't thinking big enough. Why shut down the system when we can destroy it?"

"Nine."

Scraps and Flit looked at each other, eyes wide.

"What are they doing, Adam?" Scraps demanded.

"Eight."

"We don't have remote-detonating tech. We had some volunteers step forward to ensure the explosives went off in the right places at the right time."

"Seven."

"Explosives?" Flit spluttered. They were supposed to be using EMPs, not explosives. "Fuck! Adam, stop this right now!" Flit snatched up her datapad and looked at the sites they had chosen again. The most important maglev power hubs were at key junctions in the network. Junctions built beneath subway platforms where thousands of people would be waiting for their rides to work.

"Six."

"With progress comes sacrifice. Remember, Ava, we can't get a message out by painting graffiti. You and Brian have given us a new purpose. We will shake the Government from the foundations up."

"Five."

There was a cruel, sharp tone to Adam's voice that Flit had not heard before. Judging by the alarmed look on Scraps' face, he hadn't either.

Flit swiped her comms back to the main channel. "All teams, abort mission. Abort now!"

"Four."

Scraps looked at her, eyes wide as he heard her speak next to him but not through the comms. "He's blocked our transmissions. They didn't hear you."

Without hesitating, Flit picked up her datapad and dialed Liana. "Pick up, Li, pick up," Flit muttered, teleporting over to the window and looking down into the streets below.

"Three."

Flit shook the device, as if it would somehow get her through to Liana faster. Behind her, Scraps furiously tapped at the screen of his own datapad.

"Two."

"Ava?" Liana sounded surprised when she answered the call.

The words of warning tumbled from Flit's lips. "It's a trap. I've been locked off comms. Tell them to—"

"One."

At first, there was nothing.

Then, there was an awful rumble, and the building swayed.

"Ava?" Liana's voice shook with worry and then cut out completely.

Flit watched as the power in buildings to the Western side of theirs all went out, right above that main transport hub. With her hand pressed against the glass, head spinning and heart thundering, Flit watched Citizens billow out of the street entrance to the maglev station. At first, they just look terrified, but after those scared Citizens came ones covered in soot, debris, and blood.

A strong hand settled on Flit's shoulder as Scraps stepped up beside her. Flit looked up at him, struggling to comprehend it all. "What have we done?" she breathed.

56

SCRAPS

STANDING BY FLIT'S SIDE, Scraps watched the fallout unfold beneath them. As Citizens streamed out of the subway station, Derivates and Government Officers were sent in, visors lowered, weapons raised. People who lived in the buildings that had lost power filled the streets, gawking around in wonder, trying to figure out what was going on.

The power reconnected, and the screens in Flit and Scraps' apartment flickered on. A blaring alarm tone sounded through the room.

Scraps turned, seeing the cupped hands of the Government's logo on the screen with the words 'For the good of all' underneath them. Then, a deep, calm voice spoke over the klaxon.

"This is an official Government announcement. Citizens of the Hub, do not be alarmed. There has been a malfunction in the maglev train network that we are working to repair. A city-wide lockdown has been called. Immediately return to your homes or to the nearest public venue, and await further—"

The audio broadcast was abruptly cut off, and the screen flickered with a new logo, one Flit and Scraps had become familiar with. The stylised flame of the Free Citizens wavered onto the screen, backed by a video of a raging fire.

"Good morning, residents of the Hub," a modulated voice spoke as the logo shimmered. "We are the Free Citizens. Until now, the Government has worked hard to hide our existence… but we will not operate in the shadows any longer."

Scraps took Flit's hand and led her away from the window. He snatched up his datapad and set the electrochromatic glass in the living area to full privacy. "I wonder if he changed this, too…" Scraps whispered, pressing his lips together, unable to believe Adam had deceived them again.

It was too late to fix anything, so Scraps returned his attention to the broadcast. Screenshots of documents started to cover up the video of the flames, stacking on top of one another behind the Free Citizens logo. It was all the information Flit and Scraps had fed Adam and more.

"For over a century, the Government has lied to you. They claimed that everything they do is for 'the good of all'. They have used these falsehoods to slowly take control of every aspect of our lives, from where we live, to where we work, and even who we love. But lately, new information has come to light. Not only have they controlled our lives, but they are stealing our freedom."

Images faded in over the screenshots of the documents, candid photographs of emaciated people strapped to beds and plugged into machines. Scraps had no idea where Adam got them from, but they looked real.

"So, out of respect for my fellow Citizens who are feeling suffocated by the Government's regime, this information is for you. It will play for as long as it takes the Government to get their dogs to take it down. Take it all in. Let it rip the veil of complacency from your eyes… and when you see the light, look for our flames. This is your fight. Our fight."

The Free Citizens logo shrunk and flew into the corner of the screen as the documents came back, fading in and out one at a time and in greater detail.

"Well, fuck."

Scraps watched Flit as she stood by the window, fists balled at her side, rage roiling off her.

He did not disagree with her crude assessment.

"What do we do now?" she asked.

He only shrugged in response. There were no policies or procedures to cover this sort of thing. There was no training he had undergone that had covered what to do when the rebel organisation you were helping crossed the line from acts of defiance to endorsing suicide attacks.

There was one thing that did stand out to him, though, and he clung to that. "The Government said the city was going into lockdown until they fix their systems. It is probably best that we stay here. I am guessing they won't allow us into the office for work."

Flit turned to face the window. There was nothing to be seen through the opaque glass, but she pressed her forehead against it anyway.

Scraps walked over, setting his hand gently on her shoulder. "We could not have predicted this."

"We were so caught up making a change that we didn't see what was right in front of us," she muttered, shaking her head. "We've created a monster."

"He seemed sensible when we were planning, though. I did not pick up on any hints of such madness." Scraps stepped closer, sliding his arm around her waist, hoping to forestall the tirade he knew must be building inside of her. He felt the outrage too, as it coiled and writhed in the pit of his stomach.

"I just—" Flit's entire body shook against his. "Our plan would have done enough damage for one day. I can't believe he let those people—" She choked on the end of her sentence.

"We cannot change what happened. We need to figure out how to deal with Adam and how to prevent this from happening again. We've already tried being sensible, and we are in far too deep to back out. We need to keep the leadership positions he offered. It is the only way we can make sure this does not become the norm."

"How?" Flit threw her hands up in the air as she turned around. "We already tried to fix things, but we can't know what Adam's doing behind our backs."

She was right. Scraps stepped away, shaking his head. "I don't know," Scraps admitted, "but we don't have to make any rash decisions. Let's… let's just take a while to think about it."

With a nod, Flit pulled away from Scraps and teleported to the couch. She sank down onto it with a groan.

Scraps went over to join her. He wrapped and arm around her and hugged her to his side. "We will get through this."

Flit looked up at him, the ghost of tears shining in her eyes. "We will. Together. Adam is no match for you and me," she said firmly.

He gently kissed the top of her head. She might get emotional, but she never let herself be defeated. It was one of the things that he loved about her.

They watched the leaked information from the Free Citizen's playing on the screen, over and over, for three hours before the Government finally cut the broadcast and replaced it with their own.

The order went out that all Citizens were to remain in whatever location they were in. Only emergency service workers were permitted to be on the streets for travel, and no one was to use the maglev network. They were told that there would be further updates as the day progressed.

The same message from the Government played over and over. Flit and Scraps tried to turn their screens off when the repetition became maddening, but they could not shut them down. The Government were still using an emergency broadcast channel that could not be overwritten. The cool, automated voice started to feel like an itch in the back of Scraps' neck. He had spent years listening to it when he had been younger, and it grated his nerves to be listening to it now.

While trying to figure out what to do about their situation, Flit and Scraps attempted to contact the others. It seemed that the communication networks had been switched off too. When they tried to use their datapads to search for news, they got error messages in return.

In the wake of the unprecedented attack, the Government must have assumed control of all methods of communication. It was genius, really. If people couldn't communicate, they couldn't plot against them.

So, the hours dragged by. At some point, Flit and Scraps, exhausted by the anxious, sleepless nights, fell asleep on the couch. It was a much simpler way to be.

At least, that was, until a thunderous knocking on the door broke Scraps from his sleep.

57

FLIT

AT FIRST, the knocking didn't register through the sticky sluggishness of Flit's slumber.

The banging coincided with the bomb blasts in Flit's dreams, detonations that shook the foundations of the eerie maglev network she created in her mind. She tried again and again to stop the explosions, but every single time, she found herself back at the start of a maze of unfamiliar tunnels.

It wasn't until voices mingled with the banging that she stirred. Pulling herself out of the soup of her subconscious, Flit sat bolt upright. Her back twinged from where she had been lying against Scraps at an awkward angle. He sat up when she did and eyed her warily.

There was another round of furious knocking.

Flit teleported down the hall and into their room. She ripped up the panel at the bottom of their closet, retrieved their weapon belts, kicked the panel shut, and covered it with some dirty laundry.

When Flit reappeared in the lounge room, Scraps was sneaking over to the door. She held his belt up, and he used telekinesis to float it into his waiting hand. Flit took out her pistol and dagger and teleported to the door, resting her hand on the access panel so she could open it.

"For fuck's sake, guys, open up!"

Flit blinked. "Sway?"

She looked at Scraps, and he nodded. She slammed her hand against the panel, and the door slid open to reveal Hawkeye and Sway. They dashed into the apartment.

Hawkeye yelled, "Shut the door!"

She did.

"What are you doing here?" Scraps looked between the two men, dripping with sweat, covered in dust, and panting. He didn't put his pistol away, but he did lower it.

"There were some big explosions in the Underground. They sent out recall orders for the Intelligence agents, but you guys were left off the list. We had to get you," Hawkeye panted.

Flit's stomach churned with disbelief. "They left us off?"

"I don't know why, but it doesn't matter," Hawkeye said.

"We need to leave." Sway peered around the apartment, shifting uncomfortably from foot to foot. "Now."

Scraps stepped closer to Flit. "We cannot leave the Free Citizens like this."

The responsibility of what they started weighed heavily on Flit's shoulders. What would Adam do if they weren't there to stop him?

"Hawkeye, I don't think we can—" Flit's attempt to refuse was interrupted by a low-pitched humming. "What the fuck is—"

There was a slight pinging sound, and the glass on their floor-to-ceiling living room window started to fracture. Hairline cracks raced outwards from a deep red point in the middle. Flit stared at it, not sure what she was seeing.

"Run!" Scraps yelled.

She might have said no to Hawkeye, but she wouldn't deny Scraps.

The group opened the front door to the apartment and spilled out just as the glass in the living room exploded in a shower of deadly glittering shrapnel.

"This way!" Hawkeye cried out, running down through the atrium on their level, past the elevator bank, and to the stairs in the core of the building.

He held the fire escape door open for them, just as all six elevator doors on the level pinged open, and Officers poured out. Flit, Scraps, and Sway slipped into the emergency escape and shut the door behind them. They all leaped down the stairs, skipping several at a time. They were three quarters of the way through their descent when the drumming of their pursuers' boots echoed down to them with all the urgency and malice of a hailstorm.

"Where are we going?" Flit spluttered between gasped breaths as the impact of physically jumping down so many stairs at a time hit her.

"Nearest stormwater drain. Behind next building," Hawkeye wheezed.

By the time they burst out of the fire escape and into the main lobby of the building, Flit was dizzy from the descent. She wished she could have teleported, but she would not leave her friends behind.

"This way!"

Flit followed Sway's voice. He led them through the ground floor of the building and out of an emergency escape at the back. It opened onto an alley that ran parallel to the main street on the other side, and they all did their best to flee down the narrow passage. Scraps, who was faster than her because of his height and insane affinity for running, slowed his steps to match hers. The farther they went, the more Flit noticed Hawkeye struggling. The braces on his legs were supposed to help support his body so he could walk, but what they were doing went beyond that kind of assistance.

The group reached the end of the building and rounded a corner, but Sway skidded to a stop as they were met by a wall of armed Government Officers between them and stormwater drain behind the next building.

"Fuck!" Hawkeye yelled as he stumbled and fell against Sway.

Flit grabbed the back of Hawkeye's shirt and tugged him into the alley they had left.

Sway turned, saying, "Go back. There's another entrance that way—" He pointed to a small service alley between two neighbouring buildings that they had just run past.

They ran towards their new escape, and just before they reached it, the Government Officers turned the corner and appeared at the end of the alley they were in. A second group poured out from the emergency exit of Flit and Scraps' building.

The formations rippled as Registereds stepped through their ranks, visors down, arms outstretched.

"Shit, they're closing in," Hawkeye panted.

They only had to cover a few metres to reach the service alley. The two groups of Officers surged towards them, tightening their trap. Flit grasped Scraps' hand as they ran towards their salvation. The Officers were hot on their tails.

When they reached the alley, a sudden tug on Flit's arm tore her off balance "Ouch!" she cried, her shoulder socket smarting. She looked at Scraps desperately as he just stood there. She wrenched at his hand, but he did not yield. "Scraps, please!" she begged, confused.

Why wasn't he moving?

She tugged at him again. "We have to run!"

He shook his head. "No, *you* have to run. I'll distract them."

Flit felt like she had been hit by a hover truck.

Scraps looked past her. "Get her back to safety." Then, he took her face in both hands and pulled her into a deep kiss that was over almost as soon as it begun. When he released her, they were both breathless. He ran his thumbs over her flushed cheeks as the relentless pounding of Government-issued boots marched closer.

A hand settled on Flit's shoulder. "Time to go," Hawkeye hissed in an urgent plea.

Just as he said it, windows on the ground floor of the buildings either side of them exploded. Flit dove into the service road, trying to bring Scraps with her, but she lost hold of him. She tumbled to the ground, with Hawkeye landing on top of her. Before she could pull away, she felt a sharp pinch on her wrist as he snapped a solid chrome bracelet around it.

Confused, she tried to teleport back to standing. Pain shot up her arm and lanced into the base of her brain, filling her mind with a fog of purple memories. She remained firmly in place. She tried to tear the bracelet off, but it wouldn't budge. She looked up at Hawkeye, betrayal rocking the very core of her.

From across the cascade of debris, Scraps turned to look at her. His blue eyes connected with hers and his face set with a sense of concrete resolve. "I love you, Flit."

She barely heard the words over the shouting of the Government Officers, but they didn't need to be loud when she could feel them deep in her soul.

Scraps rose to his feet and stepped into the main alley, his arms raised. "I surrender!" he called out above the barking of orders and cocking of guns. He used one hand to undo his weapons belt and let it clatter to the floor. "I am unarmed, and I surrender peacefully."

Government Officers swarmed Scraps. They threw him to the ground, and several of them knelt on his prone form as they wrenched his arms behind his back and slipped cuffs around his wrists. The debris from the explosion and the mountain of Officers piling onto Scraps formed a natural barrier at the entry to the alley that stopped more agents from swarming towards her and the others.

"No!" Flit cried, pulling herself free of Hawkeye's grip. "We can't leave him!"

But Sway stepped in front of her. "Flit, sleep." The command in his tone was so strong and unexpected that Flit's eyes closed before she could even register what was happening.

The last thing she felt was a pair of strong arms catching her as she fell, unable to do anything to stop Scraps from making the biggest mistake of his life.

TO BE CONTINUED IN...

Book Three of the Derivates Rising Trilogy

2022

The world-burning conclusion to the Derivates Rising Trilogy.

IF YOU ENJOYED THIS BOOK...

If you enjoyed The Hub (Book Two of the Derivates Rising Trilogy), please consider leaving a review on one of the following sites:

GOODREADS

AMAZON

Reader reviews are crucial for helping indie authors share their stories with the world.

If you would like more news, updates, sneak peeks, and bonus content, you can find it on any of the following sites:

www.livevans.com.au

@LivEvansWrites on Instagram, Twitter, and Facebook.